The DUKE'S TREASON

THE POISONER OF KINGFOUNTAIN

JEFF WHEELER

OLIVERHEBERBOOKS

Cover Art by Dar Albert

Published by Oliver-Heber Books

0 9 8 7 6 5 4 3 2 1

In memory of Sharon Kay Penman

ALSO BY JEFF WHEELER
YOUR FIRST MILLION WORDS

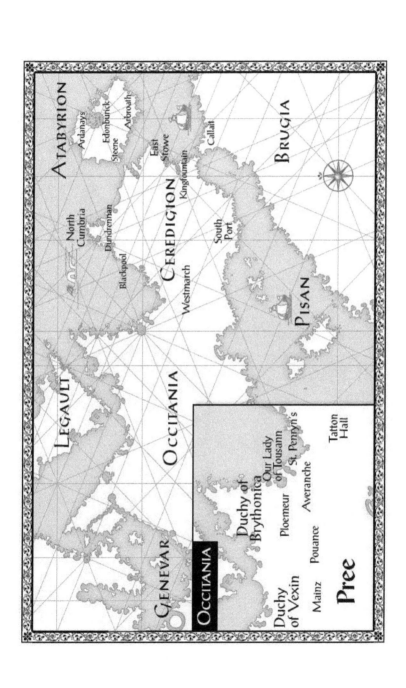

Forgiveness and trust are two very different things. King Eredur has forgiven many offenses against him. He has been neither capricious nor cruel. Some, in the past, have taken his propensity to pardon past transgressions as a sign of weakness. Lord Devereaux was such a man. He was pardoned by Eredur and made lord high constable after the first defeat of Queen Morvared's army. But he betrayed Eredur in the end, showing once again that even when clemency is granted, trust must be earned.

Devereaux failed in his attempt to rebel at Borehamwood. The once proud duke of East Stowe had gambled and lost. He is now a man without a country, but a skilled battle commander always commands a price. I've warned Eredur that when ambition sleeps, it always has one eye open.

— ANKARETTE TRYNEOWY

PROLOGUE

LORD HIGH CONSTABLE

TWELVE YEARS AGO

John Thursby crossed the bridge astride his turbulent horse, whom he'd nicknamed Truck, short for "truculent." The soldier had ridden Truck all night to reach Kingfountain, and neither of them were in a cheerful mood. The smells coming from the food stalls along the bridge wafted pleasantly to his nose—the grease of fresh sausages, the fragrance of freshly baked muffins. He'd get food on his way out, though. He had a duty to perform for his master, Lord Devereaux. The roar of the waterfall against the flagstones jarred him.

He passed the gates to Our Lady of Kingfountain, casting a wary glance at them. The worst thieves and villains lurked there, protected by the deconeus from the king's justice by the rules of sanctuary. It was said many a soldier had taken refuge there after the Battle of Mortimer's Cross. They'd feared the young king's first acts of justice, but Eredur had been surprisingly lenient. John Thursby had no reason to object to that

1

mercy since he'd benefited from it directly. His master had been elevated to lord high constable, a member of the king's privy council. Protector of the city of Kingfountain. Or was the reward merely an excuse to keep a closer eye on him? John Thursby thought that might be nearer the truth.

After crossing the rest of the bridge, he reached the gate leading to the fortress. The knights on guard wore the king's badge, the Sun and Rose. When one of them caught sight of John Thursby's badge, his lip curled slightly and his brow wrinkled, hinting at disdain.

"Is there a problem?" he demanded of the fellow. Truck stamped a hoof and looked ready to bite the man on the arm.

"Go on," said the knight, waving him through.

John Thursby nodded and continued on his way. He shouldn't have demonstrated his impatience. But he was right sick of the arrogance of the king's knights. Proud cocks, the lot of them, strutting and squawking. On occasion, they'd provoked John Thursby to the point of defiance. Devereaux had reprimanded him for the brawls, none of which he'd started. All of which had ended unfavorably for the instigators.

Truck grunted at the slope of the road leading to the palace atop the hill. His muscles quivered, and he tossed his mane with annoyance.

"Almost there, Truck," John Thursby soothed. "Steady on."

The palace loomed above them, turrets and spires and battlement walls that were impregnable. No enemy had ever taken this fortress by force. It was the seat of Argentine power and had been for generations, since the first of their brood had held power. Truck slowed pace and groaned again, and this time John Thursby had to offer a little coaxing with his spurs until the beast snorted at him and reluctantly obeyed, bringing him to the climax of the journey.

At the gates of the palace, he was met by more guards. He

rode beneath the portcullis and then dismounted when one of the king's groomsmen arrived to take his mount.

"He's a nasty temper. Have a care or he'll bite." John Thursby thought it proper to give a fair warning.

Then he tugged off his riding gloves, stuffed them in his sword belt, and marched into the palace.

When he'd stopped at the lord high constable's den at the outer walls of the city, he'd been told that Devereaux was at the palace this morning for an early meeting with the king's council. Rather than wait, he'd opted to pursue his master thither. He hadn't been to the castle often and was impressed by the tapestries, the polished floors. His boots clipped on the stone as he walked to the great hall, but the doors were closed, and servants were gathered outside.

He approached one, a lass with a jar of flowers, and asked, "How long have they been meeting?"

She gave him a curious look and said she didn't know, but the meeting had been going on for a while.

He nodded and began to pace. He'd sleep in the barracks after getting some breakfast, unless Lord Devereaux had another duty for him to perform.

Devereaux had been Duke of East Stowe under Queen Morvared's reign. Eredur had stripped that title from him and given it to one of his lackeys, but he'd made him Earl of Oxgood instead, along with its hefty income, and provided an additional title of lord high constable. But those glories didn't quite measure up to losing a dukedom. He was no longer equal in rank with the king's uncle Warrewik. Or the king's brothers. Eredur's own father had been Duke of Yuork, not a king. Though he'd rebelled against one.

The more time passed in waiting, the more frustrated John Thursby became. He regretted not stopping for food on Bridge Street now that the gnawing pit in his stomach was tormenting him. He didn't know the castle cook, nor could he guess how generous she'd be with an outsider, so he didn't bother asking.

"You're one of Lord Devereaux's men," said a woman to him, intruding on his thoughts.

"I am," he confirmed. She was a pretty thing, a lady's maid by the cut and elegance of her gown. The sleeves were tight at her elbows, but the fabric flowed long and loose by the time it reached her wrists. A subtle perfume tickled his nose pleasantly.

Her expression wasn't condescending, which was a first since he'd arrived. "I'm Mathilde, I'm a maid for the Duchess of North Cumbria. I don't recognize you."

"Lord Devereaux sends me here and there. I'm not often in the city."

"He must trust you, then." She gave him a pretty smile. It made him instantly suspicious. He wasn't an unhandsome man, as far as such things went, but his surly demeanor tended to frighten off all but the truly intrepid. Besides, Warrewik ran the king's Espion, and there appeared to be a ring on her littlest finger.

"I'm on an important mission," he said, dropping his voice confidentially.

"Oh?" Her eyes gleamed with interest. "Do tell. I can keep a secret."

Oh, he doubted that very much...

"Well, I'd tell you, Mathilde, but Lord Devereaux would be angry with me. Everyone knows he's easily vexed."

"He's quite a temper I hear," she said, dropping her voice in a conspiratorial manner.

The opposite was true. She was obviously trying to get him to divulge information. He decided to toy with her a little further to pass the time and take his mind away from his stabbing hunger.

"Well, a shipment of Occitanian wine was seized at the docks this morning on the way to the Vintrey ward. Only...one of the kegs wasn't full of wine."

"Really?" she asked, looking even more interested. News like this would appeal to someone in the Espion. A clue to be investigated. "What was inside it?"

"Ale. Isn't that terrible?" He grinned at having tricked her. "Next time, lass, remove the Espion ring first. It was a dead giveaway."

Her cheeks flushed with startled surprise. He snorted and shifted away from her, shaking his head.

"What's your name?" she asked.

"I'm not telling you that, lass. I'm a soldier. Nothing more."

"You're from North Cumbria, though. I can tell by your accent. The duke's family is from there."

"What of it?"

"The duke is in need of...loyal men...such as yourself."

He wrinkled his brow and turned back to her. "You're trying to recruit me now, lass? You think I can be bought?"

"You're a soldier, as you said." The look of intrigue was gone from her face. She'd been caught in the game and was now trying a different approach. She wanted to be useful to Warrewik. What better way than to have one of Devereaux's soldiers in his employ?

"I'm a soldier, it's true. And I do know something about loyalty. Which is why I'm going to tell my master about this little conversation, Mathilde. And you tell *your* master I'd sooner swallow a barrel of vinegar than betray Devereaux. You tell him that, lass."

"What's your name?" She pressed once again.

"John Thursby, at your service," he added with a tone of

contempt. The door to the great hall groaned as it opened. The murmuring in the entryway turned into chatter and discussion as the various household members rushed in to serve those they'd been waiting for.

"I beg your leave," he said, nodding to her formally before walking into the great hall. King Eredur and Queen Elyse were sitting on their thrones, hands interlinked. The various benches where the privy council sat were being carried away by speedy servants, who were also spiriting away the food. He gritted his teeth, wishing he'd been quicker.

He saw Lord Devereaux approaching him, wearing a hauberk beneath his tunic, hand on his sword hilt. He was a handsome fellow, about ten years older than John Thursby, and his face lifted in a smile of recognition.

"You're a long way from Beestone castle," Devereaux said. "Did something happen?"

"Aye, but we shouldn't talk here. I just met one of Warrewik's Espion strumpets, and she tried to recruit me."

Devereaux laughed out loud. "Did she now? Were you tempted?"

John Thursby gave him an insulted look.

Devereaux clapped him on the back in a friendly way. "Let's get out of here. If I have to listen to Warrewik drone on about affairs of state one more moment, I'll throttle him. You look exhausted. Have you slept yet?"

"I rode all night."

"Have you read any good poems lately?"

"How do you think I managed to stay awake all night? I think of nothing else!"

Devereaux laughed again. "Come on. I didn't dare eat any of the food. Warrewik wants to send someone to Pisan to the poisoner school. A young lady in his employ. I'm going to be wary of eating at the palace now. It might not be good for my health."

"You think Eredur wants you dead?"

"I'm jesting. No, but it will give Warrewik too much power if he pulls it off. He's paying for her training after all."

"Was her name Mathilde?"

Devereaux looked confused. "No. That wasn't it. It's Trynow-something. She's from the North. Like *you*."

"All the best come from the North," John Thursby said with good humor.

"Can't argue there. Let's be on our way."

They went out to the courtyard, and the grooms retrieved their mounts from the stable. Truck did not look pleased to be saddled again so soon.

"You're still riding that awful beast?" Devereaux said in surprise.

"We get along well. The problem's with everyone else." He patted down Truck's withers, scolding the horse when the beast tried to bite him.

Lord Devereaux mounted his bay, and the two left the palace, passing the guard house and starting down the road. They were alone now, away from ears and eyes. The sun was bright overhead. The smell of the trees flanking the road was pleasant.

"Did you warn the king about trusting his uncle too much?" John Thursby asked, cocking his head.

Lord Devereaux chuckled softly. "No, John Thursby. No, I did not. And even if I did, he wouldn't listen to me."

"He'd be a fool not to."

"Well, then he'd be in good company, for most men are fools. I tried to be helpful in the beginning. But after three years in this post, I can tell who he listens to and who he doesn't. He'll not listen to me. He won't ever trust me."

"But he listens to Warrewik?"

"Well, he *has* to. But no. There has been strain between them lately. It's naked as a babe fresh from the womb."

"If he doesn't trust Warrewik, who does he trust?"

"The queen. His father-in-law. He doesn't trust his brother, although I can't say I blame him. Dunsdworth is a..." He stopped, sighed. "He's a miscreant, let's just say. Quite a fellow. And the king trusts Sir Thomas Mortimer. I'm keeping my eye on that one. Something is off. I don't know what it is, but I'm sure I'm right." He brightened. "So...did you bring me a message, John Thursby, all the way from Beestone castle?"

"I did. An emissary arrived from King Lewis's court. Lord Hux. He's on his way to Kingfountain right now, but I beat him here."

"Ah, Lord Hux. Lewis's poisoner. He didn't offer you a drink, did he?"

"Thankfully, no. I didn't know he was a poisoner, so I might have taken it. He wanted to get you a message from Queen Morvared."

"And? What's the message? I know he wouldn't be foolish enough to write it down."

"The message was plain. No tricks. Queen Morvared wanted to know if you were ready to be a duke again."

Devereaux listened keenly, and a little smile played on his mouth.

And that was all the answer John Thursby needed, to know what had to happen next. He held Truck's reins loosely in one hand and dropped his other to the hilt of his sword.

CHAPTER

ONE

STILLBORN

All the signs pointed to one conclusion—the babe was already dead. If Ankarette Tryneowy had learned anything from her years as both a giver and taker of life, it was this: the precariousness of life favored neither the wealthy nor the poor. Duke Kiskaddon's wife had privileges at Tatton Hall that the lesser born could never experience. Some women in Ceredigion, having carried their babe to full term, had ended up squatting in an alley to give birth in the most horrible place conceivable, yet their infants survived, thrived, and became a blessing of the Fountain. Others, like Lady Kiskaddon, had a sumptuous bed, linen coverlets, a warm hearth—and a dead baby.

It was not time to tell the mother yet, however. Better to guide her through the birth before the awful news came.

"I'm so...so weary," Lady Kiskaddon panted. "This is... harder...than the last one."

Another privilege of the nobles was the skilled help to which they had access. Queen Elyse had sent Ankarette to monitor Lady Kiskaddon's pregnancy.

Westmarch was the westernmost duchy of Ceredigion, sharing borders with their enemy Occitania. Ankarette had received a whisper from the Fountain that the heir of La Marche would soon be born. She'd assumed it to be this child, Lady Kiskaddon's child—and so she'd told the king and queen. But everything now pointed against it.

"Would you care for a sip of wine?" Ankarette asked from the bedside. "To rally your strength?"

"Yes, I think so. Everything feels wrong. I haven't felt the babe move...*nnnghh*...very often."

Ankarette reached for the goblet of wine, laced with powders that would ease the duchess's pain. She helped hold the cup to her lips and watched her drink a few shallow sips. Lady Kiskaddon knew Ankarette was the poisoner of King-fountain. But Ankarette's mother had trained her to be a midwife, and Ankarette had insisted on saving as many if not more lives than the ones she'd had to end in the king's service. She'd been away from the palace for weeks to be available to help with the birthing.

Another contraction came and the goblet was shoved back as Lady Kiskaddon's back arched and she fell against the pillows. Ankarette hastily returned the cup to the little bedside table and commenced massaging the duchess's belly again.

The labor had been arduous and long. A servant who'd come in multiple times asking for news on behalf of Lord Kiskaddon peeked her head through the door, but Ankarette dismissed her with a scowl and a head shake.

It reminded her vaguely of when she'd helped her child-hood companion Isybelle give birth to her healthy son. The Duchess of Clare's boy, named Dunsdworth after his father, had come into this world, squalling and red as a beet. Hale and strong and demanding notice. Ankarette had been so relieved at the sight of this babe since Isybelle's first pregnancy had terminated in the harbor outside Callait. A gift of wine tinctured with poison. Not of Ankarette's doing, of course, but she was intensely relieved the duchess's next babe had survived and thrived. Now Isybelle was pregnant once again. Unfortunately, now that he had a son, Lord Dunsdworth, the king's brother, had become more impertinent, belligerent, and drunken than ever. He craved power and authority, and even though he was one of the wealthiest nobles of Ceredigion, he felt stymied by the king. He was not trusted, and it chafed him sorely.

Ankarette was weary of the politics. Weary of the double-dealing. She'd given her life in service to this fractious family, had watched the rivalries that plagued them internally, as well as dealt with threats from without. She needed a long rest. The sacrifices she'd endured for the king and queen had deprived her of things she couldn't get back.

"Ankarette...why isn't the babe coming?" Lady Kiskaddon panted.

"Some come more slowly than others. Time and patience. Save your strength."

Another hour later, it was over. Ankarette wrapped the dead infant in a tiny blanket after wiping the smear of blood from his cheek. A little boy. A precious little boy. She knew the word of power that could bring him back to life. But, strangely, she felt it was against the Fountain's will for her to do so. The magic restrained her. That only made her more confused. This was the future of Westmarch. Had not she believed that?

"Show me...the babe," the duchess gasped.

"I'm so sorry, my lady. He didn't survive."

She presented the listless bundle to the mother, who wept and sobbed, her heart breaking.

Ankarette's own emotions felt wrung out. She'd been so sure the Kiskaddons would have another son, one who would be important to the future of Ceredigion. But the Fountain was ever a mystery. There was no obvious rhyme or reason to its guidance. Ankarette walked to the door and opened it, found the family's eldest son sitting there, back against the door. He was about eight years old, a handsome little boy. Maybe he was to be the future duke of Westmarch after all.

"Would you tell your father to come, Jorganon?" Ankarette said.

"Why is Maman crying?" the boy asked.

Ankarette felt her throat catch, but she responded calmly and with a steady voice. The family would mourn together. It was inevitable. "Please get your father."

The boy nodded, then hastened to his feet and ran down the hall. Ankarette waited at the door, listening to the mournful sounds coming from the bed.

"Please...little one...please stay with us. You are so darling. So precious. We want you so much."

It made Ankarette's eyes sting with tears. Then the sound of heavy footfalls arrived and Lord Kiskaddon appeared, hair disheveled, eyes wide with worry. As soon as he saw Ankarette's eyes, he knew the truth. He covered his mouth, choking on a sob.

"A little boy," Ankarette said thickly. "He didn't make it. I'm so sorry. I did everything I could."

The duke nodded in misery and hurried past her, joining his wife on the bed.

"I just wish...I just wish he could have lived for a few moments," the duchess choked.

"Little one," the duke murmured, stroking the little fluff of hair on the downy scalp. "Oh, my little one!" He began to sob as well.

Ankarette stood at the door, a silent sentinel to observe their anguish.

The duchess was holding the babe to her chest, weeping and cooing, trying to coax the babe still.

"You've two brothers. Two big brothers who will protect you. Jorganon and Timond. And two sisters. Jessica and Ann. They can't wait to meet you, little one. My little one..."

"We want you, Son," Lord Kiskaddon said, sniffing. "We love you already."

Ankarette felt a ripple inside her, coming from her Fountain magic. There was a giddy little feeling inside her breast. A tingle of power. A feeling that now was the time.

Oh, thank the Fountain. She knew not why she'd been bid to wait, unless it was so the couple might know what she had done. She approached the bedside without delay. The little babe hadn't moved. Had it? No, all was still.

"Can I hold him?" Ankarette asked, feeling the urge to speak the word.

"Don't take him away," the duchess pleaded. "Don't."

"I won't. I promise. I just want to hold him."

Ankarette lifted the bundle from his mother's arms and began to pace in a slow circle, holding the baby close to her neck. She noticed, in the light, a little patch of white hair above his tiny ear. Just a splotch. She kissed it and then felt a throb of power inside her. The conviction that this was the proper moment.

"*Nesh-ama*," she whispered and then brushed her lips against the babe's.

That word had come to her mind once before, on a dark night in the sewers of Kingfountain when a flood of water had nearly drowned her. It was a word that meant, as far as she understood it, *breathe*. But it meant more than that. It was a sacred word—a word steeped in old magic.

And the little baby took its first breath and began to wriggle in her arms.

Ankarette gazed at him in surprise and wonderment, feeling the power leech from her and into him. The little boy didn't cry. He opened his eyes, which were a startling gray common in newborns. He gazed at her, intensely, then the puckered little lips opened and he yawned.

"Look, he's revived," Ankarette said, her voice thick with tears. She brought the babe back to the bewildered parents, whose faces gaped with stunned disbelief. A throb of pain filled Ankarette's abdomen as she handed him over. She needed more of the tincture that kept her alive. The effects of Lord Hux's poison, administered years ago, ravaged her still. Unless a cure was found, it would do so until the day she died.

"Oh my precious! My precious boy!" the duchess crooned. "He's awake, love! He's awake!"

"I can see that," said the duke with a surprised chuckle.

Ankarette walked to the door and opened it, finding the Kiskaddon siblings all gathered there, even the littlest, Ann, who was only two. "Come meet your little brother," Ankarette said. "He's awake."

The children charged inside, yelping with glee. Ankarette, exhausted and in pain, leaned her head against the doorjamb. She had needed to be in Tatton Hall for this, to save the boy. The Fountain had plans for this child. But what would happen to all these children to make the youngest the heir?

"What are you going to name him, Maman?" asked Jessica brightly. She was the second oldest, and she was petting the little baby tenderly.

"Owen," the duchess said, smiling with love. "Owen Kiskaddon."

WHEN ANKARETTE RETURNED TO KINGFOUNTAIN, she stopped by her little home in the city first. She was much too weary to want to climb all those tower steps in the palace to her secret room and needed time to rest. Though the ride from Tatton Hall had been uneventful, she was weary from the experience. She unlocked her door with the key and stepped inside, smelling the musty scent of disuse. The little home was a reward the king had given her after she'd helped find Severn's wife, Nanette, before they'd been wed, when she'd gone missing several years ago. She'd gotten it to be closer to John Thursby.

Thinking of him brought a familiar throb of pain that had nothing to do with the poison lingering in her body. They'd tried to create something between them. In fact, he'd proposed to her twice, but he'd kept insisting that she needed to end her service to the king. That the cost to her, personally, had been too high, especially to her health, and her missions were too dangerous. It drove him mad with worry when she was gone and even when she returned in success. His anger toward King Eredur had continued to grow.

John Thursby had never demanded she choose him over the king...but she knew it was because he already knew what her answer would be. It had been over a year since she'd last seen him, since he'd checked in on her during his duties as a night watchman. But those visits had become more infrequent even before then. It had been a while. Too long.

She plucked out the desiccated flowers from a little pot and threw them in the rubbish barrel. After seating herself at the little table by the window, she gazed outside the alley, feeling too tired to sleep.

And that's when she spied Hugh Bardulf's white hair, mustache, and goatee as he rode a horse up the alley, leading another behind him. She pushed her hand to close the curtain and lowered her head wearily. Hugh Bardulf was part of the Espion, stationed on Bridge Street. No doubt one of the other spies had seen her enter Kingfountain and rushed to tell him.

She sighed and grabbed her bag from the peg, slinging it around her shoulder, and then met him at the door.

"Ankarette," he said. "Why didn't you go straight to the palace?"

"Because I'm tired, Hugh. Is that reason enough?"

His eyebrows narrowed. "You haven't heard, then?"

The fact that he had two horses meant he expected her to take one of them.

"I've been in Westmarch. At Tatton Hall. Did something happen?"

Hugh Bardulf chuckled. "Oh, something *did*, Ankarette Tryneowy. I think an Espion was dispatched to Tatton Hall to tell you, but you must have taken different roads."

Ankarette felt frustration at being left in the dark, but she kept her composure. "And? What is it?"

"Lord Devereaux is back after all these years. He stormed the fortress of Averanche. Says Eredur is a false king and he's going to depose him."

Ankarette was so surprised she was speechless. Lord Devereaux had been acting as a pirate for years, plundering off the coast of Ceredigion, but this was a bold move. He'd likely chosen Averanche because it was a coastal fortress, about as far away from Kingfountain as one could get.

But that wasn't the only implication that struck her forcefully.

John Thursby had once served Lord Devereaux. Would he get involved, and would it be to help or to hurt the royal family? Was he already involved somehow?

Her heart squeezed painfully. She needed to go to the king. But she also needed to know where John Thursby was.

CHAPTER

TWO

THE DUKE'S GAMBLE

W hen Ankarette arrived at the palace, she was surprised to find men with the badge of Lord Horwath—the arrow-pierced lion—already clogging the bailey. They must have just arrived from Dundrennan, which meant they'd been dispatched in great haste. Sure enough, she found Lord Horwath in the great hall along with the other major nobles of the realm—all except for the lord of Westmarch. Severn and Dunsdworth were also assembled, wearing chain hauberks beneath their tunics. They all looked rather eager for battle, which increased Ankarette's worry. This was a predictable response. And that meant it was, undoubtedly, the wrong one.

Ankarette mixed among the servants, listening in on their conversations, while Hugh Bardulf approached the king to let him know his poisoner had arrived. There was another lord in the hall whom she didn't recognize right away. He stood out because he wasn't mingling with the others, even though his garb showed he was a man who enjoyed fine tastes. He had receding hair and a more scholarly aspect than a martial one. She had yet to see his face, though.

"I see you've finally decided to join the commotion, Ankarette," said a voice at her elbow in an attempt at humor. It was Bensen Nichols, master of the Espion. He picked a cube of cheese from the tray they were standing by. "Pressing matters in Westmarch? How's the duchess?"

"The family is all in good health," she answered, giving him a quick glance to judge his expression before turning her back to the table to get a better view of the hall. "Who's that lord standing by himself? I don't recognize him."

"Oh, that's Lord Bletchley, Duke of Southport. The king's distant cousin. He's the reason we're all here."

Ankarette lifted her eyebrows in surprise. His appearance had changed significantly since she'd last seen him, and he was wearing the latest Genevese fashion.

"As part of our peace treaty with Occitania, they handed over certain castles in the borderlands. Lord Bletchley was given charge of Averanche with a small garrison to maintain it. Do you know where it is?"

"It's on the borders with Occitania and Brythonica," Ankarette said. "It's changed hands many times but isn't of any major strategic significance. Why would Devereaux attack there?"

"That's the question, isn't it? Bletchley barely made it out of the castle with just a handful of his knights and rode straight to the palace to warn of the surprise attack. Devereaux has been a pirate these last many years, so it's no surprise they came by sea. Something is up. Ah, it looks like Bardulf got his attention at last."

Ankarette noticed Hugh was approaching them. "The king wants to see you in his chamber," he said in an undertone.

She nodded and left Hugh, Master Nichols, and the congregation of nobles and made her way through one of the back passages. Servants were bustling about, carrying in trays and flagons of wine. No doubt the cook, Liona, was harried in the kitchen feeding such a host.

Ankarette moved away from the throng and, once she was alone, triggered a secret door leading to the Espion tunnels. In the dark, she followed the memorized path and ended up in the king's chamber before he arrived. The hearth had seething chunks of red coals in it, and she added a few logs from the fresh pile to awaken the fire again. The room smelled of the queen's fragrance, a familiar scent of rose. It wasn't long before she heard the sound of approaching steps and then the king and queen entered, along with Duke Horwath. That was unusual. He normally wasn't invited into private conversations like this one.

"Ankarette," Eredur said with a sigh of relief.

Elyse approached and kissed her cheek. "Did the birthing go well? You were gone a long time."

"I'll tell you later," Ankarette said in response. She looked at the silver-haired duke quizzically. His ever-present taciturn expression revealed nothing. But Horwath was loyal to the family, and there had been several years of peace in North Cumbria.

"I'm glad you are here," Eredur said, brushing his hands together briskly. He walked over to the hearth, which was now snapping with sparks, tongues of flames wagging above them. "What have you heard? I don't want to bore you with details you already know."

"Lord Devereaux snatched the fortress at Averanche, one of the treaty castles. I didn't know your cousin was the castellan."

"Thankfully he managed to escape," Eredur said. She noticed the brooding in his eyes, revealing his unease at the situation. She surmised it was due to the last time he'd faced off with Deveraux—the bloody battle of Borehamwood. It had been a victory for Eredur. Barely. Many had died on both sides.

"It's no accident he's come now," Ankarette said. "There's history between you two."

Eredur gazed into the flames and nodded. The years and pressures of kingship had taken their toll, and so had his carousing. He especially liked to slip away from the palace to go drinking with his chancellor, Lord Hastings. The Espion kept to the shadows, keeping watch over him. But his habits were unwise. Reckless. Ankarette could still see the younger man he'd been, the fearless warrior who had gambled to win the hollow crown and won, but he wasn't the trim and physically menacing warrior he'd once been. The gray in his hair and beard were as telling as the liver spots on his skin. Always there was a threat to him, and he was constantly gripped by the nervous fear that he might lose what he'd won.

Eredur turned from the fire, his expression hardening. "The nobles are all clamoring to go after him. Well, except Stiev Horwath here. He thinks it's a ruse, and I tend to agree with him. The Espion said two ships attacked, and they estimate about forty men are with him to hold the castle."

"Forty is not a sizable force for such an undertaking," Ankarette said.

Duke Horwath nodded in agreement.

"But it's enough to withstand a siege. My cousin said they have ample provisions in the castle to last for months. Of course, we were all expecting to require those provisions in case Occitania broke the treaty and attacked us. Not if one of our own chose to do so."

"Do you think Morvared is behind this?" Ankarette asked. Her release had been one of the conditions of the peace treaty, but only with the assurance that she'd spend her remaining years sequestered in her own castle. Although she had been

Ceredigion's queen before Elyse, she had no right to the crown on her own. Her husband was dead and so was her only son.

Eredur didn't trust Morvared. Not in the least, especially after a killer had tried to help her escape several years back. Eventually, though, after the intercession of several deaconeuses, Eredur had been persuaded—for a price—to release her. She was living, as far as the Espion knew, in her castle in Dompier, which was west of Averanche in the heartland of Occitania.

"I don't know," Eredur finally answered. "Her? Lord Hux? Lewis? I'm in a fog and I can't see my hand before my face."

It was a reference to the Battle of Borehamwood. A deadly fog had risen before the battle, obscuring the field.

"You want me to go to Averanche and kill Devereaux?" she asked pointedly. That would be a challenging mission for anyone. It was easier to infiltrate a place when your arrival was unexpected. Getting into a fortress under siege without being detected would be a challenge.

Eredur shook his head. That surprised her.

"That's what he'd expect to happen. I've sent part of my fleet to blockade the harbor so he can't escape. I'm sending Stiev to surround Averanche and box him in."

"Why not Lord Kiskaddon? He's closer."

"But with a newborn babe, his mind will be back in Tatton Hall. I can't afford to take chances in this. Severn begged me to let him raze the castle, but I still want it in one piece." His lips quirked with a smile.

"You're going to starve him out?" Ankarette asked.

He shrugged. "If I must. But no, that's not my plan." His expression hardened. "That night watchman, Thursby, used to serve Devereaux, didn't he?"

Ankarette felt the coil slip around her chest and squeeze. "He did." She said it calmly, devoid of any of the inner turmoil she felt, pretending she hadn't had the very same thought. "I haven't seen him...recently."

Elyse gave her a look of sympathy. She knew more of the story than her husband. She knew the pain this was causing. Yet Ankarette could see that she and Eredur were a united front. The situation was grave enough that they'd ask her to use her relationship with John Thursby to serve their interests.

"He's still in Kingfountain," Eredur said. "Still at the apothecary's place. I had Nichols check."

Of course he did. She felt a tingle of outrage, but she suppressed it. "And if he refuses to help?"

"Persuade him," Eredur said flatly. "It's not going to take long before word of this spreads throughout the kingdoms if it already hasn't. I have Thomas securing the North. I'm sending Severn back to Glosstyr. East Stowe and Southport are on high alert. And I have Dunsdworth here, where he can do little except get drunk. I'm going to be patient while this plays out. But I need Thursby to find out what Devereaux's game is. Who he's working for and why."

It had been a challenge infiltrating Occitania and trying to smuggle out a renegade duke. This assignment was even more daunting. She knew how John Thursby felt about Eredur. And how stubborn the night watchman could be.

"What if he won't come?" Ankarette asked. "Are you going to throw him in your dungeon again?"

"I'm not unjust, Ankarette. No, I will not. Unless he's committed a crime. And I'm not the one who threw him in there if you remember. I won't force him to draw his sword against his old master. But I would like Thursby to reason with him. This brazen attack against our sovereignty cannot go unpunished. Devereaux is no fool, so I need to know why he did this. It will be winter in a few months. I hope he can persuade Devereaux to surrender the castle before then. If that doesn't happen, we'll take it back by force, and the outcome will not be favorable for anyone."

"Devereaux could hold him hostage," Ankarette said. "Have you thought of that?"

Eredur glanced at Elyse and turned back. His silence said he had.

"I'll be ready to leave in the morning," Lord Horwath said sternly. He knew the path of duty and was always ready to embark on it. He was getting ready for the war his master hoped to avoid.

And Ankarette had a different kind of battle awaiting her at Old Rose's apothecary.

THREE

OLD WOUNDS

After agreeing to meet Duke Horwath at the western gates of the city before dawn, Ankarette prepared herself for the journey and for her coming encounter with John Thursby.

The king's demands had rattled her. He wasn't being heartless. She knew that, and their trust in each other had been a long time in the making. But he wasn't the young king anymore. Like any father, he wanted to pass his kingdom down to his children. The Argentine dynasty was a never-ending tale fraught with family drama and sibling rivalry. But when their lands were threatened, it behooved the king to crush any sign of insurrection. Even if that meant mounting a bracing defense for a castle he cared little for.

She climbed the tower steps to her room in the palace, unlocked the door, and began gathering the vials and powders of her trade, along with a brace of extra daggers, needles, and poisoned rings. She worked quickly, her mind dreading the upcoming meeting. She already knew John Thursby would be in the city—he was always in the city and performed his duty as a night watchman with constancy and dedication. Lord Axelrod, the lord high constable of Ceredigion, had even begrudgingly offered him a command after one of his officers was killed. John Thursby had turned it down flat. He didn't trust Axelrod, not after the arrogant lord had arrested him. Once broken, trust was not easily mended. Which was why she didn't know how he was going to react to her request.

Ankarette closed the lid on the box of poisons and relocked it before putting it inside another chest and locking that one as well. She was going to her wardrobe to pack some clothes next when she heard the reverberation of footsteps coming up the tower stairwell. Very few people in the palace even knew where her room was or who occupied it, but at least the visitor was not attempting to go unnoticed. A knock sounded, so she went to the door and opened the sliding grate in the door to see who it was.

Queen Elyse was standing there.

Ankarette unfastened the lock and opened the door.

"Maybe I misjudged your expression, Ankarette. I probably did. But I grew worried. I wanted to come see you again before you left."

"You didn't have to climb the tower, Elyse. I would have come to your room."

Elyse entered and shut the door. The candles on the table provided ample light, revealing a small, curtained bed, Ankarette's stitching on the walls. A Wizr set on the table. Most importantly, there were no Espion tunnels connecting these chambers to the labyrinth beneath the palace. There was one way in and one way out.

"This was the tower the first Argentine king kept his wife in after she and her sons led a rebellion," the queen said doubtfully. "We could get you a room on the lower floors again, Ankarette. All you need do is ask."

"I'm not deprived, Elyse. And I have that little house in the city."

The queen nodded. "Are you...upset with Eredur? For what he's asking you to do?"

"Not really. One of our agreements has been that he'd never ask me to seduce anyone. I don't think he was asking me to do that."

"He may not have asked it, but it could have been implied. Did he overstep, Ankarette? I worry he may have."

It was a relief to hear her say it, and Ankarette shook her head. "I'm not going to threaten John Thursby. Or smile coquettishly at him. Neither would work. And I'm certainly not going to use his past feelings for me to sway his decision."

"Past feelings? You think he's stopped caring for you?"

"I rejected his marriage proposal, Elyse. Twice. I cannot be your poisoner and his wife. He knew that. Knew I *must* refuse him. Name me any man who'd patiently endure such a rejection once, let alone a second time. And now I must ask his favor, as a poisoner, to betray his friend. How do *you* think he'll react?"

Elyse sighed, her eyes full of sympathetic understanding. "What will you tell him?"

"I haven't decided yet. And I don't have much time to figure it out."

Elyse approached and took Ankarette's hands. "You have done so much for us. You've given up so much. When you told me he'd asked to marry you..." She wrinkled her nose and pressed her lips firmly together. "You deserve your share of happiness. If our enemies quit prowling like wolves against us, if only we had strength enough that no one would dare challenge Eredur or his heir, we could train a replacement for you. As costly as that would be." The queen shook her head. "But who would be as faithful as you are, Ankarette? I wouldn't feel safe without you watching over my family."

The two women embraced, Ankarette feeling her throat thicken. It wasn't just loyalty that bound her to the king and queen. It was shared history. It was succeeding against all the odds. Ankarette had known when Lord Hux poisoned her that she wouldn't live to an old age. Her womb had shriveled, her monthly flux had stopped and never returned. Yet still she'd found great fulfillment. Her reputation had spread throughout the kingdoms. Her name was spoken in whispers of dread. She'd overheard it happen on more than one occasion, when they didn't know she was listening in.

"I'll always be there for you and your family, Elyse. I promise." Ankarette took her friend's hands and squeezed them.

"Do you think Lord Hux is behind Devereaux's attack?"

"It's difficult to say. He's been out of favor with Lewis, and he knows too many secrets to be allowed to walk about freely. But I can't help but wonder if that disgrace is only an illusion. If they've all been biding their time."

Elyse nodded knowingly. "How did the birthing go? As I said earlier, you were gone a long time."

"The final weeks of the pregnancy were troubling, and there were...complications. But she's given birth to a little boy. They've named him Owen. He's a darling thing. It was difficult leaving him. So frail. So weak. But he's loved, and that will help."

"Thomas and Elysabeth are expecting a baby as well. Did you know?"

That was a surprise. Thomas had been Ankarette's first love. But he'd ended up marrying Duke Horwath's headstrong daughter. Their marriage had been childless up until this point.

"No. Does Eredur know?"

"We just found out after you left our chamber. Lord Horwath shared the news. They've kept it a secret deliberately."

Ankarette hoped she wouldn't be asked to attend Lady Elysabeth during her confinement. There was only so much magnanimity a person could feign before drawing a dagger. "How far along is she?"

"I think the babe is due midwinter. I don't think you'd fancy spending another winter in Dundrennan?"

"I'd rather not," Ankarette replied. "Thank you for telling me."

"I don't blame you. Well, I've taken too much of your time. Just know that we don't ask this lightly. But who else could handle such a situation as this? If Averanche must be razed to the ground, then Stiev Horwath is the man who will get it done, despite Severn's bluster. But if there's a way to prevent bloodshed, to save lives, you are the *woman* who will make it happen."

Ankarette appreciated the queen's confidence in her. They hugged again before Elyse departed. Then the poisoner opened the wardrobe. There was one gown she knew John Thursby particularly liked. She hadn't worn it since they'd broken things off. She touched the sleeve.

Strange how even fabric could conjure emotions.

It was still early enough that she suspected John Thursby would be asleep. Or reading from a book of poems. He didn't start his rounds until well after sunset.

Ankarette arrived on horseback at Old Rose's apothecary and slid from the saddle, her feelings humming like a jumble of wasps and butterflies. She tied the animal there and took a calming breath. She'd brushed out her hair, keeping it loose, and applied the scent John Thursby liked so well. The little apothecary had the smell of dried herbs, for there were clumps of them hanging from strings in the window. The apothecary had a secondary dwelling, however, and that was her destination. Thick, heavy curtains blocked the window, making it dark so the night watchman could sleep during the daylight hours. She approached his door and knocked, determined to get this over with. She still had no idea what to say. It honestly depended on his reaction.

She waited a little while before knocking again, but she heard no sound or movement from inside. Was he out and about? Or had he heard her approach on horseback and peeked out the window first?

Ankarette went to the door of the apothecary shop and opened it, finding Old Rose at work with a mortar and pestle. As soon as the woman recognized Ankarette, her eyes bulged with surprise.

"Do you know where he is?" Ankarette asked.

Old Rose's wrinkled face crinkled into a smile, but she looked worried. She'd been a mother hen to John Thursby, patching him up after fights, making sure he ate his pea soup. In exchange, no one bothered her shop. Ever. The arrangement was a mutual benefit.

"You came," Old Rose said with a sigh. "You came back. He didn't think you would." It was said almost accusingly.

"Do you know where he is?" Ankarette repeated.

"He's not on his rounds, I know that much. But no, he's been acting right strange lately. Something's chafing him."

Ankarette felt a throb of worry in her stomach. "Oh? What do you think it is?"

"He had a visitor two days ago. A soldier he knew from the war."

The throb turned into a clench.

"I need to find him, Rose." The old cat, Ani, slunk from behind the counter, making little chirping noises. Its big yellow eyes gazed at Ankarette curiously. Did the cat remember her? It padded up and began rubbing against her legs.

"You know as well as I the man never sleeps. He's been up and off at all hours of the day. I don't know where he is."

"Will he come back before his rounds?"

"Maybe? As I said, he's been acting strangely. The kind of look he gets when he's remembering dark times. He's been brooding so much since..." Her voice trailed off, her smile fading. "Since the two of you started acting like fools and pretending the other didn't exist!"

It was a fair accusation. But it didn't feel fair.

Ankarette didn't have an answer. She was inclined to wait to see if he returned, but she knew his rounds, even though he changed the order randomly so that the scum of the city didn't get used to a pattern. Better to leave and search for him. She'd hunt for him all night if she had to.

The door opened, and when Ankarette turned around, hand instinctively going for a dagger hilt, she saw John Thursby framed in the doorway. He stared at her in disbelief. There was a haggard look about him. He still wore the chain hauberk and pieces of armor he'd worn when she'd first met him. When he'd saved her from some sanctuary men who'd abducted her, believing her to be someone else. There were flecks of gray in his hair and beard now. A leanness that showed he wasn't eating well.

"Ankarette," he whispered hoarsely. They were both from the North, but whereas she'd dropped her brogue, he still let his drip from his tongue.

She'd missed hearing it.

FOUR

A STUBBORN PAST

Not wanting to discuss matters in front of Old Rose, Ankarette and John Thursby went next door to his room. He jerked open the curtain to add light and hastily swept aside the remains of an earlier meal. He'd always been fascinated by scents, and there was a little pot of mint growing on the windowsill. The room smelled of *him*, and it conjured memories of the night she'd been too ill to stand, weakened by their first run-in with the murderer Bidigen Grimmer, when the tincture that kept her alive had been stolen by a rascal thief at the sanctuary of Our Lady. John Thursby had gotten it back, risking his own life to do so.

"I don't know why you're here, Ankarette," he said after he'd tidied up just a little. "But I have news that cannot wait."

"Oh?" she asked, wondering at the source. He seemed on edge, but was it just because of her presence? She could easily reach out with her Fountain magic, as she'd done earlier, but she didn't want to intrude on his private thoughts and feelings. "Is this about the visitor you had? Rose was just telling me."

He nodded emphatically. "It was Harper. We served together under Lord Devereaux's command. He asked if I'd join in a rebellion against Eredur." He let the words dangle in the air between them.

"Devereaux has taken the fortress at Averanche," Ankarette said. With John Thursby it was always better to paint the truth in clear, contrasting colors.

"Has he now?" came the astonished reply.

"You didn't know?"

"No. He wouldn't tell me more after I refused him. I've come by your place every day, looking for you. I knew I needed to tell you. I've been worried sick you were already involved."

Ankarette gave him a half smile, unsurprised that he'd thought of her. "I was in Westmarch. Helping the duchess deliver her baby. I just returned, and now I'm going to Averanche with Duke Horwath."

His nostrils flared. "You can't go."

"I must. And I'd like you to come with me."

That roused him. He looked at her incredulously before blurting, "W-What?"

"Just hear me out."

"I'm not going to lift my sword against Devereaux! I've borne the shame of men believing I was false for all these years. He was my friend. You cannot ask it of me!"

"I'm not asking you to fight him."

"But you're going to ask me to betray him. To get you close to him so you can...you can..." He waved his hand at her, his expression wrinkling with disgust.

"No," Ankarette said. "I wouldn't put you in that position."

"Your king would," he shot back at her.

She closed the gap between them, reaching out and touching his forearm. She'd always found that a simple touch was a way to soothe him. He was riled now, that was plain to see. She needed to calm him to be able to discuss the situation and all its many facets.

"I won't lie to you, John Thursby. I do need your help. And yes, the king sent me. We're trying to avert bloodshed, on both sides. Deveraux has enough soldiers to hold the castle. But Eredur's ships are going to blockade Averanche and the fortress will be surrounded. He'll be trapped inside. The king wants to understand what Devereaux is after. And who he is aligned with, if anyone. He claims he's raising a rebellion against the king, but who does he intend to supplant him with? That's what we need to understand. We can't see all the pieces moving on the Wizr board."

"Harper didn't tell me that. He came here, tried to recruit me, and then left when I refused." He gazed down at her hand, still fixed to his arm, then into her eyes. "I can't fight against you either, Ankarette. I'd rather stay out of it." He paused, then added, "I also knew that if I didn't tell someone what I knew, I could be accused of treason."

She was so relieved he wasn't guilty of that crime. "Come with me."

"And what do you want me to do? Persuade him to give up the castle? I don't think he will. He's tossed the dice. He obviously thinks it's worth the risk."

"You think he stands a chance of winning?"

"He is no fool, Ankarette. At least, not the man I remember. But if he's changed, then so has Eredur. He isn't the man he was years ago. He's fat and complacent. If you don't keep using a whetstone, any blade will dull. And I'm not saying anything you don't already know."

Part of her bristled at the assessment, but there was truth there. Without varnish or soap. The ugly truth was that Eredur was unprepared to fight a war. He would have to rely on others to keep the peace. Also, she knew the treaty he'd signed with

Lewis had been a relief to him at the time. He'd known the situation he was in was tenuous at best and that the dice might not land in his favor if he fought Occitania. And yet he'd regretted it after the grip of fear had eased. But she could not tell John Thursby any of those things.

"So you think Eredur should siege the castle and be done with it."

"Yes. And Devereaux must believe he will not. He's probably convinced that he won't. Maybe he wants a deal. I know he's been plundering the shores from Genevar to Legault to Blackpool. Maybe he's gambling for bigger stakes now? I don't know."

"Or someone has made it worth his while to prod Eredur with a spike. To rile the bear."

"He's not a bear. Not anymore. He's like one of those castle dogs gnawing at bones under the—"

Ankarette's eyes flashed with anger. She dropped her hand, and John Thursby immediately stopped.

"I beg your pardon," he said. "That was very rude of me. I tell you, Ankarette, I can't help resenting the man who came between us. How could I feel otherwise? But you are loyal to the man and the king. I can't fault you for it. I have the same attitude toward Devereaux."

That was something else she admired about John Thursby. He'd always spoken his thoughts and feelings plainly, like a soldier. And when he'd done wrong, he'd admitted it. That was a rarity among men.

"I don't blame you," she said. "But he is my king, and he's sent me to bring you to Averanche. To see if we can uncover the truth of what's going on."

He folded his arms, giving her a wary look. "And if I refuse?"

"I hope you won't. I need your help." She thought of other

ways she could try to influence him, but she could tell he'd already made up his mind.

His voice softened tenderly. "You know I can't refuse you anything," he said, reaching out tentatively to touch her hair but stopping himself before he did.

JOHN THURSBY PERFORMED his duty as a night watchman. She went on the rounds with him so they could talk, to become more familiar with each other again. She told him about her dangerous mission to Occitania and shared some of the story of the gentle duke and the Maid. He was touched by it, as she'd known he would be. At midnight they stopped for tea at her place, settling into the comfortable companionability that had existed between them in the harrowing days after Nanette's disappearance. He had often stopped by in those days, and they'd sat together in candlelight, talking about the past, the present. But always avoiding the future.

They were at the gate of Kingfountain with horses ready an hour before sunrise. Duke Horwath was already there, impatient to be going. The duke of the North was a man of few words, but he acknowledged John Thursby with a respectful nod and introduced him to his captains. Then he sent one of them—Captain Harshem—ahead with a band of soldiers, to scout. The soldiers treated Ankarette's companion without animosity or favor. It was a duty to be performed. And the men of the North did their duty without favor or resentment.

John Thursby rode by her side as they kept pace with the duke's men. There wasn't time for idle chatter at the pace Horwath set. Even though they hadn't slept that night,

Ankarette and John Thursby pushed through their fatigue. It was several days' ride to the western parts of the realm, and the duke opted to camp amidst the hedgerows instead of trying to find softer accommodations. After making camp, Ankarette fell asleep almost immediately, the lazy flicks of the flames making her drowsy enough to collapse onto her bedroll.

She awoke after midnight to find John Thursby sitting at the edge of the dwindled flames, reading from a little book.

After she propped herself on her arm, he turned to look at her.

"Have you slept?" she asked.

He shrugged. "The snores were keeping me awake."

"You should rest."

"I rested in the saddle."

That couldn't be true unless he'd discovered a way to sleep with his eyes open.

"You should try again." She had the intuition that he was keeping watch. He just could not help himself. He was trying to protect her.

"I was thinking," he said softly, glancing at her. "Are we going to change horses? The pace we're going would challenge any beast. Except my old nag Truck."

She didn't remember him owning a horse, but he must have in the past, probably before Borehamwood. "I think the duke's horses are bred for stamina," she said. She also knew there were baggage trains coming after them, supplies and provender to help with the siege. The king would send anything needed to retake Averanche. And patrols would follow the baggage to protect it.

John Thursby nodded. "I was thinking something else. That the two of us should ride ahead. Once all these soldiers arrive and make camp, it'll be more difficult to get inside the castle. Or get him out of it."

"What are you planning, John Thursby?"

"I think he'll come out and talk to me. I would rather he come out than I go in. It's not that I don't trust him to be honest with me. But I don't want him using me as a hostage to counter you."

That was a good thought. He was always looking at a situation from different angles. Few knew of her past relationship with John Thursby. She'd kept it that way to protect him. They'd always been discreet, but if anyone did know, it made sense they'd try to use it to their advantage.

"I think you're right. In the morning, let's ride ahead. See what we can learn."

He nodded thoughtfully. "When you play Wizr against Eredur, do you let him win?"

Ankarette shook her head. "It's not his favorite game. But no, I only let someone win if it serves another purpose."

"I suspected as much. That's why I could never beat you. Devereaux loves the game. He's always thinking ahead." She watched the firelight dance in his eyes. "I'm not sure I've ever seen him lose. I remember being in his tent the night before the battle, as he was preparing for the next day. He looked at the ground. The weariness of the soldiers. How much provision we had, down to the last barrel of flour. I'm telling you, Ankarette, if it hadn't been for that fog, I think he would have won." His cheek twitched.

Was there a part of him that hoped Devereaux would win this time? And how would such a change alter things between him and Ankarette?

She knew John Thursby had been one of Devereaux's most trusted men. Was it a mistake bringing him to Averanche?

The poisoner school taught us a very simple truth and one that I've used to my advantage many times. There is nothing more deceptive than the obvious. The eye always sees what it expects to see.

— ANKARETTE TRYNEOWY

FIVE

AS THINGS SEEM

The smell of the air changed as they neared the small town of Averanche. The scent of the woods and meadows became tinged with the salty flavor of the sea. The roads and waymarkers were clear, easy to follow. She could see the haze of chimney smoke over a woody knoll, which blocked the view of the sea but not the scent of it. At the road's bend were two of Horwath's men on horseback, the distinctive color of their tunics and the badge of the pierced lion recognizable even at a distance.

She thought it wise of Captain Harshem to have left sentries on the road leading to town, to give news to the duke before his arrival. As she and John Thursby approached on their mounts, the sentries waved for them to stop. The knoll was thick with beech trees, the leaves just beginning to turn the colors of autumn. A few sessile oak trees were scattered about, the area rich with woodland life as well, from squirrels to hares, and she'd even spotted a fox during the ride that day.

"How far back is the duke?" asked one of the sentries after they'd stopped. He craned his neck to look behind her, but there was no evidence of the duke's men on the horizon yet. Ankarette expected they were still a sizable distance behind.

"Not far," she said. "Where's Captain Harshem?"

"He's in town," said the other fellow, cocking his thumb and jabbing it behind him. "He's found an inn he thinks the duke can use to command the area. Called the Respite. That's where you'll find him."

"Thank you," Ankarette said. The fellow didn't have a Northern accent, but she imagined not all of the duke's men did. It gave her pause, though. Made her wary.

"Where you from, lads?" John Thursby asked. Had he read her mind? No, John Thursby had a knack for little details.

The two soldiers looked at each other. And that's when she noticed the splotch of blood on one of their tunics and realized the danger.

She reached for the dagger at her waist, just as several men with crossbows appeared from their hiding places in the beech trees.

"Ride!" John Thursby shouted, drawing his sword.

Ankarette thought that a very bad idea. Plunging ahead could lead to a deeper ambush. And if they turned tail, they'd give the crossbowmen a clean shot at them.

Ankarette spurred her horse directly at the fellow on the left and swung her right leg over the saddle horn, coming down on the ground on the other side, to use the beast as a shield against the crossbow bolts. Gripping the dagger in her left hand, she rushed the startled soldier and jabbed the dagger blade into the meat of his thigh. Not a fatal wound, but one that would disperse the toxin on the blade's edge into his bloodstream, incapacitating him.

She heard the harsh twang of a crossbow, and the bolt skewered her horse, causing it to scream in pain, rear, and then panic and flail.

Ankarette dodged around the rump of the soldier's horse and found the other soldier frantically trying to draw his weapon to defend himself. He was right-handed, so he was reaching to pull the sword from the scabbard at his left hip, exposing his ribs to her. She grabbed the edge of his hauberk, then thrust the blade into his ribs, making him choke with surprise as she pierced his lung. She was using his and his horse's bulk to shield her again from the crossbowmen, but the horse reared at the sudden attack and bolted down the road they'd just come in on, moving away from the city, and the soldier fell off not far away.

John Thursby was charging his steed up the hill, brandishing his blade as he shot straight toward the previously concealed men.

Ankarette watched as a crossbowman hefted the heavy weapon and shot at John Thursby, but he hung low against the horse's mane, and the bolt merely glanced his horse's neck, opening a streak of red that wasn't a fatal blow. Then the furious night watchman and his equally enraged mount reached the beech trees and blows were returned.

Ankarette sprinted up the hillock, saw another man step around with a crossbow and aim it at John Thursby, who was striking down from the saddle at the men with the spent crossbows. It took too long to reload such weapons, powerful though they were. She threw her dagger and felled the man aiming at her friend. There were two more men, but both fled the scene through the trees, which made her unwilling to test her skills and lose weapons she might need later.

The man she'd caught in the neck with a dagger sank to his knees, his eyes wide with terror. She kicked him down and found John Thursby approaching on his mount, sword sheathed again. The two fellows he'd attacked were already down. He reached for her and helped swing her up onto the horse behind him.

"How'd you know," he panted, "they were false?"

"Bloodstain on the tunic," she answered, searching for signs of other enemies.

"Clever wench," he praised with a smirk. The one she'd stabbed in the ribs lay in the middle of the road not far away. The horse was galloping hotly. The fellow she'd gotten in the leg had also fallen off his horse, but only because she'd used a paralytic on him and he hadn't been able to hang on. His horse was nickering nearby, ears twitching with fear. Ankarette's mount was dead.

"Let's go to that one," she said, pointing to the fallen man nearby. "I can revive him."

"He's not dead?"

"I needed only one of them alive," she replied. "Keep watch for the other fellows in case they circle back."

"I'm tempted to run them down," he growled.

"They have the advantage in the woods and with their weapons. I'm grateful only your horse was grazed."

"I'm wearing a hauberk. It'll deflect bolts unless it's too close. You've naught but that pretty dress. You're the one I was worried about."

She'd learned from her training that in combat, weapons like bows were prone to miss their targets unless the archer was exceptional. It didn't take much skill to shoot a crossbow, but it took good aim. They were weapons favored by pirates, when aim in rough seas counted for little. When they reached the fellow, she slid off the horse and knelt by the body. From her pouch, she removed a vial with the antidote and forced a few drops onto the man's tongue. Within moments, he was blinking again and starting to twitch. Then she removed some nightshade powder and blew it into his face. The convulsions stilled and his panicked look changed to a glassy-eyed stare. He'd tell her anything now until the powder wore off.

"Where is Captain Harshem?"

The man gave her a silly grin. "He's at the Respite, like I told you."

"Where did you get the tunic, then?"

"We were hiding on the knoll and killed the sentries. They were watching the road ahead, not the trees."

Ankarette thought it rather cunning of Lord Devereaux to have left some men in hiding outside Averanche.

"What were your orders?" she asked him next, unsure of how much time she'd have.

"We were told to watch for a woman in a cloak. The poisoner of Kingfountain. To capture her." The silly grin spread. "You're beautiful."

"There now," John Thursby snarled, "don't be cheeky."

Ankarette knew it was the poison that was ravaging the fellow's inhibitions. It wasn't a surprise they'd been expecting her. They'd probably considered six crossbows enough to make her surrender. She wouldn't have. "How many men does Deveraux have in the castle?"

"There are fifty and two. No, fifty and three. I'm not exactly sure. We were told to stay back to watch for the king's men and see who was coming. Too bad the king's not coming."

"Oh? And why is that?"

"We'd have earned a thousand crowns to put a bolt in his head." The way he said it, so dispassionately, so carelessly, made Ankarette's heart simmer with fury. Devereaux wasn't interested in fighting a battle. He was content to count corpses.

"How many were on the hill with him?" John Thursby asked.

"Answer," Ankarette said to the fellow.

"Six of us. The six Ravens." He giggled. "But there's not six anymore!"

A team of mercenaries perhaps?

"What do you want to do with him?" John Thursby asked her.

"I'm not letting him go. He may still provide useful information. I say let's get to Captain Harshem, and he can search the woods for the surviving accomplices. They might be on their way back to the castle."

She bound up the wound on the man's leg to stop the bleeding, then lashed his wrists behind his back, which made him chuckle with a lopsided grin as he gazed at her. Then his ankles were secured. John Thursby came off his horse and coaxed the skittish beast nearby with some food to calm it. Once he had the horse calmed and secure, he handed the reins to Ankarette and then hefted the man up on the saddle on his stomach.

She rode behind John Thursby on his horse, holding the guide rope. Soon the man recovered from the poison and began to spew curses at them. He definitely had a pirate's tongue.

As they rounded the knoll, Averanche came into view. More men in Duke Horwath's livery were posted there. If she hadn't interrogated their prisoner with the help of nightshade, she would have been reluctant to approach, but the soldiers came to them with concerned looks, and after they related their tale, they asked to see Captain Harshem outside the town. He came in a hurry with some men, and she recognized him instantly. They related the scene of the ambush.

The captain was furious and ordered men to search the knoll for his missing sentries and then sent the prisoner to the Respite with another guard. Ankarette and John Thursby followed him into town. She discerned the Occitanian accent spoken by the townsfolk, and the style of their clothing was also decidedly different from what people of Ceredigion wore —kirtles with front-laced corsets for the maidens, exposing shoulders and bosoms and, for the men, pointed shoes and jerkins with tight sleeves but puffed fabric at the shoulders. She'd seen those styles many times on her missions among the Occitanians, and it struck her again how this town had recently been part of King Lewis's hegemony. The townsfolk had no loyalty to Eredur. The castle was their heart, and if the citizens wanted to be safe, they'd respect whoever was in command of it.

"What have you learned since you arrived?" Ankarette asked the scowling captain.

"Precious little. The mayor of Averanche is worried the king will accuse him of treason, but Devereaux arrived by surprise and quickly overpowered the guards before slamming the portcullis down and shutting the outer gate."

She could see the towers of the castle and the upper battlements as they rode through town. It was on a prominence by the shore, the town farther from the coming and going of the tide.

"Has the king's fleet arrived?"

"Aye. Got here yesterday. They've brought seventy pikemen as well as two dozen archers."

"How many ships?"

"Twelve. Devereaux's ships have already fled. I've been told he's been seen on the ramparts."

Ankarette wouldn't rely on the rumors, but John Thursby would recognize him. Now that she understood the displaced duke's intention of killing Eredur on sight, she was even more convinced that the king ought to remain behind at Kingfountain no matter what.

They reached the Respite in a trice and found the establishment full of soldiers. The serving maids were all attractive and keen to serve, but Ankarette distrusted them instantly and wondered how many of them were trying to learn secrets they could sell. Captain Harshem had a table in the corner and gestured for them to sit there while he arranged for food to be brought out.

When it arrived, she smelled it for hints of poison. Then she scraped away some of the seasoning with the table knife and cut into the flesh of the capon. Men arrived with news after they'd finished eating, and Captain Harshem sat sternly listening as the men gave their report.

"We found Teagen and Morson dead, their bodies stashed by a beech tree. They'd both been killed by crossbows, their tunics stripped away. They'd been checked on earlier, so this was a recent kill." The soldier giving the report looked furious. "I can't wait till the duke gets here and we can punish these filthy wretches."

Captain Harshem scowled. "Give the bodies the rites of the Lady. I know the duke will send word to their families in the North. Poor Morson was just married too. Ugh."

"I hope we capture Devereaux alive," said another soldier with a snarl. "I'd like to see his body go over the falls. Maybe the king will let us take him to Dundrennan for it. That waterfall is steeper than the one in Kingfountain."

"Any sign of the other crossbowmen?" Harshem asked.

"No, sir. Not a glimpse. We have four of the six if there were indeed six."

"There were," Ankarette said. "There's two more out there. Let's do a search house to house. There are enough pikemen to do the job."

Harshem nodded in agreement. "I'll tell their captain. Excuse me." He rose from the table and walked across the crowded room to another table, where a man wearing the king's colors sat.

John Thursby looked her in the eye. "This isn't going to be easy, Ankarette. He was watching for you."

"I know," she answered. "I wasn't expecting it to be easy." But she was confident in her skills. In her training. She'd outsmarted Queen Morvared. Lord Hux. And even King Lewis. Devereaux was an opponent she hadn't faced before, but surely she was prepared.

"I think sneaking into the castle would be a very bad idea," he offered. "But that's not what you're thinking, is it? I can tell by the look in your eye." He cocked his head slightly. "It's making me nervous already."

"I have an idea," she said, smiling. "Let's get a tunic from one of those crossbowmen. It's time to make you invisible."

SIX

FAMILIAR STRANGERS

A nkarette held the razor against John Thursby's throat and hesitated. A bit of lather dripped from his chin. He sat on a wooden stool in front of her, fingers digging into his knees as he gazed up at her.

"Just get it over with," he said sullenly.

Ankarette smiled and began to shave him. Bearded men were more common in Ceredigion and the opposite was true in Occitania. Ankarette had noticed this during her travels, and so she'd convinced the surly night watchman that he would blend in better in Averanche if he looked more like a local. She was careful in her ministrations, not wanting to nick his skin and draw blood. She stripped away the beard bit by bit until it was all gone and then dipped the full towel in the bowl of warm water and wiped his face clean.

With shoulders slightly slumped, he gazed at her again, a look that was confusing to interpret. She lay the razor down on the little cabinet with the remaining cup of lather and then brought a small mirror around so he could see himself.

The frown turned into a grin. "Old Rose wouldn't recognize me."

She'd combed his hair forward in the Occitanian fashion and agreed that his look had dramatically altered. He was wearing a different tunic as well, one that had been worn by one of the mercenaries—a dead man who no longer needed it. His sword belt was hanging from a post fixed to the wall. They were in a small room in the inn, one that overlooked the rear of the building. With the imminent arrival of Duke Horwath's soldiers, Ankarette had claimed the room to use for her purposes and offered to share it with John Thursby since she hadn't thought he'd enjoy bedding down on the floor in the common room. He was happy to oblige but had pledged to sleep on the floor if he slept at all.

He was still digging his fingers into his knees as if uncomfortable.

"You will blend in. We both will. We'll be able to hear things now that we wouldn't before. I can speak Occitanian fluently. Do you know any?"

"Just a little, but if I open my mouth, I'll give us away. You can do the talking, Ankarette."

"You seem nervous."

He looked away from her, shaking his head.

"What are you worrying about?"

"I'll be *fine*."

Ankarette sighed and grazed his bare cheek with the edge of her hand. "Tell me."

He chuffed, grunting something unintelligible, then turned to face her, his expression suddenly flat, his mouth a firm line. She'd never kissed him without a beard and was surprised to find herself wondering what it would be like.

"Your plan, Ankarette. It's clever and canny and cautious. But now that I see you wearing...*that*..." He opened his palm and gestured to the outfit she'd acquired from an Occitanian barmaid in the inn. "Well, I'm a little distracted. I'm sorry for speaking plainly, but you bid me to. I'm a man, a soldier, and it's rather fetching on you." His cheeks were beginning to burn as he made the confession.

Now that he'd admitted it, she did recall seeing his eyes widen when she'd opened the door of the room after changing. She felt a little throb of satisfaction at having gotten such a reaction from him. There was no denying his feelings were no longer being suppressed.

"You like it?" she asked, fiddling with the lacings of her corset.

He rose from the stool abruptly. "I'm a man, not a sexton, Ankarette. Shall we go?" He clenched his hands into fists and slowly released them.

Ankarette nodded. She had weapons concealed as well, a dagger strapped to her thigh beneath her skirt, one in her left boot cuff, and the rings she usually wore.

She motioned for the door, and he marched to it and left. The common room was more subdued than she imagined it normally being. When she approached Captain Harshem's table to tell him they were leaving to gather information, the man looked her over in surprise.

Then out into the streets they went. As they walked, she hooked her arm around John Thursby's and deliberately slowed their pace. They were two lovers out for a stroll, which allowed them to keep their voices low and intimate. She was impressed by Lord Devereaux already, at his decisiveness and risk taking. He was a worthy adversary, to be sure. Before she'd risk John Thursby in any way, she needed to understand as much as she could about his old master.

"Other than playing Wizr, did Lord Devereaux have any other interests? Hunting, hawking, archery?"

"He could do all those things, but he didn't enjoy them. No, he was more interested in people than things. It gave him energy to walk the camp at night, talking to his soldiers. He'd learn little things about them. Then, when he returned to his tent, he'd tell me. Not because I cared, because I didn't, but because it helped him *remember* those things. He had an uncanny memory, especially for people and places."

"A natural leader, then," Ankarette observed. "Those qualities instill loyalty."

"You aren't wrong. And it's one of the reasons serving Eredur rankled him so. Eredur is like that too, I've heard. Didn't you tell me he took an early interest in you when you served the Duke of Warrewik? Not romantically, of course."

"He did. His most intimate friend was Thomas Mortimer. And because he chose me, Eredur took an interest as well. He wanted to earn my loyalty."

"Devereaux is the same. When I was wounded at Borehamwood, he came to see me before he left. I could tell it grieved him to leave me behind. It grieved him personally." His voice was thick with memory. "I wasn't just a soldier to him. I was a friend."

"It will be painful to confront him, then. It's been a number of years. He's no longer a duke of the realm. He may have changed."

John Thursby shook his head. "I doubt that. His circumstances may have, but he'll still be the same man."

"Let's stop at this store first," Ankarette suggested, subtly tugging his arm to change course. It was a store that sold glass jars and vials. She'd also noticed some Brythonican glasswork in the window. "Pretend to be bored and impatient, but don't talk."

"I won't need to pretend, then," he said with a huff.

Ankarette feigned excitement and interest and quickly

struck up a conversation with the shopkeeper, while John Thursby explored the shelves with a look of pure apathy. He'd occasionally pick something up, gaze at it with indifference, then set it back down. After some talk where she learned about the shopkeeper and his family, she delicately probed for information that might be useful.

And that's when she learned that Lord Deveraux had a poisoner working for him.

"YOU RECOGNIZED HIS NAME?" John Thursby said once they were back on the street.

"No, poisoners regularly use aliases."

"That's right. You called yourself Krysia when we first met. I'd forgotten."

"The detail about the poisoner that gave him away was the lazy eye. His name is Farrit Blawn. We were at Pisan at the same time. And he came in here with Lord Devereaux. Those are the only details I needed."

"It's no accident that he knows you," John Thursby said with a snort. "This poisoner may have a lazy eye, but it'll be on the lookout for *you*."

"Exactly. And it means he'll know all the safeguards to protect Lord Devereaux's food and drink. A poisoner is expensive to hire."

"He's done well in his new career of piracy, I take it."

"Or the poisoner is on loan from another person. I don't know who Farrit Blawn was working for. It could be Lord Hux sent him."

She had been wondering whether their paths would cross

again. Before leaving Kingfountain, she'd made sure the king and queen increased the guards watching the fountains inside the palace. Lord Hux had an uncanny way of traveling through fountains.

"Where to next?" he asked.

She chose an apothecary, curious to know whether her rival had also visited there and what he may have purchased. That stop resulted in no additional information about the poisoner, although Ankarette continued to develop a sense of the town. Averanche had stronger ties to Brythonica and Occitania than it did to Ceredigion. It had once been a fortress of the first Argentine kings, although it had switched hands many times over the centuries. She could tell the owner preferred conversing in Occitanian and treated her like a local.

By the fifth store, the sun was starting to go down, and she'd heard that Duke Horwath had arrived. Word spread quickly in small communities. And the tension increased. People were asking about the duke of the North and wondering what he might do. A siege was not good for business, and a blockade was even worse. People were fearful that they'd run out of supplies and that the rulers in distant Kingfountain would be deaf to their troubles.

"We should go back to the Respite," Ankarette suggested. Dusk was a dangerous time to be out and about in a city. They walked but increased their pace, not to signify nervousness but as if they were a couple heading home.

They'd made it past the apothecary they'd visited earlier when she felt John Thursby's muscles tighten reflexively.

"What is it?" she whispered.

"The man walking toward us. I recognize him," he responded, voice low.

Ankarette wouldn't have been able to pick him out of a crowd, except he strode with confidence and strength, wearing a hauberk and bracers. He didn't have a longsword, but he did have a hefty dagger crammed into his belt. He was walking toward them, heading to the farther side of town, in the same direction as the road leading up to the fortress.

"You're sure?" Ankarette said.

"I know his name."

Since they and the fellow were walking toward each other, each moment reduced the gap faster. He'd pass them in seconds. Ankarette subtly twisted her needle ring and exposed the sharp edge.

"Are you going to...?"

Ankarette pretended to trip in the street and stumble forward just as the man stepped out of their way. His eyes were fixed on the street behind them, not on them. Ankarette grabbed his arm to steady herself, apologizing profusely in Occitanian. He rubbed his arm, having felt a prick, his eyebrows lowering in concern.

"Pardon! I'm so sorry!" Ankarette said, continuing with John Thursby the way they were going, putting him behind them.

They'd walked ten more steps before she heard the fellow collapse in the street.

CHAPTER

SEVEN

NIGHTSHADE

F our soldiers from Duke Horwath's command carried the twitching man down the center street of Averanche toward the Respite. After the fellow had succumbed to her poisons, Ankarette had asked John Thursby to summon assistance while she lingered in the shadows to see if anyone else came to the aid of the fallen man. A few bystanders had, but their reactions were typical and it was mostly women who had come to help. No one had interfered with the retrieval.

She followed behind the group at a distance. By the time they reached the inn, the man was conscious and struggling.

Stiev Horwath was there, his normally taciturn expression twisted with a look of pent-up anger. No doubt he'd learned about the deaths of his men. John Thursby wasn't there, which roused her concern, but he arrived shortly after she did and offered a curt nod signaling that all was well.

"What would you like us to do with him?" the duke asked Ankarette sternly.

"Bind him and take him to a room. We'll ask our questions

there if you agree." It was always wise to defer to the authority of powerful men.

Duke Horwath agreed, gave the order, and the fellow blanched when he saw how much trouble he was in. He was clapped in irons, both wrists and ankles, and led with shuffling steps to a room on the main floor. Two guards were posted outside. John Thursby looked hesitant about following, but she gestured for him to join her and the duke, and he did.

Their prisoner was seated in a chair, swiveling his neck both ways, trying to get a look at them since his back was to them. A candle was set on the table on one wall, offering adequate but not substantial light.

Duke Horwath stepped deliberately in front of the man, no longer suppressing a scowl, and stared at him menacingly. He did not introduce himself. He did not say a word, and that added immeasurably to the intimidation the fellow must be feeling, for his gestures were all nervous energy as he kept glancing back at Ankarette and her companion. Then, suddenly, he started when he finally recognized the night watchman.

"Thursby!"

"Quentin," replied the night watchman with a nod.

Ankarette stepped forward next. He'd given her a suspicious look, and now his brows needled with worry.

"And you're the poisoner, I assume," the prisoner said. "Who nicked me in the street."

"Do you know the punishment for treason, Master Quentin?" Ankarette asked. "What the Fountain's justice demands?"

He tried and failed to suppress a shudder. "Aye. A boat and a waterfall. Is that to be my fate, then?"

"You accepted that fate when you joined your master in

rebellion against Eredur Argentine. But the king might be persuaded to show mercy if you prove useful."

"How useful?" he asked with a sardonic tone. "Are you going to torture me, Poisoner?"

She sensed loyalty in him, loyalty to Devereaux. When he glanced at John Thursby again, it was with a glare of contempt. Of accusation.

"Whose orders is Lord Devereaux acting under?" Ankarette asked, drawing his gaze back to her.

"His own, as always."

"Why do I find that answer unconvincing?"

"You believe what you want. My master was a duke of Ceredigion, but not under Eredur. He took away his duchy and gave it to another."

"Is that not within his rights as king?" Duke Horwath said. He was one of those who'd been granted such a title for his demonstrations of loyalty to Eredur. He'd become Duke of North Cumbria, a title that Warrewik had once held.

"And what gave him that right, my lord duke? A blood-choked battlefield. What can be won can also be lost. It takes no Wizr to foresee *that*."

"Devereaux wants a fight, then?" Ankarette asked suspiciously.

"Oh, there will be a fight. Iron is tested in the flame of war. I think your king is no longer accustomed to the heat."

"You think a few pirates can challenge the might of Ceredigion? That the people will revolt and join a pirate?"

"If you believe that, Poisoner, you're not as clever as they say you are."

She'd heard enough. He wasn't going to willingly betray Devereaux. But he'd betray him, nonetheless. Ankarette withdrew her bag of nightshade powder, judged the man's health and stamina, and took a measured portion.

"What are you doing?" His arms were bound behind him, but he looked as if he'd try to stand until John Thursby clamped his hand on his shoulder, keeping him in the chair. Ankarette blew the powder into Quentin's face. He blinked, sniffed, and shook his head, confusion mixing with his look of dread.

And then the nightshade began to work. His body slumped. He gave a sleepy chuckle.

"Who convinced Lord Devereaux to attack Averanche?" she asked.

The fellow lifted his eyes, gazing up at the ceiling with a dreamy look. "An Occitanian fellow. Hawks? Pox? Something like that."

Lord Hux. Ankarette's darkest fear resurfaced. She hadn't really believed the stories that the poisoner was in disgrace with the King of Occitania, banished to Shynom castle, but she'd wanted to.

"Lord Hux?" she asked.

"Ah, that's the one."

"Why attack Averanche? What benefit does it hold for your master?"

"It needed to be a coastal city. Had to be far enough away from Kingfountain."

"Why?" she pressed.

"To draw the king out."

"So he could be murdered by your crossbowmen?"

The man yawned, starting to look sleepy. "No. So the traitor could seize the palace while he's distracted."

A jolt of energy struck Ankarette's chest. "Who is this traitor?"

"I don't know, my lady. Only my master knows. But it's all arranged. Averanche is the first piece on the board to fall. Then another. Then another. Threat and mate."

Ankarette looked at Duke Horwath, saw the fury furrowing his brow. It had been years since the kingmaker wars. Back then, it was Warrewik who had upended things and usurped power, intending to put his son-in-law, Dunsdworth, on the throne instead of Eredur. Dunsdworth had long aspired to rule Ceredigion. And now he had a son, a namesake, and another child on the way. It made the most sense that he was behind the conspiracy, but she would need proof before she could accuse the brother of the king. Irrefutable proof.

One thing made perfect sense to her. If this was a gamble to win a throne, and Lord Hux was behind it, then the strategy involved removing the poisoner of Kingfountain from the Wizr board. When Devereaux had attacked Averanche, he'd done so knowing it would draw either Eredur or Ankarette. The ambush on the road had been the first attempt to kill her. It would not be the last.

Noise from outside their private room attracted their attention. People were yelling now, a commotion.

Duke Horwath gripped his sword hilt and marched to the door, John Thursby right behind him. When the door was opened, they saw soldiers running about in mayhem and serving girls fleeing out the door.

"Captain!" Horwath barked.

Captain Harshem looked stunned, confused. "The inn's on fire! Upper floor! We have to get out!"

Ankarette smelled smoke. People were running up and down the stairs. Even the soldiers were fleeing. Panic—it was sheer panic. Ankarette didn't understand how Devereaux could have responded to the abduction of his man so quickly, not from the fortress, but then she realized this had been planned earlier.

Duke Horwath started toward the door, but she stopped him. "Wait!"

He regarded her with confusion.

"Be cautious, Stiev. There are still two crossbowmen we haven't found. They might be waiting in a window, watching the doors. If you go outside right now, they could ambush you with a bolt."

"As opposed to being burned alive? I'll take my chances," the duke said gruffly.

"The smoke could be coming from anywhere. Is the building truly on fire? It won't burn down in an instant."

"I'll go find out," John Thursby said. He rushed to the stairs and started going up.

Turning around, Ankarette noticed the shackled prisoner, Quentin, walking from the room, looking dazed and confused. The chains between his ankles dragged on the ground.

"Establish order," Ankarette said to the duke. "The smoke could be coming from anywhere. A ploy." She couldn't hear the sound of crackling flames, and there was no visible smoke that she could see.

Lord Horwath grunted in agreement and began giving orders to his men and the soldiers from the ships. He gathered them together in ranks to wait inside, while allowing the serving wenches to flee. The innkeeper was in a panicked state, but when the discipline of the soldiers returned, he quickly calmed down.

The people were all evacuated from the top floor of the inn, and Ankarette watched the stairs continuously until John Thursby came marching down. He was holding a smoldering crossbow bolt.

"What did you find?" the duke asked him.

"One of the rooms *was* on fire," he said. "But I smothered it with bedsheets. From the broken glass and the smell of burning oil, they shot a pitch-soaked bolt through the window."

Captain Harshem approached. "Someone opened the door and shouted 'Fire,' saying a room was on fire upstairs."

"And there was," John Thursby said. "But it would have taken time to burn. It might have gone out by itself."

Duke Horwath scowled. "Captain, take your men. Search every building on both sides of the street. Find those crossbowmen. And put that prisoner back in the room before he wanders off!"

"Yes, my lord!" the captain said and saluted. He began giving orders to the troops to begin the search. Quentin was escorted back to the room where they'd interrogated him.

Within the hour, one of the crossbowmen had been apprehended and brought back to the Respite. They'd found him skulking in an alley. He'd run for it, causing an uproar, but he'd been blocked by another set of guards and had surrendered. The other man was still at large, and the search for him was ongoing.

After much of the commotion had settled down, Ankarette saw John Thursby coming down the stairs again, this time wearing his regular armor and cloak. She wrinkled her brow when she saw him.

"Where do you think you're going?" she asked. It had been a strenuous day. She was tired, on edge. Her mind was whirling from all they'd learned. A traitor was at large. She had to find out who it was. She had to know.

"I'm a night watchman, Ankarette. It's time to start my rounds."

"This isn't the Hermitage, John Thursby."

"I know, lass. But the night carries secrets. I'm going to see what they teach me."

EIGHT

THE SECRETS OF WAVES

It wasn't until after midnight that the Respite became true to its name again. Duke Horwath was a formidable battle commander, and he'd established a rotation of the guard to patrol the town, while others worked through the night to construct picket lines as defensive measures. The inn was full, and Ankarette had to step around snoring soldiers who'd bedded down on the floor since all the rooms were taken. Every time the inn door opened, she glanced over in expectation of seeing John Thursby arrive, but he did not, and she could not help but feel the nagging sensation of worry.

It was nearly dawn when Ankarette went to her room, deciding to get some rest and take another sip of the tincture that eased the ache in her stomach from Lord Hux's poison. Her mind whirled as she stared at the little bottle. She hadn't really believed Hux had been neutralized as a threat, but she'd thwarted his plans before, most recently with her daring infiltration into Occitania seeking information about the Maid of Donremy, which led to her killing several of his accomplices. She could do so again.

Still, there was a nagging doubt that pulled at her mind. A fear that the end was coming soon for her king. Years ago, she'd heard a whisper from the Fountain that Severn's wife would become Queen of Ceredigion someday. It was a secret she'd clung to, dreading its eventuality, because the Fountain was never wrong. Maybe it was a distant future, one that was unavoidable because Ankarette herself would no longer be there to stop it from happening...but each time a new threat to Eredur reared, she thought of what she'd heard. She feared it.

She pushed the stopper back into the vial and slipped it into her pocket. She took the candlestick to the bed and was about to douse it when she heard the bootsteps coming up the stairs. The sound headed toward her door, so she walked to it and waited until the soft knock sounded.

After twisting the handle, she was surprised to find a member of the Espion she knew and trusted. Bennet, tall and built like a farmer. She'd known him since she'd starting training with the Espion herself, knew he was capable and totally loyal to Eredur.

"Hello, Ankarette," he said. "I hope I didn't wake you?"

"I hadn't gone to sleep yet. Did you just arrive?"

"Yes. I'd just returned from an assignment in Brugia, and Master Nichols sent me to see if you needed any help. I heard about the fire earlier. Interesting times."

"To say the least. Come in. It's too crowded down below."

He accepted, entered the room, and glanced around before deciding on the chair.

"What were you doing in Brugia?"

"Chasing rumors. As always."

"Rumors of what?"

He tilted his head. "Of an uprising. There's a young fellow, a descendent of Henricus Argentine's wife—the famous one, who won the Battle of Azinkeep. After his death, it seems she married one of Henricus's men, got with child, and bore a daughter. That daughter had a son, the fellow I was looking for. Claims to be an heir of Ceredigion." He snorted. "However that works."

"Did you find him?" Ankarette asked.

Bennet shook his head. "No, unfortunately. The trail went cold and since that whole skirmish a few years ago between our realms, there weren't many who were interested in helping me chase smoke. This assignment, however, seems much more promising. So Devereaux is here?"

"Yes, and he's been sighted in town, so we're not chasing smoke. He's proving to be rather cunning."

"I wouldn't doubt it."

"Does the Espion have a way into the fortress?" Ankarette asked.

He shook his head. "No tunnels that I know of. I think it was built before the Espion even existed. Were you thinking about sneaking in and disposing of the duke?"

"They're on the lookout for me. I don't think I could move around the castle without being noticed."

"Probably not. I'm glad the king chose Horwath to lead the assault. He's the solid sort. What can I do to help?"

Ankarette had been considering this since Bennet had arrived. "I need you to get a message to Master Nichols. We learned this evening that there's a plot afoot. A traitor in league with Devereaux."

Bennet scowled. "Do you know who?"

"I suspect the king's brother."

"Dunsdworth?"

"The same. We captured one of Devereaux's men in town and learned about the traitor from him, although he doesn't know who it is. I think they were expecting the king to come here in person. He confirmed the traitor is in Kingfountain, however, and we need to find out who it is. We need proof, Bennet."

"I've never liked Lord Dunsdworth. The Duke of Clare is, as they say in Legault, an eejit." He clapped his hands on his knees. "So I've just arrived and now you're sending me back. I should probably get some sleep first."

"The inn is full, I'm afraid."

"I got that message loud and clear. I'll bed down in the woods. It's quieter anyway." He rose and Ankarette walked him to the door.

"It's good to see you," she said, putting her hand on his arm, holding the candlestick with her other hand.

"You too, Ankarette." He twisted the handle and opened the door, startled to find John Thursby standing just outside with a brooding look on his face.

Bennet looked chagrined. Ankarette wondered why she hadn't heard him come up the stairs. Perhaps the conversation with Bennet had distracted her.

John Thursby's eyes were full of menace.

Bennet was taller than him but much less powerfully built. He looked back at Ankarette in confusion, sensing the tension. He made a subtle hand signal in the Espion way to ask if the fellow was trouble.

Ankarette responded with a simple gesture, meaning no.

"Very well. I'll be on my way then," Bennet said. He nodded to John Thursby, who didn't nod back, only glowered at him until he was gone.

"Did you just get back?" she asked.

John Thursby nodded, lips pressed firmly together. He looked altogether different without his beard, but she recognized his moods. It didn't require much imagination to realize he was acting out of jealousy.

"Come in," she invited, opening the door.

He shook his head.

"Bennet is part of the Espion," she explained. "He just arrived on orders from Master Nichols."

"I don't care who he is," John Thursby said brusquely. "Wanted to show you something. Get your cloak. We'll be walking near the beach." Then he turned and walked away.

Ankarette blew out her breath. She retrieved her cloak and her things and then snuffed out the candle and left it in the room. John Thursby was standing near the door leading out when she reached the bottom steps, and she had to traverse the ground carefully to avoid kicking sleeping soldiers. There were probably thirty men sprawled out on the floor, and the noise was obnoxious.

When she reached him, he opened the door and went outside. The air was brisk and the scent of smoke from the earlier emergency was still recognizable.

She walked alongside him as he kept a sturdy pace.

"You seem upset," she said when the silence became tiresome.

"Can't imagine why that would be."

"Can we talk about it?"

"There's nothing to talk about, Ankarette."

"I think there is." She touched his arm and noticed him flinch.

He paused midstride and turned. "I've no claim on you. I know that. But just consider for a moment that I left my duty in the city because you asked me to. That I came all this way to confront someone I've considered a friend. Not because the king commanded it, but because you asked. If you think I'm not conflicted, you don't know me at all."

She applied pressure to his arm. "But I do know you, John Thursby. And I appreciate what this is doing to you."

There was noise from the street as a group of Horwath's soldiers approached with a lantern.

"We can talk later." He chuffed.

When the soldiers arrived, John Thursby gave them the password of the watch and the soldiers continued on their way. No one else was in the streets. No lamps or candles were lit in the homes they passed. A dog barked in the distance. The town was much smaller than Kingfountain, so they reached the edge of it quickly enough, the smell of the ocean getting stronger, the sound of the surf getting louder. They spotted a work crew with lamps building pickets, approached them, and then went beyond into the darkness.

"How far away is the fortress?" she asked. She couldn't see it yet or the ocean, but the road had the gritty texture of sand now.

If she didn't trust him absolutely, she would have anticipated he was leading her into a trap. There was a temptation to use her Fountain magic on him, to reveal his motives and any danger they might pose to her. Yet when she'd used her power on him the first time, she'd discovered his feelings for her. What a surprise it had been. She'd come to learn his moods and feelings just through observation and listening. He wasn't a deceiver. He'd rejected the very thought of joining the Espion. It wasn't in his nature to be duplicitous.

After they passed over a little rise, the beach opened in front of them. The tide was higher, the waves crashing on the shore before making the distinctive shushing sound as it retreated. There was the fortress, on the left, built on higher ground. She could also see the king's fleet in the distance, the lanterns glowing against the starry night. There was no moon that night, but there was ample starlight to see. She didn't notice bootprints in the sand, but then she realized the tide must have come and washed them away.

"Where are we going?" she asked him.

"A little further. To those rocks." He pointed.

Her instincts screamed ambush. She halted. "Did you come here already?" she asked.

"Of course I did. That's why I'm bringing you back."

The unsettled feeling wouldn't go away, so she summoned her Fountain magic. Her power revealed they were utterly alone at that moment. She didn't sense another person. It was just the two of them. But the magic revealed John Thursby to her again. The aching of his heart, the suffering he was enduring from being near her, smelling her, seeing her wearing the Occitanian bodice. He was heartsick but faithful. As he'd always been.

She shut off the flow of magic, feeling her own emotions getting tangled up in his.

"Show me what you found," she said, coming forward to close the gap between them.

He brought her to the boulders. She realized they were at the junction of a cove. The stony cliff to the left was gouged and blocky to a certain height and then the lower part was smooth. It showed where the tidewater rose to. Bits of drift-wood were scattered everywhere, along with fronds of seaweed. The smell was strong but pleasant.

John Thursby brought her to the smooth edge of the boulder and then sat down on the damp, packed sand, the rock to his back. She dropped down beside him. The water came close but did not touch them. The smell of juniper was very strong. She'd learned in Pisan that juniper berries were edible, not poisonous, and could be made into alcohol, but it was otherwise aromatic and harmless.

"I smell juniper," she said.

"Is that what it's called? I didn't know." He was gazing at

the cliffs where the fortress was nestled. Then he pointed. "There."

"What am I looking for?"

"We won't know until morning," he said. "When I came here, I saw tracks in the surf and followed them here. Single person. Thought it might be our missing crossbowman. I hid here, behind the boulders, and just watched and waited. It took a long time. But then I saw the glow of a lantern. The light disappeared into a cave. I think there's a secret entrance into the fortress. If they see us, or anyone, bumbling around the beach tomorrow, they'll reinforce the door, and then it'll be useless." He sighed. "I was going to wait here all night so I could see if anyone else tries to get in or out before dawn. Then I thought you might want to wait here with me." He wrapped his arms around his knees, rocking slightly.

And when he'd come back to the Respite, he'd found her with another man.

NINE

GAMBIT

"I've missed you," Ankarette said softly, leaning against him to share body heat. The rush and roar of the waves continued its ebb and flow. "I've missed our talks. Our walks in Kingfountain after midnight. Listening to your poetry."

"It's not *my* poetry, lass. It never was." He sounded a little embarrassed.

"But you own it in the way you say the words. I've missed *you*, John Thursby."

He sighed, his head drooping. "I've missed you as well. I was a fool, Ankarette. You told me you weren't free. But I still wanted more than what you were able to give. I wanted your whole heart. I wanted to give you mine. Just the idea that you'd found someone else made me furious. I shouldn't be jealous."

"You have nothing to be jealous of. Bennet is part of the Espion, like Hugh Bardulf and Master Nichols. I've known and trusted him a long time. But there is nothing between us."

"Are you so sure of that, Ankarette? He's handsome. Maybe *too* handsome."

She butted her shoulder against his arm. "And so are you, John Thursby."

He snorted. "I wasn't searching for praise, lass. I couldn't be part of all that mischief. I'm blunt, forthright. I don't know how to be any other way."

"And I like that about you." She yawned, feeling the lateness of the hour. "And I'd rather be here with you than anywhere else."

He adjusted and put his arm around her. "I've been thinking a thought. About how to get to Devereaux. You see, getting in isn't the problem. It's getting out that has stymied me."

"I agree. I don't want to use you as bait."

"You don't, but the king does. You've told me before that knowing someone truly is the only way to discern what they're going to do. I know Devereaux. At least the man he was. Everything he does has a reason. Here's my thought. Devereaux cares about his men, especially those loyal to him. Mercenaries he'd throw to the wolves. But we've captured one of his faithful ones. Quentin. He's arrested for treason and will be judged at the Assizes. So we offer Devereaux a deal. We'll give him his man back, freely, if Devereaux agrees to meet with me first. He lets me go. We let Quentin go. He has nothing to lose, and it saves his man's life."

"But what if you are worth more to him than Quentin?" Ankarette said. "What if he uses you as a hostage?"

"I don't think he will," John Thursby said. "Not if the terms were agreed on in advance. I don't think he'd go back on his word. And if he follows through, he's gaining something, not losing something."

Ankarette thought in silence, listening to the waves crash. It was an interesting plan. "I don't know Devereaux enough to trust him to keep his word."

"How could you? But I served with him for years. I remember going to Kingfountain to inform him of an overture from Queen Morvared. It was Hux who delivered the message to me, actually. Wish I'd known back then what he'd do to you; I would have run him through with my sword."

"He hadn't poisoned me yet," Ankarette said, touched by his sentiment. "He was Lewis's herald. It gave him access to many people."

"Sad but true. Devereaux trusted me to deliver messages like that. Things that were sensitive. Messages that could have gotten him killed."

"He knew you had integrity."

"And he knows I still have it. He sent his man to try and recruit me, after all. If I had a chance to talk to him, to try and find out what he's up to, I might be able to persuade him to part ways with Morvared or whoever is behind this scheme. If I cannot, I think he'd let me go."

Ankarette thought some more. "We'd need to ask Duke Horwath. He might not be amenable to the gambit."

"But isn't this why you brought me? To use my knowledge of Devereaux to try and sway him? If he's got that poisoner with him, Farrit Blawn, he'll probably use nightshade on me. But I don't know anything that would be dangerous for me to divulge. Just think on it. And get some rest."

"Are you going to sleep?"

"You think I can?" he answered with a chuckle. "I'll keep watch over you, Ankarette. I always will."

She believed him. Resting against his body, his arm draped over her, she felt the pull of weariness. And with the shushing of the waves, she fell asleep.

John Thursby roused her before dawn as the gray sky gave hints of color. The tide was higher now, coming ever closer. He looked haggard but had a special smile. During the night, his whiskers had sprouted, his hair more messy than stylish.

"You want a poem, lass?" he asked, his mouth twitching.

"You have one for me?"

"I've been chasing it all night. I wish I had my books, for I might have it wrong. But I know one about the sea."

"Let's have it, then."

He nodded. "*The Fountain made the earth. Shaped the beautiful plains marked off by oceans. It made the proudly setting sun and the gentle moon. Each to glow across the land and to light it. Light makes quick with life. But the sea is the Fountain's memory. The sea whispers in all men's ears.*" He turned his head, gazing at the surf as it rumbled.

"That's lovely."

"I mixed up some parts, I'm sure I did. Now, I want you to look yonder." He stretched out his arm and pointed to the cliffs. "See that rough part of the cliff? It's shaped like a crooked staff."

She searched through the gloom and thought she saw what he meant. "Is there a bit of broken-off rock above it?"

"That's the cleft where I saw the light glowing from. You can't see the cave from here. It blends in. But that's the spot. If we stay here much longer, the sunrise will reveal us."

"We'll need to ask Duke Horwath about your plan. I don't know what he'll say."

"We can try. No more than that." He gripped her arm and

started to round the boulder, when he suddenly jerked back, his eyes wide.

"Someone's coming," he whispered.

Ankarette peered around the rock and saw a man walking along the beach toward them. A crossbow was gripped in his hands. The last mercenary.

"He'll come this way," he whispered again. "The tide is already covering the boulder on the far side. And he knows it'll cover his trail within the hour."

"Agreed," she said. "This is a good spot for an ambush."

"But if he makes a fuss, they'll know we know about the cave."

"I can be discreet, John Thursby," she said.

"Let me tackle him. I'll wrestle the crossbow away, and you can prick him with a needle."

She cupped his cheek. "I can manage this on my own."

He huffed but didn't argue. As the mercenary drew closer, Ankarette began to hear his footfalls in the sand. John Thursby pressed against the boulder, keeping out of sight, and Ankarette crouched lower, listening to the man's footsteps. She would wait until she saw him to be sure the bolt in the crossbow was pointed away from her. Drawing a dagger, she readied it.

She judged the timing of his arrival, and he came around the edge of the boulder, oblivious to their presence. He had the crossbow aimed their way, but his eyes were fixed on the cliff wall ahead.

Ankarette leaped at him, using a subduing technique she'd learned from the poisoner school, a choke hold that would prevent him from crying out and render him unconscious in seconds. He grabbed at her arms, and she felt his fingers dig into her skin, but she was behind him, levering his body against her back, hoisting his feet off the sand. She felt him pass out and go slack, and he dropped the crossbow onto the sand.

John Thursby picked it up and then hoisted the man over his shoulder. "Let's walk back to the pickets."

She took the crossbow from him, and they both followed the footsteps in the sand. Already, ahead of them, the tide had begun washing the tracks away. That meant the cave in the cliff would be submerged for the next few hours.

When they approached the soldiers at the pickets, Ankarette ordered two of them to help carry the man back to the inn. They complied, relieving John Thursby of his burden. He was huffing with the exertion, but the two men did the job well enough.

When they reached the Respite, Duke Horwath was in the common room talking to his captains. He looked surprised when the men entered carrying the unconscious fellow.

"This is the last mercenary," Ankarette said. "We caught him trying to sneak back to the fortress."

The duke looked at his captains with a frown of disappointment that none of them had been able to accomplish the task. "Well done," he told her. "I have the town guarded. We're going to set up a camp closer to the fortress. Out of range of their crossbows. My best sappers say the wall is very thick. It'll take months to breach it."

"You're going to mine beneath it?" she asked.

"It's on higher ground," Horwath said simply. "That gives them all the advantage, and I'm not going to throw away lives recklessly. If we can undermine one of the corners, we can collapse the wall. It'll be easier to repair later."

"It's a good strategy, but we'd like to offer another."

"I'm listening."

Ankarette quickly related the plan and the terms of the deal. By releasing Quentin, they would only be adding one more soldier to Devereaux's defense of the fortress. That was insubstantial. The information they could get, if John Thursby was successful, might provide a different strategy for retaking the fortress of Averanche. Or reveal the traitor.

Horwath rubbed his goatee. "What if he sets you free by way of a catapult?" he asked the night watchman.

"It's faster than walking, I suppose," John Thursby replied. "I don't think he will."

Horwath shrugged. "It's your neck. I'm not going to stall my preparations for the siege."

"I'm not asking you to," Ankarette said. "Quentin is in your custody. You have the authority to release him. You have a reputation, Lord Horwath, that will aid in this situation. Deveraux will trust your word."

"I'll honor the terms if he will," Horwath said. "You have my permission to make the offer. See to it."

Ankarette nodded. She asked the duke to keep the crossbowman in custody so she could interview him later. In the interim, she wanted to be at the castle when terms were offered. Only after she was confident in the agreement would she permit John Thursby to enter the fortress.

Going back to her room, she quickly changed her clothes and prepared herself. Then she went down into the common room, and they got permission to talk to Quentin. He was still in his guarded room, sitting on the edge of the bed, wrists and ankles in irons. He looked at them glumly, then hung his head again.

"Are we riding to Kingfountain now?" he asked nervously.

"Change of plans," John Thursby said, folding his arms. "Is Devereaux the same man he was before Borehamwood? Will he keep his promises?"

"He's a gambler. Always has been. But he honors his debts. He's no cheat."

John Thursby nodded. "He always did like betting on dice. We're taking you to the castle. Not inside, just so he knows we have you. I'm going to talk to him. If he lets me go, we'll release you back to him. You think he'll take that bargain?"

The man's eyes widened with hope. "Are you serious, Thursby?"

"You know I'm not a liar. Will he honor the terms?"

"Of course he will! He still talks about you sometimes. We all do. You should have been in the castle with us."

John Thursby looked at Ankarette. "Let's see if this works."

They had the guards unlock his ankles so he could walk, but his wrists remained chained. A troop of soldiers were assigned to escort them, with heavy shields, to the fortress.

The sun had risen, and smoke lifted lazily from chimneys. They walked through the quiet streets of Averanche and then passed the pickets on the way to the fortress. Ankarette walked alongside her friend, while the soldiers escorted the prisoner. She felt the throb of discomfort as the effects of the tincture wore off and knew she'd need another sip soon.

The gritty road led up to the battlement walls of the fortress. The front portcullis and doors were recessed beneath a stone arch. There were turrets flanking it, the lower half protruding from the walls in nested rings of stone. The battlements were shielded by crenellations, which gave the defenders ample protection from missiles from below while also providing a great perch to lob them down.

Ankarette and her company approached the walls but kept a safe distance. Still, they were amply prepared, and some of the soldiers held longbows rather than swords.

John Thursby glanced at Ankarette, giving her a tender but nervous smile. "I like the odds, but I'm still nervous."

"If he doesn't let you out, I'm going in after you," she said softly. There were signs of life on the walls, men patrolling and more gathering by the minute. They'd seen the delegation approach.

John Thursby took Quentin by the arm and walked him closer. Then he paused and raised his voice.

"It's John Thursby! I wish to speak to Lord Deveraux."

Murmurs came from the walls. A confident voice sailed down from the heights.

"Well met. Did you come to join us?"

John Thursby scratched his neck. "I just want to talk. We captured Quentin last night. But we'll release him if you agree to the terms."

"If you came to negotiate a surrender, you've wasted your time."

"No. I just want to talk. Man to man. Soldier to soldier. You let me walk free, and Quentin can trade places with me. A few words for one of your men. What do you say?"

Ankarette couldn't tell which of the men up there was Devereaux. There were at least a dozen gathered atop the battlements, hidden by the shadows of the stone.

"Is that really you, Quentin?" asked Devereaux.

"Aye, my lord! 'Tis I!" said the other. "I'd be grateful if you accept this bargain. They were going to send me to Kingfountain. Something about a river."

More murmuring voices.

"Let's have breakfast, John Thursby. We can talk."

Ankarette felt both a thrill and a wave of worry.

John Thursby nodded for Quentin to walk back down to the soldiers, and he did. Then Thursby turned and marched toward the fortress doors.

"Let him in!" Devereaux ordered.

The men of the North by Ankarette shifted nervously, preparing for a sudden attack. As John Thursby approached the doors, she heard a chain rattle. The doors wouldn't need to open much to let in one man. The defenders were also poised in case of any mischief—everyone ready to act at the drop of a pin.

John Thursby reached the door, one hand on his hip, the other on his sword hilt. She saw his cloak flutter in the breeze.

Come back safely, she thought in her mind while her heart tingled with apprehension.

The door groaned. John Thursby sidled through it, and then it shut resoundingly. She heard the chains again as they were dragged back into place. She wondered how long the conversation would last. An hour? More?

She'd know no peace until he was free.

And then she felt the unmistakable tingling of Fountain magic coming from the castle. The revealing presence of another Fountain-blessed. A feeling she recognized instantly as a spike of fear shot through her.

It *must* be Lord Hux.

I learned during the kingmaker wars that fear and hope march in unison, like a prisoner and the escort he is shackled to. Fear keeps pace with hope. Both belong to a mind already in suspense. None of us can help being anxious looking into the future, but that is a trap. Fear and hope—both spring from projecting our thoughts too far ahead instead of adapting ourselves to our present circumstances.

— ANKARETTE TRYNEOWY

CHAPTER

TEN

THE KING'S RING

"Retreat from the castle," Ankarette said, her voice suddenly husky as she battled the spike of anxiety jabbing into her heart. None of the soldiers she stood near could sense the dangerous foe lurking in the fortress of Averanche. Only her.

On the surface, the mission had gone as planned, but she realized now that she'd been duped. Lord Hux clearly had disguised himself by pretending to be a recognizable poisoner. Farrit Blawn. And he'd probably sensed her presence the night before when she'd used her Fountain magic. In revealing John Thursby's feelings, she had also revealed herself.

Now the fear of losing someone important to her triggered an avalanche of concerns. The thought of John Thursby being killed by Lord Hux was enough to drive all temperance from her mind. If he dared do such a thing, she would hunt the other poisoner to the ends of the earth and plunge a dagger into his chest.

Of course, that thought did the opposite of calming her.

They did retreat back to the Respite. As they walked down

the main street, which was now occupied with townsfolk going about their business, she tried to reason things through. Yes, she was sure that Lord Hux must have sensed her using her magic the previous night. Instead of invoking his own Fountain magic, sending an echo back to her, he'd remained silent, anticipatory. So he'd known something was afoot. He'd had a warning; she had not.

When they reached the inn, Duke Horwath was discussing siege preparations with his captains. He didn't even seem to notice her return.

"I want sappers digging two trenches on opposite sides of the fortress," he said.

"That will divide our efforts and slow the progress of the siege," Captain Harshem rebutted.

The duke nodded in agreement. "But Devereaux has proven he's clever. If we rely on just one tunnel, he'll focus his energy on thwarting it. I want both. I want him to feel our victory cannot be stopped."

Another captain nodded in appreciation of the tactic. "Should we summon more men from Dundrennan to help?"

Horwath frowned. "I'll not leave the North vulnerable or draw more strength from Lord Mortimer than necessary. We have enough. All we need is time. I want our work guarded night and day. Don't give them any hope of an easy target. Now, get to it."

With the orders given, the captains dispersed to fulfill their various assignments. Ankarette caught Captain Harshem by the tunic as he was passing her.

"Captain. Can you send some men to retrieve the Espion camping outside the city? His name is Bennet."

"I don't have a man to spare," he said apologetically. "You'll have to take it up with the duke." Then he left the inn.

Ankarette was still roiling inside, her mind a tangled mess.

Duke Horwath had noticed her and lifted an eyebrow questioningly. "Any news?"

"Some. Master Nichols sent an Espion here, and I prematurely sent him back. I'm going to need more support from Kingfountain. Can we send someone to fetch him before he leaves? I have new information he needs to know."

"Anything that will help with my siege?"

"Not really."

He motioned for one of his squires to approach. "This is Davern. You can send him on your errands. I didn't bring as many men as I need for this effort, and I'll need all the king's men who came for guard duty. But he's yours."

"Thank you, my lord. Once I have some Espion here, I can return your squire."

He nodded and turned away. The young man was probably seventeen, looked inexperienced but eager, with a mop of curly hair atop his head.

"There's an Espion named Bennet camping outside the city," she told the lad. "Can you go to the sentries and see if you can find him? I need to speak to him immediately."

"Yes, my lady," he said and left with alacrity.

What was Lord Hux doing in Averanche? Was he here on Lewis's business? She had no idea. But she had to believe he was part of the plot. Maybe he was advising Deveraux just as she was advising Duke Horwath. Two poisoners of Pisan, matching wits once again.

Captain Harshem burst into the inn, holding a crossbow bolt in one hand and a rolled message in the other. He took it immediately to Lord Horwath, so Ankarette intercepted him.

"What's this?" the duke asked.

"A message fired from the castle. A sentry just brought it to me. I think it's for her." He gave Ankarette a wary look.

Duke Horwath took the message, read it, and his brow furrowed. He offered it to her without a word.

She recognized Lord Hux's handwriting. He had very elegant script, which was necessary for his disguised profession of sending messages on behalf of a king. It wasn't in a cipher code, so he was delivering his ultimatum to all.

Bring me the ring or the watchman dies. You have four days. SHX.

THE THREE-LETTER SIGNATURE was written with a flourish. She brought the paper to her nose and smelled it. The writing was recent, the ink still moist. No sign of poison.

"Can you make sense of it?" the duke asked her warily.

She could. He could only be referring to one thing—the ring she'd taken from Bidigen Grimmer, the killer who had come to Kingfountain years before. The ring possessed a magic of the Deep Fathoms that allowed the wearer to be protected from water. Grimmer had used it to travel the river above the falls without succumbing to the force of it. The magic harmed the wielder, causing pain and disfigurement of the finger it was worn on, but the power was a worthy prize.

She'd learned from Deconeus Tunmore that it was a prize of the Occitanian royal family. Losing it had contributed to Lord Hux's disgrace, as had his failure to secure the release of Lewis's sister, Morvared. Although she had ultimately been released—it had been at the mercy of the king, which hadn't done much for the poisoner's reputation.

"This was signed by Lord Hux, King Lewis's poisoner. We now know another piece on the Wizr board."

"And the ring?"

"I know what he's talking about. So does Eredur. It takes

nearly two full days to ride to Kingfountain. This means it will only be possible for me to fulfill his demand if I travel by boat. He wants me gone."

Horwath's brow wrinkled further. "Why would he think we care if Thursby lives or dies? It's a man for a man. He kills Thursby, we kill Devereaux's man."

Ankarette saw the interested expressions on the duke's and captain's faces. They could sense something more was happening but couldn't make the connection.

"Can we speak privately, my lord?" Ankarette asked.

He nodded and they retreated to his private room, which was on the first floor of the Respite. His battle armor was on a rack and one of his squires, who'd been tending to it, was promptly dismissed. When the squire left and shut the door, they were alone together.

"Hux was involved in the abduction of Dunsdworth's wife, Lady Isybelle. My friend. It was all part of a ploy to win Morvared's release from Holistern Tower. He'd hired a murderer to see it done."

Horwath nodded. "I recall. My son-in-law was rather interested in the whole mess. Sometimes I think he regrets giving up control of the Espion. Go on."

"The ring is a magical artifact I took from the murderer. Hux wants it back. He also knows that John Thursby and I are...more than just friends. The king and queen also know about our...situation. I've never withheld anything from them. It was the king's demand that I bring him with me because of his past allegiance to Devereaux."

A wizened look came on the duke's face. "Now I understand. That puts you in a compromised position. To say the least."

"Which is why I'm telling you all this privately," she said.

"I've never put anything above my loyalty to the Argentine family. They trust me, and I will not breach that trust."

"That's why you need the Espion fellow."

"I need to send him by ship, not by land. The current will be in his favor for a speedy voyage to Kingfountain The king must know what's happened. This is no ordinary siege. It's a diversion."

"Clearly," Horwath agreed. "If Bennet has already left, I can send a rider after him. Because you're right. Sea is the only way to get to Kingfountain and back in so short a time. I take it you plan to stay here?"

Ankarette nodded. "Lord Hux has a way of traveling between fountains within sanctuaries or holy chapels. It is a magic he possesses. I don't know if the fortress has such a place, but we should find out if possible."

"The mayor should know," Horwath said. "I'll summon him."

"Thank you. There is also the back entrance to the fortress, the one concealed by the tide. I have to assume that Hux knows that we know about it and will have it guarded."

"It's a fair assumption. That means the only way into the castle is through the main doors with a battering ram and a terrible toll in lives. It would take weeks to get a trebuchet here. But that fortress is on a cliff, so a trebuchet isn't the ideal siege engine in this situation."

"And if you brought it too close, it would be a target for their crossbows."

"As I said, it's not ideal." He stroked his goatee. "I must be clear on this, Ankarette. My duty is to take back the castle. I've already lost some men and stand to lose more. They are every bit as precious to me as your night watchman is to you. Unless the king tells me to hold back, I'm going to move forward with the siege and bring Devereaux back in irons for justice. Sometimes duty compels where our hearts pang hardest."

She was grateful for his forthrightness. The risk to John Thursby's life wouldn't change his plans in the slightest.

"Thank you for your candor," Ankarette replied. "I would never ask you to defy the king."

"Good. For I will not."

Ankarette nodded in farewell and went back to the common room. Her stomach was growling, but she felt no hunger for food, not when John Thursby was trapped in the castle. He had felt confident that Lord Devereaux would honor his end of the bargain. But Lord Hux would have no compunction in harming Ankarette's companion.

Was John Thursby already in the dungeon beneath the fortress, hearing the surf, wrists in shackles? Probably so.

He had four days left to live.

That gave Ankarette only four days to save him.

CHAPTER

ELEVEN

STOLEN TIME

Ankarette sat at the table in the tumultuous common room, sipping from a cup of calming tea. Four days. Barely enough time to fetch the ring had she been disposed to do so, and she was not. Lord Hux was a notorious schemer, quick to mislead and direct attention away from his true aim. Was he trying to get rid of her so he could assassinate Lord Horwath and remove another ally from Eredur's inner circle? Or was he trying to keep her in Averanche so he could travel to Kingfountain and murder the king?

Alone, she could not thwart Hux's plan, so as long as she knew he was in Averanche, that's where she would remain. The ring was hidden in a place only a Fountain-blessed could touch. A lesser fountain within the palace. Not even Deconeus Tunmore knew where she'd hidden it, but since he was Fountain-blessed himself, he could retrieve it if the king commanded it. But she didn't imagine Eredur would agree to exchange such a potent artifact for John Thursby's life. No monarch would. No, Hux was using her friend to get her to act foolishly. To defy her king if she must.

After taking another sip, she saw young Davern enter through the door of the inn, Bennet at his heels. They scanned the crowd, clearly looking for her, so she held up her hand to catch their attention and invite them over.

"I found him, my lady," Davern said proudly. His quaint Northern brogue was charming. "What else would you have me do?"

"I will need you again soon. Stay nearby while I discuss this mission with Bennet."

"As you will, my lady," he said before trotting off well out of earshot, his hands clasped behind his back in an attitude of attention and respect. She liked him already.

Bennet hooked a chair with his boot and then slid down near her, leaning forward. "I had a horse ready to depart, Ankarette. What's changed?"

"Lord Hux is here," she said and watched him start with surprise. He was one of the few people who knew about her special rivalry with Hux, including the poison he'd dosed her with.

She unfolded the paper that had been fixed to the crossbow bolt and gave it to him. He scanned it quickly, and his brow wrinkled. "What's this ring?"

"I'm not at liberty to tell you. But the king knows about it," she said. "He also knows where it is hidden. I doubt he'll accept the terms of the deal, but it's his choice to make. If Lord Hux is involved in this, then we have even more reason to assume that the traitor within Kingfountain is preparing to make a move."

"It'll take three days just to reach the palace. Two if I kill a horse."

"Which is why you'll be going by sea," she replied. "Take this message as proof. Show it to the king and Master Nichols. Tell them we sent John Thursby into the fortress to negotiate with Lord Devereaux, and this bolt was fired in response. Tell them I *know* Lord Hux is in Averanche right now. But that doesn't mean he'll stay."

Bennet frowned. "He can't leave. There's nowhere to run."

"He's very capable of coming and going as he pleases," Ankarette said. "And the king knows it. So does Master Nichols. He travels by the water, so all the fountains in the palace must be guarded night and day."

"What's his game?" Bennet asked.

"I have no idea. We don't have all the clues we need."

"I think what you said yesterday about Dunsdworth isn't far off the mark."

"Which is why I want him watched."

"Oh, we were already watching him," Bennet said with a bemused sigh.

"Really? What aren't you telling me?"

"The last time he spent the night in the palace, an Espion was watching through the spy hole. Watched him manhandle his wife. He was drunk. He's quite mean-spirited when he's intoxicated. Lady Isybelle said some provoking things, as I understand, and he lost control."

Ankarette felt her stomach clench with fury. "Why wasn't I told?"

"We know she's your friend, Ankarette. Nichols had us relate the matter to the king. If anyone was going to tell you, he should have been the one."

And yet he had not. Ankarette bristled at the withholding of information. What did Eredur think she would do, confront and threaten Dunsdworth again? She'd had to do so during the hunt for Isybelle's sister, Nanette, but that had been a matter of life and death.

"I'm sorry you didn't know," Bennet said softly.

"Thank you for telling me. The tide has come in, so it's

imperative you leave at once for Kingfountain. Find the fastest ship and be on your way. Tell Nichols I'll need more support over here."

"He'll know by this dawn. I promise." He clapped his palms on the tabletop and then stood. She gave him a nod of thanks, and he departed. Being part of the Espion entitled him to certain privileges, including the ability to countermand a ship's captain and divert the vessel for another mission. Besides, the ships were all at anchor in the harbor. It would infuriate the Genevese, but such things were of little consequence when larger affairs were pressing.

She took another sip from the tea and spied Davern looking her way. But he resumed his posture and didn't approach the table. He was waiting to be called over. Yes, he would do nicely indeed.

Four days to rescue John Thursby. Or to set in motion a plan that would lead to his release. He'd be guarded, undoubtedly. Hux would expect a plot. She wished she didn't feel that she'd played into his hands.

In her head, she went over the different ways there were to enter the castle. The duke had thought of only three—the front door, the cave near the shore, and bringing a wall down. But it was also possible to scale the walls, was it not?

Ankarette mused about the last option. In many sieges, the attackers used hastily constructed ladders to throw up against the walls and climb, but that was a very dangerous method, as the defenders could shove the ladder away. A rope with a grappling hook could also do the trick.

To develop a plan, she'd need more information. She finished off the tea and rose from the table. Another quick glance revealed that Davern was regarding her once more, and she gave him a subtle nod to follow her. He grinned and sprang into action.

They left, side by side, and she noticed some of Horwath's archers patrolling the rooftops across the street. The townsfolk were going about their business but with subdued manners. They were nervous, ill at ease. Did they even have true loyalty anymore, or were they used to this dilemma of being handed over and back again? She had the memory of a distant Argentine king, Jon-Landon, being particularly fond of Averanche for some reason, but could not recall why.

The young man followed her stride easily and didn't ask any questions until they'd left the town and crossed the pickets. There was a line of dusty-looking soldiers returning from their efforts to undermine the fortress. It would take weeks before they were even close enough to the walls to make any difference. A sapper's skill was rare and valuable. It took patience and deliberate planning to excavate a tunnel that far. The entrance to the closest tunnel was surrounded by pickets and a group of soldiers. Right now was the easy part, using pickaxes and shovels to dig through dirt and sand. As they neared the castle, they'd be fighting for every inch against solid rock.

She and Davern went past the sappers' checkpoint to get a view of the fortress from another angle. She'd already seen the rear of it from the seashore. It was a standard double-bailey castle. A lower outer wall defending an interior structure. Even if they breached the difficult outer wall, there would be another line of defense.

They reached the edge of town where only a few small shacks were present, and there she stopped, gazing up at the fortress. They were well out of range of weapons from the castle. It was huge and blocky with round turrets evenly spaced around.

"What are we looking for, my lady?"

"I'm looking for another way to get inside," she said. The

mere height of the structure added to the defenses of the castle. They'd see anyone approaching with ladders or siege equipment.

"I don't think castles like this are meant to be easily gotten into."

"You serve in Dundrennan?" she asked.

"Aye. The blackguard Atabyrions have tried to take her. But they do naught but weep. She'll hold until the Lady of the Fountain returns or the waterfalls freeze over."

She knew that to be true, or close enough to the truth, but not every fortress was as impregnable as Dundrennan. She hadn't been to the North in years.

"Do you like serving Lord Horwath?"

"Aye, my lady. He's the best of men. But I also like Earl Thomas. Sometimes we get to go on hunts with him. But he doesn't leave much nowadays. Not with his lady in a...delicate way. If you know what I mean."

She gave him a look that coaxed more from him than words probably would.

"She's always moaning about how painful it is. How uncomfortable. I'm the third in a line of six sons, and my mum was churning butter, plopped out the youngest, then went right back to churning again. I think the duke's daughter just likes the attention is all." He rocked on his heels, gazing at the fortress. And went quiet, likely realizing he'd said too much.

"I won't tell anyone what you said, Davern."

"I shouldn't have said that last part," he confessed.

"It's usually best to keep your feelings about your master's family to yourself. Even if others gossip. You'll be trusted more if you keep family secrets."

"Huh," he said, pursing his lips, as if the thought were entirely new to him.

They stood at enough of a distance from the castle that she

could see the towers and walls were made of varying sized blocks of stone. It had been assembled in a hurry. She could tell from the variegated stone that the outer walls had been damaged and repaired multiple times. Because it had so many irregularities, it would be possible to climb it. The arrow slits were too narrow to enter, so it would require going over the wall. Climbing it would be difficult. Strenuous. There was no moat to fall into. But perhaps it could be done with the aid of a grappling hook and rope.

"I have your next assignment, Davern."

"I shall do my best, my lady."

"I want you to stay here for several hours and observe the guardians on the wall. How often do they pass? Do the guards change regularly? Are there any parts of the wall they do not protect? I need you to pay attention and focus on the details. Can you do that?"

"I can. I will."

"Very good. Come see me this afternoon after you've been at it during the day and have seen at least two changings of the guard. If anything strange happens in the meantime, let me know at once."

He nodded solemnly and gazed at the walls, trying to take in the whole scene at once.

"Start in sections," she advised. "The space between those two turrets, for example. Just study that part and count to one hundred. See how many people pass by during that time. Then move to the next section. Then the next. You're gathering information that's important."

"Are you going to try climbing the wall, my lady?" he asked nervously.

"That depends," she answered, "on how well you do your task."

TWELVE

INTRACTABLE

There were only two blacksmiths in Averanche, and Ankarette was able to learn from one of them that he'd made a grappling hook for a fisherman who'd used it to dredge the harbor. From there, she visited the fisherman, and he was able to produce it. It was a bit heavier than she'd wanted, but it was sturdy. It would work. The fisherman was eager to sell it to her for more than it cost him and provided some sturdy rope as well. She put both in a bag she'd brought and set off on her other errands.

Memories of climbing walls in Pisan flooded her mind. Climbing was tedious and wearying. One bad move could be devastating. Breeches were better suited for such a task than skirts, and she knew from experience it was more dangerous in the dark—but also less likely to draw notice. If she ascended the castle's rear wall, she'd have an easier time hiding, but that would require scaling the sea cliffs as well. The energy it took would be daunting.

It would help considerably if she could persuade Duke Horwath to feign an attack on the other side of the castle, giving her time to slip over the wall, enter the grounds, and possibly find John Thursby's cell before the commotion had ended. A few scaling ladders could be an adequate decoy. But her interactions with Duke Horwath led her to believe he'd be unwilling to stage such a trick. Especially if it put his men at risk. He'd said as much himself.

Ankarette visited the apothecary next, to purchase some powders that would be helpful to her once she was inside the castle. It served no purpose for her to deceive herself into thinking that she could incapacitate the entire garrison on her own. If there was a way to poison the castle's well or cistern, a poison that would render everyone inside sick, it would end the siege in days. But she had no idea where it was. Still. Powders could be flung in someone's eyes or choke them. The apothecary didn't have on hand what she needed, but he was enthusiastic about earning some coins from her and promised he'd procure what she'd requested by the end of the day.

Then she went back to the Respite to train and rest. Climbing was especially hard on the shoulder muscles, so she did exercises to help loosen hers for the exertion of climbing a wall. After resting, she was able to secure some breeches that fit her and a belted tunic to aid in the disguise. She could not use her Fountain magic on this mission. Doing so would reveal her to Lord Hux and bring the entire garrison down on her head.

It was late in the afternoon when she stored her supplies in her room and went out to the common room. She found Davern milling about, and he noticed her immediately when she entered the room. His expression was excited.

"Walk with me," she said, guiding him outside for the return trip to the apothecary. As soon as they were alone in the street together, she asked, "What have you learned?"

"My lady, they are mostly patrolling the walls, not the

towers," he said brightly. "They have two men stationed at the tower overlooking the bay. That's it. No patrols at all on that side. It's the front they're worried about and the front that's well guarded."

That made sense. With limited manpower, Deveraux would have to be prudent and run the guard in shifts.

"How often did the guard change?" she asked.

"I saw it change thrice, so every four hours or so? It changed again before I came back to the inn. I'd not been back at the inn very long when you came out of your room."

Changing the guard that frequently was a sign of vigilance. Keep a man posted in one spot too long, and he grew bored and inattentive. Again, another sign of Deveraux's wisdom. "Tell me about the guards patrolling the walls. How quickly did they walk?" She guided him down another street.

"Not quickly. Each had a section, and they'd walk down to one end, turn around, and walk back again."

It was so much easier to infiltrate a place that wasn't expecting it. Maybe her best chance was to climb the cliff at the rear of the castle, where there were much fewer men. Of course, perhaps Lord Hux was expecting her to do just that. He'd also expect a diversion.

She'd talked to the fisherman about the timing of the tides after her negotiations for the grappling hook. According to him, it was coming and going at sunrise and sundown. It would be dangerous trying to climb the cliffside at night with the tide coming in. However, it would provide more protection in case she fell. Well, not if the ocean smashed her against the rocks. She could, perhaps, hire the fisherman to row her there under cover of darkness. He knew the beach and the reefs.

"Well done, Davern. Is there anything else you noticed?"

"I was wondering, my lady, if I might accompany you."

She gave him a surprised look. "I think that would be unwise."

"You're part of the king's Espion, aren't you? I would rather help you than be on guard duty all night."

"What I'm doing is very dangerous, Davern."

"I know," he said with a grin. "Just...I thought you should know I'm willing to help."

They reached the apothecary shortly afterward, and she found the man hadn't made even half of the quantity he'd promised her and looked alarmed at her early arrival.

"I'm sorry, but I had to tend to an injury earlier. I'll make it up, I promise!"

She wasn't sure how honest he was being with her, but she paid for the batch he'd already produced. Time was running out.

She wished she had some trained Espion with her. Men who'd be useful in a fight, who knew the arts of stealth and intrigue. But Bennet would only just be arriving in Kingfountain the next morning. Davern was useful, at least.

After she'd paid, she thanked the apothecary and left. Davern didn't press the issue and just walked silently next to her.

"I'll consider it," she said to him when they returned to the Respite. Her next task was convincing Lord Horwath to help. She still thought it unlikely that he'd agree.

He wasn't there, however, but she learned he was at the command pavilion set up near the sapper works. So she and Davern went there next. She kept her eye on the sky and the position of the sun as they walked. It was sinking fast, meaning the tide was coming in. The transition at dusk was the perfect time to stage a feint because the human eye was more careless in shifting light.

John Thursby had been in the fortress all day. It made her

restless thinking about what he was going through. What he had already endured because she'd brought him there.

They found the command pavilion, where Duke Horwath was deep in conversation with his captains. He noticed her arrival but ignored her, continuing to hear reports on the activities of the day. They'd dug a considerable distance in just a single day, but the progress would halt soon enough, and it would take days and weeks to carve through the stone.

"Wait outside," she told Davern, and he obeyed promptly. The shadows were thickening in the pavilion, but no lamps had yet been lit. She fidgeted with impatience.

Captain Harshem remained behind after the others were dismissed.

Duke Horwath looked at her. "What is it?"

"I would like to try and infiltrate the castle," she said. "I need a diversion."

Harshem smirked and said nothing.

Horwath shook his head. "They'll be expecting it. The answer is no."

"Will you hear me out?" she asked patiently.

"I don't think it will help. I am not rash nor reckless by nature."

"Of course you are not. The king needs you because you are so steadfast."

"He needs *you* as well, Ankarette. Tell me truthfully. Would he approve of this mission you've given yourself?"

She stared at him, impressed by his sound judgment. He'd cut right to the quick with a disarming blow. "The king trusts my judgment," she answered after too long a pause.

Horwath studied her. "I don't think he'd approve of this. A night watchman is no replacement for a poisoner. If he were here, he'd refuse you. And so will I. The answer is no."

Fury began to ignite in her veins, but she shrugged,

keeping her reaction neutral. "You are in command, my lord. I cannot pressure you to do something you're unwilling to do. But the king didn't know Lord Hux was here. The situation is graver than we originally thought. I was considering poisoning the water supply while I'm in there. They'll come out of the fortress if they're thirsty enough. It'll save months digging in the dirt. Time we don't have."

She'd judged pivoting was the right approach, and she was pleased to see the subtle wrinkling of his taciturn brow. Captain Harshem frowned more blatantly.

"You don't aim to rescue Thursby, then?"

"My aim is to bring the king's enemies to justice," she said. "I can befoul the waters and make them undrinkable. I won't kill them, at least not intentionally, but I can make them all sick and weak. Imagine how easily you can scale the walls if they're cramping too much to stand."

"What if Hux has the antidote?"

"It will be useless if he's dead, my lord."

He was considering her suggestion now. If the siege concluded early, he'd have time to get back to Dundrennan before his daughter gave birth.

"I'm listening," he said carefully. Cautiously.

She began to relay her plan. Her acquisition of the grappling hook. Her ability to climb walls and Davern's information about the patrol frequency and guard change. How a perceived threat from the opposite side of the fortress would summon soldiers quickly, creating an opening for her to scale the wall and get inside. Her first target would be poisoning the well in the keep. Her second would be killing Lord Hux. She'd hide in the castle until the men became so disabled they'd be helpless. She said nothing about John Thursby.

"Harshem. What do you think of her plan?" His arms were folded, his look contemplative.

"Would the king approve, do you think?" the captain asked. He also seemed convinced.

"He might. It's clever." He shook his head. "I'll let you do it after the four days are up. We need to plan it. Prepare for it. I don't have siege ladders, so we'll have to make some. And I don't want your connection to Thursby tainting your judgment. Besides, if we wait, we may have reinforcements to help."

She was furious at the delay. Once again, he'd removed the option of saving John Thursby. But she didn't let it show. "Very well, my lord. It was just a suggestion."

"And a good one. I'd like you to stay at the inn tonight. No acting alone. I'm going to order Davern back to his duties too."

She'd never played Wizr against Duke Horwath before, but she suspected he was a canny player. He had a sharp mind.

There was commotion outside the tent. Raised voices. Shouting. The duke scowled and was heading for the flap when Davern came rushing in, eyes afire.

"My lord!"

Ankarette sensed something out of order. Was this another trick by Devereaux? Were they in danger? She reached for her dagger.

"What is it, lad?" the duke asked.

"A man just jumped into the sea! From the castle walls! The scout saw him. The men are rushing to the beach!"

Ankarette was the first to sprint out of the tent. The soldiers were all agog, talking about what had happened, but there was a stream of soldiers running toward the beach. She could hear the loud twang of crossbows being fired and her heart began to race. When she reached the beach, she noticed the tide had risen considerably, the waves smashing against the boulders along the cove.

Soldiers were cheering. There was a man in the water, swimming toward the shore, being carried by the waves.

And then, to her astonishment and relief, she saw John Thursby's face after the next wave passed. He was struggling in the water, but he was deposited onto the shore with the next wave, where gleeful soldiers helped drag him to his feet.

How had he made it that far wearing a chain hauberk? But she saw his shirt clinging to his skin. The hauberk was gone. Water dripped down his face. He looked exhausted but triumphant.

Their eyes met as she reached the scene, panting. A little smile quirked on his mouth. She knew if she rushed into his arms, every soldier throughout the camp would be talking about it, but oh, she wanted to.

He was panting, weary, but victorious. Once again he'd defied the odds.

And he'd come back to her.

THIRTEEN

A WARNING

After returning to the duke's pavilion, Ankarette grabbed a fresh tunic and handed it to John Thursby. She was still amazed at the change of events and, like everyone else, wanted to know what had happened. Duke Horwath fetched a flagon of wine and handed it to the night watchman, who took a long and thirsty drink from it. He eyed a tray of broiled meat hungrily but didn't ask to share the duke's supper.

"That was a bold gambit, Thursby," the duke said with a reluctant smile. "I don't think anyone expected you to jump into the sea to escape. Still, it's perplexing they let you get anywhere near the outer wall."

John Thursby finished the drink and set the flagon down, wiping his mouth on the back of his hand. A puddle was forming where he stood, and he looked uncomfortable.

"I'll be honest with you, my lord. If Devereaux hadn't arranged it all, I'd be living on limited time."

"Devereaux was behind your escape?" Ankarette asked in surprise.

"Aye. He ordered his men to strip away my armor, my weapons. He treated me disdainfully, but it was all a show for Hux." He gave Ankarette a pointed look. "He's in the fortress right now. Met him once, long ago." What he wasn't saying was conveyed in the angry pitch of his voice.

"What happened after you were brought inside?" the duke asked.

"I was promptly detained. That poisoner is with the duke at all times. I guess you could say Hux tricked us by disguising himself as another man." He stuck his finger in his ear and wiggled it violently to dislodge some water. "They took me to a cell and questioned me. Devereaux never left me alone with him, but I could see he wasn't free to speak plainly."

"Is he a prisoner himself?" Ankarette asked.

"I wouldn't say that. But I can still read his face after all these years. They asked trivial questions at first, then demanded answers I didn't know. That's when Hux pulled out some powder and blew it in my face." He shook his head, wrinkling his nose. "It wasn't pleasant. And I don't remember anything he asked me afterward. My mind was a fog, but I still had some sense. Apparently, I was a disappointment to Hux, and he told Devereaux that I was to be bait to catch *you*." He looked meaningfully at Ankarette.

"What does the poisoner want with her?" Horwath demanded.

"I couldn't rightly tell. But he's no idiot. He knows she stands in the way of his plans." He splayed his hands. "Look. I was given permission to abandon my cell once a day to walk with an armed escort. He took away my armor. The timing of the walk coincided with the coming of the tide. From what I heard the men say, I only had a few days before the poisoner killed me. They didn't say it so openly, of course, but I'm no fool. I think Devereaux was hoping I'd get the message."

And he had. Ankarette was so relieved. She wanted to hug him still. "Did you overpower the guards and rush up the steps to the upper wall?"

He shook his head no. "They took me up there. Deliberately. One of them gave me a look. Like if I didn't jump, I'd be the world's greatest bungler. They fired their crossbows at me, but that was just for show. And trust me, I feared I was going to ruin everything by drowning." He shook his head and chuckled. "But there's one more thing. Something I overheard."

"Go on," the duke said.

Captain Harshem was there as well, eyes glinting with eagerness, along with the duke's other captains. Ankarette had seen Davern outside of the pavilion before they entered. If the lad had as much mettle as she thought he did, he was listening to everything going on.

"I don't know if I was meant to hear it or not. But some guards were talking about needing only to wait a little longer for help to arrive. They said the *boar* was coming."

Duke Horwath frowned. Ankarette felt a jolt.

"Severn?" she whispered. The king's brother wore the emblem of a white boar as his symbol.

She'd never told John Thursby of the whisper she'd heard from the Fountain. That someday Nanette would be Queen of Ceredigion. That insight now caused a feeling of foreboding to bloom in her chest. Would Severn rebel against the king? Was he plotting to overthrow him?

Although loyal in the past, he had been offended by Eredur's capitulation to Occitania. It had strained relations between the brothers, a strain that Lord Dunsdworth was aware of.

Ankarette saw her concern mirrored in Duke Horwath's eyes. Severn and Nanette had a child now, a son.

"This must stay between us for now," the duke said in a

low voice. "No one will speak of it. Captain Harshem, take some riders on the road to Glosstyr. With our attention fixed on Averanche, I don't want to be taken by surprise. Go now. Tonight."

"Yes, my lord," the captain said worriedly. And then he was outside the tent and following his orders.

Duke Horwath was clearly brooding about the implications of this new information. When loyalties and allegiances shifted, everything became unstable, like a table with a mismatched leg.

"I could use another hauberk, my lord," John Thursby said. "And a sword."

"My master-at-arms will provide what you need," the duke said generously. "If there's trouble with Glosstyr, I'll need every able-bodied man. This isn't your fight, though."

"I go where she goes," John Thursby said simply. "And I'm feeling rather naked without either at the moment."

The duke grunted and nodded. "Get some rest, Thursby. You're in dire need of it." He nodded to the tent, dismissing them both.

Dispatching Captain Harshem was the right decision. But the mere thought of Severn rebelling against his brother made Ankarette feel weary and worried. The Fountain had given no indication of when Nanette was to become queen, but now it felt like events were unfolding quickly.

She and John Thursby walked quietly through town, so close that their bodies kept touching. It wasn't the embrace she wanted, but it would have to be enough for now.

"You didn't tell the duke everything, did you?" she asked in a hushed voice. The sun had fallen, and people were hunkering down inside their homes again.

"I did not," he confessed. "The rest I wanted to tell you. Were you planning a way to rescue me?"

"Of course. I even bartered for a grappling hook."

He sighed, shaking his head. "I knew you would. Which is why I knew I had to escape. I didn't much like being the bait for their trap."

"Hux asked for the ring I got from Bidigen Grimmer. That's what he wanted. He said we had to hand it over, or he'd kill you."

"I'm not worth a ring," he said in a flat tone.

"You are to me," Ankarette said boldly. They looked at each other in the shadows of the street, and she felt her world lurching, tilting. If Eredur died, everything would change. She would be free to make her own choices. At least until she died, and she'd already reconciled herself to the reality that she'd die young.

"Are you saying I have a chance to be with you yet?" he asked huskily.

"I don't know what tomorrow brings any more than I knew what today had in store. But this much I do know." She reached over and took his hand in the dark. "I don't want to lose you."

When they reached the Respite, she let go of his hand and they entered together, walking to her room. As soon as she shut the door behind them, she grabbed his tunic and pulled him close, thinking of how she'd have felt if Lord Hux had killed him to spite her.

She felt his arms wrap around her, and her throat clenched. It took all her willpower not to break down and start weeping.

THE SOFT KNOCK on the door broke through her reverie. John Thursby's tunic was in her lap. She'd mended the rips with her needles and thread before starting to add some embroidery to the cuffs and neckline while she waited for him to finish bathing. Needlework was how she replenished her Fountain magic, and she'd found doing such work for John Thursby even more enjoyable and fulfilling.

She rose from the chair, leaving the tunic behind, and opened the door. He was there, dry and clean and smelling of soap, and wearing the tunic she'd grabbed from the duke's pavilion.

"Sorry I was gone so long," he apologized. Judging by the darkness and the snores coming from the common room, it was probably after midnight. "I may have dozed in the tub for a while." He grinned sheepishly. "The maid gave me my pants but said you took my tunic after she'd cleaned it."

"I have it over here," she said. He followed her inside and gently shut the door. "I'm almost done. Sit on the bed while I finish it."

"What are you doing? It's just a shirt."

"A little embellishment. Oh, and the master-at-arms came by and brought a hauberk and a blade. I asked him for a dagger too since you prefer using two weapons." She pointed to the glimmering links of mail on the table with a dagger nestled on it. The longsword was leaning against the edge.

He walked over and examined both blades, nodding approvingly.

She sat down and continued working on the design. There was a metallic clinking as he examined the chain mail before folding it and setting it down on the table. He came to stand behind her and gazed at her work.

"You didn't have to do that, Ankarette. I'm no nobleman. I don't deserve something so fine."

"You had some holes that needed patching. And then I got carried away." She was working quickly now, trying to finish the last bit of the collar. "I'm glad you finally slept, though. It gave me enough time to work."

He sat on the edge of the bed. "I like it when your hair is down like that."

"I know," she answered, feeling heat tingle inside her.

When she'd finished the edge of the neck, she stood up and shook out the shirt. He dragged the borrowed tunic off, and she felt her pulse quicken as she beheld the edges of his muscles. There were battle scars on his arms, his chest, his back. He looked at her with discomfort and extended his hand to take the shirt.

She kept it from him. "Which is the scar from Borehamwood?"

"Ah," he grunted, nodding. Now he looked even more embarrassed. "This one," he said, tracing a large puckered scar below his ribs. Then his fingers continued around to his back, where she saw its twin.

"A sword?" she asked.

He shook his head. "A pike. He was aiming for my horse but got me instead. Lifted me clean off the saddle."

"Your hauberk didn't stop it?"

"Oh, it made a hole in that too. Can I have my shirt now?"

She gave it to him, and he quickly yanked it on. He admired her handiwork, gazing at the little design she'd sewn in. When he looked back up at her, his eyes were full of warm emotion. Vulnerability.

"I'm sick of war and trouble, Ankarette. I don't want to fight Glosstyr. Fought him at Borehamwood too. I don't know why Devereaux is siding with him now. The two have nothing in common."

"Men will do many things for the promise of a duchy. I'm sure he's wearied of playing the marauder."

"He may be weary, but he's not stupid. It doesn't make sense to me."

"Maybe he didn't arrange it," Ankarette said. "Severn doesn't trust the Occitanians. He never has. Maybe there's another voice he's listening to. We need to know his true aim. But he knows who I am, and he won't let me question him. He's distrustful by nature."

"One thing is for sure," John Thursby said, sitting back down on the bed. "We can't let these two armies get within a league of each other. Or there will be blood."

CHAPTER

FOURTEEN

THREAT

T here was no knowing when they could expect word
from Captain Harshem, who was watching the road
to Glosstyr. The siege progressed and the tunnels to
the castle grew longer with the hour. Duke Horwath kept his
men vigilant, ensuring no lapses in discipline or security.
Without the pressing need to infiltrate the castle, Ankarette
had time to think, time to watch, and time to spend with John
Thursby.

She was enjoying a late supper with him inside the inn
when Davern came bursting through the door, his cheeks
flushed from running.

His surprise arrival made her tense with dread, but it was
immediately eased by the grin on his face.

"Th-The ship! It's back from Kingfountain," he said after
reaching the table. "I saw Bennet. He's coming this way. I ran
ahead to find you."

"Thank you," Ankarette said. "Have him come here."

He nodded eagerly and sprinted off again.

"He reminds me of a pup dashing to and fro," John Thursby said with a smile. "It seems you won him over."

"He wants to be part of the Espion," Ankarette told him.

"Does he realize who you really are?" he asked, arching an eyebrow.

Ankarette shook her head. "He's been helpful. Young men aren't given many chances to advance."

"That's because most young men don't survive their first battle," he said grimly. "They stay up all night, imagining glory and triumph. And then they see what war is really about."

"He was too young to fight in the kingmaker wars," Ankarette said. "He doesn't have your wisdom."

Shortly afterward, Bennet arrived with three other members of the Espion. They were two men and one woman, all unfamiliar to Ankarette.

Bennet noticed John Thursby sitting at the table with her, and he opened his eyes wider in surprise. "I came as fast as I could, Ankarette," he said, taking a chair opposite her. "Did you take matters into your own hands?"

Davern went to the bar and waited over there, out of earshot.

"Devereaux let him go," Ankarette explained.

"Why would he do that?" Bennet asked incredulously.

"Because some men have honor," John Thursby said. His posture had altered with the new arrivals. His mood had soured.

"It seems the lord didn't take kindly to Lord Hux's decision to use our friend as bait. And now we have further information. Devereaux is expecting the Duke of Glosstyr to come."

Bennet's brow furrowed and he leaned back in his chair. "I spoke with the king. There was no mention of his brother coming here. He was convinced Duke Horwath could handle the situation. Forgive me. I should make introductions. This is

Balmor Tranz of East Stowe. He's good in a fight. Matthew Hopkins of Southport. He's one of the best infiltrators and climbers we have. And the lass is Giselle. A picklock from Our Lady of Kingfountain. A newer *recruit*."

Ankarette was impressed with the varied skills that had been assembled on short notice. She could tell by the inflection in Bennet's voice that there was a story behind Giselle's inclusion in the Espion. "Thank you all for coming."

"You think Severn is turning on his brother?" Bennet asked, his voice low. "I know things have been strained between them since the treaty."

"We know nothing for certain," John Thursby said. "I overheard some guards talking. It could have been deliberate or not, there's no way of knowing."

"How did Horwath take the news?" Bennet asked.

"He sent one of the captains to watch the road," she said. "Supplies keep arriving from Kingfountain every day, and none of the couriers have heard anything strange."

"Do you think Lord Hux is still inside the fortress?"

"I do," Ankarette answered. "He's in our territory, either acting alone or with Lewis's knowledge. It's a provocation of war."

"You think Lewis wants to break the treaty already?"

"Lewis wants more than to break a treaty. He wants to break Ceredigion," Ankarette said. "But there's no direct evidence he's behind this. Yet. I have an idea about breaking into the castle. I like our odds better now."

Bennet grinned. "I was hoping you'd say something like that."

ANKARETTE HAD ASKED Davern to bring over cups from the bar, and they'd made a makeshift replica of the fortress on the table, the cups representing the different towers of the outer and inner walls. She then let the young man explain to the Espion members about the rotation of the guards based on what he had observed over the past few days. Giving the squire some recognition in front of the Espion made him nervous, but he rose to the occasion and then answered questions.

"The duke is digging two tunnels, one to knock down this wall," Ankarette said after Davern's explanation was over. She pointed to one side of the fortress. "I acquired a grappling hook and rope from a local fisherman. I spoke to the duke about causing a diversion of some kind here"—she tapped the cup nearest the duke's pavilion—"in order to draw the guards from the wall over here." She tapped an upside-down cup on the opposite side. "It would have to be at dusk."

"I don't need a grappling hook," said Matthew with a thin voice, arms folded confidently. "I can scale it." He was lanky but looked like a sturdy fellow.

"And what if Lord Hux shows up?" Balmor asked. "We need a group of us to take down a poisoner of his caliber."

"If Matthew climbed the wall first, he could lower a rope so the others could get up more quickly," Ankarette said. "I would need to be one of them so I could be there to deal with Lord Hux. We need to capture him alive."

She noticed the scowl on John Thursby's face had deepened.

Bennet's brow was furrowed in concentration. "You

mentioned poisoning the cistern. That would require getting into the keep." He pointed to the fortress within the fortress. "I imagine they only have one door going in or out."

"There's a porter door in the back," John Thursby said, pointing. "It's made of iron, and it's kept locked."

"Locks won't be a problem," Giselle said.

"What I like about the plan," Bennet said, "is if the diversion feels real enough, they'll draw all the knights to defend the walls. That would give us a chance to sneak in through the back door, find the cistern, and pollute it. They wouldn't even know we did it." He tapped on one of the cups. "It's brilliant."

"Lord Hux would recognize poison, though," Ankarette said. "I would like to prevent him from escaping. There has to be a fountain inside the keep. One he uses to travel."

"How does he travel from inside a fountain?" Giselle asked, looking confused.

"We don't know how he does it, only that he can," Ankarette said. "If he believes the castle is going to be breached, he might flee. If we could damage the fountain or drain it, it would trap him inside Averanche."

"How much poison would you need to befoul the water?" Bennet asked.

"I have some that the apothecary made for me. Also, I have another kind. An irritant to the eyes. I was going to use it in case I was outnumbered."

"Now you won't be. We have the manpower to do this. If we can stop the siege, we can end the conflict before Glosstyr comes. I think Duke Horwath will see the wisdom in this plan of action."

"I hope you're right." She noticed the dark look on John Thursby's face, but he said nothing.

"I'd like to help," Davern offered meekly.

John Thursby rolled his eyes, but he still didn't speak.

"Better sit this one out, lad," said Balmor Tranz with a look of disdain. Davern blinked, his expression crestfallen.

"You've been a great help so far," Ankarette said. "But the duke would need to give his permission. I think we should speak to him soon. Now that we control the town, there have been no further disturbances."

Davern smiled but he looked defeated.

"Or we could just wait out the siege," John Thursby suggested, but the Espion gathered at the table frowned at the suggestion. "It's only a matter of time before they lose the castle. And Hux might already be gone."

"I don't think he'd stand much of a chance against all of us," Bennet said.

Balmor cracked his knuckles.

"We have enough of a plan to show the duke," Ankarette said. "He is not impulsive. But I think he will heed us if we ask and give him time to think. Tomorrow night at the earliest."

"I think we can be ready by then," Matthew said. "I'll inspect the castle tonight. These border castles are the easiest to climb. Lots of handholds and footholds."

The more she thought on it, the more she liked the idea. But she could tell by John Thursby's expression he didn't like it at all. He was good in a fight. But he didn't want to fight his brothers-in-arms. That was to be expected.

"Bennet, why don't you speak to the duke," Ankarette said.

"It's your plan, Ankarette."

"I know, but I've already shared the general concept with him. If the encouragement comes from you, someone Master Nichols trusts, he's more likely to act on it. Everyone else should get rest."

"There aren't any more rooms left," Bennet said with a sigh. "We'll be bunking outside of town again. Where the lad found us. Maybe he can take the others there while I talk to the duke?"

"Agreed," Ankarette said, rising from the table. "If we can capture Lord Hux, we remove a huge threat to Ceredigion. I don't like how he continues to interfere in our realm. It's time we put an end to it."

Even if it cost her life.

The founder of the poisoner school had a saying that every initiate had to memorize. "The dose makes the poison." All things are poison, and nothing is without poison. Too much water ingested by a body will kill it. Too much salt. Too much wine. A poisoner understands that all things must be in their proper ratio and applied in the proper amount. The seed of an apple is poisonous. But it takes many, many seeds to be fatal. With hemlock, very little. The dose makes the poison.

— ANKARETTE TRYNEOWY

FIFTEEN

THE BREACH

After shutting the door to her room, Ankarette turned and faced John Thursby. He looked restless, agitated, and defiant.

"I haven't asked you to be part of this mission," she told him. "You don't have to fight your friend."

His lips pursed. "I'm already tangled in this spider's web, Ankarette. I can't escape it now."

"I don't want you to look at it that way." She countered. "Please tell me how you're feeling. I can see you're upset."

He raked his fingers through his hair. "It's not just about Devereaux. I wish him no ill, but he made his choice to breach the castle."

"Then what is it?" She approached him and touched his arm.

"I'm daring to hope," he said. "And it frightens me."

That was not the answer she'd been expecting. Her confusion must have shown because he grabbed her by the shoulders. "You don't know how *badly* I want to get my hands on Lord Hux, Ankarette. When I was in irons, there was nothing I could do. But just knowing he's there, so close, has been tormenting me. If he knows a way to cure you...I would do anything to force him to reveal it. And I mean *anything*. I hate how he holds a grip on your life with that tincture."

She saw the feverish intensity in his eyes. His grip on her shoulders wasn't painful, but it was firm. "There may not even be a cure," she said softly.

"But it's the hope that's killing me. I'm going on this mission with you, Ankarette. And if I can get my hands on him, if I can make him wear the shackles this time..." He had a savage look now, one that promised pain.

"He's just as capable of stabbing you in the heart," she said. "There are poisons that can kill a man in seconds. Leave the fight to me."

"No, not this time," he said, releasing her and turning away. "I had to listen to you fight Bidigen Grimmer in that sewer. Helpless to aid you. No, we'll take him together. You've mentioned before that poisoners often carry a suicide ring. Well, I'll just cut off his hand so he can't use it. I need this, Ankarette. I don't want you under his power anymore. Forced to take sips of that foul-smelling drink to stay alive."

His concern for her made her heart burn with gratitude. But in his present state of mind, he'd be unnecessarily reckless. It was no easy task capturing a poisoner. Especially one with Hux's formidable skills.

"He may not be inside the keep. He may have already left."

"I don't care. We'll find another way to get him if we have to. I just want you to understand what motivates me. I want a chance to be with you, Ankarette. These last few days with you have reminded me of what I've been missing. I'm coming. There's no other choice."

She studied him for a moment, then said, "Part of me

thinks it would be wise if you helped Duke Horwath with the pretend attack."

"Hang the duke! You are not going in there without me. You know I'm good in a fight."

"I do know that. And you're a good man, John Thursby."

"A man who loves you. Who'd do anything for you. I don't want us to be apart after this." He started to tremble. Then he surprised her with his intensity of feelings by taking her in his arms and embracing her. She was lost in his scent, in the wildness of her feelings for him. His words had conjured a different life in her mind. One where he read her poetry every night, and they grew old together. Where they walked hand in hand in the dark of the night. One where she was his and his alone. Where no other duty bound her.

His lips found hers. His fingers pulled her tightly against him. She couldn't think in that moment; she could only feel. And her feelings were aroused by his fervor, his simplicity, his utter lack of disguise. She kissed him back, feeling her breath coming in quick gasps as her heart began to gallop recklessly in her chest. The room was reeling, and she felt her back pressed against the door as she slid her fingers up his chest. The anguish of desire blazed inside her, an ache she'd nearly forgotten. Not even with Thomas Mortimer had she experienced such powerful feelings. Feelings that once again nearly made her abandon reason.

He'd just started kissing her neck when a knock sounded at the door they were leaning against. It jarred her senses, making her aware they were inside a crowded inn during a siege.

John Thursby pulled back, half frowning, half smiling at the unwanted interruption. He hung his head and sighed. His mouth was near her ear, so his whisper was very soft.

"Can we have no moment of peace?"

Ankarette felt her cheeks were flushed, but she tried to steady her breathing. A knock sounded again, this time more urgent.

"My lady?" It was Davern's voice.

John Thursby let out a disappointed sigh. He stepped back away from her, his eyes still smoldering with pent-up desire. He gestured for her to answer it.

She didn't want to. But she did so regardless of her feelings. She opened the door and found the young squire looking at her with hopeful eyes.

"Duke Horwath wants to see you. He said to bring you straightaway. I think he's going to go along with the plan. That's my sense anyway. I saw some men working with a carpenter from town on building some ladders. Will you come?"

"Tell him we're on our way," Ankarette said and then shut the door. She put the key in the lock and turned it.

John Thursby's eyebrows lifted. "But the duke...?"

"He can wait," she said. "I'm not finished kissing you yet."

STIEV HORWATH GAVE them both a look of impatient curiosity when they arrived at the command tent near the siege. The men had been working on the tunnel night and day. The duke's captains were there, all except for Harshem. Bennet and the other Espion were also already gathered in the tent.

John Thursby looked a little too proud of himself for the situation, but she knew he just couldn't help himself. Dissembling just wasn't in his nature.

"I think your plan may work," Horwath said. "A night attack would be the least expected. Do you agree?"

"I do," Ankarette said. "Devereaux knows you are patient and determined. He's not going to expect this."

"What do you think, Thursby?" Horwath asked. "How will he react?"

"He'll defend the walls. His men are doing patrols all the time. If they believe an attack has come, they'll come rushing together to repel it."

"Captain Thueson said he can have three siege ladders done by midnight," the duke said. "I'd like to do this tonight."

Ankarette blinked in surprise. "Isn't that...hasty?"

"There's been no word from Captain Harshem. That means Severn is still far away, presuming he's coming. Devereaux is waiting for support to arrive. Better if we strike before that happens. Tonight is perfect. The young Espion says climbing the wall will be no trouble. He's already had a look at it. Even the darkness won't be a problem."

"I usually climb at night, my lord," confirmed Matthew Hopkins. "I can be atop the wall in a trice."

"Which begs the question of which comes first," the duke said, gazing again at Ankarette. "Do we create the diversion so you can get inside or do it after you're already in?"

All the other gazes shifted to her.

"If we're not discovered, then the extra time would certainly be useful," Ankarette said. "Might I suggest this is where your squire would be particularly helpful?"

"Davern?"

"Yes. He could take watch. Once we're over the wall, he can tell you we've made it inside. We could time the attack that way."

Horwath brooded on her suggestion. "You trust the lad to deliver your message accurately?"

"I do. He's been diligent so far, which is a trait I value highly."

"He is that, to be sure. Very well. I'll have my men pretend to bed down for the night, but no one will sleep. We'll finish those siege ladders and be ready to hit the eastern part of the wall. Your Espion will breach from the west. See how far inside you can get. Send Davern with word of when you want my men to attack. But I won't put them at needless risk. We'll have shields to ward off crossbows."

"Then it's determined. We'll wait until after midnight to try and slip in."

"Agreed," the duke said. "I hope this ruse works. We need it to."

THEY'D HAD ONLY a few hours to prepare. Ankarette had provided her grappling hook and rope, but Matthew had another line he'd managed to acquire in the interim. He'd tied grip knots at even spaces along the length to make it easier to climb. Balmor Tranz had grabbed two shields, one for himself and one for John Thursby so that they could also defend against crossbows. Darkness was another shield they could use, but if guards came, they'd be bringing torches. Giselle had her pick and tools ready, as well as a brace of daggers for close-range fighting. Ankarette had gathered her poisons and powders, she had enough now that so many people were coming with her, and changed into the breeches she'd arranged for earlier. Their appointed messenger, Davern, was enthusiastic about the role he would play. Just before midnight, the small band retreated from the duke's camp and approached the castle's western side quietly.

They made it to the edge of the wall without rousing any alarm and crouched down there to wait for the night sky to shift. There was a little bit of moon, so they had adequate light, especially once their eyes had adjusted to the darkness. They spoke in whispers and only then when necessary. The night was frigid, but Ankarette was warmed by the presence of John Thursby. The night was his time. He seemed calm and at ease, not the frenzied man from earlier that evening. When she'd decided to make the duke wait on them, he'd taken that as the highest of honors.

Bennet tapped Ankarette's wrist and made an Espion hand sign to see if she was ready to proceed. She gave the counter-sign to indicate that she was.

Bennet nodded and pointed to Matthew, who tilted his neck back and forth, causing little popping sounds, and then took off his boots and stuffed them in his pack. He hoisted the backpack onto his shoulders, which also contained the ropes and grappling hook, and stretched and shook out his hands. Then he pounced on the wall like a cat and began to shimmy up the little crevices and seams of the stone wall. He was nearly soundless, his bare feet and fingertips providing the feeling and delicacy he required. She hadn't even considered the possibility of going barefoot.

While he was climbing, the guards returned in their rounds. The sound of their boots and murmured conversation carried down the stone wall. Ankarette felt her stomach twist with worry. They were working around the guards' schedule, which was precarious, to be sure. Before the men came back, Balmor and Bennet would need to climb up, followed by Ankarette and John Thursby. Giselle would remain below with Davern, and someone would hoist her up while the others used the other rope to descend into the courtyard on the other side. Bennet would stay at the wall to safeguard an exit and take out the two guards.

That was all they could plan for.

After the guards passed them, a coil of rope came down the wall and thumped on the ground. Noisily. Ankarette gritted her teeth.

"D'you hear something?" asked a voice from atop the walls. The guards holding the torches turned and started back.

SIXTEEN

CHAINS OF OPPORTUNITY

Ankarette didn't hesitate. She jumped up to grab the dangling rope and began to pull herself up, knot after knot. The hiss of John Thursby's breath sounded after he saw what she'd done. The rope held her weight easily, yet she felt the strain in her arms, the burning sensation in her muscles.

She heard the guards above her, saw the glow of their torches. This one moment could dash her plans if one of them shouted in alarm. If Matthew had Espion training, he could likely dispatch them himself, but all it would take was one startled cry for a voice to carry, alert the other defenders, and then their surprise attack would be foiled.

Hand over hand, she gripped and pulled the rope, letting her legs dangle as she relied on her arms to do the work. Memories from Pisan surfaced, guiding her actions. This was a time for quick action, not silence.

She heard the gasp of surprise, followed by a scuffle, and cursed herself for not being fast enough. A grunt of pain sounded above her, and then a body came plummeting down, so close it nearly brushed against her before landing violently on the grass below.

Ankarette reached the edge of the balustrade, saw Matthew grappling with the soldier holding the torch. The glare of the light illuminated his face and his look of intense concentration as he tried to subdue the other man.

She vaulted over the edge, twisted her ring to expose the needle, and jabbed it into the guard's neck just as his open mouth was about to cry out. He jolted with surprised pain, stiffened as the toxin immediately incapacitated him, and then slumped and fell unconscious. Matthew wrested the torch from his grip and mouthed a silent thank-you to her.

"Take the torch and go that way," she said, pointing in the direction the soldiers had originally been intent on going. "I'll get the others up."

He nodded obediently and dropped his sack with the other rope in it once he'd taken his shoes out. Then he proceeded down the wall, pretending to be one of the guards they'd dispatched by taking the man's jacket. Ankarette knew the poison would render the man unconscious for quite a while, so she focused on retrieving the other rope and tying it around a crenellation. Because there wasn't anyone to hear it fall this time, she dropped the bulk over the wall into the darkness below.

The first rope and grapple were quivering with the strain of a climber, and soon John Thursby poked his head over the edge, giving her a scolding scowl.

She gripped his arm and helped him climb over the edge. He saw the comatose body on the wall and crouched near the fellow, looking at his face.

"That's Kennion," he muttered in a whisper.

Soon Bennet joined them, having climbed the other rope she'd dropped. That left Balmor Tranz and Giselle down below with Davern. Matthew had reached the edge of the next tower, whereupon he turned and started walking back slowly.

Ankarette looked down into the bailey yard. There was no sign of anyone down below, though she worried the starlight might not be bright enough for her to discern shapes. But there didn't seem to be anyone camped in the bailey. That meant Devereaux's men were either in the barracks or in the keep—or both.

"What next?" John Thursby whispered at her side. "Down there?"

She nodded, and then Balmor was clearing the wall. Only Giselle still had to come over, so they had an extra rope, and no time to lose. "Pull up that rope and send it over the other side," she told Thursby, and he leaped into action.

Bennet and Balmor tugged up Giselle and the second rope. They'd timed things so well that Matthew approached just after she came over the lip of the wall.

"Everyone duck down," Ankarette ordered. With the torch coming, they'd be visible to anyone watching from another part of the wall.

It was exciting to be in this sort of action again. Her preferred approach had always been infiltration, getting into a place in advance, sneaking in undetected. There was a certain thrill with having the danger and risk so imminent.

As Matthew approached, he looked for guidance on what he should be doing. Ankarette glanced at her Espion friend. "Bennet, take the torch and continue on. You stay on the wall for now so you can see the lay of the land from above and relay orders to Davern. Agreed?"

He nodded and rose just before Matthew reached them. He took the torch and continued walking past them, the tongues of flaming pitch hissing as he went by. Once the light was past,

John Thursby sent the second rope over the other side, lowering it carefully so it didn't make a noise.

Ankarette nodded to Matthew to go first, and he slipped over the wall and was down the rope in seconds. Balmor went next. He took longer, but descending was much easier than going up. Giselle followed him down at Ankarette's nod.

Once they were alone, John Thursby sidled up her next to her, both of them sitting with the upper part of the wall to their backs. They left the original grappling hook in place so they could use this part of the wall to escape if needed.

"You just had to jump into danger, didn't you?" he whispered.

"I'm trained for this work. If I hadn't come, that man would have cried an alarm. I got here just in time."

"And scared me out of my wits," he said. "What are we going to do with Kennion? Can't leave him lying there."

He was right, of course. Every instinct she had warned her that leaving him would only cause problems later.

"Was he your friend?" Ankarette asked.

John Thursby shook his head. "He was a bit of a git. But that shouldn't matter."

"Your feelings matter to me," she said. Giselle disappeared from sight as she swiftly climbed down. "You next."

He nodded in agreement and grabbed the rope, swinging over the wall and starting down. That left herself and the body. Bennet was reaching the other tower and about to turn around. She thought about what poison to use on the guard and decided on hemlock. It was one of the most lethal poisons in her arsenal and fast acting. It was the same poison she kept in her jeweled ring, the dose suitable for killing herself in case she were ever captured. She retrieved a tincture of it from her pouch, dipped a needle into it, and then pressed the needle through the man's shirt into the skin near his neck until she saw a little drop of blood well up. She cleaned the needle and replaced the vial.

Doing this kind of work always filled her with guilt. This was why she'd insisted on working as a midwife and went to places like Tatton Hall to help birth children. It didn't clean the blood from her hands. But it helped ease her conscience that while her skills were used to end life, they were also used to help foster it.

Bennet slowed as he approached. "I haven't seen anything out of order," he whispered. As he neared, he stopped beside her, gazing out into the night.

"Stay nearby. Don't have Davern go just yet."

"What are you waiting for?" he questioned. "And what are you going to do with the body?"

"Leave it here for now. There doesn't seem to be anyone down below. I think they're putting too much trust in the guards on the wall."

"Are you going after the porter door, then?" he asked. It was the most likely entry point they could use from the interior courtyard.

"I will, but I want to check something first."

"What?"

"The main gate. I want to see how they're guarding it. The information could be useful to the duke. Keep Davern at the ready. I'll send someone back to give further instructions."

"You know I trust you, Ankarette. It's good to be on a mission again together." He gazed down at the body. "I think he stopped breathing."

"It's very fast acting, especially when it goes straight into the blood."

"Remind me to stay on your good side," he quipped. "The guard doesn't change for several hours still. I'll keep watch and make sure the ropes are here to get you all out."

"Thank you. Now keep going."

Bennet nodded and continued on his patrol. After the glare from the torch was gone, she slipped over the wall and quickly descended. John Thursby was waiting at the bottom, the shield still strapped to his back, and he grabbed her by the waist to hoist her down. The others were flat against the wall, looking in both directions.

"The porter door is that way," John Thursby said, pointing.

"I know. But I want to see how they're guarding the main gate."

"I can go check," Matthew volunteered.

Considering his earlier mistake, she decided against it. "You three stay here. John Thursby and I are going to follow the wall to the gate. I promised Bennet I'd send someone to tell him our next move after that."

Balmor gave a frustrated sigh. "You're taking him?"

John Thursby began to bristle, but she didn't intervene. "You'll have your chance. We won't be long. If the alarm is raised, climb the wall and get out."

She didn't wait to acknowledge their acceptance before she started walking along the wall, following the perimeter. The interior keep was taller than the outer wall, more imposing, and she saw light filtering in from some of the arrow slits. But all was quiet, which wasn't surprising considering the late hour. Still. It was unnerving.

"Just another night patrol," John Thursby murmured. She'd chosen him as her partner because she trusted him, but also because he was a creature of the night—accustomed to its sounds and the lack of light.

"Do you smell anything off?" she asked.

"Just the sea," he said.

They reached the tower, went around it, and continued toward the front. They walked quickly but quietly, trying not to scuff or make noises. They spoke only in whispers. The tension mounted the farther they strayed from the safety of the escape ropes. But Devereaux didn't know they were coming. Did Lord Hux?

They continued down the way, keeping close to the wall. The outer wall had five towers on the western side. The keep had three. So by the time they reached the corner tower of the keep, she could tell they were going to be within sight of the gatehouse soon. She tugged on John Thursby's sleeve, and they crossed the yard to the inner keep as they approached the round turret base in the corner. About three-quarters of the tower was separated from the inner wall, so they had to go around its circumference. She slowed, pressing her back against the rough wall, trying not to expose herself.

The front of the keep had two guard towers and an interior gate, plus a set of stairs leading up to the door that would make it an uphill slog for a battering ram. The castle had been designed very well. The huge sturdy gate, which she'd seen from the other side when they'd delivered John Thursby, lay unprotected.

"There's no one there," Ankarette whispered in surprise.

Devereaux had put all his guards on the wall and none at the gate. Why? She suspected he was trying to project that he had more guards than he really did. Making them walk the top of the walls lent to that deception.

John Thursby craned his neck. "It's very dark, though. And the gatehouse is deep. We should get closer."

She nodded to her friend, and they snuck across the gap to the outer wall and quickly paced toward the gate. The alcove was thick and deep, just as he'd said, and guarded by a single man who'd fallen asleep. Why they'd trust the defense to one man was quickly discerned. Heavy chains had been dragged within to secure the gate. She'd heard the chains when they had opened the doors for Thursby, but she hadn't know they would be so thick. They were the same kind of chains you'd find on a ship. The interior of the gatehouse was deep and filled with shadows, so entering it kept them concealed. She exposed the needle of her ring and jabbed the man in the neck to incapacitate him. He jolted awake before becoming paralyzed. A quick search of his body showed he did not have the key. Then she ran her fingers over the chains, feeling the rust and grit of the iron. In the middle of the nest of chains was a huge lock. That was how Devereaux had chosen to defend the entrance. He'd known Lord Horwath wouldn't try to breach the gate since they could defend from the heights, killing men with arrows and crossbow bolts. Making it too costly for the duke of the North.

All that was defending the door now was a lock. A single lock.

"We need Giselle," Ankarette whispered, feeling a throb of triumph in her chest.

SEVENTEEN

THE RIOT OF AVERANCHE

"But I thought the plan was to get inside the keep and spoil the water?" Balmor Tranz whispered, his brows furrowing with concern. "The front gate is where they'll go first to defend the castle. Our people will be slaughtered."

"All we need is to buy enough time for Duke Horwath to get some men in there," Ankarette said. She was a little surprised by his resistance to her plan. Now that they were past the first barrier and could see the defense for what it actually was, there was an opportunity of weakness to exploit. She felt confident Duke Horwath would agree. So confident she'd dispatched the hapless guard at the gate.

"I can unlock that contraption," Giselle said confidently. "The way you described it, it sounds like an ordinary ship lock. The kind they use to secure precious cargo."

Balmor was still frowning. "I don't like it."

"I don't think she was asking for your opinion," John Thursby said dryly. "Let's not stand here and dither. It's a sound plan."

"Are you calling me a fool?" the sizable Espion asked in a challenging tone.

It was common in moments of high tension for impulsiveness and self-preservation to override companionability. The last thing they needed was to be at odds with each other. And a few hasty words could throw their advantage to the winds.

"This plan won't work without you, Balmor," Ankarette said, trying to mollify his pride. "Both you and John Thursby are seasoned warriors. You're right, as soon as they realize a night attack is underway, they'll rush to defend the gate. That's why we need to act and move quickly. We need to be ready to pull open that door when the duke's forces arrive. You're not wrong. This is risky. But it's a risk we must take."

He was still frowning, but he'd begun nodding in acceptance.

She turned to Matthew. "I saw how quickly you scaled the wall. I want you to get up there and tell Bennet the plan. He needs to communicate to Davern the urgency of getting some men to the gate as quickly and quietly as he can."

"The duke doesn't strike me as the risk-taking type," Matthew said.

"If I've judged his character correctly, he'll leap at this opportunity. It will make sacking the rest of the castle much easier, give us freedom of movement and protection from their archers and crossbowmen. He'll do it. I promise."

Matthew nodded, hurried to the dangling rope, and immediately began scampering up the wall.

Balmor let out a sigh, readied his shield, and nodded for them to get going. Time was critical. Ankarette led the way, John Thursby at her side, followed by Giselle and Balmor.

"Well said," John Thursby whispered to her. "I could have been more helpful back there. I'm sorry."

People tended to act within their natures. Thankfully, she'd learned enough diplomacy over the years to help her get ahead of ill feelings. It didn't always work, but she was grateful it had. She touched his arm and gave it a gentle squeeze of acknowledgment.

Moving quickly, they kept to the shadow of the wall as much as they could until they reached the angle of the corner tower. This was the most dangerous section, where they'd be exposed. She halted the group, trying to tamp down the growing tension in her chest, and gazed ahead, watching for the telltale torchlight that would reveal the pattern of the watch. They'd timed their initial infiltration to take place just after a guard change, knowing that would give them the most time and the group previously on duty would have gone to bed and were probably snoring by now.

She spied the torchlight, then waited until it was going back the way it had come before signaling to the others to move. In a trice, they were concealed by the murk of the gatehouse.

She motioned for John Thursby to take one edge of the gatehouse and Balmor Tranz to take the other. Both had their shields out and swords in hand.

"Do you need light?" Ankarette whispered to Giselle.

"Wouldn't be very good at my trade if I did," the Espion girl replied. She reached out and traced the chains with her fingers until she came to the ship lock. "Good. I've done this kind before."

Ankarette felt a throb of relief and let her go about her work. She imagined Davern was sprinting to Duke Horwath's tent already to relay the message. Ankarette's greatest power from the Fountain was her ability to discern people's strengths and weaknesses. She knew enough about Duke Horwath that she didn't even need to use her magic on him to understand how he'd react. If the Duke of Glosstyr was indeed coming with ill intent, having command of part of a fortress was better than having none at all. He wouldn't want to risk his men in open battle against the king's youngest brother.

If they took the castle back, he wouldn't have to.

She heard a snick behind her, and then the lock came open. "Help me with the chains," Giselle whispered to Ankarette.

Together they began to loosen them from the crossbar pieces. The iron rattled a bit, and Balmor hissed at them to be more quiet. Ankarette and Giselle slowed their work, being meticulous in unwinding the chains and setting the heavy coil down in the corner of the gatehouse. The massive oak crossbar was still in place, so both women hefted it up and slid it to the right. The piece was very heavy, and so it took the two of them, but they slid it far enough that it was no longer over the center slit between the doors. The doors would be heavy. It would likely take all four of them to get them open.

"Here's Matthew," John Thursby whispered.

The climber arrived, slinking into the area with them.

"Any trouble?" Ankarette asked.

"Bennet agreed with the plan. He's going to guard that side of the wall in case we need to flee. The boy ran like a dart."

"Horwath better hurry," Balmor said tonelessly.

They waited, feeling every moment keenly, anxious for the dread of waiting to end, but knowing they'd be in the thick of battle as soon as it did. If Horwath's men arrived undetected, they could open the doors and launch a surprise attack. But getting that many men to move in unison and quietly was too much to ask. Devereaux's men would not be so careless.

"Ring the bell! Ring the bell!"

The shout came from the upper walls, a cry of panic. Ankarette felt her chest muscles constrict. "Open the door," she said.

She, Giselle, and Matthew pulled on one of the door

handles. It groaned but didn't move. Matthew huffed with the effort as all three of them strained against it.

The bell in the tower began to clang loudly. Whoever had been stationed there had responded instantly to the command. The noise echoed down from the shaft of the tower, loud and booming to their ears.

"John!" she cried out, trying to get more help.

He came at once and threw down his shield and sword to join in the task of budging the hulking door.

She heard a muttered curse come from Balmor as he stood there. "They're coming."

The door they were guarding began to squeal on its hinges. She saw Balmor loosening himself, preparing for a fight. Soldiers came rushing out from the keep to defend the very gate the group was trying to open. One was carrying a torch, and it illuminated the shadowed alcove instantly.

"The gate!" one of them screamed. "Intruders at the gate!"

Balmor rushed to strike them head-on. Ankarette thought that incredibly foolish, exposing himself to the archers at the wall. Her muscles quivered as she lent her strength to move the door. She couldn't hear the sound of anyone approaching from the other side, but at least having the door open would allow them the chance to escape if all of Devereaux's men came rushing at them.

The clash of arms sounded as Balmor struck out at the oncoming soldiers. The fellow with the torch was cut down first, but three others quickly took his place.

"Almost," Matthew seethed. The door was moving ponderously, but it had opened a small gap now, enough that they could get their fingers into it.

"Help him," Ankarette said to John Thursby.

A roar sounded from outside. It was the battle cry of

Dundrennan. But it wasn't coming from beyond the doors. It was farther away.

"Ladders! They have siege ladders! To the walls! To the walls!"

The bell started clanging again.

Siege ladders? Ankarette's heart ticked faster. Why was the duke attacking the walls now? She needed him at the gate!

John Thursby grabbed his sword and shield and rushed into the yard, skewering one of the men who'd been attacking Balmor from behind. Now the odds were improved.

And then she felt the thrum of Fountain magic coming from within the castle. She recognized it instantly as coming from Lord Hux. He was using his magic to size up the danger. To determine where the threats were coming from. And she felt her own magic respond to his, reflexively, resonating like the echoes from the clanging bells. Metal did that sometimes, thrumming in harmony with invisible tones.

Lord Hux knew she was within the castle precincts, and they still hadn't gotten the door open.

All three of them pulled with their might, but the door continued to protest. The twangs of crossbows began to sound, and bolts came rushing down into the bailey. Ankarette glanced back and saw the first rush of guards who'd come had all been killed. John Thursby and Balmor Tranz held up their shields and swords and backed into the alcove.

She felt Lord Hux approaching. He was running. He knew the gate had been breached. And he was coming in person to handle the situation. Excitement and fear wrestled inside of her.

"Hux is coming," she said aloud. The others might not understand, but John Thursby would.

More cries from the outer walls. Devereaux's men were gathering quickly. Confusion was hindering the enemy.

Perhaps Devereaux himself had been abed and was having to clear the fog of sleep to think quickly and rightly. They might take the entire castle tonight if they acted well.

Lord Hux was at the door now.

Ankarette knew she had to join the fight. She backed away from the effort and drew two daggers, both having been treated with incapacitating poison.

"I see him," John Thursby growled.

"What's he holding?" Balmor asked.

There was a twang, but a softer sound than that of a crossbow. Balmor hissed in pain and Ankarette saw a small bolt protruding from his knee. And then the poison hit him, and he collapsed to the ground.

Lord Hux was standing at the door, holding a strange weapon she'd never seen before. It was like a crossbow but much smaller. And equipped with poisoner bolts that would allow him to strike them from a distance. He wouldn't need to engage them at all.

John Thursby seemed to realize this at the same moment. And he charged.

EIGHTEEN

OLD FOES

Ankarette was about to send a poisoned dagger hurtling at Lord Hux, but she risked hitting John Thursby with it and stayed her hand.

"Get the door open!" she shouted to Matthew and Giselle.

John Thursby did an unlikely maneuver, dropping and rolling over his shield before springing up, shield first, to collide with Lord Hux. It was a bold move, but the canny poisoner dodged out of the way. She heard the click of the bolt being fitted into place and watched Hux aim the short crossbow directly at her friend's back. The dagger sailed from her hand, aiming for the weapon's taut cord. Her aim was true, and the contraption recoiled from the expelled tension, the bolt toppling harmlessly to the courtyard stone.

John Thursby swept his sword around, trying to nick the poisoner across the cheek, but again Hux's reflexes kept him out of range.

Ankarette rushed her enemy, throwing another dagger while drawing a third from behind her back. Hux was equally skilled at blades, but she had years more experience since the last time they'd fought face-to-face in the palace of Kingfountain. She'd taken down the giant Bidigen Grimmer. She'd bested knights and Espion. She *knew* she could defeat Hux. She had to believe it.

"If I die, your queen dies," Hux told her, his face betraying his agitation. Of course he'd threaten Eredur or Elyse. Anything to rattle Ankarette's emotions.

She dropped and swung her leg around in a reverse sweep, hoping to knock him off his feet. He'd dropped his miniature crossbow but hadn't drawn another weapon yet. She knew better than to take heart from that, though—he was just as deadly with hands and feet.

John Thursby lunged at him again, aiming for his heart or vital organs. He was trying to draw blood, to incapacitate the poisoner.

Lord Hux twisted, grabbing his opponent's wrist, and then threw John Thursby to the ground. Ankarette lunged at him. All she needed was to manage a little cut with her blade, and he'd be unconscious in a second. She hadn't expected his reaction, though, his backward kick that caught her in the stomach, knocking the wind from her.

She tried to jam her blade into the meat of his leg, but he retracted it and popped her in the jaw next. An explosion of stars crossed her vision. Unable to see or breathe, she swiped the dagger in front of her, trying to find him. For a dizzying moment, she feared she'd black out.

"I knew we'd face each other again, Ankarette. I've been looking forward to it."

She heard the whoosh of clothing and ducked reflexively. She shifted her dagger to an underhand grip and lashed out at him again. Her stomach muscles were quivering, but she managed to get some air in.

John Thursby rolled onto his feet. He'd dropped his sword

as he went down. Now he pulled the shield off his arm and flung it at the poisoner's head. Hux ducked, and the shield sailed past him, clanging loudly against the wall. John Thursby took the time to grab his sword and then drew a dagger from his belt. Using two weapons had always been his preference.

"We attack him together this time," Ankarette said, her throat tight. "Now!"

She rushed Hux and so did John Thursby. Two against one would be a challenge for anyone, but Lord Hux was equal to it. She didn't recognize the fighting technique he used but was amazed by his ability to sidestep and swerve, altering the point of attack so that Ankarette found herself confronting her friend instead. It was like trying to scoop up a glob of quicksilver that danced away.

She feinted high, then reversed the dagger and brought it on another plane of attack, aiming for Hux's middle. He caught her wrist, danced around again, and she was suddenly caught in a spiraling move, landing on her back. Her dagger clattered and her wrist stung.

"I've trained in the East Kingdoms," Hux sneered, "and know their ways."

Ankarette rolled to the side, confused but determined. As she came to her feet, she watched John Thursby attack again, but this time, Lord Hux didn't evade him. He came forward into a horse-riding stance and struck his palm against the night watchman's chest, a blow so hard that she saw John Thursby's cheeks quiver, his eyes bulge, and he flew backward in disbelief, a grunt of pain followed by a crash against the stone floor. The two men were not comparably sized. John Thursby had been knocked down by a much smaller man.

Lord Hux turned his gaze on Ankarette, his body in a tight, rigid stance. One fist was at his waist, his other arm extended still.

Ankarette flew at him. He parried her attacks, one by one, his motions a blur as he let her wear herself out, his movement vastly superior to hers. John Thursby didn't rise again. He was on his back, his expression stunned.

"You think I am a doddering fool?" Hux said to her. "Past my prime? I've been patient with you, Ankarette. But that patience is at an end. You could be so much more."

She wanted to kill him now instead of taking him captive. Even if that meant no more tincture. Even if it meant she would die. She tried to grapple him, but he wouldn't budge. It was as if his legs were welded to the stone. A blow to her cheekbone came. She summoned her Fountain magic, trying to find a weakness in him. In the haste of combat, she'd been too focused on winning to summon it.

Her magic coursed through her body, into his, and she began to unmask him. He had trained beyond Pisan. He'd spent years in the deepest reaches of the East Kingdoms, studying under a cruel master who had hardened his body and his mind. He'd learned an ancient discipline that could even make his skin invulnerable to a blade or needle for short bursts of time. He'd practiced it for hours and weeks and years, hardening his body, making himself insusceptible to another poisoner's attacks.

He had one weakness.

And that weakness was Ankarette herself.

He saw promise in her. Saw the potential to be even greater than he was. Someone he could share his secrets with. Someone he could mentor and mold into the greatest poisoner who had ever lived.

That's why he'd never killed her. Even when he'd had the chance. Even when Morvared had ordered it.

The glimpse into his soul connected them. He could sense her magic. And she could sense his. His training, his Fountain magic, made him immune to blades. That was what he had desired more than anything else and what had driven his training. And he desired to teach her. To share what he knew. But mastery of such skills and secrets would require her to surrender to him, to obey him completely in all things, to betray even her king and queen. He would do the same, but *she* never would.

He grabbed her wrist and twisted her arm around, her shoulder exploding in pain. She felt his breath against her cheek. "How often I have tried to bring you to my side, Ankarette. You could be the greatest of us all! But you will not. There's a plant in the East Kingdoms that can heal the damage done to you. It is a secret few know about. But you continue to defy me. You scorn me when I want nothing but to see your perfection. You could be even better! But you will not!"

He shoved her to the ground, his voice thick with rage. There was nothing he could say or do that would turn her to his side. He knew it and it galled him.

She looked up at him, no longer fearing for her life. He wouldn't kill her. But he would take away everything she loved.

The barricade door groaned, and soldiers wearing the lion of Horwath surged into the bailey, roaring with the battle cry of the North. She saw Bennet at the head of them. Duke Horwath had pulled off a feint by using the siege ladders against the far wall, to draw attention to that side while he sent men to the gate. She saw Davern rushing forward, sword drawn, coming toward her.

Relief coursed through her. Not even Lord Hux, with all his power, could subdue that many.

"Take him!" Bennet yelled, pointing at Lord Hux.

The poisoner stood defiant against the onrush. He looked down at her once more, the magic still binding them.

"Too late," he said to her. "You're already too late."

She saw him reach into his belt for a metallic cylinder, which he gripped in his hand. And then he vanished, no words spoken, no power uttered. Nothing. If he'd gone invisible, like Dragan, the Fountain-blessed thief who hid in the sanctuary of Our Lady, she would have still been able to sense him. But the void, the absence, was striking in its suddenness. He was gone, whisked away by a magic she didn't understand.

The soldiers flooded the bailey. Ankarette was still trying to get up, her ribs moaning in complaint, when Davern arrived and put her arm around his shoulder. Bennet, after seeing Lord Hux disappear, went to where Balmor Tranz was lying immobile on the stone. He dropped and touched his neck.

"He's dead," Bennet said. The soldiers were flooding the courtyard now, while arrows began to rain down on them from above.

"Get John Thursby," Ankarette pleaded, letting Davern help her to the safety of the gate. The soldiers on the wall were yelling and sending down shafts, the fire quickly returned by Horwath's man. Cheers began to erupt. The Northerners were taking the outer walls. It would be over soon, with just the men in the keep to stand against them. Averanche would fall swiftly now.

Only...Hux's words spread like poison in her mind. The Fountain magic had bound them together, and she knew there had been no deception in his thoughts. Hux wasn't loyal to King Lewis like she was to Eredur. He was acting in his own interests, concealing knowledge from his king. And he saw in Ankarette a kindred spirit of sorts. One that he thought he could mold and develop. It wasn't a physical passion. But a passion of ambition. Of seeing what she could become if taught his ways. He could heal her and had been willing to do so all along. That knowledge was tantalizing. If she was healed, she could be with John Thursby. She could be whole again. A wife instead of just a midwife. And she was scared by how much she suddenly wanted that.

She looked over and saw Bennet and Matthew carrying John Thursby toward the gate. He was listless, his eyes vacant.

Ankarette reached out with her dwindling magic, and when she touched John Thursby with it, she realized he wasn't breathing. And hadn't been breathing since Lord Hux had struck his blow.

NINETEEN

BROKEN PROMISES

Within the alcove of the gatehouse, there was a door on each side that contained a little guard room and the stairs leading up to the walls. Duke Horwath's men were flooding through the breach, and many were rushing through the door and up the steps to attack the defenders on the wall. Ankarette's heart raced with shock and worry as she guided Bennet and Matthew into the little room.

"Put him on the floor," she ordered and then knelt beside him as they laid him down. It was just registering that Bennet had abandoned the wall to join in the fight. She saw Davern peering down at John Thursby, his eyes wide and full of concern, his mouth showing dismay.

Ankarette wondered if the night watchman's ribs had been crushed from the blow to his chest. With the clang and clatter around her, she pressed her ear against his mouth, trying to hear or feel his breath. There was none. His eyes were fixed open, the blinking reflex no longer working. Then she pressed her hand against his heart and felt the galloping race of his pulse.

Thank the Fountain, he was still alive, but his lips were turning blue.

"What happened to him?" Bennet asked, panting, crouching next to them.

She knew what she needed to do. But she felt a warning from the Fountain not to do it in front of everyone.

"Go help Duke Horwath," Ankarette said. "Take Giselle and see if you can unlock the porter door at the rear of the keep."

"I'll come too," Matthew said, and the three Espion rushed out into the maelstrom of arrows. Davern looked hesitant but started to edge away.

"You may stay," Ankarette told the young squire. "But turn around."

"Yes, my lady," he said and assumed a sentry pose, hand on his sword hilt.

Ankarette gazed down at her friend's face. Her heart clenched with dread and hope, Lord Hux's words still clattering around inside her. There was a plant that could heal her from the poison. Could make her whole.

But none of that would matter if John Thursby died. She reached and took his gloved hand, squeezing it.

She knew the word of power to restore life. It had brought the Kiskaddon boy back from the dead, but a tiny infant required less magic to revive than a man.

"Come back to me, John Thursby," she whispered, bending over his face. Then she whispered, *"Nesh-ama"* and pressed her lips against his. The swirl of Fountain magic rushed through her. She felt the power gush out of her, depleting her, abandoning her. Waves of darkness lapped over her as she felt her strength vanish. She gripped his hand, trying to stay conscious.

Hoping that her magic would restore him as it had done the babe. Hoping for a sign.

She collapsed on top of him, utterly spent.

A VOICE ROUSED HER, but it was garbled, as if the words had been spoken underwater.

Ankarette felt she was floating in a lake, carried by gentle water that was neither cold nor warm. She tried to awaken, but the water tugged her down. She was sinking into it. Drowning.

And then it felt like she'd burst from a cocoon. She could hear again. Could sense the candlelight against her eyelids and lashes. And she heard John Thursby's voice reading a poem.

"...*and the sky sipped the smoke and smiled,*" John Thursby said aloud. "Is that a flutter I see in your eyes, Ankarette? Is it?" He sounded excited. "Are you awake at last?"

"I am," she croaked, surprised at how tremulous and difficult it was to say those two words. As her eyes opened, she beheld the little room in the inn, a candle by the bedside and John Thursby sitting in a chair next to her, a folded book in his lap. He reached down and laid his hand on hers.

"I've never seen you so helpless. It frightened me."

She felt no strength, so it was difficult lifting her hand and grazing his stubbled cheek with the edge of her finger. "You're alive," she whispered.

"I thought I was done for," he said. "When Hux hit me like that, I think he shook my soul loose. I couldn't breathe. Felt like I'd taken the brunt of a battering ram." His eyebrows raised in astonishment. He set the book of poetry down and then knelt at the edge of the bed. "What did you say to me? I was hovering over my body, feeling the tug of the Deep Fathoms. Then I saw you there. Saw the lad. I was getting pulled away, but you said something, and it tethered me back inside my body."

Ankarette was so relieved it had worked. She felt tears gather in her eyes. In all her training in Pisan, she'd learned to hide her emotions, to bury them. Lately they'd been too near the surface. "It was a word of power," she said listlessly. "Only the Fountain-blessed...can use them."

"It was powerful indeed," John Thursby said. He took her fingers and kissed them. "Thank you, Ankarette."

"You're welcome, John Thursby. Put a coin in the fountain. We must honor this miracle."

He nodded. His smile was pained. "I hoped we'd capture him. With all the men rushing through the gates, I could have sworn we'd nab him. But he fled. How?"

"I don't know," Ankarette answered. "He had some magical artifact with him. One that took him away. I felt he was gone immediately."

John Thursby bared his teeth as a look of disappointment crinkled his brow. "So much for finding a cure," he muttered.

Ankarette bit her lip. She felt powerless to do much more than lie there, but she stroked her fingers through his hair. "There *is* a cure. He told me of it. My magic tells me he spoke the truth."

His eyes blazed with purpose. "Where?"

"In the East Kingdoms," she said. "Far, far away. I'm sure that's where the poison comes from too. And his training. What he did to you, he did not learn at the poisoner school."

"The East Kingdoms are on the other side of the world," John Thursby said, amazed. "I know a merchant who has been as far east as Chandleer and the East is farther still. Not even *he* has gone all that way. Through desert and storms and hurricanes."

"I know," Ankarette said. "I could tell Hux isn't loyal to King Lewis. He serves another master. Or he serves himself, I guess. He...he wants me to join him."

John Thursby swore softly, gazing at her. "And he promised to heal you, didn't he?"

Ankarette nodded. "But he knew I wouldn't go with him. He won't kill me, though. It's like he can't." More of his words came to her memory. She tried to sit up but felt a wash of dizziness.

"Easy, lass," he said, pushing her shoulders back onto the mattress. "You need to rest."

"The king is in danger," Ankarette said. "Or someone is. The last thing Hux told me was that it's already too late. I think he went to Kingfountain."

"And not by ship."

"Not by ship. I warned Master Nichols to be vigilant. I hope he heeded me. Help me sit up."

"Whatever you need, let me fetch it for you. You must rest."

"I have to see the duke."

"I'll send Davern to get him. He hasn't left your door all night."

Ankarette felt a flicker of warmth for the young man. She watched as John Thursby rose from her bedside and hurried to the door.

As soon as the door was opened, Davern poked his head inside, and she managed to get herself up on one elbow and give him a little wave. Upon receiving his instructions, he took off at a run.

"It's midmorning," John Thursby said after shutting the door. "Are you hungry?"

"Famished. Help me sit up."

His forehead wrinkled with concern, but he returned to the bed and gently lifted her into a sitting position. She flopped against him, her limbs still exhausted. He cradled her for a moment, stroking her hair and then rubbing her back.

"I wish Old Rose were here to make you some of her soup," he said, and she could hear the smile in his voice.

Slowly, ever so slowly, she was able to move again. He arranged some pillows, and she managed to sit up without falling over. How grateful she was for John Thursby's protection.

Sitting up, she sensed the ache from where Hux had kicked her bruised ribs. Massaging it helped. A little grunt of pain came.

"I underestimated him," John Thursby confessed. He leaned forward and touched their foreheads together. "Next time I won't."

"John..."

"If there is even the littlest hope that a cure can be found, I must pursue it. You deserve to have a life, Ankarette."

"This isn't the same as that night in Kingfountain when Dragan stole my vial," she said. "You can't go to the East Kingdoms to find it. You must promise me you won't."

"You can't make me stop loving you," he said with a fierceness that took her breath away.

"And I love you, John Thursby. But we mustn't be swayed by Lord Hux's attempt to send us off on a wild chase. I have to stay. I made a promise to the king."

"I'm not saying I'm leaving today," he told her. "But I have to. How can I love you and not try to help you? I'd travel to the ends of the earth."

"I know," she whispered thickly, tears spilling from her eyes. "But promise me you won't. Not yet."

"Lass, it's unfair to bind me in such a way."

"I know it's unfair. Please. Don't go. I need you near me. I need your help."

He chuckled softly. "I've fought against my old companions. What more do you want?"

"You," she said, pulling back to gaze in his eyes. She felt a tear streak down the side of her face. "I just want you."

The look of tenderness in his eyes was powerful. Gratitude mixed with hope. And relief. She'd said something that had touched him deeply. Touched the core of his heart. "Oh, lass. I'll always be yours. So long as you'll have me. Always."

His fingers slid through her hair, around her neck, and he kissed her deeply, hungrily. There was poetry in the way his mouth moved against hers.

They were still kissing when Duke Horwath arrived.

We believe in the Deep Fathoms because we want to believe there is something after this life. Bones will molder into dust. Songs will fall silent. Even the ink in the pages of books will fade. We cling to life because it is a gift. But death is either extinction or change.

— ANKARETTE TRYNEOWY

TWENTY

THE COMING OF THE BOAR

There were not enough places to sit in Ankarette's cramped little room, so Duke Horwath fetched a chair from the common room and seated himself near her bedside. She was dizzy again, weakened well past the point of vulnerability. John Thursby stood by the dresser, elbow leaning against it.

"I'm glad you are sitting up at least, lass," the duke said. "I wouldn't want to explain to the king how I'd lost his poisoner."

Ankarette smiled at the words. "How goes the siege? How many men have you lost?"

"A dozen to arrows or sword blows. Twice that number are wounded. The Espion girl managed to get the porter door open, but there were guards waiting on the other side preparing a counterattack. Another Espion fell during the fight, and they managed to barricade the door. Bad luck."

Ankarette flinched. "Bennet?"

The duke shook his head. "No. It was the other fellow. Got in the way so they couldn't kill Giselle."

"Matthew," John Thursby said with a sigh. "Poor cove."

That left two Espion dead—two that Bennet had brought with him. "I'm sorry for the loss of your men," Ankarette said to the duke.

"We've claimed the outer wall. I have archers on the turrets now. The keep is surrounded. The sappers have quit digging the twin tunnels. Now we're going to work on a battering ram big enough to breach the front gate. Devereaux has lost. We have protection from the walls now, and he's not going to have enough men to repel our assault. It'll be over in days."

Ankarette nodded. "We need to send word to Kingfountain. Lord Hux got away."

"I don't see how," the duke said. "He must be holed up in the keep with the others."

"No, he's not."

"How can you be so sure, lass?"

"Because he has a certain magical gift that allows him to flee. I thought it was limited to the fountains, but it is not. He disappeared before my very eyes, and I sensed him leave. I think he's going after the royal family, and I'm not there to protect them."

The duke frowned. "Do you think Master Nichols is up to the task?"

"He'd better be," Ankarette said. "I would go there myself, but I'm in no condition to defend the king's family. I need rest. Time to recover."

The duke rose from the chair. "I'll have a ship sent at once."

A fist hammered against the door, making the duke scowl at the interruption. John Thursby hastened to open it, and in came a flushed and distressed Captain Harshem.

"Glosstyr's on the move." He panted raggedly. "He's coming this way. And he's coming fast!"

"This is ill timing," the duke muttered.

Ankarette agreed. The duke's baggage and supplies were all

outside the walls. If their suspicions about Glosstyr proved true, it could become a siege within a siege. "Devereaux knows he's coming. It's his last hope."

Duke Horwath clenched his fist. "We need to get the supplies inside the walls. And we need to knock down that gate before Severn gets here. How long do we have?"

"At his pace, he'll arrive tonight," Harshem said.

"With how many men?"

"I would say well over a thousand. Knights, pikemen, and archers. The knights will get here first."

"That's not enough time to get a message to the king and back," Horwath said. "Or to get reinforcements." He gave Ankarette a hard look. "Get your rest, lass. I need you to be ready to poison the king's brother if he's come to fight."

Her stomach began to ache with dread and the effects of Lord Hux's poison.

ANKARETTE'S FINGERS were deftly sewing another series of decorative lines in John Thursby's tunic. The weakness and fatigue were fading now. Her Fountain magic was trickling in to replenish the lost stores, but she didn't feel anywhere near ready to face the Duke of Glosstyr. Using her magic to restore John Thursby had cost her much. Although she didn't regret it, it put her at an unfortunate disadvantage.

A little knock sounded on the door, and she rose from the bed to answer it. She'd locked the door after John Thursby had left, not wanting to be caught off guard by anyone. She imagined he'd returned, but it was Davern instead.

"Is there a message from the duke?" she asked worriedly. It

had been many hours since he'd come to her. Now he was conducting a siege and preparing to possibly face Glosstyr's army.

"I was just checking on you, my lady," he said, looking a little embarrassed. "Can I get you anything?"

What she needed was solitude and time to think about the situation. Her best insights usually came when she was working with her hands.

"I still haven't finished what was brought earlier," she said, gesturing to the tray atop the bedsheets. "But maybe you can help in another way. Come in."

He brightened at that and entered at once, looking around the room. He scratched his arm and then sighed. "I'm sorry for what happened to Matthew and Balmor."

"Are you still interested in joining the Espion?" she asked him with genuine curiosity.

"More than ever," he said. "Even the little I did to help…I really enjoyed it."

"It's dangerous work."

"I know," he said with a grin. "I'm not afraid to die for the king."

Gazing at him, she saw the same exuberance and ambition she'd once had. She'd been called into the service of the Duke of Warrewik when she was practically still a child. She'd been enmeshed in a conflict for the throne that had led to Eredur's fall and rise—twice. Davern had been little more than a child when she'd first been sent to Pisan to study. Now, all these years later, she felt the prickling of regret. She didn't get to visit her mother regularly. She'd broken off her relationship with John Thursby because he'd wanted too much from her. The sacrifices she'd made to protect the king had taken an awful toll on her body and her heart.

"If you stayed in the duke's service, you could have a normal life," Ankarette said.

His lips pressed together. "Maybe that scares me the most," he confessed. "Bennet started teaching me how to disarm someone. How to yank on someone's littlest finger to break it. I'd never even thought of that. They don't teach such things in the training yard."

"They do not," Ankarette said, smiling. "I'll tell you this, Davern. When I go back to Kingfountain, I'll tell Master Nichols that I was impressed with you. It's taken time to cull Warrewik's lackeys from the Espion. We need more young men to join."

Davern beamed. "Thank you, my lady."

"But I'll say this as well, Davern. If I could go back and do it all over again, I might not have made the same choice that I did. That's not what you want to hear, but it's the truth."

He looked startled by her words. He considered them and then nodded gravely. "I can't imagine it's been an easy road."

"No. It hasn't been easy at all. Now, here's how you can help. I need you to listen. I've been considering the situation all day. By speaking my thoughts out loud, I'm hoping I can expose any flaws in my reasoning. You'll help me the most by listening and asking questions. Do you understand?"

"I do, my lady. And I'm happy to help."

"The king has two younger brothers. One has always been faithful. The other has always been feckless."

"Pardon me, my lady, but I don't know what that word means."

"'Feckless' means *unreliable*. Weak-willed. Easily persuaded."

Davern nodded. "Duke Severn is the faithful one. Dunsdworth is the feckless one. Why would the faithful one betray him?"

179

"There are many reasons a man will betray his own family. Some do it for wealth. Some for power. Some for love."

"Love?"

Ankarette gave him an enigmatic look. "I've read legends of King Andrew and the knights of the Ring Table. That's all we have left...legends. We don't truly know the circumstances anymore, for it all happened before the founding of Ceredigion. But the legends say his most favored knight, a knight who was Fountain-blessed, betrayed him because of his love for the queen."

"Th-That's awful," Davern said, his expression showing his horror.

"His name was Sir Peredur. And it happened a long time ago. Our king's name is a derivative of it. Eredur. A knight who was never defeated in battle. It's a strange truth that we always long for forbidden things. That we desire what is denied us. So I've been asking myself, what does Severn want? What has been denied him?"

"He doesn't lack for wealth," Davern said, shaking his head. "The king's been very generous. And didn't he refuse to take any of King Lewis's treasure?"

"He's the only noble who did," Ankarette said. "He thought we should have fought Occitania even after Brugia forsook the war. That we could have ended the rivalry once and for all."

Davern had a thoughtful look. "All right. That's something. I don't know Duke Severn very well, but he's got quite a waspish tongue."

"He does indeed. I've witnessed him using it."

"Do you think he wants to become king, Ankarette?"

She wouldn't tell him about the whisper she'd heard from the Fountain. She hadn't even told John Thursby that. "Severn and Eredur have been at odds since that conflict with Occitania. He hasn't been to court as often, but then, he's a young father and has been doting on his wife and child. When he has come, he's shown disdain for Eredur's privy council."

"Even my master?" Davern asked, surprised.

Ankarette shook her head. "Not Lord Horwath. He's always had a deference to him."

"Deference? I'm sorry, I feel I should have paid more attention to my reading tutor."

"It means *respect*. Admiration. But Severn grew up in the North. Lord Horwath was the castellan of Dundrennan when Severn was a boy. A childhood bond is very powerful."

"Ah, I see. So why would Duke Severn come and attack my master? His loyalty to the king is unflinching."

"Now we've reached the crux of the matter," Ankarette said. "If Severn does want to become king, he'll have to face his own brother in battle and also a man he's admired all his life. In the game of Wizr, if you remove a powerful piece before you challenge the king's piece, there are less available pieces to thwart you. If he wins, Severn can return to Kingfountain with an army, wearing Horwath's tunic instead of his own, and he could launch a surprise attack against his brother with Lord Devereaux as an ally."

Davern gaped in surprise. "The king would be unprepared."

"Exactly. What Devereaux gets is no surprise. He'd become a duke again and a powerful ally to King Severn. That is what I see happening. And what I must prevent. I don't think Devereaux expected the siege to end quickly. He thought he'd have more time."

"No doubt on that front," Davern said. He tapped his chin. "I wonder what Dunsdworth would do if his younger brother became king?"

His question caused a cold splash of reality. One that jolted her. Dunsdworth craved the throne. He'd been promised it when he'd joined Warrewik in rebellion. He had a son and another child on the way. He would not stand idly by and let Severn take the hollow crown. No, he'd do everything in his power to prevent Severn from seizing it.

He'd...

Ankarette realized the truth in a flash of insight. Pitting Severn and Horwath against each other would serve Dunsdworth's interests most of all. Dunsdworth was at his manor, the Arbon, in Kingfountain. He'd been cultivating favor among its citizens for years. The traitor was in Kingfountain. And Severn was not.

"The look on your face," Davern said. "Have you thought of something?"

Lord Hux's final words haunted her. *You're already too late.*

TWENTY-ONE

THE PIERCED LION

By nightfall, Ankarette had regained enough strength to appear unafflicted. But her Fountain magic was still depleted. Conflict had raged all day between Horwath's men on the outer walls and Devereaux's men on the interior. When John Thursby arrived with news that the battering ram was finished, he also said the duke wanted to see her.

The poisoner and the night watchman walked briskly through the town of Averanche. A curfew had been announced earlier in the day, so the streets were clear of townsfolk. Word had spread of another army coming, and the people were rightfully feeling the stress.

Ankarette shivered from the cold despite the cloak around her shoulders. Her body was still recovering from the strain it had been through. When she'd changed back into her dress, she'd seen the bruises marring her skin. But the dwindled feeling, the emptiness of missing her magic, caused even more concern. Lord Hux had proven to be a formidable foe once again—and if he were to reappear, she would not have the reserves to fight him.

"I'm not keen on Horwath's strategy to breach the keep tonight before Glosstyr gets here," John Thursby said as they approached the encampment where the duke was leading the siege.

"Why do you say that?" she asked. "Timing is everything right now."

"Aye, but it'll tire out the men. They were kept up last night, have fought all day. They need rest. Weariness breeds mistakes."

It was a valuable insight spoken from a soldier's heart. "I don't think Severn is the enemy here. I think it's his brother Dunsdworth."

"I'm pretty sure I could tell the brothers apart," John Thursby said. "It was mention of the boar that I overheard."

"I don't doubt it. But I think it is more important to consider this based on who has the most to gain."

"Both brothers do. Whoever prevails gains a kingdom."

"Yes, but Severn has never *wanted* it. And that's the difference. They may be sowing false information to mislead us."

They reached the pavilion, and the sentries nodded for them to enter. Inside, they found Duke Horwath and his captains, except for Harshem, who'd been sent to patrol the northern road. After the duke acknowledged her arrival with a nod, he laid out the situation.

"The battering ram is ready. I think if we press the advantage, Devereaux's grip on the keep will fail tonight. That gives us a defense for when the Duke of Glosstyr arrives. I hope we can resolve any attitudes of conflict he may have. I have fondness for the king's youngest brother but a duty to perform here. The men are tired, but they smell victory in the air. Do you agree, Ankarette? What would you advise?"

As she glanced from man to man, she saw the eagerness in their eyes. They all wanted to be done with this and get back to the North.

Giving a contrary opinion wouldn't be received well. So it mattered how she couched it. "There is no doubting the bravery of the men of the North," she said. "Devereaux is down at the heel surely, but desperation adds conviction, and fear of death emboldens courage. They'll fight for that gate."

"They'll lose," snarled one of the captains.

"There is something else going on here," Ankarette said, turning her full attention to Stiev Horwath. He was the only one she needed to convince. "Your men are exhausted, and Glosstyr's men will be fresh. If things turn violent, you need to be prepared. Instead of attacking the castle, I think we should ride to meet the duke."

Horwath frowned. "Why should we do that? We have defensive pickets here. The men are encamped within the castle walls. There's no advantage in leaving a defensive position."

"There's one advantage, my lord. It hastens the two of you meeting."

"I only see disadvantage in that," the duke said. "I want bulwarks between our forces."

"What better bulwark is there than distance? My lord, hear me out. It will catch Severn off-guard. He's not expecting it. He won't even know how many men have come with you. In the dark, a smaller force can seem larger. We need to understand what his intentions are. Better to discern that when your armies are still far away so we can possibly avoid a battle. We can bring fresh horses with us and be prepared to flee if he acts hastily. But I don't think he will."

His brows furrowed. "And what makes you say that?"

"Because I don't think he's allied with Devereaux. I believe his coming can help you. The threat is only perceived."

Horwath stroked his goatee and cast a look at his captains.

"It's too risky," said the most unconvinced captain.

"But the *king* trusts her," said another.

Their opinions varied. But in the end, it was Duke Horwath's decision. And the duke had always been a decisive man. "I like her plan," he said. "It gives the men a chance to rest a little. But let's keep some of them up and working, as if preparing to use the ram. Devereaux's men will be up all night worried, while most of ours are sleeping. I'll go north with Ankarette and a few good knights, with spare mounts. We'll see what Glosstyr has to say. We all know this. He's honest to a fault."

Ankarette felt a surge of relief. "As you will, my lord." She looked at John Thursby and saw that he was going to come as well.

CAPTAIN HARSHEM LOOKED beleaguered and weary. Their force was small—only his outriders and the knights the duke had brought—and they were all wearing light armor. It allowed for faster travel up the road. They chose a spot where they could await Glosstyr's arrival. There were not many trees around their position, so it was easy to see and hear things, but there was a nearby copse to aid in an escape if one were needed. Duke Horwath sat rigid on his stallion, his tunic and badge revealing his station and rank as a peer of the realm.

Ankarette's mount was positioned next to his, and John Thursby was next to her on the other side. His dark cloak and armor helped him blend in with the night. He had a distrusting scowl on his face. Most of the knights held torches, creating a wall of light that would be seen at a distance. They wanted Glosstyr to know they were waiting for him.

It was just before midnight when the army arrived.

"I feel them," John Thursby murmured. Moments later, she sensed the throbs in the ground signaling the approaching riders. They were not carrying torches, so their approach, in the black night, was invisible to the eyes but not to other senses. The grunts of weary horses announced them, followed by the jangle of arms and spurs.

"Raise it high," the duke ordered, and the knight holding his banner unfurled it and began to wave it. The rippling sound of the cloth was soon drowned by the arrival of men-at-arms.

Ankarette recognized Severn Argentine leading the soldiers, wearing battle armor and carrying a lance. His men were also similarly armed.

"I don't like this," Captain Harshem muttered, and indeed, there was no denying the approaching iron-clad men looked dangerous. Ankarette recognized the symbol of the white boar on their pennants. The air seethed with tension as the advancing army slowed and then stopped, the leaders pausing to keep a distance between their forces.

"I wasn't expecting to find you blocking the road, my lord duke," Severn said, his voice throbbing with distrust.

"I thought we might talk," Duke Horwath said in a milder tone.

"While your men scurry to the sides and flank us? I don't think so."

So Severn had come expecting conflict. That did not bode well.

"I came to Averanche on your brother's orders," said the duke. "Why have you come?"

"I come because of treason," Severn said sharply. Ankarette felt a plume of Fountain magic begin to swell. Not from her. Not from Lord Hux. It was coming from Severn Argentine. "Lay down your arms, Stiev. Do not challenge us. I come to arrest you of treason."

Ankarette was startled by the stark display of magic. She'd sensed the growing power of the Fountain in Severn once before, but he was much stronger than he'd been. That meant he'd been experimenting with it.

She felt the power of his words, the power to influence the minds of those he spoke to. He was using it against the duke of the North.

"We shouldn't have come here," Captain Harshem moaned. The horses were getting fractious. The knights were gazing at each other with suspicion.

"I've committed no treason," the duke said sternly.

"If what you say is true, then submit yourself to the Assizes. I warn you, Stiev. Do not attempt anything foolhardy. We may be tired, but we are determined. Lay down your arms. Now."

Ankarette heard some of the duke's knights begin to unbuckle their sword belts. She craned her neck, watching the confusion. Some even looked guilty, as if convinced they were villains because they'd been told so. That their master had done something wrong and they were culpable for it. It was the Fountain magic at work, persuading them.

"Who accuses me of treason?" Lord Horwath said, his tone throbbing with anger.

"Your own hand, my lord. Ratcliffe, do you have the note? Lovel, prepare the men to fight."

"We will not fight you," Lord Horwath said.

"My lord," Captain Harshem pleaded in an undertone. "Let us fly!"

The Duke of Glosstyr looked at them sternly, his whole posture ready for violence. "This is your last chance, Stiev. Submit or perish. We will carve our way to Averanche if we must. Stand down!" Another throb of Fountain magic filled the air. Ankarette had so little of her own to counter it with, but she gazed at the Duke of Glosstyr. He was convinced he was right. He was convinced this was an ambush.

Lord Horwath looked at her, his eyes imploring. He wasn't guilty of anything. They both knew that. But Glosstyr would not be appeased with his assurance. He demanded obedience or hostility. There was no other way.

"He won't hurt you," Ankarette said. "He's acting under false information himself. Submitting to him will be the fastest way to resolve this. And it will earn his trust."

"My lord!" Captain Harshem gasped in dismay, gazing at Ankarette as if she were mad.

The duke of the North was one of the most powerful men of Ceredigion, his stronghold in Dundrennan a nearly invincible castle. She was asking him to humble himself when he wasn't at fault. When he'd done nothing but obey his king's commands. Severn may be the king's brother, but he was an equal.

And this was the test, she realized. A ruse had been played to pit these two men, these men with shared history, against each other. It made her even more convinced that Dunsdworth was the true traitor. If Severn and Horwath fought, it would weaken the realm considerably. It would foment division when the kingdom needed to be unified. Especially if a revolt was about to happen within Kingfountain itself.

Ankarette realized that Severn's magic wasn't being used to manipulate Horwath for a selfish cause. He believed his old mentor was wrong. Traitorous even. But that old loyalty was powerful. He hoped to persuade Stiev to surrender, to prevent bloodshed.

"I'm trusting you in this," Stiev murmured to Ankarette. He reached down and unbuckled his sword belt, letting it fall to the ground with a thump.

Then he nudged his stallion with his spurs to approach the Duke of Glosstyr alone.

CHAPTER
TWENTY-TWO
LOYALTY

"You're letting him do this?" John Thursby said in a low voice, his tone dripping with doubt.

Ankarette's gaze was fixed on Duke Horwath's back as his horse plodded forward, approaching Severn Argentine. The tension in the air was so thick it throbbed.

It was uncomfortable taking such a risk. She was putting Duke Horwath's life in another man's hands. Severn was known to be acerbic, brash, and strong-willed. But was he a traitor to Eredur? She did not have the conviction he was.

Still, the stakes were high. Horwath was a loyal man, and soon to be a grandfather. If anything happened amiss, it would be on Ankarette's heart for having given the wrong counsel.

The duke's horse slowed and then came to a halt. He was just a few paces away from Severn and his front guard. The torchlight from the men of Dundrennan glimmered off the armor of Glosstyr and his men.

"Speak your accusation," Lord Horwath said. "I tell you, I am innocent."

"Ratcliffe, the letter." Severn's eyes were piercing. He held out his gloved hand. Ankarette noticed the young duke's other hand was nervously fidgeting with his dagger. Loosening it from its sheath and then slamming it back in. Was Severn contemplating attacking? Or were his nerves also over-wrought?

Another rider came forward, one of Glosstyr's men. He had a calculating look, his head covered in a chain hood. He handed a rolled scroll to the duke and then stayed next to him.

Severn nudged his war horse forward and handed the scroll to Duke Horwath. All eyes were focused intently on the exchange. Lord Horwath took the scroll and unrolled it. He squinted, trying to read it in the dim light.

"That is not my seal, although it is similar. The lion's tongue is wrong. This one curves down, not up. It's a forgery."

"I know," Severn said, breaking into a smile. "I knew it. I knew you wouldn't have betrayed my brother. Not the faithful constable. Not you. But I had to test you. I had to be sure."

Ankarette heard John Thursby's stifled groan of relief.

"Be it known to all present," Severn announced. "I hold Duke Horwath innocent. And I will swear it on the Fountain. Some evil attempts to beguile Ceredigion. So I've come with men-at-arms to help you. You command the siege, my lord duke. How can we help?"

Ankarette allowed herself a relieved smile. She glanced at John Thursby, who was staring at her with wonder. "That could have ended badly. I confess...I thought you were wrong. Well done."

Captain Harshem was mopping his brow with his glove. He gave her a chuckle and a look of relief.

"We are close to retaking the fortress," Duke Horwath said. "My men are weary, but we're preparing for an assault at dawn."

"We are ready to storm the walls with you, my lord,"

Severn said. "Tell us where, so we can bring the traitor in chains to Kingfountain." Then Severn swiveled in his saddle and looked at one of the armored men nearby. Ankarette suddenly recognized the Duke of Southport among Severn's men. "You were right, Lord Bletchley. I owe you due credit as well."

"Lord Bletchley?" Duke Horwath asked, gazing at the other man. "You were in charge of the fortress."

"I was, my lord. We were caught unawares by Devereaux and his pirates. While in Averanche, I've fostered a relationship with certain Genevese merchants, those who lead trade between Occitania, Brythonica, and Ceredigion. I paid handsomely for that letter when I heard it was for sale in Glosstyr. We didn't have time to return to Kingfountain and warn the king. I didn't believe you'd betrayed us, and I attempted to convince Duke Severn of that fact. Others were more... doubtful."

Ankarette noticed Ratcliffe's expression turned instantly sour.

"How was I supposed to know it was a forgery?" he complained.

"It was a clever ruse," Severn said. "One meant to pit the two of us against each other. You've proven your integrity again today, my lord duke. Let's show these knaves they're no match for us despite their schemes. Lead the way, Lord Horwath. I march under your banner now."

CAPTAIN HARSHEM HAD BEEN SENT AHEAD to alert the other captains to the change in situation. The two dukes rode side by side and arrived back in Averanche with the bulk of the knights of Glosstyr. The foot soldiers and archers continued their slow but steady march and would arrive hours later. Back at the camp, they found the soldiers of the North rested and spoiling for a fight. The battering ram had been brought to the alcove of the main gate, where it was shielded. Ankarette saw a few lonely sentries patrolling the upper walls of the keep. She assumed Devereaux and his men were waiting at the inner gate.

While the knights from the dukes began to mingle and talk, Ankarette found Lord Bletchley in the command pavilion with the other two dukes and their captains.

"Lord Bletchley, may I have a word with you?" she asked.

He was a dour, middle-aged man with receding hair combed back and a pointed beard, all flecked with strands of gray. He had intelligent brows, a rather bulbous nose, and a look of concentration, which he turned on her. "Oh, Ankarette," he said and then retreated with her to a farther corner of the pavilion.

He gave her a smile that didn't reach his eyes.

"I'd like to know more about where you got the letter," Ankarette said. "Who is your source?"

"A merchant named Lisono. The Genevese, I've found, care more for coin than they do for politics. Since I was put in charge of Averanche, I've dedicated resources to currying favor among the merchants. Paying handsomely for important news tends to invite more of it."

"What kind of merchant is Master Lisono?"

"A wine merchant. Bottles, not barrels."

"Does he do business in the Vintrey ward of Kingfountain, then?" Ankarette asked. Vintrey was where Lord Dunsdworth had his manor, the Arbon. The duke had a certain fondness for expensive wines.

"I believe he does," Lord Bletchley said. His brows narrowed. "Why do you ask?"

"Can you arrange a meeting for me with Master Lisono?" Ankarette asked.

Lord Bletchley nodded. "Of course. It may take a few days if he's already left Kingfountain. He was headed there from Glosstyr."

"Is that where he gave you the letter?"

"Indeed. Naturally. I'm loyal to the throne, Ankarette. I think the Espion have been too distrusting of Genevese sources. Do you agree?"

Ankarette knew he was a consummate politician, eager to show his importance. And she could hardly fail to notice his disdain for the Espion and their current leadership.

"I'd like you to arrange that meeting," Ankarette said. She didn't want to give away her own opinions on the state of affairs. She wouldn't trust Lord Bletchley until he'd proven himself trustworthy. A political marriage to the queen's sister wasn't enough to ensure it.

"I will. How should I contact you? Through Master Nichols, I assume?" There was a slight flaring of his nostrils as he said his rival's name. He was trying to be discreet, but his disdain was palpable. He coveted the other man's job.

"Yes. Thank you."

"My pleasure, Ankarette. If I can be of any further service, do let me know."

There he went again, offering to do her favors. His ambition was not at all disguised. Very well. She could use that to her advantage.

She walked over to where the other two dukes were conversing about the plan to storm the fortress.

"If Devereaux only has twenty or thirty men left," Severn

was saying, "he'll put them all at the door. He can't escape by sea. He's trapped in the keep with his men."

"They have some crossbowmen on the walls who keep trying to pick off my men," Horwath said.

"I've a fellow who is expert with a longbow," Severn said. "Best archer in all of Glosstyr. Let me have him take out those foes. He can fire fast as you blink. Then no one harries us while we man the battering ram. Your men want the honors to lead that charge?"

"They do, my lord. They'd be disappointed if they weren't the first to breach the fortress."

"Rightly so," Severn replied. "You said you've made some scaling ladders as well. Can I have my men try and get over the wall in another spot? They can't resist all of us hitting at once. We'll crack this nutshell before dusk. I promise you."

Duke Horwath folded his arms and nodded. "Very well. You man the ladders. My men will hit the gate."

"By all means. There is enough glory to share. Then we need to send riders back to Kingfountain to warn my brother there's a plot afoot."

"Sending ships will be faster," Lord Horwath said.

"Indeed so. I didn't have enough ships in Glosstyr Harbor to bring my force here. We'll send some by boat to Kingfountain and the rest by land. Whatever mischief is being plotted, we'll spoil it."

Ankarette was relieved to see the old camaraderie had been fully restored between the two men. Duke Severn left the tent to give orders while Horwath relayed the battle plan to his captains. They'd been warned about Lord Hux. Even though Ankarette had not felt his presence since he'd vanished, she didn't underestimate him. Whatever power had borne him away could bring him back again. She had to trust Master

Nichols and the Espion to protect the king. Warnings had been sent. It was all they could presently do.

The men were eager to attack. As Ankarette and John Thursby walked amidst the camp, she could feel the air tingling with excitement. Shields were being prepared. Pikemen assembled to rush the gate after the door was smashed through. It would be over quickly. As they walked, she saw the sullen look in her friend's eyes. His brooding mouth revealed he wasn't elated by the events.

"Are you glad you're not inside the keep right now?" she asked him.

"Aye. But defeat isn't honeyed mead. It's bitter all the way down the throat. Devereaux seemed confident of victory when I saw him."

"He likes to gamble. The hope of victory is alluring."

"Luck is a fickle lady," John Thursby said.

Then they heard cries from the camp. Cheers even. The two of them looked at each other, not understanding what was going on. It took some time for the word to spread.

"What happened, man?" John Thursby said, grabbing a knight of Glosstyr by the shoulder.

The knight was grinning fiercely. "Devereaux is wounded!" the knight exclaimed. "Old Bonner got him with an arrow! Nasty blighter got him in the face!" The whole camp was in an uproar now. Everyone was on their feet, coming to the walls for the last time.

Ankarette put her hand on John Thursby's arm, saw the look of devastation on his face. His eyes were gazing at the fortress, grieving for the men inside who were about to lose everything.

Just as he had.

TWENTY-THREE

THE DEATH OF COURAGE

The cacophony of conflict was loud, ever present—the clash of arms, the thud of the battering ram against the doors, the hiss of arrows and crossbow bolts, the sudden screams from the wounded. The splintering of the door reverberated all the way to Duke Horwath's pavilion which was empty except for them since everyone else was participating in the end of the siege.

John Thursby sat on a camp stool, his gaze not fixed on anything in the tent but on inner visions from past battles. Through it all, Ankarette stood by him, stroking his hair, waiting for the end.

After the gate to the keep was broken open, the knights of the North surged inside. The desperate screams of Devereaux's knights met them. It was anguishing to hear, even though it meant the siege was nearly over. An operation they had presumed would take months had happened much sooner. The fortress of Averanche had fallen, while the sea crashed against the cliff walls.

Then the cheers began. That was the moment she'd been waiting for. There was always a cost in blood, iron, and courage. But the cost had been paid, and the dukes of Ceredigion had prevailed. The cheers echoed throughout the camp, the cause lifted up by those who had come.

"It's over," Ankarette murmured.

John Thursby lifted his chin and looked up at her. "Fighting Eredur in this way was a fool's errand. And they'll all pay the cost with their lives."

"The king won't send everyone over the falls," Ankarette said. "He will punish the ringleaders, though. He must."

"Aye, lass." He looked at her glumly. "I'm on the winning side this time, but my heart still aches for them. It still feels like losing."

Ankarette squatted in front of him, looking up into his face. They were alone in the duke's tent, so she allowed herself the familiarity. She stroked his cheek, wishing she could heal the scars inside him. "If Devereaux survived, he may have useful information. I'm going to encourage the king to spare his life if he cooperates."

The night watchman blinked in surprise.

"I'm not saying he'll go free," she continued. "It will take time to unravel the strings in this plot. Eredur kept Morvared imprisoned for a very long time."

"And prison can break a man," John Thursby said. "I'm not sure which fate is worse."

"Time will tell." She rose, pressed a kiss against his hair, and turned, for she heard a growing commotion outside the tent. John Thursby stood, and together they went to the tent flap and gazed outside.

The soldiers were still cheering and celebrating, but some of the men who'd led the charge were coming back, their armor dented and spattered with grime. Then Davern rushed up to the tent, puffing out air from his run.

"Lord Devereaux survived," he panted when he reached. "They're bringing him here. He's gravely wounded. The duke wants you to try and save him. They're coming behind me!"

Ankarette gave the young squire a nod of acceptance, and he tore into a run to relay the message. The cheers of triumph turned to jeers of contempt as a litter approached bearing the injured Devereaux. Duke Horwath walked in front of the bearers, his face dark with soot and a fierce scowl.

Ankarette recognized the knights carrying the body, and she and her friend held the tent flaps open as they marched in. Devereaux's face was contorted with pain, and a gaping wound in his face was raw and glistening.

"Any sign of Lord Hux?" Ankarette asked Duke Horwath.

The leader shook his head curtly. "My men are scouring the castle. Even if he's hiding in a privy hole, we'll find him."

She didn't think they would. At least, they wouldn't find him *alive*.

The men carrying the groaning earl set him on the floor. Davern gazed down at the fallen man, his face a mixture of pride and horror. A quick glance revealed the biggest part of the damage. Devereaux had taken the arrow in his cheekbone. Someone had pulled it out, and the sight was grotesque. But she'd seen worse.

Ankarette told them to leave so she could get to work. Duke Horwath ordered guards to be stationed at the tent door and surrounding it.

"Think he'll live?" Horwath then asked Ankarette.

"Too early to say," she replied. But she crouched down by the wounded man and asked Davern to fetch some water in a cup and some in a basin.

John Thursby knelt by his old comrade and gripped his hand.

"Th-Thursby," grunted Devereaux. "If you'd been with us... we'd have won! I know it!" It was an unlikely sentiment, but Ankarette appreciated that Devereaux was showing kindness to his old brother-in-arms despite the extreme pain he had to be in.

"Looks like a little scratch on your face is all," John Thursby said. "You'll hale in no time."

"I doubt that," Devereaux wheezed. One eye was nearly swollen shut, and he turned the hale one to Ankarette, who accepted the water cup from Davern. They helped her lift Devereaux's head. He took a frantic sip, but then tried to back away.

"Drink it all, my lord," Ankarette coaxed. "You've lost a lot of blood."

"It tastes...strange," he said, looking at her worriedly.

"Medicine for the pain," she replied. "I was trained as a midwife before going to the poisoner school. I'm here to help you."

His heart was racing so fast that if she'd tried using night-shade on him, it would have probably killed him anyway. She bent her head and got to work.

"Davern, can you light the lamp and bring it closer?" she asked. It felt like the shadows were thickening inside the tent, and she'd need as much light as possible for the stitches. Devereaux was exhausted from everything that had happened and had dozed off again.

Davern lit the lamp and brought it nearer. John Thursby sat on camp stool close to the palette, gazing down at his friend with sympathy. Ankarette prepared her needles and suture string. With delicate fingers, she began the final part of her efforts. His various wounds had been cleansed and bandaged, but now it was time to close the wound on his face. The prick of the needle roused him again, but he didn't struggle during the procedure. She made the stitching very tight and small, which would leave a smaller scar.

"Help me hold the skin," she requested of John Thursby. He came off the stool and knelt next to her, using his fingers to press the cuts closed while she did the needlework. As she worked, she felt her Fountain magic swell inside her as her work further restored it.

When she'd finished, she lathered some salve against the stitched wound until it glistened. The salve would hopefully prevent infection. It was still too early to tell.

"How's the vision in the injured eye?" she asked him.

"I still can't see anything from it," Devereaux said. "Am I partially blind now?"

"Things take time to heal. You may get your sight back in that eye. I can't promise when."

He gave her a calculating look. "Why bother, though? Why heal me if Eredur is just going to kill me? I know the penalty for treason."

Ankarette screwed the lid back on the tub of ointment and stuffed it back into her bag. "I don't think you'll be pardoned, my lord. Not this time. But if you have information that is helpful, I think the king can be persuaded to spare your life."

"Holistern Tower? I think I'd rather swim."

"Either way, I'm going to find out what you know," Ankarette said. "If you cooperate, there might be better options than Holistern."

Devereaux grinned and then winced in pain. "You're persuasive. And I've nothing left to lose except my life. But I don't think the king will like what I have to say."

"You'll find he bears the truth better than falsehoods. Your men, at least some of them, seemed convinced that Glosstyr was coming to join the revolt. But that wasn't true."

"No, but it was plausible," Devereaux said. "I don't make a habit of sharing my plans loosely. And it was done to keep the rascals from deserting me. Pirates aren't known for their loyalty."

"If it wasn't Glosstyr, who were you expecting?" John Thursby asked.

"I'll tell you, but it will do little good without proof."

"Say on," Ankarette said, dropping her voice lower.

"I was to be given East Stowe and Southport," Devereaux said. "Westmarch would return to Occitania. They'd have to conquer it, of course, but with no one to oppose, they'd make quick work of Kiskaddon's lands. I was tasked to kill off Horwath here if possible. That would leave the North open for Severn."

Ankarette felt a chill in her heart. "I thought you admitted he wasn't part of the plot?"

"He wasn't. It was to be a consolation gift from the new king of Ceredigion. To secure his allegiance."

"The new king?" Ankarette asked.

"Aye. Dunsdworth Argentine."

Ankarette wasn't surprised to hear this. It was exactly as she'd expected. But how would the king react to the news? What would he do with his treacherous brother this time?

"I see you're not surprised. I wasn't expecting you to be."

"What proof do you have he was involved?"

"My man was at the Arbon before the siege. Before he visited you, John Thursby." Devereaux winced in pain again.

"The duke has been bringing his men into Kingfountain. Hiding them throughout the wards of the city. Waiting for the sign for them to rise up."

"And what is the sign?" Ankarette said, feeling urgency gripping her heart.

"The death of the king," Devereaux said. "That's when he was going to seize the throne."

"But the king has two heirs," Ankarette said.

"He's already contrived a story. Of a previous marriage prior to Elyse. There are documents. Forgeries. Enough to give credibility to claims that the king's children are bastards. Which leaves Dunsdworth as the heir to the throne. Glosstyr gets the North. I control the East and the South. And Kiskaddon falls to Lewis. This was the plan. Now you know all of it."

"Lewis was part of it?"

"No. Hux contrived this all."

"Is that where Hux went? To kill Eredur?"

"Yes. He said he has someone he trusts in Kingfountain. I don't know who it is. Hux never revealed it in case the siege failed. But the proof that Dunsdworth was behind it...the letters...the forgeries. They were stolen by a Genevese merchant days ago. Someone knew they'd be of great worth. Hux came to tell me of this. Genevar is flexing their power in this game of succession."

Lord Bletchley knew who had the letters. He might not know what was in them, but he knew about them. His alliance with the Genevese was about to pay off.

"Lord Hux went to Kingfountain to kill the king," Ankarette said.

"The king is the only one who stands in the way now," Devereaux said. "Dunsdworth is terrified of his brother. He doesn't want to face him in battle. He knows he'd lose." He paused, then added, "Hux wants something you took. A ring. A ring that Lewis wants at all costs."

"Why does he want it so badly?"

"I don't know. Hux never told me. Some superstition, I think. A fear Lewis has of drowning."

TWENTY-FOUR

A FINAL ACT OF COURAGE

"I arrest you, Simon Devereaux, on a charge of high treason against His Majesty, King Eredur of Ceredigion. You will be remanded to Kingfountain, where the Assizes will be held to determine your fate. If you attempt to escape, expect a hasty execution."

Duke Horwath made the pronouncement gravely, as befit the circumstances. Lord Devereaux had his wrists shackled. His armor and weapons had been stripped away, and he was wearing a fresh but very simple tunic.

"What will happen to my men?" Devereaux asked. "Those who are left?"

"I can build a gibbet in a few hours," Severn drawled nonchalantly. Devereaux's eyes widened with dread. "But...as Lord Horwath and I had already decided, I'll take the prisoners to Beestone castle and then rejoin you at Kingfountain."

This was a public spectacle, held outside the duke's command pavilion in front of the soldiers. Many had lost comrades in the siege. They were hungry for justice and proud of what they'd accomplished. In addition to the victorious dukes of Ceredigion, Lord Bletchley and Bennet were in attendance, as well as the mayor of Averanche, who was relieved that the siege was over and trade ships could return, although it would take days or weeks for that news to spread. A perimeter guard held torches to dispel the dark of night, preparing to escort Horwath and his prisoner to a ship bound for court. Ankarette and John Thursby would be going with them.

Devereaux's shoulders slumped. Even though Ankarette had said Eredur might spare his life if he proved to be useful, it did not require much imagination to know that he could also be assigned a rendezvous with a boat and a waterfall.

"Take him to my ship," Lord Horwath commanded. The soldiers of his army began to cheer at the news. Some spat on the ground as Devereaux was marched by the guards, escorted to the beach where a skiff awaited them.

Duke Horwath waited to confer with Severn. He put his hand on the younger man's shoulder in a rare show of affection and solidarity. "Hasten to Kingfountain, my lord duke. The plot hasn't ended here. Your brother will need us to finish the job."

"Don't be surprised if I beat you there," Severn answered with a smirk. "My brother knows he can depend on me. Loyalty binds me."

"The men of Glosstyr are never to be underestimated," Horwath said with a nod of approval. "They're men of honor, as is their lord."

"And so are you, old friend," Severn said. "I'll race you home."

Ankarette watched the exchange with satisfaction. A greater bond had grown between these men because of what had happened on the road to Averanche. Severn had tested

Stiev Horwath's integrity, his honor, his loyalty and found him abundant in all three. It had shifted their standing with one another and increased the power of both men. Lord Horwath would be an implacable ally should Severn become king.

The thought made her shudder anew, anxious to return to court. There had been no word from Kingfountain, and she found the silence most alarming. What was Hux up to? Where had he gone? Had the precautions she had put in place to safeguard the royal family been enough?

She had withheld information from both of the dukes after she'd treated Devereaux's injuries, telling them the man was more dead than alive at present. If Dunsdworth was indeed plotting to overthrow his brother, she wanted the king to decide his fate before Severn arrived. The relationship between the three brothers was strained at the moment, for different reasons. Severn was still brooding over what he considered a devil's bargain with King Lewis. And Dunsdworth had caused more than enough flare-ups in the family regarding Warrewik's lands and inheritance. But his ambition to become king had never left. If he was truly guilty, and Ankarette believed he probably was, it would be a breach that could not be repaired. But she needed proof. Lord Bletchley was coming to Kingfountain too, to gather evidence from his contact. Such evidence would provide irrefutable proof of the betrayal. Only then would she reveal the full matter.

Lord Horwath turned to Captain Harshem. "Now that we've secured the castle, I want you to leave two companies here to defend it until Lord Bletchley returns from Kingfountain. Once he's relieved you of command, return to Dundrennan."

"Yes, my lord." Captain Harshem looked a little disappointed that he'd been chosen to remain behind, but now that they held the fortress, he could oversee the repair of the gate and make sure the castle was defended.

Lord Horwath turned to Ankarette and John Thursby and gave them a nod, signaling it was time to go to the ship.

"The Fountain go with you, my lord," Duke Severn said.

"Until we meet again," replied Horwath.

THEY ARRIVED at the royal docks of Kingfountain midafternoon the next day, bringing with them the ships that had been blockading the harbor in Averanche. In those ships, Duke Horwath was bringing the remainder of his army, except for those left behind to guard the fortress and the men who would bring the horses and baggage back to Kingfountain.

When Ankarette saw the castle perched atop the hill, she felt a strong sense of foreboding. It would take Severn several days to reach the palace with his entourage, despite his boast. And she needed to confirm Dunsdworth's complicity before he arrived. Time was short.

"Do you want to stop and check on Old Rose while I go see the king?" Ankarette asked John Thursby, who stood with her at the railing of the ship as they neared the harbor.

"I'd rather stay with you and see this done. If that's all right." She could see in his eyes that he didn't want to part from her. Not again.

She nodded, touching his hand.

Davern approached from the foredeck. "You will introduce me to Master Nichols? Bennet has been showing me so much. I want to be part of the Espion more than ever."

John Thursby chuckled and shook his head. The overeager squire was bursting with energy.

"When it's time," Ankarette said. "Be patient."

"I'll try, my lady. I'll try." Grinning, he marched away as they prepared to disembark.

After the ship docked and the sailors were preparing to lower the gangplank, Ankarette recognized Hugh Bardulf awaiting them with a look of dread on his face.

"This doesn't bode well," John Thursby said, catching her eye.

"Indeed, it does not," she said. "Bennet," she called, spying him in conversation with Davern farther away. Her Espion friend hurried over to her. She noticed Devereaux standing by Lord Horwath, the shackles and chains still securing his arms. She'd dabbed more healing ointment on his wound during the night, and it seemed to be healing well.

As soon as the gangplank was down, she, John Thursby, Bennet, and Giselle hurried down to meet with the Espion.

"You look serious, Hugh," Ankarette said. "And you weren't expecting our return."

"I wasn't expecting it, but it's most appreciated, under the circumstances. Nichols is dead. He was murdered yesterday."

Ankarette felt her chest constrict. "Where?"

"In the Star Chamber. It's been ransacked. I sent a ship to summon you back, but I wasn't expecting the whole armada. The king put me in charge of the Espion temporarily until Lord Thomas gets here."

Ankarette was surprised again. "His wife is nearly due, isn't she?"

"Aye, and the head of the Espion was murdered *inside* the palace of Kingfountain. Like I said, I'm *relieved* you are here. There's more. Two other Espion were found dead in the tunnels today. I think Hux is here, and he's trying to find a way to the king."

"How did Nichols die?" Ankarette asked.

"Poison."

"If Master Nichols is dead, the king is vulnerable." It was Lord Bletchley who'd said it. He'd approached the conversation discreetly, but clearly, he'd overheard enough. "How many Espion know how to get to the king's room through the tunnels?"

"It's common knowledge where the royal suite is," Ankarette said. "But only a few know how to open the secret door. We need to hurry. I can find Lord Hux if he's in the palace."

"Let's catch this blackguard while we can," John Thursby said angrily. "We'll need a dozen men."

"Tell Duke Horwath what's happened," she told Bennet. "Then meet us at the palace. I want all his men to come stand guard. The uprising might already be underway." Then she turned to Lord Bletchley. "Get your contact to the palace. Now."

He nodded gravely and departed.

Killing the spymaster of Ceredigion was a declaration of war. Ankarette and the others hurried to the network of stairs leading up from the docks to the palace embedded in the hillside. The roar of the falls felt like ominous thunder.

"Where is Nichols's body?" Ankarette asked. "You haven't sent it over the falls yet?"

"No," Hugh replied. "There hasn't been time to even think about his last rite. It's still in the palace. In the crypt."

"We'll go there first. I want to see it."

"Why?" he asked, confused.

"To see what Hux used to kill him." She was tempted to summon her Fountain magic, but that would alert the other poisoner that she was back. It would be better if she gathered enough Espion and guardsmen to do a proper hunt. But it would be a wary one—they had to surprise Hux and disarm him, or he'd just disappear again.

"Shouldn't we tell the king you are back?"

"We will. I need information first."

She hoped to give Lord Bletchley some time as well to produce the Genevese merchant who had the incriminating evidence. First things first. She had to stop the threat.

They were all a little winded when they arrived in the crypt. Only a pair of sentries were on guard. They looked askance at the sudden arrival of so many people, but Hugh showed them his Espion ring.

The crypt, which was belowground, was dark and musty. She could smell the decomposing body before they got there. John Thursby, who'd always been especially sensitive to scents, grimaced with disgust. There, on a stone shelf in the wall, was Master Nichols's corpse. His eyes were closed, his skin pallid and rigid. Rigor mortis had set in.

"There were no marks on the body," Hugh said, his nostrils flaring at the stench. "He was on the floor, sprawled out."

"Did you search his body?" Ankarette asked, reaching for the stiff hand. She looked for traces of dust around the nostrils. "Hand me the torch," she asked.

John Thursby grabbed one from the wall and brought it close to Nichols's face so she could see better.

"Yes, I did search him," Hugh said. "But I don't know what would have been missing if something was missing."

Ankarette didn't see any traces of dust. Looking at the hand, she saw the Espion ring remained on Nichols's finger. The jewel was missing, though.

"He wasn't murdered," Ankarette said in relief.

"Clearly he was," Hugh countered, astonished.

Ankarette pointed to the ring. "The jewel is missing. He swallowed it. Probably still in his stomach. He died of hemlock poisoning." She saw the look of realization on Hugh's face. "He killed himself to keep the king and his family safe. To prevent Hux from pulling information from him. Nichols is the only reason that Eredur is still alive."

TWENTY-FIVE

SECRETS REVEALED

Ankarette learned that Eredur and Elyse and their children were keeping to their rooms for added protection. After they'd learned of Master Nichols's death and that Lord Hux was likely on the loose in the castle, the king had increased the number of guards, and ongoing searches were being conducted to find the Occitanian poisoner. The fact that Hux hadn't already killed the king suggested to her that his device had limitations. What they were, she didn't know.

Ankarette and John Thursby arrived at the door leading to the royal family's private chambers. There were six guardsmen on duty, armed and ready for action. The guards knocked on the door to announce their arrival, and they were admitted immediately. Elyse looked fraught with worry, with bulges under her eyes showing lack of sleep. Their eldest child, the daughter named after her mother, was reading a story to the young princes, Eredur and Eyric. They were sitting near her, by the hearth, their young and innocent faces glancing up at the new arrivals before turning back to their sister, who continued the story.

The queen stood by her husband, holding his arm as if she were seeking comfort in his presence. Eredur looked haggard and unsettled.

"You couldn't have gotten my message already and returned this quickly," Eredur said to Ankarette. "I've heard the ships have all returned. Are we expecting an attack?"

Ankarette realized he didn't know the siege was over. "Averanche has been reclaimed," she said. "I've come with Lord Horwath, who is coming up from the docks with the bulk of his army. Your brother Severn will be here in two days with his."

The look of astonishment on Eredur's face quickly transformed to one of relief. He wiped his mouth, registering the impact of the news.

Elyse squeezed his arm, then gave Ankarette a grateful look. "You bring welcome tidings. I didn't think the siege would be broken this quickly."

"I was expecting it," Eredur said, giving Ankarette an approving smile.

"Things worked out as well as they could, I suppose." She realized she'd forgotten to introduce her companion. "You remember John Thursby?"

"My lord," the night watchman said brusquely, bowing with courtesy.

"You were Lord Devereaux's man once," Eredur said. "I hope you don't blame Ankarette for drawing you into this affair. I asked it of her and of you."

"She made that abundantly clear," John Thursby said. "And I did my duty. And now, if I may, I would ask you to spare Lord Devereaux's life."

"He's alive?" Elyse said with shock.

"He was wounded in the siege," Ankarette said. "But yes, he's alive. And the request is not without merit. He helped John Thursby escape the fortress. Allowed him to. As you know, Lord Hux was using him to pressure me into returning Lewis's ring."

Eredur frowned, which showed he was not inclined to honor the request.

"Secondly, he has provided useful information about the plot and plans afoot. Lord Bletchley is arranging a meeting for me shortly to validate what Devereaux told me. If what he's said is true, it is information worth having. He could be of use to us still."

"What sort of information?" Eredur pressed.

Ankarette had to be delicate here. She didn't want to expose Dunsdworth as the treacherous duke until she had definitive proof.

"Information about an uprising within the city itself. It's another reason we hastened back with reinforcements."

"Where is Devereaux now?" Eredur asked.

"Lord Horwath is bringing him to the palace," Ankarette answered.

The king struck his palm with his fist. "I want to see him. Now. Captain Barrent! Have him brought to me."

"Yes, Your Majesty," the captain of the guard said and hurried to obey the order.

Eredur began to pace. She could see his mind working, trying to decide who his enemies were. He stopped midstride. "It's not Severn, is it? There was an Espion report that he'd left Glosstyr unexpectedly." His eyes were flaming with worry.

Ankarette shook her head. "He's loyal to you, Eredur. Before Stiev arrives, let me tell you what happened." She quickly related the scene on the road to Averanche. How Lord Horwath had submitted himself to Severn in order to prove his allegiance. And how the two dukes had made quick work of the fortress and secured it the next day.

"Just think what would have happened if Ankarette wasn't there," Elyse murmured in disbelief. "You deserve recognition for handling that situation so ably. You were the one to advise him to do it. And to his credit, he listened to you."

"I did what I believed was right," Ankarette said. "Your enemies are making their move. I hope to catch Lord Hux here and finish his meddling."

The king sighed. "No one has seen him. Every servant has been interviewed. Every guardsman questioned. I even sent men down into the cistern with lanterns. The Espion tunnels have been searched and searched again."

"He has a device, a magical artifact," Ankarette explained, "that allows him to disappear. It's not invisibility. It transports him somewhere else. With it, I'm sure he's been able to elude your search parties."

"Then we have no hope of catching him?" Elyse said worriedly. "We can't keep living like this."

"Now that I'm here, you won't have to. If he uses magic, I'll be able to sense it. I want to catch him unexpectedly. He doesn't know I'm here yet."

The king frowned, looking helpless and frustrated. Then he gazed at his children, huddled together, listening to their story. His eyes glistened with tears. "If anything happens to me, before they're ready..." he whispered.

Elyse buried her face against his shirt. Ankarette saw the king was wearing a hauberk beneath it. He had his sword strapped on, as well as a dagger. He wasn't in his prime anymore, but he was still deadly. Still noble. He would fight for his family to the end.

Silence prevailed for several minutes as the king and his wife comforted each other. The tromping of boots down the hall revealed the arrival of newcomers. Elyse composed herself, her mood shifting from worry to strength and ferocity. The king was equally fixed in purpose, showing no signs of weakness or lack of courage.

The door opened and Captain Barrent entered first, followed by Lord Horwath and the prisoner, Lord Devereaux, who was still wearing chains. The sutures on his face and the hardened scabs gave him a frightening aspect. Ankarette noticed the two princes sidled up closer to their sister, who put her arms around them and held them protectively.

"Welcome to Kingfountain," Eredur said with a tone of hostility, addressing Devereaux.

Lord Horwath stood aside. The door was closed again, but Ankarette saw that many men out there wearing the badge of the pierced lion. More soldiers to help in the search.

"It's been some years since I've been here," Devereaux said with a sigh. He glanced around the room. "Under different circumstances." He noticed John Thursby's presence and offered him a weak smile.

"Is that my fault?" Eredur said, his tone holding a challenge.

"No, my lord. You were generous. Merciful even. And I betrayed you."

"Why?" Eredur said. "I was trying to make peace between our people. To stop a civil war. Your actions led to so many deaths. Was it pride?"

Devereaux looked defeated. "I have none of that left. Do you want honesty, my lord, or something trite?"

"I'm debating sending you over the falls forthwith," Eredur said. "Honesty is your best card to play."

"I figured as much," Devereaux said. "Then let me play my most valuable card first. This was part of Lord Hux's plan. Me. You. Here. Now."

Ankarette felt a throb of danger and reached for her dagger.

"This isn't helping your cause," Eredur said.

"Allow me to explain, then. Lewis's ex-poisoner has a device he acquired in the East Kingdoms. It's called a Tay al-Ard. It allows him to transport himself and anyone touching it to another place, but only a place one of them has been before. When we had John Thursby in custody, he was poisoned with nightshade. So he won't remember this part." Devereaux turned and looked at his old friend. "Hux used Thursby to get inside the dungeons. He willingly revealed information because of the power of the poison. He knew about the Star Chamber as well because he'd visited it before with Ankarette." He turned back to the king while everyone in the room experienced a jolt of shock at the revelation. "My part, my lord, was meeting you here. You see, now that I've been here, I would have the ability to bring Lord Hux with me the next time."

He didn't say the rest, not with the children now staring at him. But the implication was clear. Hux would come and murder the entire royal family. That was the spark that would signal to Dunsdworth he was free to seize the throne. No doubt he was sitting in the Arbon anxiously, awaiting news of Hux's success in slaughtering his brother, sister-in-law, nephews, and niece.

Eredur was staring in astonishment at the traitor who had just revealed the plot.

"I don't remember any of this," John Thursby announced. "I swear it!"

Devereaux smiled with fondness. "I know you don't, old friend. There were plans upon plans, of course. If you did this, then we'd do that. But we knew the siege didn't stand a chance. This was my part to play in return for the duchy I'd be getting back. I've provided your poisoner with other helpful information. Actionable information."

"You held back this part in our conversation in Averanche," Ankarette said dryly.

Devereaux shrugged before a cocky grin flashed across his face. "I was bluffing so you wouldn't use nightshade on me."

"Your plan might have worked," Eredur said, no longer looking hostile. In fact, he looked stunned and sympathetic. "If you hadn't revealed it."

"I don't really care for Lord Hux all that much," Devereaux said. "I care for my friends more. He needed me to get the job done, but I quickly saw that he was not to be trusted. That he'd leave me without sails the moment it benefited him to do so. If I help you capture or kill Hux, perhaps I can earn a lesser sentence. I'm not asking to go free. And I know you can never forgive me, Eredur. Trust isn't an option. But I would rather not go over the falls. Or see more of my men perish. I've stopped in Brugia now and then. In disguise, of course. Maybe you could send me there until this all blows over and you decide how valuable my help really was?"

He was referring to the garrison at Callait, which was Ceredigion's only stronghold in Brugia.

"Do you know where Lord Hux is hiding?" Ankarette asked.

"He's probably hiding many places," Devereaux said. "And with the Tay al-Ard, he can move from place to place quickly. However, it has limitations. If you use it too much, the magic jewels can break. These constraints I learned from him while discussing his plans."

Ankarette looked at the king. An idea had been taking shape in her mind. "I think we should send Lord Devereaux to the dungeon after all." Then she smiled at John Thursby. "Or someone who looks like him."

Loyalty should be earned, not demanded. I have served the Argentine family not because the king or queen insisted on my loyalty but because they expected my integrity.

Ankarette Tryneowy

TWENTY-SIX

TO CATCH A POISONER

T he effects of the nightshade were beginning to wear
off. Lord Devereaux was starting to look around the
room now, taking notice of the objects in the king's
chamber, saying less and less. After his confession, Ankarette
had felt it only prudent to confirm his tale through use of the
poison, which she'd done in the king's dressing chamber, away
from the sight of his children. Eredur and John Thursby had
borne witness to it, and they'd heard all he had revealed.

Mainly, they'd learned that he'd spoken the truth.

"I'm not surprised he reneged on the deal in the end," John
Thursby said. "He wasn't wrong to doubt Lord Hux's willingness to deliver on all his promises."

Devereaux was seated on a cushioned stool, shaking his
head as if trying to rouse himself from a dream.

"He must have realized the value of the information he
held," Eredur said. "And what he said about my brother
Dunne...that is worth more than you know." His voice had an
edge of anger to it.

Ankarette put the nightshade powder back into her

poisoner's bag. "While it only proves he *believes* Dunsdworth was going to betray you, the situation merits further action."

"It's enough to persuade me," Eredur said flatly.

"Evidence. We need more evidence. If Lord Bletchley produces what the Genevese merchant told him about, then we will know for certain. And then what will you do?"

"I haven't decided yet," the king said. "The sting is still fresh. I have forgiven my brother over and over again, but this is treason. The blackest kind. He was willing to murder my entire family."

Ankarette agreed but said nothing.

"Where am I?" Devereaux asked at last, his brow wrinkled in confusion, which was a side effect of nightshade powder. He wouldn't remember anything he'd said. Or even how he'd agreed to be subjected to such questioning.

"The king's wardrobe," Ankarette said, gesturing at the chests of clothes, the robes and fur-lined capes hanging from pegs.

Devereaux frowned. "And why am I in here and not the dungeon?"

"How much of our previous conversation do you remember?" Ankarette asked.

"I told you about Lord Hux's plan. And the Tay al-Ard. Didn't I? You used nightshade on me, I assume?"

"I did," Ankarette answered. "We need to catch Hux while he's here. If he's expecting you to be sent to the dungeon, then he is no doubt waiting for you to arrive. But you won't go to the dungeon. John Thursby has agreed to go in your place."

John Thursby nodded. "I'll need your clothes."

"Ah. That makes sense." Devereaux turned to the king. "Have you decided what you'll do to me yet?"

"If you're expecting a pardon for this..." Eredur said and then paused. "You'll be disappointed."

"I don't expect a pardon," Devereaux answered. "Just a nicer cell than Holistern Tower."

"Since you have a penchant for seaside fortresses, I've a mind to heed your request and send you to Callait."

"Lewis is afraid of Brugia," Devereaux said with a nod. "I think that's the best option for me. I hope what I said was useful."

"It was," Ankarette said. She'd taken the key to his manacles from Lord Horwath, who was personally standing guard over the queen and the children in the other chamber. She unlocked the chains, and Devereaux quickly stripped his simple tunic away. The king provided him with one from his own supply—a gesture that seemed to humble Devereaux.

John Thursby tugged off his shirt, the one Ankarette had added embellishments to. Then he put on the one he'd been provided.

Ankarette had John Thursby sit on the stool next, and with her supplies, she began to implement the disguise, replicating the bruises on Devereaux's face and using a kohl pencil to imitate the sutures and scars on the other man's cheek.

"This is not going to fool Hux if he gets too close," John Thursby said, gazing at her.

"If he gets that close, put a dagger in him," Ankarette said. She concealed his dagger beneath his shirt and then put one of her dirks in his boot. That done, she picked up the manacles from the floor and arranged them on his wrists but did not lock them.

"Walk us through your plan again, Ankarette," he said.

"Lord Horwath is going to march you to the dungeon. You'll be put in a cell, but it won't be locked. They'll only pretend to secure it. All you need to do is wait for Hux to come. We'll have Espion put in as guards—disguised, of course. I'll be nearby with a poisoned crossbow." She turned to the king.

"I think Elyse and the children should wait in my room. It would be safer for them."

The king nodded. "And I'll keep Devereaux with me and my guards."

"Do you dice, my lord?" Devereaux asked with a wry smile.

"No. But you can teach me."

EVERYTHING HAD BEEN PUT in motion. The trap was set with bait. The spring was coiled. The claws were ready to snap shut. Lord Horwath had brought the prisoner to his cell in person, and word was being sent through the castle that Devereaux was in the dungeon. Ankarette didn't know how Hux would learn of it, but she had no doubt he had his own means of gathering intelligence. Bennet was disguised as the chief warden in an ordinary soldier's uniform, a wig, and a false mustache. At the changing of the guard, other Espion were brought in through the normal doors, all of them in disguise.

The Espion tunnels also led in and out of the dungeon, which is how Ankarette arrived. She picked the cell opposite John Thursby's and hid in the shadows with a loaded crossbow, the bolt treated with a fast-acting poison. Now she needed patience. To wait for Lord Hux to arrive.

She knew he wouldn't come through the doors. If he'd infiltrated the dungeon previously, then the Tay al-Ard would allow him to travel undetected. She doubted he even needed a key to the cell. He'd explained the device to Devereaux already, so he'd anticipate that the man would know what to do—he could reach through the bars to touch the magical device, and both men could disappear. It would be quick, an escape that would take only a few moments, and perhaps even the guards would be confused as to what was going on. It was a clever plan. It would have worked.

It made her think about how much she'd missed. Of course, she hadn't even known about Tay al-Ards, and so she couldn't have prepared for them. Once again she realized that the other poisoner had access to information she didn't have. Poisons from a distant land. Cures. And magical artifacts. If she could take the Tay al-Ard, she would have a way to travel to the East Kingdoms—either by finding someone who had been there or to travel there herself—and then get back quickly. The device could help her discover the cure to the poison she'd been infected with. And that meant she and John Thursby might be able to have a life together...

Gazing across to the other cell, she watched him pacing back and forth. They'd been down there for an hour at least already. To force Hux to make his move, and also throw Dunsdworth into a panic, the king would proclaim that Devereaux would be sent over the falls at sunset.

The king's guards were stationed at the gates and the docks and would prevent the Duke of Clare from leaving Kingfountain if he tried.

As she sat still, listening and waiting, her mind wandered to the newly vacant position of the head of the Espion. The king had summoned Thomas to Dundrennan and was going to ask him to take the job. With Master Nichols dead, someone of his capabilities was desperately needed at the helm. He was about to become a father. Would he put the interests of his family over his duty to the king? She wasn't sure what he'd decide, but she secretly hoped he'd refuse. She wouldn't want to work closely with him again.

And, if Thomas refused, did that mean Ankarette could also choose her own path? If Lord Hux were dead, if his threat was removed, would she be able to change her fate, to live a life with John Thursby at her side? Hadn't she given enough to Eredur and Elyse? Would she have to protect their children and their children's children? If she was free of the poison's taint, would she be able to conceive and have children of her own?

The thought caused an ache inside her to flare up. She'd been a witness to the birthing chamber for so many years. But to experience the pangs herself? To see a child brought into the world, a child of her own womb? She realized, in that moment, she would give anything to make that happen. If she could remove the biggest danger to Eredur's family, if she could be healed, she would choose to live life to its fullest. It would not be an easy conversation to have with the king and queen, but she knew Elyse would be sympathetic. She had five children of her own.

What if she were to find a replacement for herself? Someone who could be trained at the poisoner school. Someone young, ambitious. Someone determined. Would Davern be interested? She'd been younger than him when she'd gone to Pisan, and she could mentor him, prepare him for the dangers...

Hope tingled inside her. She wouldn't abandon the family all at once. But if there was even a small chance of success, it was worth it. She wanted to give herself totally to someone, not to have her loyalties so divided anymore. Was it a foolish hope? All she knew was that if it were even remotely possible, it was worth chasing.

She felt the surge of Fountain magic as Lord Hux arrived. He appeared in the corridor, right in front of John Thursby's cell. The feeling of his magic was palpable, exciting. There he was, standing with his back to her.

"Did you worry I wasn't coming?" Hux asked dryly.

Ankarette lifted the crossbow and stepped to the bars. She

positioned the tip of the bolt between them so that it wouldn't, accidentally, ricochet off the bars and ruin her shot. There was only time for one.

She saw the shadow of John Thursby move, and suddenly his face was visible in the glare of the lamplight. She'd warned him not to say anything. Nothing that would reveal himself and make Hux flee.

She pulled the trigger of the crossbow, and the dart hurtled toward Lord Hux. She'd aimed for his lower back, hoping to cripple him with a single shot.

Maybe he'd heard her. Maybe his instincts were just wary enough.

Hux vanished, and her crossbow bolt impaled John Thursby instead.

TWENTY-SEVEN

SHATTERED DREAMS

A nkarette gasped in shock as she watched her companion stiffen and then slump to the cell floor. She threw down the crossbow, yanked open the door, and rushed into the corridor. Espion were already charging toward her location.

"Bennet! Get the king's surgeon!"

She flung the opposite cell door open and rushed inside. John Thursby was on his back, eyes wide, but the paralytic poison had already done its work. He couldn't move. But she knew from experience that he could feel everything. The feathered bolt was protruding from his tunic. It had pierced the chain hauberk.

The shot had been fired at close range, and blood was spreading quickly. Guilt raged in her heart. Guilt and sheer panic.

She had to stanch the bleeding quickly, but that required the delicacy of removing the bolt. Without hesitating, she gripped it by the haft and pulled it out. John Thursby didn't even groan, but she saw the expression of suffering in his eyes. The disguised Espion arrived at the cell door.

"Help me remove his hauberk," she said, and she heard her voice quaver. With her dagger, she slit the tunic in order to peel it away. Two Espion nudged past her to help. "Lift his arms. Quickly now!"

They obeyed her, and she helped drag the hauberk up above the wound. The bolt had gone through his abdomen. Had it not been fired at such close range, his mail shirt would have deflected it. She saw the punctured links and felt dread seep into her bones. Judging by its location, it had pierced either his stomach or his liver.

She had pulled the trigger. She had been aiming for Lord Hux, but she'd injured, maybe even killed, someone she loved. While the two Espion tugged and wrestled with the hauberk, Ankarette wadded up part of the tunic and pressed it firmly against the wound to try to stop the bleeding.

John Thursby's skin had gone white. Normally someone with such a wound would go into shock, but the paralytic was preventing it. His chest was rising and falling quickly. The Espion got the hauberk over his neck and head and tossed it to the cell floor with a hissing sound as the links settled.

"I need more light!" Ankarette shouted. Another Espion approached with a lantern. Her fingers were slick with blood.

She had to stop the bleeding. But she knew his injuries were internal as well. While her skills in midwifery were helpful in such situations, this was more of a battlefield injury, and it would take more than sutures to treat it. When internal organs were damaged, they often failed, which could lead to death. She closed her eyes, feeling like weeping, but commanded herself not to.

"Help is coming," she whispered soothingly. If they were in the city, she would have called for her apothecary friend,

Danner Tye. She'd call for him anyway. She trusted him and his skills. But it might be too...

No, she couldn't let herself believe it was too late. She could not.

"What else can we do?" asked one of the Espion helpers.

"Water. Bring a pitcher of water and a bowl." She pressed the wound harder. The thought of John Thursby dying before her eyes was unbearable.

After a significant delay, Bennet finally returned. "He's coming," he said reassuringly.

Thank the Lady.

Ankarette felt every moment keenly. The noise of boots announced the surgeon had arrived. She recognized the fellow but couldn't remember his name in the mayhem of the moment. He'd been with Eredur since his rise to king.

"He's not moving," the surgeon said. "Is he dead?"

"He's breathing if you look," Ankarette said, her voice wavering. "The bolt may have pierced his liver. I can't tell." She looked up at Bennet. "There's an apothecary in Queenshithe. Danner Tye. He's an expert on battlefield wounds. Hugh Bardulf knows how to find him."

Bennet nodded curtly and sprinted away.

"I need to examine the injury," the surgeon said, kneeling down next to Ankarette. She lifted the blood-soaked tunic, and the surgeon lifted John Thursby's undergarment so he could gaze at the location of the wound.

His immediate frown froze her heart.

A KNOCK SOUNDED at the door. Ankarette was still seated at John Thursby's bedside, although the location had changed. After the surgeon had done his work and treated the injury, the Espion had carried John Thursby to Ankarette's old room in the palace, the one she'd occupied before she'd moved to the tower, and laid him on the bed. The place had a dusty, unused smell, but a gentle lamp burned fragrant oil nearby. It was probably almost midnight by now, but she had no sense of timing since there were no windows.

He had passed out during the surgery and hadn't yet regained consciousness.

Davern, who'd fallen asleep on the chair by the door, roused from the knock and hurriedly stood. He unbarred the door and then opened it.

"It's the queen," he said, eyes full of wonder.

Ankarette didn't rise. She had her hand on John Thursby's cold one. He had blankets smothering him to try to keep him warm. Danner Tye was asleep in the next room, getting some much-needed rest after he'd arrived to help.

"Has he awakened yet?" Elyse asked, entering.

Ankarette shook her head.

"He's had the best care possible," the queen said. She approached the bed and gazed down at the listless body before touching Ankarette's shoulder. "You should get some sleep, Ankarette. You need it."

"I can't," the poisoner murmured. "Not while it's uncertain."

"It's not your fault."

"It's *exactly* my fault," Ankarette said. "In all aspects. It was my plan, *and* I'm the one who fired the bolt."

The queen smoothed some of Ankarette's loose hair from her shoulder. "Do you think Hux heard you?"

"I don't know," Ankarette answered miserably.

"If we hadn't acted, things might have turned out even worse," the queen said. "I know you don't want to hear that right now. I know you're suffering because you love him. But your efforts might have saved our lives tonight. I'm grateful for that, Ankarette, but I'm still hurting for you."

The queen knelt by the bedside, slipped her arms around Ankarette's waist, and hugged her. That act of kindness softened something inside of her. After all she'd done for Elyse and her family, she was grateful the sacrifices she'd made were being recognized.

"Thank you," Ankarette said, trying not to sniffle. Davern was standing at the door, watching the scene silently. Lord Horwath had ordered him to remain available to help in any way possible.

Elyse continued the hug but eventually rose again and pressed a kiss to Ankarette's hair. "I put a coin in the fountain tonight. We're all praying he'll recover."

Ankarette smiled sadly, gazing down at John Thursby's shadowed face.

"I'll stay awake if you need to rest, my lady," Davern said simply. "Danner Tye said there's naught we can do now but wait."

"Thank you, but I'm going to continue my watch. You should get some rest."

Davern yawned and stretched. "I'm not so tired anymore. So much has happened these last days. Who can think to sleep? But it'll take more than a crossbow bolt to take John Thursby down. He's not going to leave you, my lady. I know it."

Weariness eventually prevailed. Her friend Danner had done all he could do. The wound was grievous, and he might not make it. But he'd seen worse in the war, and some soldiers had survived a similar injury. Ankarette slid next to John Thursby on the bed, keeping her hand on his, and tried to fall asleep. His breathing was light and troubled, as if he were deep in the fog of dreams, struggling to resist the pull of the Deep Fathoms on his soul. If they claimed him, she would get Lewis's ring, and she would go into the Deep Fathoms to find him and bring him out again.

That was her last thought before she fell asleep.

A FEATHER-LIGHT TOUCH on her hair woke her instantly. She was nestled against John Thursby's shoulder, smelling the aroma of the yarrow poultice that had been applied to his abdomen.

"Ankarette," he whispered tenderly. His hand had awakened her.

She lifted herself up on her elbow. Davern was asleep in the chair by the door. She saw light coming from the crack above the floor. Dawn had come.

"You're alive," she breathed.

His crooked smile made her heart ache. "I'm not going anywhere, lass."

She brought her mouth to his and kissed him soundly.

A noise from the chair and a squeak on the floor told her Davern was awake. "I think I'll fetch some breakfast in the kitchen," he said and hurriedly slipped away.

Ankarette gazed down at John Thursby and brushed hair from his forehead. "I'm so sorry," she said. "I'm the one who shot you."

"I gathered that," John Thursby said with a subtle groan. He winced. "Did we catch the blackguard?"

"He got away," she said with a sigh.

"Another dawn. Another day. We'll catch him yet. I know

we will." He reached and cupped her cheek, and he added, "Every day with you is a gift I don't deserve."

"You don't deserve love? I think everyone deserves love."

"And I think every man feels undeserving of a *woman's* love. Or her touch. I'm the luckiest fool in Ceredigion. The way you are looking at me. It's worth a king's ransom to me."

"I don't want to lose you, John Thursby."

He tilted her chin. "You can't lose me, Ankarette. I'm yours, heart and soul and blood. However much I have left. Always. Nothing can change that. The Fountain gives us one day at a time and bids us use it well."

"You've claimed my heart."

"Hearts must be given freely, lass," he said. "I can't claim anything."

"It's yours, nonetheless."

"And I'll be gentle with it." His eyes roamed her face and then her room. "Is this your room in the palace?"

"No. Mine is up in a tower," she said, stroking her finger down his chin, then his chest. "I've kept it a secret. I don't want too many people to know where it is. But I'll gladly show you when you're able to climb steps."

"You have too many enemies. And now I can't protect you." He slid his fingers into her hair and began to pull her close again for another kiss.

"Then I'll have to protect us both," Ankarette murmured.

They were still kissing when Davern returned with a tray from Liona in the kitchen. It had enough food for four, and he had to balance it carefully.

"The cook is generous," Davern said after setting it down. Then he grinned. "I don't know what the rest of you are going to eat. This is my helping."

Ankarette smiled and scooted to the edge of the bed. She

looked inquisitively at John Thursby to gauge his interest in eating.

"A drink," he said to her.

Ankarette rose and went to fetch him one.

"Oh, and I saw Bennet in the kitchen as well," Davern said. "He was talking to Lord Bletchley and some other man I didn't recognize. He looked well-to-do but wore a different fashion, like Lord Bletchley's. They said something about having some news for you. News you'd been asking for."

The Genevese merchant had come.

TWENTY-EIGHT

UNDENIABLE

While Ankarette was relieved that John Thursby had woken up, he'd lost a substantial amount of blood, and the risk of infection was high. After so many injuries in his life, he'd seemed nigh on indestructible. But lifting his head was too much effort right now. And the pallor of his skin alarmed her more than she could say.

She'd asked Davern to find Lord Horwath so he could meet with her and Bletchley in the king's solar. Eredur had a meeting with the nobles scheduled for later in the afternoon and had business to attend to with the lord mayor of Kingfountain that morning. She was the first to arrive, and while the room was familiar to her, she felt an impending sense of doom. The king's Wizr board sat on a little table, the pieces arranged midgame. She wondered whom he'd been playing with. Restlessly she paced, awaiting the arrival of Bletchley, the merchant, and Horwath.

The three arrived at the same time. Davern waited at the doorway for an invitation to be admitted, but she shook her head surreptitiously, and he nodded and shut the door after the last guest arrived. Lord Horwath gave Ankarette a questioning look.

Lord Bletchley took the Genevese man by the arm and escorted him to her. The fellow had a broad chest, a grizzled beard, and a fashionable plaited hat with plumes arranged rakishly in the band. The jewelry he wore on his fingers and wrists signaled his wealth. He had a cunning smile and a rather bulbous nose.

"Master Lisono, may I introduce you to Ankarette. She is the one who wishes to speak with you." Lord Bletchley made a grand gesture, as if he were introducing the merchant to one of the ladies of court.

"My pleasure, surely," said the merchant, bowing low. "It is, certes, an honor and a privilege. Your reputation in Genevar is...shall we say...exceptional." He put his hand on his velvet jerkin with brass buttons and bowed once more.

"Master Lisono, have you met Lord Horwath?"

"The estimable duke of the North? I had the pleasure of meeting His Grace just now in the stairwell. And to congratulate him on the victory at Averanche. Trade can resume now, which is always good news. My lord, the honor is mine!" He bowed to Lord Horwath.

Ankarette felt his deference was feigned. The Genevese did not want to cause offense, and so they tended to be superlative in their manners.

"You were already in Kingfountain when we arrived?" Ankarette queried. "You had not left yet?"

"My ship is ready with cargo to leave for Genevar at the moment. But I felt impressed by the situation that lingering might be prudent. We're scheduled to sail tomorrow."

"I understand you're a wine merchant?"

"Yes. I trade with all the famous vintners to provide the best quality wines to my customers."

She looked at Duke Horwath and then back at Lisono. "Tell me how you came across the forged letter. The one you sold to Lord Bletchley."

"I will tell you, my lady. One of my most profitable customers is Lord Dunsdworth Argentine at the Arbon. He has a taste for extravagant wines, as you may know."

She nodded in agreement.

"He recently placed a rather large order. Not his typical size." He reached his hand into his jerkin pocket and produced a receipt of sale. Then he cleared his throat. "He ordered sixty barrels of wine. Not bottles. That's enough to last quite a long time. I know his cellars were not built for such capacity. I was intrigued and had a messenger confirm the delivery arrangements in advance. I brought the shipment myself." He handed the receipt to Ankarette.

The handwriting was elegant and very professional, and it revealed Lord Dunsdworth's name and the shipping location. "Did he say what the wine was for?"

"A celebration fit for a king. His words, my lady. Not mine."

Ankarette felt her pulse throb. "You said his cellars were not big enough to contain that many barrels. Where were they delivered?"

"To a warehouse in the Vintrey ward owned by one Master Skimpole."

Lord Bletchley raised a finger. "I took the liberty of assigning some Espion to keep watch on the warehouse. The kegs are still there. Skimpole used to work for Warrewik's household. I checked."

Ankarette returned the receipt. "And the forgery?"

"I found it on Lord Dunsdworth's desk," Master Lisono said, his eyes glittering with intrigue. "It was written in his own handwriting, no? He would not trust a steward to write such words. I kept pushing him to reveal what the celebration was for, but he would not tell me. So I plied him with wine. We enjoy...drinking together. Lord Dunsdworth is a jovial man."

"You got him drunk," Ankarette surmised.

"Yes, my lady. But I kept my wits. After he was deep in his cups, he told me that he would soon be King of Ceredigion. He boasted of it. I asked him how, but he would not say, no matter how innocently I asked. Then he dozed in his chair. That's when I snatched the letter from his desk. I could tell he was trying to set his brother at odds with other nobles, such as Lord Horwath's esteemed person. I even found the seal of the duke that was used in the forgery inside a drawer."

Ankarette's brow wrinkled. "Did you know what was going to happen here in Kingfountain?"

"I know nothing but what was written in that letter. But I surmised something terrible was about to happen to King Eredur and his family. So I sent a message to my friend, Lord Bletchley, with the news and the letter and told him I was in Glosstyr."

"Help me understand something," Ankarette said pointedly. "Why would you turn against your largest customer, who had just paid you for your largest order? Surely, if he became king, you would profit even more."

Lord Bletchley smiled at her question, reflexively, and then muted his look.

Master Lisono regarded her carefully. "War is not good for business, my lady. Ceredigion has prospered under Eredur's reign. It has made many Genevese merchants very rich. Myself included. The last civil war was very costly. My people could have prevented it by sharing what we knew earlier. This time, we decided to take action and prevent it from happening again."

"Does Dunsdworth know you took the letter?"

Master Lisono grinned like a wolf. "He sent his steward to

my ship asking if I had seen any correspondence when I came to visit. He said something was missing. I lied to him. That is another reason I did not leave Kingfountain quickly. Lest the duke suspect something."

Everything Master Lisono said was believable. And it looked like the Genevese were now taking a more active role in the politics between the kingdoms. Peace did benefit those who worked in trade, for if money wasn't being funneled into defenses, there would be more of it for wine and other luxuries.

"Is there anything else, Master Lisono?" she asked, keeping her air unconcerned.

"I would just ask to keep my involvement in this affair confidential," he said. "I would prefer the Duke of Clare not know of my involvement in his undoing."

"Thank you for the information," Ankarette said. "Your assistance has been valuable. We'll safeguard knowledge of your involvement."

"And will you tell the king about his brother's treachery?" Lisono asked.

"That is something you need not concern yourself with," Ankarette replied. "If there is further need of you, we know where to find you?"

Lord Bletchley nodded vigorously.

"Very well. Thank you."

"I shall escort my friend back to the docks," Lord Bletchley said.

"Thank you, kind sir. My lord, my lady." He bowed deeply to them both and followed Bletchley out of the solar, leaving Ankarette and Lord Horwath alone.

As soon as the door was shut, Horwath let out his breath in a prolonged sigh. "The evidence is condemning. Based on the merchant's word alone, I would find Dunsdworth suspected of treason. The forgery of my signet...that only amplifies his guilt."

"And we have the barrels of wine as evidence of the conspiracy. The letter implicating Severn as a ruse. There is no room for doubt. He's guilty."

Lord Horwath nodded. "We must tell the king what we learned."

There was no other option.

I̲t̲ ̲w̲a̲s̲ in that same solar that they shared the news with Eredur as soon as his business with the mayor was concluded. He already knew about the letter. But once he learned about the wine and how it was tied to the attempted murder of his family, the anguish and anger in his face was unmistakable. Elyse was with the children, still hidden in Ankarette's tower because so few knew where it was or how to get there. Ankarette had used her magic to sense for Hux in the palace and had discovered nothing. She was convinced he was gone.

For now.

"We have a meeting of the nobles this very afternoon," Lord Horwath pressed. "Your brother intends to come. That would be the perfect opportunity to arrest him."

"He sent me a note earlier today complaining his wife has a stomach ailment," Eredur said. "I replied that I expected them both to come. If he doesn't, I'll send my guards to fetch him."

"He'll come," Ankarette said. "He doesn't know that you're aware of his treachery."

Eredur nodded. He was pacing now, battling terrible emotions. He'd forgiven his brother so many times. But this...

this was unforgivable. He'd seen his own children cower in fear. He and Elyse had nearly lost their lives. Murdered in their own palace by Lewis's poisoner. All so a greedy younger brother could finally claim what he felt he deserved. What he felt entitled to.

"Who would you like to preside over the Assizes?" the duke asked.

"You, Stiev," Eredur said wearily. "With your credibility and integrity, no one will question the verdict. But I'll not arrest him today. Maybe he will come forward and confess. He's done things in a stupor before. Things he's regretted later." His voice thickened with emotion. "He's still my brother."

Lord Horwath nodded, sympathy in his expression. "I won't go back to Dundrennan until this is resolved."

Ankarette knew he likely wanted to return home for the birth of his grandchild. Now both father and son-in-law would be away from home, since Thomas had been summoned to the castle.

"Thank you," Eredur said, putting his hand on Horwath's shoulder. The duke left them alone.

"I'm sorry to bring such tidings," Ankarette said. "It grieves me too, to watch your family fracture like this."

Eredur nodded, but he looked miserable. "Even with a public condemnation, with all the evidence, there will be some who believe he is innocent. That I'm condemning my brother because he's a rival."

"There will always be those kinds of people."

He shook his head and sighed. "I can't believe it's come to this."

"You've been more than patient. The hollow crown is a fever dream to him now. He can't let go."

"I know. I thought common sense would eventually win

out. But it hasn't. It won't." He looked at her. "And there is a sizable faction, here in Kingfountain, who would prefer him as king. He's good-looking. Popular. Generous with his wealth. That's how the people see him. But we know him to be a drunken git. And now his ambition has led him to murder, and he won't stop there. Not only is my family at risk but Severn's too. He'll remove all obstacles to power."

Ankarette couldn't disagree. She remained silent and just nodded.

"I know what I should do, but it's so painful. So painful."

"In my opinion, I think you should have him arrested today. Publicly. In front of the peers of the realm."

Eredur shook his head.

"Delaying will only make it hurt worse," Ankarette said. "And give him time to compose his lies. He's condemned himself. It's not your fault."

"He'll challenge the proceedings," he replied miserably. "Drag them out. He'll turn it into a spectacle."

"Yes. But in the end, he will be found guilty of crimes he's committed."

"He is guilty. The reason I told Stiev not to arrest my brother was because I wanted to buy *you* time to end this. To end this *today*."

Ankarette could not help but gasp.

He looked her in the eyes, tears quivering on his lashes, his voice choking with emotion. "I'm going to let him think he's beyond suspicion. And while he is here at the palace, you will go to the Arbon. And you will make sure his next cup of wine is his last!"

TWENTY-NINE

THE ARBON

"How long have you been considering poisoning your brother?" Ankarette asked, her voice barely more than a whisper. She could sense it was not an impulsive decision. It was something he'd been battling with for quite some time.

Eredur cast his gaze to the floor, unable to look her in the eye. "I have fought against this decision for years. He's my brother, Ankarette. But he has no loyalty to anyone but himself."

"That's true." She was wrestling with the implications herself. At the poisoner school, this was how one handled recalcitrant and scheming family members. But the same conflict that tore Eredur's heart also tore hers. Isybelle was her friend. Her husband could be a boor and a brute, but she would not want his life ended in such a way. Or would she?

If Dunsdworth was accused of treason, brought to the Assizes for it, and condemned by the peers of the realm, his lands would be forfeit to the crown, his heirs stripped of their rights of inheritance. Even Isybelle's station would be reduced because, whether or not she was guilty of treason herself, some would assume the worst.

Those in Dunsdworth's favor, on the other hand, would accuse Eredur of being grasping, of claiming his brother's lands and wealth for his own. Even the blackest of treason could be plastered over.

He was looking at her again while she mused. "I've never wanted this, Ankarette," he said. "But if you do this, it would preserve Isybelle's station. It could give their children the right to claim their father's station. No Assizes. No verdict. It's too late to win over my brother. But it may not be too late to win over his son. In time. This is for the best. And it must happen today. Take a few trusted Espion if you need them, but be discreet. Keep them ignorant of your mission if you can."

Ankarette tilted her head. "What will Elyse think? Is that why you didn't want her to be here for this?"

Eredur shook his head. "She's been suggesting this for years. Not maliciously. To protect our children. The Argentine legacy has been rife with conflict since the founding of the dynasty. My ancestor, the first Argentine, lost his throne to his son. The right to rule has sometimes skipped a generation. Factions, infighting, treachery, betrayal—that is our legacy. I must do this to safeguard my children. My wife. Elyse has told me that when I die, her first act will be to flee to sanctuary at Our Lady of Kingfountain with the children." He shook his head. "She doesn't trust my council to act in her interests. Or our children's."

"I know you don't ask this lightly," Ankarette said. "This is not something I wish to do."

"But you will. I'm counting on it. We've always had an agreement, Ankarette. That you save more lives than you take in my service. Is there someone you want me to pardon? I will do it. You've served me faithfully for so many years. I don't take that for granted."

Did he, though? She wanted to ask his permission to marry John Thursby. To find a way to disentangle herself from the politics of Kingfountain. But she would not ask for it now. When she was done with this awful task, she'd be in a better position to make such a request.

"I will go," Ankarette said. "I'll take a few to go with me. I don't want to be caught off guard."

Eredur nodded, his lips a firm line. He was determined to do this. But was this action only putting his family more at risk? She remembered the whisper from the Fountain she'd heard about Severn. But she still felt constrained not to tell her king. Not to tell anyone.

"AND WHERE ARE you off to, Ankarette?" John Thursby said from her bed. She'd just checked the wound again and didn't like the color of it or the smell. She'd added more salve, hoping against hope that it would drive off infection. It was rare to see him so lethargic. His listlessness was another bad sign. He needed sunshine. He needed to be up and about again. When the threat of Dunsdworth was over, she'd take him back to Old Rose's apothecary, knowing he'd be in good, caring hands. Or maybe she'd take him to her little home in the alley, where the fragrant smells from the planter boxes outside would help soothe him.

"The king has given me an assignment," Ankarette said. She'd taken some poison from her stores in her tower and packed several supplies into her bag and now used them to prepare her weapons and needles for action.

"What kind of assignment requires those little bottles?"

She'd tried to stow them away surreptitiously, but the night watchman's eyes were ever alert. She tucked away her bag, came and knelt by the bed, and smoothed his brow and kissed it. "I'll tell you when it's done."

"Will you be gone long?" he asked.

She shook her head. "I'm off to see Hugh Bardulf on Bridge Street. I'll be back soon. Get some rest."

His hand lifted to her hair and stroked it. "Be careful. I'll worry until you return."

She liked the feeling of his rough hand. Its gentleness to her. "I'm always careful."

She rose and left him alone. When she opened the door, Davern was still waiting there. "Keep watch on him, Davern. He's in your charge. Keep the door locked when you need to leave." She handed him a spare key to the room.

"Aye, my lady." He hooked his thumbs in his belt after accepting the key and gave her a nod that showed his commitment.

She then went to the Star Chamber, the Espion's main chamber in the palace, where Bennet was waiting for her. With him was Giselle, the picklock he'd brought to Averanche. Ankarette thought her skills would be useful for the mission. She'd proven herself capable.

"Off to Bridge Street, then?" Bennet asked.

Ankarette nodded, and the three of them departed the palace through the secret tunnels. It didn't take long to reach the bridge. The roar of the falls made her think of the king's justice. Not many days ago, she would have predicted that Lord Devereaux's fate was intermingled with the waterfall at King-fountain. Now the man was likely to be incarcerated instead.

Only someone Fountain-blessed, it was said, could survive a boat plummeting from the waterfall.

They reached the inn and found Hugh Bardulf waiting in the common room. He looked harried by all the responsibilities that had settled on his shoulders. The strain of sleepless nights was taking its toll on him.

Ankarette sat down at a table near the windows by the front door, one that would give ample view of the street. Bennet slouched in a chair next to her, and she saw the short sword belted at his waist along with a brace of knives. He was good in a fight. Even better, they had a shared history of defending Eredur's throne.

Giselle sat more demurely and brushed hair over her ear. "What's the job?"

"We're breaking into the Arbon to look for evidence of treachery," Ankarette said to them in a low voice. "We have ample reason to suspect that the Duke of Clare was involved in Devereaux's plot. The king wants evidence. The false seal of Duke Horwath. Anything else we can discover."

Everything she said was true, but it was not the true reason for their visit to the Arbon. She was going there to poison him. But they didn't need to know that. Yet.

Hugh came to the table and planted his palms there. "Do you want to eat anything before we head out?" he asked.

Ankarette wasn't hungry. In fact, she felt a little sick to her stomach. She shook her head. The others followed her example.

"You had men search the warehouse?" she asked, gazing up at him.

He nodded. "It's all still there. Just as was said."

"What's where?" Bennet asked suspiciously.

"More proof," Ankarette said.

Hugh backed away and went to talk to some other guests.

They waited another hour or so before an Espion on horseback came up to the inn and dismounted. He hurried inside, spotted Hugh, and came to him. Hugh nodded and then approached Ankarette's table.

"He's on the way. Will be passing by shortly," he said confidentially.

Ankarette turned her gaze to the window. Sure enough, the arrival of the Duke of Clare's entourage soon claimed all the attention on the street. Ankarette recognized Dunsdworth, noticing the look of ill health and worry that made his features tense. However, he was putting on a show for the commoners, riding with a straight back and wearing a very expensive doublet. His knights were flanking him, and Lady Isybelle rode alongside her husband, wearing a beautiful green silk gown that didn't hide the bulge of the babe in her womb. They had brought at least thirty knights with them, a sizable show of force, and the polish and glistening arms made it look like a king and queen returning in pride to their city. Ankarette gazed at Isybelle's profile, taking in her pale countenance and serious expression.

Ankarette was grateful that Eredur had insisted both of them attend his council. With all the guards they'd brought, there would be very few left at the Arbon.

"I have your horses ready," Hugh told them after the entourage had passed. "In the alley next to the inn."

Ankarette rose from the table, and her two companions did the same. "Have someone stationed here, watching the road. If we're not back before the duke returns from Kingfountain, send word and help."

"I will," Hugh said.

Ankarette's group left out the side door, found the three horses waiting for them, and took off down the street at a quick pace, hurrying toward the Vintrey ward. Ankarette knew the side alleys and took them to disguise their path in case anyone was following him. At a blind turn in one alley, she waited for several minutes to see if anyone was indeed coming after them. No one was.

They brought their horses to an Espion handler whom Hugh had left near the Arbon for that purpose. The plan was to approach on foot.

She couldn't help but think of the time she and John Thursby had hunted this same area for Lady Nanette. Then a familiar throb filled her stomach, a reminder that she hadn't had a sip of her tincture in a while. Even when she had other important things to do, Lord Hux was always meddling with them because of the poison. Speaking of Lord Hux, where was he concealing himself? She shook her head to rid herself of thoughts like these now. She needed to concentrate.

As they approached the porter door, she gestured for the other two to fall back so she could arrive first. She lifted her cowl to conceal her face and walked up to the gate. The shadowed interior nearly concealed the guard stationed there. It wasn't Moser, the guard who'd been employed by the family during the last crisis. He was still living with his sister, Agnes, and her children.

Ankarette came to the gate. "Excuse me? I'm looking for Master Trollop's estate? Is this it?"

"Master who?" asked the sentry, rising from his stool and coming to the bars.

"Master Trollop? This is the Hermitage ward, is it not?"

"No, ma'am, this is Vintrey ward. I've never heard of the man." He gripped the bar, exposing his bare fingers.

Ankarette twisted her needle ring and put her hand atop his. "Am I really that turned around? I'm so sorry to bother you, but do you know which direction I should go?"

The man flinched from the poke of her needle. He yanked

his hand back and started massaging it a second before he crumpled to the floor.

Ankarette motioned for Giselle to unlock the gate, which she did in seconds. The gate creaked as they pushed it open. Bennet hoisted the guard beneath his arms and dragged him near the stool, setting him down in the shadows.

"How long will he be out?" Bennet asked.

"Long enough. Stay here with him. You watch the street while Giselle and I go inside."

"What if there are knights in there?"

Ankarette gave him a look. "If there's anything we can't handle, you'll know about it soon. This is our way out. You keep guard."

Bennet nodded and began pacing.

"Have you been inside here before?" Giselle asked as they quickly walked the cobblestone path leading to the rear door. The yard was still overrun with bushes and brittle weeds. Dunsdworth wasn't paying for a gardener, and it showed.

"I know the way," Ankarette said. They walked to the door, and she opened it, revealing the quiet interior. They didn't keep a lot of servants. A banging sound echoed from the area leading to the kitchen, as if from pots clashing against each other. Voices lifted and laughed. The servants had gathered for a rest and some refreshments while the master and mistress were gone.

Ankarette's conscience began troubling her. Not about what she was about to do but about how easy it was. People were so set in their habits. That was their biggest downfall. Eredur's summons to the palace had created the perfect opportunity for her to poison his brother. The servants were gleefully enjoying some wine and cake, no doubt, and would be oblivious to the intruders coming to do harm.

Ankarette gestured for Giselle to follow, and the two stole

through the great hall where arms and banners were fixed to the walls. At the other side were the stairs leading to the private rooms. They went up quickly, Giselle looking around as they went, and reached Dunsdworth and Isybelle's chamber. It was unlocked, as Ankarette had assumed it would be. They went inside, shut it quietly, and examined the mess on the floor, the rumpled sheets, and the strong stench of wine in the air.

Giselle tapped an empty bottle on the floor with her boot and gave Ankarette a look of disdain at the slovenly mess.

"I imagine the evidence we're looking for will be in a locked chest or drawer." Ankarette gestured to the writing desk and cushioned bench. "Start there. I'm going to inspect the changing rooms. See if you can find a seal with a lion on it."

Giselle nodded and got to work.

From her earlier interactions with Dunsdworth, Ankarette knew he didn't drink directly from bottles. He liked his fine things, his displays of prestige. There were two golden chalices, one near the bed on the floor and another on a table by the door. She walked over to it and saw it still had a large splash of wine within it. She lifted it to her nose and smelled. In her mind, she imagined Dunsdworth taking a final calming drink before leaving for the palace.

She turned around and saw Giselle with her lockpick set, working at a small chest on the table, eyes fixed in concentration.

Ankarette glanced back at the goblet. It would be the first thing Dunsdworth drank when he returned from the palace. And then he'd drink some more. She knew from her private conversations with Lady Isybelle that she loathed wine because of her husband's indulgence in it. The smell made her nauseous.

She'd already thought about what kind of poison she'd use.

Not one that caused suffering. No, it would be better for everyone if he died in his sleep. That's what had led her to choose mandrake. People reacted to it in different ways—some with vomiting—but it was a poisoner's favored choice for making a death appear natural. It often gave the victim fevered dreams.

While Giselle was working to open the lock on the chest, Ankarette removed the little vial of mandrake oil, twisted off the cap, and poured the whole thing into the cup of wine. She'd added some syrup to sweeten the sharp taste of the poison.

She was confident in her abilities and the dosage. *The dose makes the poison.* She was equally confident that with his already compromised internal organs, the Duke of Clare wouldn't wake up in the morning.

Then she stuck the vial in her pocket and pretended to continue looking for evidence of Dunsdworth's guilt.

"Found the seal," Giselle announced, grinning.

CHAPTER
THIRTY
THE MANDRAKE

Ankarette was back at the palace before the king's council had even ended. It was followed by a meal in the great hall, which would occupy the royal couple for some time. So she stole back to her room to relieve Davern of his vigil and found, to her added alarm, a fever had set in. John Thursby had wrestled off his sheets and was dripping with sweat.

"How long has he been like this?" Ankarette asked, touching his scorching brow with the back of her hand.

"Since you left," Davern said. "I've offered to bring him water, but he refused to drink it."

"Thank you for watching over him. Now go to the kitchen and get yourself something to eat."

"I don't mind staying, my lady. In case you need me."

"If I need you, I'll call for you. I'm going to stay with him now. You may go."

He nodded and left.

"I've had worse than this," John Thursby muttered. "I'm

just a little dizzy is all. I want to go back to Old Rose's. Can I borrow a horse?" He tried to sit up.

"You aren't fit to ride one," Ankarette said, pushing him back down. She added more salve to his wound, but what he really needed was rest. "I can make you some tea. It will help you sleep."

"I know what my body needs, Ankarette. It's too quiet here. I need to be back in my ward. With familiar sights and smells. I can walk my rounds tonight. I know I can. That will help me recover. There are too many ghosts in this palace."

She didn't feel it was safe for him to return to the Hermitage, not while Dunsdworth still breathed. If he suspected John Thursby was dear to her, then she knew by the Lady the king's brother would use that against her.

"Tomorrow," she promised. "I'll take you there tomorrow."

"How did your...task go?" he asked, his voice sounding frail.

"I think it went well. Just try to rest, John. Rest."

He closed his eyes but continued to fidget on her bed. She waited at his side for several hours, unaware of time, feeling no hunger, just the raw anticipation of impending news. Finally, a gentle knock sounded at the door. She rose to answer it and found Bennet standing there.

"The king wishes to see you."

She glanced back at John Thursby, listless on the bed.

"Can you go find Davern and tell him he's needed again? I don't want to leave my friend alone."

"It'll take time for him to heal, Ankarette," Bennet said, not without sympathy. "But I'll send someone to fetch the lad for you and will wait until he gets here."

"Thank you. Have the guests left yet?"

He nodded. "The feast ended an hour or so ago. Dunsdworth and Lady Isybelle left in good spirits, from what I observed. The porter guard woke up none the wiser."

She touched his arm, smiled, and then hurried to the king's private chamber. When she got there, she found both the king and queen, still dressed in their finery from the council meeting. The hollow crown, the symbol of the Argentine family's rule, lay on a cushion on a small circular table. It would be put away by the royal chamberlain soon. Eredur was removing a necklace from the queen's slender neck when Ankarette arrived.

He looked at her with expectancy but didn't ask the question they both knew needed to be asked.

"I've done my part," Ankarette said. "Now all we can do is wait."

Elyse looked from one to the other. "Is this about your brother?"

"Yes," Eredur said curtly. He set the necklace down on the dressing table. "I don't know if I'm going to sleep tonight. I'm still very conflicted about this."

Elyse shot him an intense look. "Husband. You are doing this to protect us."

"I know," he said with a sigh. "Call my fascination morbid, but what did you do, Ankarette? Will he...suffer?"

Ankarette shook her head. "I used mandrake and syrup. I think his liver is totally ruined by all the wine he drinks. I made sure the dose was sufficient. He'll die in his sleep tonight."

Eredur nodded but still looked to be wrestling with his feelings.

Elyse stroked his arm. "I don't want this any more than you do. But he left us no other choice. An inquest, the Assizes, would have turned many against us. He might have fled the kingdom to avoid justice."

"I know. I know." He rubbed his brow. "Yet it feels awful. I had to pretend he was in favor during the feast. To smile at him and praise him publicly. Just to avoid casting a shadow of suspicion."

Ankarette understood that must have been difficult. But it was a burden a king needed to bear to safeguard the succession, although that was almost an afterthought in this case. Eredur knew his brother would be a *terrible* king. Not only was he safeguarding his children, but he was trying to safeguard the realm. Dunsdworth's wouldn't be the first life Ankarette had ended to protect the throne. On Eredur's command, she had also poisoned the mad king. His one child with Morvared, a son, had died in battle. There was no more legacy of that line to contend with.

"How did Dunne react to your praise?" Ankarette asked.

Elyse had an incredulous look. "He was nervous when he came to the council. As tense as a hare poised to flee. But he's just as thirsty for praise as he is for wine, and his countenance changed when the king talked of his good standing. During the feast, Eredur invited him and Isybelle for a private conversation, just the four of us."

Eredur cut in. "I mentioned I'd heard reports of some treachery at Averanche from Lord Devereaux but that I wouldn't hearken to such gossip. I told him I was grateful for his support and his goodwill. He looked so relieved, so elated, it was torture to see how much he'd craved hearing words like that. Even though he doesn't deserve them."

How true it was. Even the most unworthy craved recognition. In fact, she'd observed that the desire to be considered, esteemed, praised, beloved, and admired was probably the keenest disposition in the heart of every man. It was that unyielding lust that had driven Dunsdworth to try to claim the throne for his own. Little did he realize that attaining it would not sate his hunger. It was an endless appetite—one destined to end in disappointment.

"I'm sorry it has come to this," Ankarette said. "Truly."

"We know," Elyse declared. "Were you seen by anyone at the Arbon? Servants perhaps?"

Ankarette shook her head. "They were celebrating their master's absence in the kitchen. I took one of the Espion inside with me. Not even she noticed me slip the poison in the cup."

Elyse looked relieved at the news.

"Thank you, Ankarette," Eredur said. "I've asked Hugh Bardulf to keep an eye on the Arbon tonight. He knows about the investigation. But we probably won't hear any news until midmorning. I know my brother likes his sleep—"

He stopped abruptly because a commotion outside the door had grown loud enough. The door opened and one of the guards poked his head in.

"It's Lord Mortimer, Your Majesty. He's just arrived."

The man was yanked away from the doorway, and Earl Thomas barged in, his eyes full of fury. He looked out of breath from the pace he'd kept. He started when he saw Ankarette, but then shifted his angry glare back to the king and queen.

"I've come all the way from Dundrennan, as ordered, and I wasn't going to be detained by some idiot guardsmen." He still had that dusting of a Northern brogue in his tongue. Ankarette wished she had a Tay al-Ard herself and could whisk herself away from the scene with magic.

"Tom," the king said, his brow wrinkling.

"My wife is ill and I've left Dundrennan unprotected, but I came because you commanded it. I know what you're going to ask, and you needn't have dragged me away to hear the same answer I told you before."

Ankarette saw Elyse was struggling to keep her composure. The rudeness of Thomas's manners would have rankled anyone. She normally tried to reconcile people, but Ankarette saw she wouldn't intervene this time.

"Tom, I wouldn't have summoned you if the situation weren't dire. My family was nearly murdered by Lord Hux. Nichols is dead."

"Nichols wasn't much of a swordsman, then," Lord Thomas shot back with a look of contempt. "Is that why you want me? To hunt Hux down and kill him like a dog?"

"Master Nichols is dead because he used the suicide ring," the queen said, her voice throbbing with indignation. "He saved our lives!"

That was news, and it blunted some of Lord Thomas's anger. His eyes widened with surprise, and he fell silent.

Ankarette had rarely seen such a display of animosity. It was a sign he was under considerable stress. No doubt he and his wife had had words before he'd left.

"I know your babe is due soon," Eredur said placatingly. "But this is serious. The fate of Ceredigion is at stake. If Hux had been successful, you would have arrived to find my brother, the Duke of Clare, wearing the crown. He was part of the conspiracy, Tom."

It was another blow. Thomas had the good grace to look abashed now. "I d-didn't know."

"There is more at stake here than you or me," Eredur said forcefully. "What kind of kingdom do you think this would be if the succession happened now? Would not Occitania turn against us and try to reclaim land? Would not Atabyrion be tempted to strike again at the North? I need you, Tom. You're a natural leader. You can smell intrigue like garlic on the breath. And admit it, man, you *miss* the work!"

That was the blow that made Thomas crumple. He *did* miss it. Ankarette knew that he did; she could see it in the shift in his countenance. He missed the subterfuge and plotting. The danger. She could see the glow of ambition still in his eyes. The hunger.

"I promised my wife that I would tell you no," Thomas said after a long and painful pause. "I'm about to become a father. I *want* to be a father. And my family deserves more than the dregs of my time and attention." He shook his head, muttering to himself. Then he lifted his chin and faced the king, his friend, with boldness. "I'm honored by your confidence in me. But I have to refuse. I'll take your punishment. Your fall from favor. I do want it. Truly." He shook his head in defeat. "But I promised I wouldn't. And if I can't keep my promises to my wife, then you can't trust me to keep one to you."

Ankarette saw Elyse glance at her husband, but she said nothing. It was his decision to make. Eredur looked disappointed but not surprised.

Thomas rocked on his heels. "Shall I report to the dungeon, then?" he asked, a grin threatening before revealing itself.

Eredur chuckled. "I'm disappointed by your answer," he said. "And rightfully wroth with you. This does vex me enough to send you to the dungeon. But I won't. I don't reward loyalty that way."

"I might suggest, as a friend, that you confine your brother there instead," Lord Thomas said, this time with no hint of joking. "He doesn't even deserve the prison tower. You've been too forgiving for too long. Blood is thicker than water, as they say. But you're truly thick-headed if you delay punishing him if he's guilty of treason *again*. That advice, my lord, is free."

Elyse offered a knowing smile but said nothing.

Eredur stepped forward, and the two men embraced. Despite their dispute, they were brothers-in-arms. Friends to the last.

"I need your advice on who I should have run the Espion, then," Eredur said, afterward, draping his arm around the other man's neck.

"I'd suggest Ankarette if I didn't think she'd stab me for saying it," Thomas said.

"What about your father-in-law?" Eredur asked.

Thomas winced. "I like him, truly. But he's not devious enough. You need to be able to think like your opponents. He's more apt to want to bludgeon them to death."

Ankarette agreed. She wanted to leave, but it was enjoyable having them all back together again. It felt like old times.

"What do you know of Lord Bletchley?" Elyse asked. "He's been helpful in this situation. He paid some Genevese merchants for information. In fact, their information is what led us to Dunne."

Thomas thought on that a moment. "I don't know the man, so I can't proffer an opinion. But if he wants the job, by the Lady, let him have it!"

Ankarette rather thought Bletchley wanted the job *too* much, and that lessened him in her eyes. But given the difficulty of the task, there might not be a better option.

The secret door leading to the king's chamber clicked, the wall moved, and Bennet came in, eyes wide. "Tom!"

"Bennet! You look pale. What's wrong?" Thomas's smile began to fade.

Ankarette felt a surge of unease. More bad news. She could see it in Bennet's eyes.

The Espion looked at the royal couple. "Something's happened at the Arbon. There's been shrieking since the duke and duchess returned there after the feast. Lady Isybelle has fallen ill. A knight from your brother's household is on his way to the palace, begging that Ankarette come at once. I wanted to warn you before he arrived."

Ankarette worried for her friend and former mistress, knowing she'd already suffered one stillbirth. Of course, that one had been due to poison...and then an insidious thought struck Ankarette like a slap to the face. What if Isybelle had drunk from the poisoned chalice?

THERE WAS nothing that would stop the mandrake from killing her. Not even Ankarette could forestall that end.

In the poisoner school, the adage was taught that every obstacle, every impediment, every setback can be turned into an advantage and used to help achieve our goals.

I used to believe that. But no heart can bear the weight of too much disappointment.

Ankarette Tryneowy

THIRTY-ONE

MOST FOUL MURDER

The realization of what she'd done to her friend and childhood companion struck Ankarette to her core. She knew the properties of mandrake. Knew it should *never* be given to a pregnant woman. It would not only be lethal to her but the child. Horror seared her mind and must have shown on her face.

The king realized the truth at once. "You will not go to her, Ankarette. I forbid it."

"Who else can help her in such a situation?" Thomas declared, looking between the two of them. "If you don't, Dunne will have grounds to accuse you of having..." And then he stopped speaking, realizing himself what must have happened.

"I have to go, I have to try," Ankarette said, her voice sounding hollow in her own ears.

"No!" Elyse countered. "We'll send our surgeon instead." She grabbed Eredur by the arm and shook him to get him to look at her. "We'll say she's away. If we send our own surgeon, it'll be enough."

The noise of bootsteps coming down the corridor alerted her to the fact that Bennet's warning had come just in time. If the knight saw Ankarette in the king's room...

Thomas gripped Ankarette by the arm and propelled her toward the secret door. Bennet preceded them through it. The king and queen had begun to compose themselves, but she could see the awful emotions surging inside them. No one had expected this outcome. Ankarette hadn't imagined for an instant that the cup had been Isybelle's or that she'd be the one to drink from it.

Thomas led Ankarette through the secret door next and then gently shut it behind them.

"Go to the Star Chamber," he whispered. "I'll stay here and listen in."

"I need to hear it too," Ankarette whispered back. "It's my fault."

"I'll warn Hugh," Bennet said in an undertone, grabbing the lantern from the floor by the secret entrance. He retreated swiftly down the corridor, leaving the two of them alone in the dark.

Ankarette's guilt was torturing her. She'd killed her friend. And the baby. She'd seen what mandrake had done to the mad king. The peaceful look on his face still, all these years later, gave her nightmares on occasion.

Thomas slid open the spy hole and looked into the chamber. The familiarity of the moment wrapped around her and squeezed, making her feel even more wretched, because she'd killed her other childhood friend. She had *killed* Isybelle.

"It's not your fault," he whispered, not looking at her. "I know that's not helpful now, not when the grief is so raw. But it's the truth."

The raised voices from the other room came through the small gap easily. "My lord! Your brother has sent me to bring back the poisoner, Ankarette Tryneowy. Lady Isybelle has fallen ill suddenly. She's having seizures, my lord. We fear for the baby. I beg you, in my master's name, to send her at once!"

She tried to rein in her thoughts, to consider all possibilities. This could be a ruse. Perhaps Lord Hux had found the poison and changed cups? Or what if this was something else? A pregnancy complication. The uncertainty stabbed her mind like so many knives.

She wanted to go to the Arbon. Needed to. Her Fountain magic was still drained from her last usage of it when she'd revived John Thursby. She doubted she had the strength to do it again.

Her king had told her she mustn't.

"Ankarette isn't at the palace," Elyse said, her voice throbbing with concern. "Or we'd send her straightaway. Who could we send instead?"

"Doctor Spora?" Eredur suggested, referring to the king's surgeon.

Elyse joined in. "Yes! We'll send him to the Arbon at once. I'm so sorry to hear the news. Lady Isybelle looked fine at the banquet."

"She wasn't feeling well beforehand, Your Majesty, but it was insisted upon her that she come. This pregnancy has been difficult for my ladyship."

"We will send Doctor Spora immediately," the king said. "You can escort him back to the Arbon yourself."

"Thank you, my lord! That is gracious. But is there no way to summon Ankarette? My master was adamant that she be brought at all costs."

Ankarette felt sick to her stomach listening to the conversation. She leaned against the stone wall of the hidden corridor, trying to calm her breathing.

"She's not here," the king said. "I have her on an assignment elsewhere. Doctor Spora is very capable. And we will throw coins into the palace fountains for Lady Isybelle, that she might recover."

"Thank you, Your Majesty. A thousand thanks!"

It would take time for the doctor to collect his things. And Isybelle would likely be dead before he even arrived. Perhaps he would discern that it was poison, but he was loyal to the royal family. Any suspicions he had he would keep to himself.

"You need to sit down," Thomas said after sliding the cover back over the spy hole. Only little cracks of light penetrated the hidden hallway, and her eyes were still adjusting. "Let's go to the Star Chamber. I know we can both find it in the dark."

He was right, and they walked without speaking, traversing the secret tunnels honeycombing the palace of Kingfountain. Up and down stairs. Through side passages and hidden doors. They arrived at the Star Chamber and found it empty, but at least a fat candle had been left burning inside a shielded lantern, providing light.

Thomas sat down in the master's chair, gazing at the heaps of papers and scrolls on the desk. Reports were still coming in from Espion stationed throughout the realms. Hugh Bardulf had been unable to keep up. Thomas picked up one, looking at the seal on it before tossing it back on the pile.

"Remember the nights you stayed up with me, going through all this?" he said, gesturing at the mess, invoking a memory she cherished still.

There were three other chairs in the room, but she didn't feel like sitting. She couldn't sit. Couldn't do anything but pace, feeling a hollow ache in her heart.

Thomas rose from the chair and gazed at her. "I'm grasping here, but if I understand what I heard and what I saw, Eredur asked you to poison his brother. And his wife drank it instead. Is that about it?"

Ankarette couldn't bear to look at him. She nodded. She felt tears pressing at her eyes but refused to cry in front of the man who'd broken her heart.

"The rest of the Espion don't know yet, do they?"

Ankarette shook her head. She still didn't trust her voice. She was going to burst into tears. She had to leave.

"I must go," she whispered thickly, starting for the door.

Thomas rushed around the table and put his hand on the door to stop her from opening it. "You can't leave. Not right now. How many times have you stopped to tend the wounds of others? Now you need comfort." He gripped her by the shoulders and turned her around to face him. She felt a tear trickle down her cheek.

"I wouldn't have encouraged Eredur to poison his brother. I'm sure you counseled against it as well. The decision was made by him and Elyse. They bear the responsibility for this. Not you. But she was your friend. *Our* friend. And it is no sin to mourn those we love. I'm so sorry, Ankarette. I am so sorry this happened."

Upon saying that, he wrapped his arms around her and held her while she shook and her tears spilled out. She buried her face in his shirt, gripping the fabric in her fists, wishing she had refused the king's orders. That she'd had the courage Thomas had shown in refusing to bend. There was nothing she could do to take back her actions, but she could do something different in the future.

Ankarette couldn't remember ever being comforted like this by Thomas before. Marriage had changed him. His empathy was a balm. And she needed it. In that moment, she felt a spike of jealousy, a feeling she wasn't proud of but couldn't deny. It was because they'd known each other so long. Because only someone who'd shared her history like he had— who'd been there with her, while Dunne and Isybelle had bantered, flirted, and fallen in love—could comfort her in such a moment.

She felt Thomas stroke her hair. "Don't let yourself be numb to this grief. We must feel what is only natural. Grief is a river, and it will take us on its course."

"I know," she said, stifling a hiccup. "And it leaves scars."

"It does," he agreed. He released the hug and put his hands on her shoulders again. The look of sympathy on his face made her raw feelings even more tender. "Thank you, Thomas."

A grin quirked on his mouth. "You haven't called me *that* in a while."

"We haven't spoken in a while."

"A visit from you isn't typically a good sign," he said, then winced. "Sorry. With our baby coming, I've thought of you more often. I've considered asking for you to be near when it happens."

"Why haven't you?"

He hesitated. "Because you know my wife. You knew her, back when Stiev was the castellan of Dundrennan. She wasn't always kind to you. Or to anyone actually."

Ankarette said nothing but gave him a knowing smile.

"There have been no complications thus far. Just... complaints." His tone said more than that.

"Have you decided on names yet?" Ankarette asked.

Thomas nodded enthusiastically. "If he's a lad, Stiev Thomas Mortimer. If a girl, we've agreed on Elysabeth *Victoria* Mortimer. I have a kenning she'll be a girl, though. Because I promised you, a long time ago, that I'd name a daughter Victoria after all you did to help Eredur secure his throne. Do you remember that?"

Ankarette did and was pleased by the confirmation that he did as well. "I like that name."

"I'm glad you approve. I'm going to leave with the tide to

land at Kennit in the morning. Maybe we could go through some of these notes in the meantime, like we used to do together. It would be nice to talk to you for a while."

"It would. But I need to check on someone who was injured earlier. I want to see if the fever has gone down."

"Someone. Who?"

"I don't think you'd know him."

"*Him?*" That made Thomas's eyebrows lift. Was he... jealous?

"He's my friend," Ankarette said simply.

"What's his name? If you'll tell?"

"John Thursby."

Thomas nodded in recognition. "He's from Yuork. He's the night watchman who found Nanette a few years...ago..." His voice trailed off. "Actually, I've always suspected *you* were the one who found Nanette. And didn't want to take credit."

Ankarette looked away, abashed. "You see through everything still."

"Let me come with you if you don't mind. I'd like to meet John Thursby of Yuork."

"Come, then."

They left the lantern burning in the Star Chamber, knowing they'd be back to sort through all the unread missives. They walked the byways of the palace corridor and encountered a few sentries on patrol. The castle was quiet. Most of the servants had gone to bed, but torches lit the corridors at intervals.

She took him to her room in the more secluded area of the castle, feeling all the comfort of being with an old friend, especially given the likely fate of her other old friend. It was nice to be on familiar terms with Thomas again. It had healed some of the rift that had opened between them.

Turning the final corner, she saw a body sprawled next to her door in a pool of blood.

It was Davern.

CHAPTER

THIRTY-TWO

THE CISTERN

Ankarette knew he was dead before she knelt by the
young man's body. He'd lost too much blood. Still,
she touched his neck anyway and felt the coolness
of skin, the absence of a heartbeat. Thomas crouched by her
side, gazing in concern at the scene. She turned the body over
and saw the death wound. He'd been stabbed in the back.
Judging by the angle, the weapon had pierced his lung, so he
hadn't been able to cry out.

Ankarette rose, feeling grief for the young man, terror for
John Thursby, and anger against whoever had done this. The
repeated blows she'd endured in so short a time made her feel
as if her whole life were careening out of control. She tried the
door handle and found it locked. Reaching hurriedly into her
pocket, she produced her own key and unlocked the door. She
drew a knife and Thomas drew his sword.

"Let me go in first," he said.

Ankarette shook her head and opened the door. The dim
torchlight from the corridor revealed two things immediately.
John Thursby was off the bed, on the floor about halfway

across the room. She instantly noticed his shoulders rising and falling. His breathing was ragged. The next thing she saw was the other key she'd left with Davern. It was on the floor inside the room.

Together, she and Thomas hurried to the night watchman and helped lift him back to the bed. There were no signs of injury, but his face dripped with feverish sweat. She hadn't felt Hux's presence in the castle. She suspected one of Dunsdworth's men might have been trying to get to her...or to her love.

"He's burning up," Thomas said.

Ankarette had an idea. "The cistern."

"Let's go." Thomas hoisted the other man over his shoulder, and they set off down the corridor. They came across some sentries almost immediately, and she alerted them to Davern's body and told them to bring it to the crypt and alert Duke Horwath about the murder. One of the sentries followed them and helped Thomas carry John Thursby through the castle until they reached the door leading to the queen's gardens.

There was a hole in the middle of the garden floor where rainwater from the palace was channeled during storms and helped fill the cistern. A swarm of stars filled the night sky above. There was another door in that yard that led to some steps. Ankarette opened it and held it ajar for the two men to carry John Thursby inside. She struck a spark and lit a torch suspended on a wall sconce. The smell of wet stone was strong.

"Strip him," Ankarette said.

The two men obeyed and then carried the half-naked man down the steps to the edge of the water and waded in. The cistern water soaked their boots and pants as they immersed John Thursby into the enormous bath. The torchlight could not penetrate the entire depth of the cistern hall, which was a network of buttresses that held up the massive castle above them. The noise of the sloshing water came as the water struck the stone.

John Thursby hissed out his breath, jolted to consciousness by the chilling plunge.

Ankarette came closer, gazing at his pallid skin. The bandage around his waist wasn't specked with blood, which suggested it was the internal damage that was ailing him.

Thomas and the sentry set the wounded man down on a lower step. Ankarette handed the sentry the torch and stepped into the water herself, which immediately soaked her boots and hem. She crouched by John Thursby, watching his feverish eyes as he gazed around with a disoriented look.

"Ankarette," he whispered hoarsely.

"I'm here," she said. Worry and sorrow clashed inside her, along with a dozen other emotions. So much had happened so quickly. Her feelings were in turmoil.

"What is this place?" he asked with confused eyes.

"This is the palace cistern. You're burning up with fever."

"I thought...I thought I was in the Deep Fathoms," he admitted. His whole body began to tremble with cold.

Ankarette looked at the sentry. "Go find a blanket and bring it to me," she said. "Back the way you came. But leave the torch."

The sentry handed the torch to Thomas and then jogged back up the steps.

"Something happened to Davern," John Thursby said.

"He's dead," Ankarette confirmed. "We just found his body."

John Thursby frowned and shook his head. "He went to get me something to drink. I heard another man's voice. Then Davern cried out. I thought someone was coming to kill me, so I tried to get my sword. I collapsed on the floor."

"That's where we found you," Ankarette said.

"I thought I was a dead man. Then the key came under the door. I think Davern dropped it and kicked it so the person couldn't get to me. I called for him but heard nothing. Poor lad."

Ankarette crushed the feelings of sadness deep within her. She would have thought it Lord Hux's doing, but she hadn't felt him in the palace. She hadn't sensed his magic or the magic of the Tay al-Ard.

"He saved your life," Thomas said.

"Aye, he did," John Thursby agreed. He wrinkled his brow. "Who are you?"

"Tom Mortimer," he said. "I've heard good things about you, John Thursby. My pleasure."

"You're from the North. You're not...*the* Thomas Mortimer?"

Ankarette nodded in confirmation. She'd told John Thursby about her early days in the Espion. About her first love. She had never expected the two men might meet each other.

His teeth were starting to chatter. "I'm cold."

"We need to break this fever," Ankarette said. "You have to stay here longer."

"I'll bring back that blanket," Thomas suggested. He hung the torch in a wall rack and then hastened back up the steps, leaving her with the feverish man.

She smoothed some wet hair from her friend's forehead. "You need to get better," she said, her voice thickening.

"I'm trying, lass. I feel so weak. So helpless."

"You are not weak." She felt tears sting her eyes as she stroked his cheek.

She waited there, feeling the chill of the water as it seeped into her clothes. Trembles began to shake her, but she endured them.

"Take me to Old Rose's," John Thursby whispered. "She can heal me. I know she can."

"You're not safe there," Ankarette said. "I need to keep you safe."

"You can't save everyone, Ankarette. Maybe...maybe I could go to that little house in the alley. Your house. She could tend to me there."

Her little house in the city was a secret she'd guarded well. It should be safe for him there...

She thought about Dunsdworth and Isybelle. About what would happen if Ankarette's friend died. Dunsdworth would be furious. He'd seek revenge. On her, if he learned she was the one who'd poisoned the wine. She feared he'd come for John Thursby, but he wasn't safe in the palace either. There was someone who wanted to get to him. Who had killed poor Davern?

"We'll see," Ankarette said. She heard the sound of others coming, and Thomas returned with the sentry, another torch, and a blanket.

Now, it was time for a different kind of fight.

THE COOLING BATH had helped with the fever and even managed to conjure back John Thursby's appetite. Ankarette had helped bring him back to her room. Poor Davern's body had been removed, and servants had mopped up the blood. Two Espion stood guard at the door. She'd changed into a fresh gown, and Thomas had brought her a stack of correspondence to read while she watched John Thursby begin to eat. And then eat some more.

He was sitting upright now, no longer as weak as he'd been. Ankarette had always fancied Liona's cooking.

"What are those letters you're reading?"

"Correspondence from the Espion throughout the world." She picked up one missive she'd just set down. "This one's from Legault. Some faction is stirring up trouble against the rulers. That kingdom is prone to violence."

"I knew a Legaultan soldier. Had these quips he'd say in his mother tongue. Kept calling everyone eejits."

Ankarette smiled and set down the paperwork. She walked over to the bed and saw he'd eaten most of his second helping.

"Are you hungry, Ankarette?"

She shook her head. She'd lost her appetite after learning she'd poisoned her friend by accident.

A gentle knock sounded on the door before it opened, revealing Thomas, this time without more letters.

"You aren't finished going through them, are you?" Ankarette asked.

"Actually, yes. But I had more help."

"Who?"

"Lord Bletchley. He offered his services and was quick and efficient. He even corroborated some of the information with news he'd learned from his Genevese contacts."

His tone signified he was impressed and had taken a liking to the man.

"Are you going to recommend him to Eredur?"

"I'd be a fool not to. Especially since I don't want the job. I don't think the king will need much encouragement to choose him in such circumstances as this. I believe Severn pushed for him as well recently." He tilted his head and gazed at John Thursby. "You look a dram better, sir. Well enough to ride?"

"Give me a horse," John Thursby said, his head drooping

with weariness. Bravado. That was all. He'd collapse out of the saddle if he rode on his own.

"Hugh Bardulf is arranging to bring him, I think. Ankarette...can I have a word?"

She rose from the bed and followed him out into the corridor and away from the two guards, both of whom she recognized from the Espion inn on Bridge Street.

Then he leaned back against the wall, folding his arms. His genial expression changed to one of sadness.

"You have news," she surmised.

"Isybelle died. Doctor Spora just came and told the king. There was nothing he could do for her or the child. I wanted to be the one to tell you."

She'd known this was inevitable. But it didn't make the news any easier to hear. She sighed, her emotions so bludgeoned she didn't feel anything yet.

"Dunsdworth sent his knight again to beg the king's permission to leave the city and take his wife's body to the North, to the place of her childhood, and send her over the falls by Dundrennan."

Ankarette remembered jumping off a boulder into the river near those falls. It felt like a fitting end. She wanted to attend the burial rite but knew it would be too dangerous.

"Thank you for telling me," she said.

He nodded, gazing at her in sympathy. "Eredur granted permission for his brother to leave the city and he will go with me by sea to Dundrennan to be there for it. My father-in-law will travel north with Dunsdworth. I hope this puts an end to his ambition. But I doubt it will. Once he's processed his grief, he will react...violently."

Ankarette met his gaze. And knew in her broken heart that he was right.

THIRTY-THREE

VENGEANCE

The fever returned. And, upon examining the crossbow wound once again, Ankarette saw the skin around the sutures was inflamed and leaking pus. She had done all she could to heal him and realized that more help was needed. She had the Espion summon Danner Tye again, and he confirmed her fears. The wound was infected and getting worse. He made another poultice, helped wrap the wound, and said rest was the best remedy in such cases.

"I'm sorry, but there's no more I can do," the apothecary said with a sigh. "You've taken all the steps I would have, Ankarette. For some battlefield injuries, we'd use moldy bread against the injury, but that's not common anymore. Not when we have better medicines here."

"Thank you for coming," Ankarette said, trying not to let the strain reach her voice. She was worried about John Thursby. Terrified that she might lose him too, and so soon after Isybelle.

"It's in the Lady's hands now," Danner said. He nodded to

John Thursby, who was sitting up in Ankarette's bed with a brooding expression. Then he departed.

She reached over and took his hand. The death of the squire was also weighing on her. Davern had been young, ambitious. He'd have made a great Espion. There were no clues about his murder or who had done it. No dagger left behind. No witnesses. The palace guards had been interrogated about who had been wandering the corridors that evening, but they'd noticed nothing. Did that mean the killer had used the Espion tunnels? If so, there was a deceiver among them.

"'*Pride, o flower of warriors, beware of that trap. Do not give way. For a brief while, your strength is in bloom. But it fades quickly. Soon follows illness or the sword to lay thee low. Or a sudden surge of fire, a plume of water, or jabbing blade or javelin from the air. Or repellent age. Soon thy piercing eye will dim. And darken. Death will arrive for thee, dear warrior, to sweep you away over the falls.'*"

She lifted her head, looking at John Thursby's face, feeling menace in the familiar words of the poem this time.

"That was the first poem I shared with you," he said softly with a bittersweet smile.

"I remember. You've shared it with me many times."

"I'm not getting better, Ankarette. And you have duties you must do. Old Rose will take care of me."

"*I* want to take care of you," she insisted, squeezing his hand harder.

He raised her hand to his lips and kissed it. "You have. This place...I'm not going to get better here. It's too quiet. Too much like a crypt. I can smell all the poisons that used to be in here." His lips pressed together.

"I'll take you to my home in the Hermitage, then. The flower boxes are in bloom."

"Aye. That's what I need right now. Winsome smells. But I'll go alone. All I need is a horse."

Ankarette shook her head. "Too risky."

"I'm just a night watchman, Ankarette. No one will pay me any heed."

"You are *my* night watchman, John Thursby. And I won't risk your life. Not after what happened to Isybelle. She died this morning." She hadn't wanted to burden him with it while he was so ill.

John Thursby didn't know the full truth, but he did know they'd been friends. "Sorry, lass. Truly. Can you help me put my shirt on?"

It had been cleaned by one of the laundry girls. She helped him put it on, then smoothed the fabric, admiring the needle-work she'd done to embellish it. Pain, grief, confusion swirled inside her. But love shone through it all. She adored this man, his bluff manners, his character.

"Thomas Mortimer is a good man," John Thursby said. "Good as they come. Has it been difficult being around him again?"

"Do you mean painful?"

"I suppose." He watched her with inquisitive eyes.

"He made his choice a long time ago, and I've grown accustomed to it. The king offered him the job of head of the Espion, but he turned it down. He wants to be a good husband, a good father. To rule the North someday."

John Thursby shook his head and chuckled. "He turned Eredur down? Imagine that."

Ankarette cupped his cheek. "His wife made him promise to. He wants the job but not at the cost of his marriage."

"And what do you want, Ankarette Tryneowy?" he asked her huskily.

"I want to be yours, John Thursby. To share whatever life

we have left together. When I saw my friend stand up to the king's demands, I could not help but feel a little envious. I think it is time I made my own demands."

John Thursby nodded, giving her a tender look. "I think the promise of that can make me well again."

"It better," she replied, hooking her hand behind his neck. They kissed softly, tenderly, and the ache and the worry began to melt away.

The king had promised her a boon. She knew how she intended to claim it.

THE AFTERNOON SUN shone down on the courtyard within Kingfountain. She stood by the horse, checking the straps to make sure they were secure. John Thursby was mounted on one of the palace stallions, which was calm and gentle. He wore his cloak, squinting in the sunlight as he gazed down on her. Bennet was astride another mount, which was more fractious.

"Dunsdworth left Kingfountain hours ago," Ankarette said. "Along with the cortege for his wife. Duke Horwath went with him with some of his men. It will take several days for them to get to Dundrennan for the funeral rites."

"That's all I'll need to recover," John Thursby said. He gripped the saddle horn as his body swayed slightly.

"Be careful," she told him.

He gave a her a slow smile. "I'm not planning any horse races if that's what you're worried about."

"I'll come check on you this evening," Ankarette said,

reaching up and touching his hand. She didn't care that Bennet was watching. She felt emboldened.

"I'll see you then."

Ankarette gave Bennet a stern gaze that implied that she would hold him accountable if anything happened along the way. He would make sure Ankarette's home was safe and secure before fetching Old Rose to tend to John.

He nodded to her, and the two men began a languid ride down into the city.

Ankarette folded her arms, watching them depart, enduring the fear and doubt she felt. After they were both out of sight, she went back into the palace and made her way to the Star Chamber. She found Lord Bletchley in there with Thomas, the two men deep in conversation.

"Ah, Lady Ankarette," Bletchley said, bowing to her. She lacked such a title, but he was being gallant.

Thomas was sitting leisurely in the chair, a sprawled-out pose she'd forgotten was normal for him. "We were talking about what Dunsdworth might do next. It doesn't seem very politick to arrest him for treason straight after his wife's body has been sent over the falls."

"I agree," Bletchley said. "I'd suggested having the Espion raid the warehouse where he's keeping all that wine, to give a pretext for recalling him back to the city. What do you think?"

"We have the evidence of the letter," Ankarette said. "We have the seal. Those alone are enough to condemn him. But since he doesn't know we have them, the investigation could increase his worries about the missing letter. He'll let himself hope we don't have it. Then, when it is *found*, he'll feel his guilt all the more."

"I agree," Bletchley said. "It's good thinking, Ankarette, but that doesn't surprise me in the least. How do you think his brother Severn will react? Do you think he'll be against the verdict of the Assizes?"

"Sev has always been a little unpredictable." Thomas butted in. "But as long as the Assizes are done formally, I don't think he'll contend the outcome. I know he's not motivated by money, but if Dunne is attainted for treason, the bulk of Warrewik's holdings will divert to Nanette, Severn's wife."

"I hadn't considered that," Lord Bletchley said.

Thomas grinned and pushed some letters across the desk to the other man. "You will after you've been doing this for a while."

"Has the king decided, then?" Ankarette asked.

Lord Bletchley flashed a pleased smile, which he quickly suppressed. "He has indeed. Duke Severn has full confidence in me and the king now trusts his brother even more. He will announce my new appointment to his council tomorrow. I hope I can count on your support as well?"

She nodded. She imagined the expense of running the Espion was going to increase. That he'd bribe for people's loyalty more than his predecessors had, especially if he wished to lean on his Genevese connections.

"Thank you," he said, trying to appear meek but failing to disguise how gratified he was by his new responsibility.

"The young lad who was murdered," Bletchley said. "I haven't had any new information on it. I know he was a particular friend of yours, Lady Ankarette. One of Duke Horwath's squires. This act will not go unpunished. I've made inquiries throughout the Espion, naturally, but they are still getting used to things. I will hunt down his killer personally."

He was trying to show a willingness to do her a favor. He wanted her as an ally. That softened her view of him a little. Clashing with others who had authority could be bothersome.

"And that's the hardest part of the job," Thomas said,

shaking his head and looking disappointed. "The double-dealing. The fractured loyalties. I myself pretended to serve Warrewik while secretly serving the king's interests."

Lord Bletchley nodded sagely, his expression showing his deep interest in the topic. "It must have been difficult to maintain the ruse."

"You could say that," Thomas said, giving Ankarette a knowing look. "Well, off to Kennit when the tide comes in. The king and I will be back at Dundrennan before the cortege arrives." His expression turned sad.

"Safe journeys, Thomas," she said.

"I cannot tell you how much your advice has meant to me," Lord Bletchley said. "I hope it won't trouble you if I defer to your wisdom and experience on occasion in the future?"

The flattery was being spread a bit thickly for Ankarette's taste. But she preferred it to the animosity and pride shown by other members of Eredur's council.

"It's no bother. I'm grateful you'll be sitting in that chair instead of me." Thomas stretched and then rose to his feet. "I should say good-bye to the queen. And you," he added, nodding to Ankarette.

"I'll go with you," she said. She'd see him off and then return to her home in the city to check on John Thursby.

"Will you be staying in the palace?" Lord Bletchley asked her.

She shook her head but didn't provide any further explanation. He was still a new quantity to her and needed to prove himself over multiple interactions before she'd trust him like she did Hugh Bardulf, Bennet, and Thomas.

It was a quick journey to the king's private chamber, but the royal couple wasn't present. The servant said the king had already left for the ship and the queen was dining with her children. So they quickly went to the dining hall. The young princes seemed nervous, but Princess Elyse was in a sunny mood. It wasn't a formal dinner, so other nobles weren't in attendance, just the royal family with Captain Barrent and a few guards on duty. Ankarette would also watch over them while Eredur was away.

Ankarette admired the royal children, their good-natured spirits and regal bearing. They shared their parents' good looks, and their richly attired outfits were the best money could buy. Ankarette hovered in the background while Thomas bid a farewell to Elyse. But as the sun slanted to the horizon, she knew he needed to be on his way. And, in the end, he realized it too.

She walked with him to the king's docks, where a ship bound for Kennit was waiting. Ankarette could see Eredur on board already, talking to the ship's captain with good humor. She was grateful for the time she'd had with Thomas. The hurt of the past felt diminished now that she'd fallen in love with John Thursby.

"I wish you well, Ankarette. Truly. I'm glad we've been able to talk. I always feel better leaving knowing you're here."

"I do what I can," she said.

Before mounting the plank, he gave her a friendly hug and then nodded farewell as he climbed aboard. The captain of the vessel seemed eager to be underway, but Eredur gave her a wave.

Ankarette didn't wait until it departed but immediately started her journey across the town. The golden sunset was pleasant to look at. As she crossed the bridge over the falls, she paused to gaze at the majestic sanctuary of Our Lady. The noise of the falls had always been a soothing sound to her, one she associated with home. She passed through the different wards of the city and reached the quiet neighborhood in the

Hermitage. There were no candles lit, no glow revealing anyone was home.

There was no horse there, by design—Bennet had returned, per the arrangement with Hugh Bardulf beforehand, and he'd reported that all had gone well and that her friend was safely ensconced there with the old apothecary. She wished she'd thought to pick up some meat pie for supper, but knowing Old Rose, there was probably soup already cooking in the little kitchen.

She twisted the door handle and opened it, catching the smell of soup in the air.

"It's me," she called out, coming inside and shutting the door. There was a little kettle hanging over some coals, seething with fragrant flavors.

No one answered.

Ankarette felt a throb of uneasiness. "Rose?" she called out.

She heard an unnerving creak in the floorboards upstairs. Ankarette summoned her Fountain magic, which had been rejuvenated since she'd last used it. There were intruders in the house, many of them, armed and skilled.

Turning around, she pulled open the door to retreat outside.

And found one of the Duke of Clare's knights standing there menacingly, sword pointed at her.

THIRTY-FOUR

REVENGE

Ankarette drew a dagger, ready to plunge it into the knight's body. He lowered his blade slightly in response to her dagger.

"Think carefully, Poisoner," the knight said. "Your friend and the old woman are already in our power. But it's *you* Lord Dunsdworth wants to talk to. They will be set free if you come with me. If you don't, you'll all three perish tonight."

She heard the sound of boots thudding down the stairs at the back of the house. They had her boxed in. She sensed from her Fountain magic that there were more knights concealed outside. If she attacked, she could kill many of them. But it was equally likely that they'd leave her bloodied corpse in the street for the Espion to find.

So Dunsdworth wanted to talk to her, did he?

"I thought your master was already gone," Ankarette said, risking a few moments before making a decision whether or not to fight her way clear.

"He left these orders before he departed. And he's close

enough to the city to return once we've assured him you've been captured."

"I'm not that easy to capture," Ankarette said with a voice full of warning.

"We know, Poisoner. He has questions for you. Questions only you can answer. Now, are you going to cooperate, or does this end badly for us all?"

If it were just her life at risk, she might have made a different decision. Dunsdworth had found her secret house. He'd had his servants observing the alley. They'd seen John Thursby and Old Rose go inside. And in his weakened conditioned, the night watchman was no match for them. Had he fought? Was he even alive?

"How do I know my friends are alive?" she said. If they'd already been dispatched, fighting was the better option.

"The night watchman has a festering wound," the knight replied. He lowered the tip of his sword. He was still tense as a crossbow, but she could see he didn't relish the thought of fighting her—and dying. "The old woman, the apothecary. We had to keep her too, so she wouldn't warn you. You have my word as a knight that they're both alive. As I said, it's you my master wants to talk to."

"Do you know why?"

He shook his head.

The other men had joined the confrontation. They all wore the duke's badge. She recognized some of them from previous visits to Isybelle.

Ankarette lifted her ring finger to her mouth and bit off the jewel with the hemlock poison. She felt the little glass orb and pushed it to her cheek with her tongue. The crystal encasing the poison would crack if bitten, and the delicate flesh inside of her mouth would be cut, putting the poison directly into her bloodstream.

The knight swallowed reflexively. "Don't do it," he said, his eyes betraying fear.

"I will take my secrets to the Deep Fathoms," Ankarette said. "If I bite on this, I'll be dead in minutes. I'll come with you, but on my terms. I will not reveal anything I don't want to."

"That is acceptable. And in good faith, I will release the old woman if you come willingly."

"Where is she?"

"They're both at the Arbon. That's where we've been ordered to take you."

"I want my friends released," Ankarette said.

The knight shook his head. "I won't do that, mum. The night watchman's my guarantee you don't do anything rash. If we wanted to harm you, we would have by now. Come with us so I can summon my master."

Ankarette felt the fake jewel in her mouth. She would not betray her king. After all she'd given up for him, to surrender now would make it all meaningless. What she really needed was to stall for time. Surely Hugh Bardulf would send someone to check on her or provide news from the palace. She could rely on him for that.

"What's your name?" Ankarette asked the knight. The captain.

"Rufus," he said. "We met a few years ago."

"You're a man of honor?"

"I am."

"Then I'll go with *you* as my hostage. If any of these men betray me, you'll be the first to die. And I'll kill as many of them as I can before we're all dead. Is that clear?" She raised her voice loudly enough for the others to witness.

Rufus nodded and sheathed his sword. He offered her his arm. How gallant. She stepped outside, noticed the two other men flanking the door, and accepted the proffered arm but pointed her knife at his ribs.

"Let's not dally," the knight said to the others. "To the Arbon."

It wasn't long before they were all standing in front of the porter door at the back of the Arbon. None of the knights carried lanterns or torches, but the noise of their hauberk rings and the rattle of armor was deafening in the dark night. She kept a firm grip on Sir Rufus's arm, the tip of her dagger a hair's breadth from his ribs. They paused before the gate.

"Bring out the woman," Rufus ordered the keeper. Ankarette recognized the man and watched as he disappeared and went into the manor house. A few minutes later, Ankarette saw Old Rose being escorted by a single soldier. She looked frightened.

"Is John Thursby all right?" Ankarette asked her.

"Ankarette? Thank the Lady! Yes, he's well enough. They didn't harm us."

"How is his fever?"

"It's come back again."

Ankarette prodded Rufus with the dagger. "Let her go as you promised."

"Release her," the knight said.

The guard at the door unlocked it, and the hinges creaked as it opened. Ankarette watched Old Rose take a few tentative steps outside, looking at Ankarette questioningly.

"Return to your shop and stay there," Rufus said to her, "if you know what's good for you."

Old Rose nodded meekly, but Ankarette saw the gleam of defiance in her eye. She wasn't happy about this at all. But she kept her feelings to herself and hurried down the street, away from the gate.

"In we go," Rufus said, gesturing to the gate.

As soon as they were all inside, the man at the door closed and locked it.

And that's when the bloom of Fountain magic from Lord Hux revealed itself in the small courtyard full of dead plants and broken cobbles. Of course he'd be there. Of course he'd arranged for her capture. This also explained why Dunsdworth was so confident in his ability to quickly get back to King-fountain.

"You betrayed me," Ankarette said. She jabbed the dagger into her prisoner's side. Rufus coughed in surprise, and the poison incapacitated him instantly.

"Take her," Hux ordered, stepping into sight. "I need her alive."

In that cramped space, surrounded by Dunsdworth's men, Ankarette knew she didn't stand a chance. But she was determined to take as many of them with her as she could. And she would *not* let Hux have any of her secrets. She fought against her captors, using her skill with blade and boot. After all she'd suffered, she fought with cruelty and skill, stabbing, blinding, kicking. But they overpowered her, tackling her to the ground, wrenching the dagger from her grip.

She sensed Lord Hux coming closer and bit down on the vial of glass in her mouth. She felt it pop, felt the bitter taste flood her mouth. Felt the sting of pain as the shard cut her cheek. It tasted like spoiled carrots or parsnips. That surprised her, although it made sense that she didn't know—victims didn't survive the dose long enough to describe its flavor. This was how Bensen Nichols had perished. And it was how Ankarette would perish too.

She swallowed the bitter taste and stopped fighting. The weight pressing on her made it nearly impossible to breathe.

The poison began its work immediately. Her muscles began to spasm.

"She ate poison," one of the soldiers said worriedly.

"Tilt her head," Lord Hux answered, coming to crouch nearby.

Ankarette knew she'd be dead in minutes. Some of the guards backed away, relieving pressure from her back and legs. She reached for a hairpin, but a man grabbed her wrist and arm and wrestled it down again.

Hux was crouching in front of her. He had something in his hand, what appeared to be a little tuft of moss. She'd never seen the plant before.

The pain in her stomach intensified. Wave after wave of anguish spread through her as her heart began to thump erratically.

"Open her mouth," Hux said. One of the soldiers twisted her head and squeezed her cheeks to force her lips open.

Hux put the moss inside her mouth. It tasted strange but sweet. It had a honeyed smell.

Immediately she felt a rush of magic surge through her. Magic that stopped the hemlock instantly. Magic that healed her injuries. She even felt the sickness, which had been caused by Lord Hux years before, vanish. It was like part of her body that had been clenched tightly had now opened. Health and vitality were restored to her. Energy too. She felt she could fight off a hundred men.

Lord Hux lifted his other hand and blew powder in her face.

Nightshade. Her sense of awareness, of self, began to alter.

IN THE POISONER SCHOOL, they'd all been exposed to the powder. She knew the effects and the aftereffects. Ankarette's sense of her surroundings had changed. She was bound in a chair, her wrists secured behind her back and ankles tied together with rope. The faint memory of having spoken something came to her mind, but she couldn't remember the question or her answer. She blinked rapidly, seeing unnatural whorls of color come in halos from the lamp.

She smelled wine. Lots of it. She blinked again, trying to clear her thoughts. The cellar at the Arbon. Was that where she was?

"Ah, I see you're coming around."

It was Lord Hux. She stiffened with fear. She probed her cheek for the glass vial, but it was gone. Hadn't she crushed it with her teeth? But there was no cut against the soft inner flesh of her mouth. She felt good actually. Wonderful even. Where was she? One of the aftereffects of nightshade was disorientation. A loss of memory.

She'd already revealed things. But she didn't know what.

Lifting her head, she saw Lord Hux standing near her. She saw the cylinder stuffed in his belt. The one he'd used earlier. It took several moments for her foggy brain to remember its name.

"You've been most helpful, Ankarette. I've learned what I came here to learn. I know the fountain where you hid Lewis's ring. Now I can be restored to his good graces again. And Devereaux, of course, will pay the price for his treachery. This little adventure has been costly. But it's been a productive evening, wouldn't you agree?"

"I hate you," Ankarette whispered, wishing she had the strength to break the rope. She felt her poisoner ring was gone. She imagined Hux had been thorough in his search and had completely disarmed her of her other weapons as well.

"I know, my dear. And I can live with that knowledge. How do you feel, though? The pangs from the poison I gave you earlier are gone now."

His words made her mind foggy again. But she *did* feel different. The constant ache of her lower abdomen was gone, after all these years, and the relief nearly made her choke with emotion.

"How does it feel to be whole again?" Hux said. "The captain you stabbed in the side is completely uninjured now. This is what I promised to give you if you joined me. You see? I wasn't lying."

"You think I will join you now?" Ankarette said, gasping with disbelief.

"No. I *know* you will not. But I did want you to remember what it felt like to be whole again." He came closer and stroked the edge of her cheek with his finger. He was conflicted about her still. "You could have been the best of us. My protégé. My equal. You could have subverted kingdoms, principalities, gained power beyond your comprehension in this world or others."

Others? What did he mean by that?

His gaze hardened. "You could have had your night watchman too. Could have shared his love in ways you've never known. Ah, Ankarette. It saddens me that you've chosen to give up. All because you believe loyalty is worth the cost." His eyes flashed with menace. "Well, then. Drink the reward of loyalty. You will find the taste to be bitter in the end."

He produced a vial from his pocket. She recognized it instantly. He'd forced her to drink its noxious ichor before. This was the poison that had shriveled up her womb and stopped her monthly flux.

"No," Ankarette moaned, straining against her bonds. If she was finally free of the malevolent power of the poison he'd given her, he was about to dose her with it again.

"Trust is worth more to me than loyalty," Hux said as he unscrewed the lid. "You can buy loyalty. A man may be loyal out of fear. You cannot buy trust." He was standing so close that she could smell the oily liquid once again. It made her gag involuntarily.

He dug his fingers into her hair and yanked her head back. She wrenched against her ropes, but it only tightened them, cutting off circulation to her fingers. Ankarette fought against the vial still as he pressed it against her mouth. Panic, desperation, fury—all availed her nothing.

She felt the liquid enter her mouth, trickling to her throat, where she tried to stop it. He didn't ask for her allegiance. He didn't try to tempt her. What he'd learned from using the nightshade must have exposed her deepest self to him. And whatever he'd learned had convinced him they could never work together. They were implacable enemies to the last.

She tried to spit it out, but he torqued her hair violently until she reflexively swallowed.

And wept as the poison burned down her throat once more.

"There," he sighed, satisfied. "You've drunk it all up. Someday, when your king is dead and the Ceredigion you know and love is no more, just remember that I can help you. That I will *always* be able to help you. If you beg me to."

He screwed the lid back onto the vial and stuffed it back in his pocket. From another pocket, he withdrew a familiar-looking vial. The horrid tincture that kept her alive...barely. A fresh supply. He inserted it into her bodice front, plunging his finger into the gap to embed it deeply. She shuddered with revulsion at his touch. Then he drew the Tay al-Ard from his belt and invoked its power.

He was gone in an instant, leaving her in the wine cellar alone, choking back sobs.

CHAPTER
THIRTY-FIVE

MOCK ASSIZES

How much time passed in the cellar, Ankarette didn't know. She was still working on the knots when the sound of footsteps came from above. The tromping of boots. Then the glare of lantern light stung her eyes as Captain Rufus arrived with two other men. As Lord Hux had said, he showed no sign of injury from when she'd stabbed him.

"Release me," Ankarette said forcefully. "Or you will be accountable to the king for what you do."

"Bring her upstairs," Rufus said to the men. They grabbed her by the arms and hauled her away from the chair. The captain had a greenish cast to his skin and haunted eyes. He was the one holding the lantern and leading the way.

She knew the configuration of the Arbon and realized they were taking her to the great hall. Her ankles were still bound, so they dragged her down the corridor, her legs useless to her. Rufus opened the door, and she saw the hearth fire raging.

Dunsdworth was seated behind a table, which had been

dragged to the center of the room. There was a bench before it, and sitting on that bench was John Thursby, also trussed up. She saw the sweat stains on his tunic, his glistening skin. He was feverish. The enormous fireplace was roaring with oak and cedar logs.

Dunsdworth had dark circles under his eyes. He looked awful. When he saw her, his lips twitched into an expression of scorn.

When Rufus pointed to the bench, the two soldiers hoisted Ankarette onto it, seating her near John Thursby but not close enough to touch him.

"The Assizes will commence," Dunsdworth said formally, "now that the accused are here. State your names."

There was a clerk of sorts at a nearby table, quill in hand, an ink bottle near his wrist.

"You have no authority to conduct the Assizes," Ankarette contested. "They are under the king's purview."

"For the record, write Ankarette Tryneowy, poisoner of Kingfountain," Dunsdworth said to the clerk.

The scribe hastily did so. "A-And the other?" he stammered. He looked very nervous. He should be. What he was doing was treasonous.

"John Thursby, night watchman of the Hermitage ward," Dunsdworth said. "Her *accomplice*."

John Thursby chuckled to himself. He twisted his neck a little and met her gaze. The glare from the fire danced in his eyes. He'd had nothing to do with her assignment from the king. Nothing at all. But that didn't matter. This was revenge.

"Release us, Dunne. You are in enough trouble as it is," Ankarette said.

He ignored her words. "You are accused of poisoning Lady Isybelle, my wife. Your friend. Dregs of mandrake were discovered in the cup she drank from. Identified by smell by a local apothecary." He glared at her. "Do you deny the charge?"

"This is an illegal proceeding," Ankarette said. "In defiance of the king's orders. Once again, release us. I answer to the King of Ceredigion."

His nostrils flared when she invoked Eredur's title. "Very well, for I *am* the true king of Ceredigion. That means you are under my authority. And so is this meeting. Do you deny poisoning my wife?" His eyes were murderous as he said the words. There were no wine cups on the table in front of him. If he had stopped drinking, his body must be experiencing acute tortures caused by his past overindulgence. His reason was clouded by revenge and the cravings of his body.

"I answer to Eredur Argentine, the true king of Ceredigion."

Dunsdworth leaned back in his chair. His gaze softened, his fingers tapping the tabletop. "Did you know I watched her die? Watched that incompetent doctor minister to her. And then she was gone. A candle snuffed out." He made a sad little laugh. "I'm sure it was an accident, Ankarette. That mandrake was meant for me. She was so relieved when we returned from the banquet, you know. The babe was causing her pains that night. She just wanted a little sip of wine to dull it. She'd told me that climbing the stairs. Just a little drink of sweet wine to help her fall asleep." He wasn't looking at her, his eyes seeing the horrors he'd witnessed. "And there was the cup, right where I'd left it. She liked the sweetness, she said. And drank every drop."

His eyes focused again. His upper lip quivered. "She did sleep a little while. Then the convulsions started. The spasms. I sent for you. But you didn't come. He said you were *away.*" He shook his head. "Another lie. Another trick."

"I am sorry Isybelle died," Ankarette said. She felt her

throat clench with sorrow, and she struggled to steady her voice. But the danger was tempering. She had to think if she were going to survive. "She was my friend."

Dunsdworth leaned forward and slammed his fist on the table. "Your friend! How dare you call her that! You murdered her. And you were trying to murder me. On my brother's orders, no doubt. Well, Ankarette Tryneowy, I find you guilty of the charge, and I condemn you. I have every bit as much royal blood in my veins as my brother does. I am an Argentine as well. You poisoned my wife, and you will die for it. Unless, as everyone says, you are truly Fountain-blessed and you survive the plunge off the falls."

Ankarette saw the madness in his eyes. There was no reasoning with him. There was no hope of convincing him to stop. She glanced at John Thursby, head hung low, stunned but not surprised. She glanced at Captain Rufus, who was caught up in the insanity of the moment. If he fulfilled his master's orders, he would also be found guilty of treason.

"Captain," Ankarette breathed. "You have the power to stop this. You will all face the king's justice if you go through with this."

"I am the king's justice!" Dunsdworth roared, rising from his chair. His eyes were livid as he came around the table and towered above her. "The throne was meant to be mine. It was *always* supposed to be mine! It's your fault I was robbed of it. Captain! Drag them to the river. I am coming to watch. I have two boats already prepared."

"Two, m-my lord?" Rufus said.

"One for her and the other for her lover," Dunsdworth snarled. "Now you'll know what it feels like to lose someone dear to you. And you'll watch him go first. Take them!"

The indecision in Rufus's eyes lasted a moment longer, but then he acquiesced. Soldiers were summoned into the room again, and both she and John Thursby were hauled to their feet. Ankarette could hardly believe what was happening. More time was needed. Time for the Espion to be alerted.

"Is this what Lord Hux promised you?" Ankarette said sharply. "That he'd make you king after all? He cannot fulfill his promises."

Dunsdworth leered at her. "He said you'd come, and you did. Everything he's promised me has come to pass. I *will* be king. And I have my own poisoner now. I don't need you."

Ankarette struggled against her bonds, which were starting to loosen, but there was nowhere for her to go. She and John Thursby were hoisted off their feet and carried. Real and fervent panic jolted through her limbs. Had Rufus known this would happen when he'd come to capture her? No, she suspected he had obeyed his master's orders without knowing Dunsdworth's true intentions. Now he was like a man badly in debt, rolling the dice once more to try to free himself from a bitter outcome. If his master became king, he wouldn't be punished for helping execute the queen's poisoner. If not, he'd learn firsthand what her fate had felt like.

She tried to quiet her mind as they carried her into the dark streets. There was a faint glimmer of dawn coming. The streets were quiet, save the noise of their boots, the jangle of their armor, the huff of their labored breathing from having to carry their victims.

Then she noticed that John Thursby was whispering something, over and over. The next moment, she realized it was a poem.

"*Death is not easily escaped from by anyone. All of us with souls, earth dwellers and children of men, must make our way there. All must make our way there. Death is not easily escaped from by anyone. All of us with souls...with souls...earth dwellers and children of men, must make our way there. All must make our way there.*"

He was reciting the lines over and over. Trying to comfort both of them as they faced their fate. He'd always found comfort in poems. It caused her eyes to burn and throat to thicken. She knew death was not the end. There was the Deep Fathoms, a place of rest and relief. There, perhaps, they could be together.

Dunsdworth and Captain Rufus led the way, the steady captain holding the lamp. She heard the noise of the river, the ever-present murmur of the falls.

"Over there," Dunsdworth said, pointing. Ankarette craned her neck, saw them approach an alley next to a warehouse that, if she could judge by the smell, contained barrels and barrels of wine.

The soldiers hoisted their prisoners, grunting with the effort of carrying them so far, and brought them to the edge of the alley where a dock had been built. It was small and tidy, and two canoes did indeed wait there.

"Death is not easily escaped from by anyone," John Thursby murmured. He'd settled on that line now. Repeating it over and over.

"Put him in first," Dunsdworth ordered. "I want her to watch him go in. Now!"

"John Thursby," she said, her voice thick.

He stopped his incantation, turning his neck to look at her, as the soldiers carried him to the first canoe. He, too, was bound with ropes.

"I love you," she said.

She saw his broken smile as he looked back at her. He didn't seem afraid. No, he'd been death's silent companion for many years. He was the most comfortable at night. On his watch.

Oh, blessed Lady, spare him!

"And I you, lass. Always."

Her heart seized with pain as she watched the soldiers lower him into the boat and out of her sight. But she could still hear him. Still heard the words. *"Death is not easily escaped from by anyone. All must make our way there. All must make our way there."*

Ankarette felt tears trickling down her cheeks. The two men holding her lowered her legs to the dock planks, where she knelt, her skirts taut against her skin. Her heart was breaking as she watched the men heft John Thursby's canoe into the water.

"See you in the Deep Fathoms, my love," she whispered.

The splash of the boat came as the men tossed the heavy burden into the river. The current swept it away in a rush.

"Put her in," Dunsdworth ordered. His jaw was clenched. He looked fearless, as if there would be no consequences to his actions. He truly believed himself invincible.

The two men lifted her by the arms and lowered her into the boat. The struts were painful against her back.

Dunsdworth towered over her, holding a bottle of wine in his hand now. He twisted free the cork and then took several heavy gulps from it. A sigh of relief came as the wine went down his throat. He lowered the bottle, but she knew he'd end up drinking all of it. He'd been saving it for this moment. He wanted to remember it. "My wife is dead because of you," he rasped. "You failed, Ankarette. Now embrace my revenge." He knelt down by the edge of the canoe. "I should have done this long ago," he said spitefully, the stench of his wine-infused breath floating down on her, making her want to vomit.

He straightened, gave a jerk of his chin, and the soldiers grunted and lifted her canoe.

A feeling of weightlessness came as they hurled her into the river. Water splashed on her face when the canoe landed.

She heard the roar of the falls distinctly now, coming closer and closer as she gritted her teeth and fought against her bonds. The ropes on her wrists were finally beginning to give, loosening under the strain and pressure of her movements. She'd been trained to escape bonds. But never had she needed to do it so urgently.

Jerking hard one last time, she freed her wrists and quickly unraveled the ropes. The confinement of the canoe hedged her in, but she managed to sit up, just enough to see the stunning sanctuary of Our Lady, its tall spires lit by torches in the night. It sat on an island in the midst of the churning river, at the head of the falls. The palace was to her right—dark, foreboding. Was the king still on the ship with Tom heading north to the fortress of Dundrennan for Isybelle's funeral, or had he already landed? He was too far away to learn about her plight. Too far to save her.

The blush of dawn made it possible to see farther downriver. She'd freed herself from the rope, but the pull of the river was merciless. Without King Lewis's ring, she was helpless against it. And that ring was probably on Lord Hux's hand by now since he'd learned where to find it. Maybe he'd forced her to take him there, as he'd done to John Thursby in the dungeon. Now that Lord Hux had gotten what he wanted from Dunsdworth, he'd leave the king's rebellious brother to his fate, clinging to his dream of being King of Ceredigion.

The gentle duke had told her he'd watched from the shore as the Maid had gone over the falls. And she'd survived.

It was her turn to watch someone she loved go over the falls, helpless to prevent it. Gripping the sides of her canoe, she gazed at John Thursby's canoe as it rushed midriver and then disappeared over the edge. Her heart heaved in her chest. Her chin quivered with a suppressed sob. *No. No. Not like this.*

He was gone.

Ankarette lay down in her canoe, bracing her boots against

the sides, gripping the struts with her fingertips. She clenched her eyes shut, feeling the thrill and terror of the boat as it raced her toward the edge.

Then she, too, was falling.

Falling.

One breath. Two. And then everything shattered.

Some things rush into existence, like the hasty delivery bed of a woman in labor who'd born children frequently, while others rush out of it. Change and fluctuation are constantly remaking the world, just as the incessant progression of time makes up eternity. Our lives are moments spent in a river. Which of the things around us should we value when none of them can offer a firm foothold?

Love. Love is the only thing that endures in the Deep Fathoms.

— ANKARETTE TRYNEOWY

THIRTY-SIX

SAYING GOOD-BYE

The canoe shattered as it struck the river below. Because Ankarette was lying down in it, she felt her neck crack with the impact, felt the pain shoot down her legs, up into her chest. The tumultuous force of the water-fall shoved her under, where the churning, relentless waters made it impossible to tell which way was up or down. Breathing was out of the question. Her eye sockets throbbed, her ears could hear nothing but an omnipresent roar. She struggled to swim, seeking to get away from the deluge. The need for air became desperate. Was that the sunrise she saw through the foam? She reached, trying to pull herself through the torrent.

A hand grasped hers. And then she was standing in a place she'd never been. The pain of the violent fall was gone. She was on a beach in a strange land, her gown no longer wet. John Thursby had a halo of light around his head, as if the sun had already risen partway into the sky and fixed behind him. She recognized the feel of his hand, the rough calluses. The tenderness.

"Ankarette," he said gently.

She was astonished by the feeling of peace and tranquility that overshadowed the fear and panic of moments before. There was no waterfall now. Her boots were on wet sand. The surf crashed to her right. Ahead, farther along the beach, she saw a strange protuberance of rock jutting out, like a giant natural wall. The surf crashed against it, spraying foam and salt water up its height but not over. She had traveled to many countries, seen many shores—but never one that looked like this.

"Come," John Thursby said. "Don't you feel it? We're supposed to go there."

She *did* feel it. A gentle tugging at her soul, a desire to walk along the beach to that rocky wall. Something beckoned to her beyond it. With that thought, they were walking side by side, hand in hand.

"This is the Deep Fathoms," she said, understanding swelling in her heart. "We've died."

"This isn't at all what I thought death would feel like," the night watchman said, chuckling softly. He looked carefree. Relaxed. Rested. She gave him a smile, leaning into him as they walked together along the shore. The crashing surf ahead didn't terrify her. She felt safe. She looked back and didn't see any footprints in the wet sand. Strange. But lovely. An uncanny sensation whispered for her to go back.

But all her worries were gone. The things that had nagged at her with anxiety suddenly felt unimportant. She thought of Eredur and Elyse. Her mother. Thomas. Bennet. She had fond feelings for all of them, but as she walked along that beach, holding hands with John Thursby, she felt as carefree as a young maid in the first bloom of love.

The pain inside her was also gone. No poison racked this spirit self. No broken spine. The feelings she had now were more ephemeral. Wistful. Satisfactory. The feeling of the Fountain was all around her, gentle and loving. In the mortal world, it had been so difficult to hear it sometimes. Here, in the world beyond, it was omnipresent.

As they approached the wall of rock, the tide went out, retreating back to the sea. Something was repelling it. She didn't understand how she knew it, but she sensed it.

"Do you see that little girl?" John Thursby said in wonder, gaze fixed ahead.

Ankarette did. There was a young girl, perhaps eight years old, with golden tresses hanging loose over her shoulders. Her gown was pretty, simple, and she walked barefoot on the sand toward them. Ankarette sensed the girl's Fountain magic radiating like a beacon. It made her want to shield her eyes from its radiance.

The surf roiled in the distance, the ocean yearning to come back and smash against the odd wall. But it was restrained, prevented by a higher power from coming back. Wave upon wave built behind it as the ripples of the sea joined together, but they were held back by an invisible wall that was mystifying in its power. The only way she could tell that wall was there was when the waves dispersed around its shell.

"Hello," the girl said, smiling at them. She had serious eyes but a kind smile. "Welcome."

"Who are you?" Ankarette asked with poignant curiosity. She felt she should know but didn't understand *how* she could have known her.

"My name is Sinia," the little girl said. "You are Ankarette Tryneowy. And you are John Thursby."

"Hello," the night watchman said reverently.

Ankarette's feelings began to shift. The sense of well-being was leaving her. She felt the little girl's magic repelling her.

"You have to go back," Sinia said to Ankarette. "Your time

isn't over. There is something else you must do to prepare for the coming of the Dreadful Deadman. For the rebridging of the worlds. You must go back to Kingfountain."

That's what she had felt. A preternatural awareness that she was going to be separated from John Thursby. Sadness engulfed her.

"I'm ready to die," Ankarette pleaded. "Please. Can I not come now?"

Sinia looked at her with serious eyes. "I can see the future, Ankarette. I can see what is coming. You are needed still. The little boy you helped deliver at Tatton Hall is special. He will help the Dreadful Deadman return. He will help open the breach between the worlds again. You saved his life once, and you must do so again. Your work is not yet finished."

I don't want to go back, Ankarette thought, her sorrow growing, but somehow she could not weep. In this state, she could not.

"You have sacrificed so much for the Fountain, Ankarette. But there is more it needs from you. That babe will become a little boy. And he will need you. You will come back here when your time is done. I promise you. There are other friends waiting for you here. Your father. The gentle duke of La Marche. The Maid of Donremy. Squire Davern. They all paid the price the Fountain asked of them. John Thursby will be waiting for you too."

She squeezed his hand, feeling like they were being tugged apart. Always, they were being tugged apart.

John Thursby stepped in front of her. He reached out and cupped her cheek. "I was dying anyway, Ankarette. I held on as long as I could. I felt the call of the Deep Fathoms and refused to answer it. It's my time."

"I don't want to leave you," Ankarette whispered huskily.

He stroked his fingers through her hair. "It's a parting, that is all. I will wait here for you. I will wait until you return. Then nothing can separate us."

That thought was worth any treasure. "D-Do you promise?" she pleaded.

He nodded and leaned down and kissed her gently on the mouth. "There is nothing to fear in death, Ankarette. It's a...a relief."

She knew he was right. She knew Sinia was right. Part of her still balked because she didn't want to return to her body. To the pain that was waiting to torment her. But she would do it. For a little babe she hardly knew.

She pulled John Thursby into a hug, pressing her cheek against his chest. The pull of the mortal world was growing stronger. Water lapped around her ankles.

"I love you, John Thursby," she murmured.

"Always," he answered gently.

The little girl, Sinia, stood by him, taking his hand. Ankarette felt the tug of the water, the same sensation she got when she stood barefoot on the beach and felt the surf retreating and sucking sand between her toes. She was being pulled away from them, dragged off by the mysterious tide of the otherworldly realm.

And then she was choking, vomiting water. Her hair and dress were heavy. She was listless, powerless, in excruciating pain from her neck and back. Dirt and small rocks pressed against her cheek. Each breath was a torture, but she endured it, unable to move. Her body had floated downriver. She heard some ravens squawking nearby.

She tried opening her eyes. It took several tries to succeed. She was breathing laboriously, aching, wincing. Weeping. She saw a little girl with golden tresses standing near her, hunched down. She looked...familiar. At first she thought her mind was playing tricks on her, but then she remembered her visit to the Deep Fathoms. She even remembered the little girl's name.

"Over there! She's over there! Hurry!"

Ankarette recognized the voice as Hugh Bardulf's. There was birdsong amidst the raven squawks. Was it midmorning?

It felt cool. Actually, she was shivering. Her fingertips were pruned.

When the Espion arrived, Ankarette saw the little girl was gone. A butterfly with blue wings was perched on a piece of driftwood. No...a broken part of the canoe she'd been inside. The blue butterfly flittered away, but it felt significant.

"She's alive?" Bennet gasped in disbelief. "She survived the falls?"

"Praise the Lady of the Fountain," Hugh said reverently.

"DRINK SOME MORE BROTH," the queen urged, pressing the bowl to Ankarette's lips. The saltiness was pleasant and soothing. There were chunks of carrots and celery in it too, chopped into tiny bits. Ankarette's back ached with each swallow. But she needed nourishment. Her body was healing, though she wasn't sure her heart ever would. The poison Hux had made her drink the second time was working on her again. When he'd dosed her with the strange mossy plant, she'd felt like she'd completely recovered. Now the poison was taking its toll again. She guessed the temporary reprieve had prolonged her life by several years. But it would, in the end, kill her.

"Thank you," Ankarette said, laying her head down on the pillow. She was back in the tower again. Her place of convalescence. Away from the tumult and noise of the castle. Alone with her thoughts, her grief, her ghosts. The queen spent time with her every day. Hours, actually.

"I heard some shouting last night," Ankarette commented. "Was there a riot in Kingfountain?"

"There was," Elyse said. "Dunsdworth started it. He and his knights tried to attack the castle. It was a pathetic attempt, actually. Disorganized. Reckless. I think he was expecting the people of the city to rise up, and when they didn't...he began to panic."

"Is Eredur back?"

Elyse shook her head. "But Severn arrived with his forces from Beestone. When he saw the commotion, he acted promptly and put the insurrection down swiftly. Dunsdworth is in Holistern Tower at the moment. His men have all been arrested."

"I'm glad to hear it," Ankarette said. She winced as she shifted in the bed.

Elyse looked at her with compassion. "I'm so sorry for what he did to you. To John. It's unforgivable. Stiev Horwath arrived last night as well. After Dunsdworth disappeared from the honor guard, he came rushing back to the palace to protect us. But Severn had already taken care of it."

Dunsdworth was now fully implicated in the treason. Not only did they have evidence of his previous treachery, but he'd compounded his guilt with the mock trial and executions, followed by his attempted insurrection.

Ankarette had asked the queen to conceal the fact that she was still alive. It was a secret she wanted kept even from Lord Bletchley, the new head of the Espion. After all she'd endured, she was ready to stop playing a prominent role in supporting the kingdom. It would take months for her to heal. Even longer to mourn her losses.

Ankarette heard the sound of little footsteps coming up the

tower steps. A child. The memory of the little girl on the beach was fading. She couldn't even remember her name for a moment, but then it came back and she hoped she wouldn't forget it.

The new arrival was the princess, named after her mother.

"Papa is home," she said breathlessly.

THIRTY-SEVEN

THE END OF DUNSDWORTH ARGENTINE

Ankarette gritted her teeth as she climbed the tower steps to her room. She still needed one hand on the wall to steady herself, but each day she completed the task of going down the steps to fetch her food and then climbing back up again. Her back was healing, slowly, its pain mingling with the acute sensations in her stomach from Lord Hux's poison. It had been over a month since she'd gone over the falls. A month since John Thursby had gone to the Deep Fathoms. That was the worst ache of all.

As she finished the last step, she heard the door at the bottom of the shaft open and someone start up. Listening, she recognized the lightness of the tread and knew the queen was coming for her daily visit. She'd be coming with news. The Assizes had been going on for weeks, and today was the day Duke Horwath would pronounce judgment. This was the moment Ankarette had been waiting for.

She twisted the door handle to the tower room and went inside, her heart pounding fast as she massaged her neck and lower back and then did some stretching.

Then she walked over to the little table where the Wizr set was laid out and sat down in the wooden chair to await her friend.

Only three members of the Espion knew she was alive. Hugh Bardulf, Bennet, and Giselle. The palace cook, Liona, also knew, as did her husband, Drew. They were the ones who left food for her, and she would sometimes go to the kitchen after all the other scullions were gone and sit by the fire. It was better if others believed she were dead. If Lord Hux ever returned and used his Fountain magic inside the palace, she would know.

And she would kill him. No matter what, she would kill him.

The sound of the steps grew louder as Elyse made it to the top. She knocked first, even though she didn't need to, and entered. The smell of her perfume crept inside with her. The queen looked relieved.

"Was the verdict not to your liking?" Ankarette asked, tilting her head. Although she could not suppress the pain in her body, she could limit how much she revealed it in her expression.

Elyse took the chair opposite her and stared down at the set—they'd started a game together on her last visit and hadn't finished. The queen had never beaten her yet.

"Dunsdworth was found guilty of treason, conspiracy, murder, and misprision."

"Misprision?" Ankarette said, feeling a smile tug at her mouth.

"I think the official charge was 'misprision in the highest degree.' Guilty on all charges."

Ankarette nodded. Part of her wished she could have observed the trial. The queen had come every day to talk about the witnesses, the evidence, as well as additional matters revealed during the investigation. Lord Bletchley had been thorough, and had uncovered even more information, which had made the evidence overwhelming.

Dunsdworth had defended himself during the Assizes. Had made outlandish accusations that Eredur's children had been born out of wedlock due to a prior agreement of marriage. He'd claimed a deconeus had told him the information, but when that man was questioned and brought to the court, the claim was denied. There was no defense in the end. Dunsdworth's crimes were undeniable. He'd blustered about his wife being poisoned and claimed he'd had the right to execute Ankarette and John Thursby. That act alone had invoked Eredur's full wrath upon his return from Dundrennan. He had pardoned men for treason before. But he would not pardon his brother. He would not banish him.

"So Horwath judged him guilty on all counts. Did anyone speak on his behalf?"

"No one did."

"I'm not surprised."

The queen moved a piece on the board. "He was defiant to the end. Denounced the justice as false. Said he was being persecuted by those who were jealous. He claimed the Fountain would prove his innocence. That he would not perish going over the falls. That your death, Ankarette, proved your guilt." She frowned as she said that last part, showing the bridled rage behind her lovely eyes.

"Is Eredur going to send him over the falls, then?" It was the usual penalty for treason.

"He will go over the falls. But only after he is dead. Eredur wants him killed in Holistern Tower. Because of his crimes, the crown will reclaim the duchy of Clare. The boy cannot inherit anything. He'll be kept in the palace as a ward of the crown.

The Warrewik inheritance will go to Nanette and Severn." Her expression darkened as she said it.

"That puts a lot of wealth and power in Severn's hands," Ankarette observed.

Elyse nodded, deep in thought. "Too much. But there's nothing that can be done about it."

Ankarette moved another piece on the board. "Threat."

Elyse blinked in surprise. "I didn't see that one coming."

"How has the verdict affected Severn and Eredur's relationship?"

"They're both heartsick over Dunsdworth's fall. I think this experience has strengthened the bonds between them."

Just because there was peace between Eredur and Severn now didn't mean that would always be the case. She knew what would happen in the future. Nanette would be queen one day. She just didn't know how it would happen.

The two continued to play the Wizr game, passing the time in quiet for a little while. "What of Devereaux? His witness against Dunsdworth must have been particularly damaging."

"It was. Forgiveness is not possible, but mercy is. Eredur is sending him to the fortress at Callait. It will stop him from marauding again, and it also gets him away from Lord Hux. Brugia, as you know, is no friend to the poisoner. In time...we will see."

Ankarette finished the game. "Threat. And mate."

Elyse shook her head and sighed. "I must practice more, I think. Maybe against a child?" She gave a self-deprecating smile. Then she reached over and put her hand atop Ankarette's. "How is your heart? It's been nearly a month since we lost Isybelle and you lost John."

Ankarette was grateful to be asked. Some days, she hadn't wanted to talk about it at all. Other days, she dreamed both of them were still alive, and she'd awaken with a surge of hope before the truth came crashing down and made her weep.

"The pain of loss never truly leaves," Ankarette said. "When my father died all those years ago, it hurt a great deal in the first weeks. The pain ebbs and flows. It will for this as well." Despite having seen evidence of the plant that could cure her, she no longer desired to seek it out. The East Kingdoms were too far away. Besides, such a voyage would separate her from the royal family, whom she had a duty to protect. And a little girl named Sinia had told her what her future was to be.

"I've lost family too," the queen said. "We bear the grief as best we can."

"You don't have to keep visiting me every day," Ankarette said. "I need to sell the house in the city. It...it would be too painful to go there now."

The queen nodded, still holding her gaze. "This is your home. You are part of our family."

"You've always made me feel so," Ankarette said softly.

They sat in companionable silence. But eventually the chair became more and more uncomfortable, and Ankarette rose and began to pace the room, pressing on her lower back to relieve some of the discomfort.

"I should be going," Elyse finally said. "Are you certain you wish to remain up here? There are other rooms in the castle that require fewer steps to reach."

"But so few know about this one," Ankarette said. "It's steeped in history. Tell Liona I'm grateful for her bread. And for Drew hauling up the fuel to keep me warm at night."

"I imagine it can be drafty up here. Well, I'll be going."

"Thank you."

Elyse was about to leave but Ankarette stopped her.

"How is Eredur going to execute Dunsdworth?"

"Lord Bletchley is going to handle it. Drowning, I think.

That way, when his body is recovered from the river, he will show those signs."

Ankarette furrowed her brow. "He doesn't want me to do it?"

Elyse shook her head. "I wouldn't let him ask you. You've done enough, Ankarette. You saved my children, my husband, and myself from murder. You safeguarded the crown. We cannot ask you to do this. Not when you are still so weak."

It was a kindness. But Ankarette would not have it. This was one assignment she *needed*. "Tell him Dunsdworth will be poisoned tonight."

A<small>NKARETTE WALKED</small> through the palace of Kingfountain in a serving maid's gown, her hair carefully braided in a youthful style. She carried a tray of food and drink against her hip and passed guards and others who didn't give her a second glance. Taking the Espion tunnels would have attracted notice. She'd have to be careful when she used them now, to avoid alerting Lord Bletchley that she was still alive and mostly well.

When she reached the entrance to Holistern Tower, she was allowed in by the guard after she revealed her name— Krysia. That was the watchword that she and Eredur had agreed on. Her fake name. Her false identity within the city of Kingfountain.

"You're a pretty thing," one of the guards said with an admiring look.

She gave him a passive smile in return, sizing him up with her magic to be sure he wasn't a threat to her, and then began to walk quietly up the stairs, feeling her back muscles throb.

But all her practicing going up the stairs of her tower had strengthened her, and she endured the journey. When she reached the top, she heard the jailer in conversation with Dunsdworth.

The last time she'd come up these stairs was when Morvared had been imprisoned there. The memory brought a pinch of hate in her gut for the vile woman.

"You seem out of sorts tonight," said the jailer. "What ails you?"

"I don't want to fall asleep again." Dunsdworth sounded weary. Worried even. Was he experiencing pangs of dread? "My dreams have been dark of late."

"Oh?"

"I broke out of this tower and fled to Brugia. I was with my brother."

"The king?"

"No, Severn. Why I should dream about him, I don't know. In my dream, I fell off the boat and into the sea. I flapped and flailed, sinking like a stone."

"Drowning in the depths of the sea. A miserable fate." The jailer did not sound sympathetic.

"You would fear it too," Dunsdworth snapped. "There is a dreadful noise in the ears, from the waters. And what sights I beheld."

"What sights? What do you mean?"

Ankarette stayed by the door, listening in to the conversation, balancing the tray.

"I saw a thousand corpses that fishes were gnawing on. Fearful wretches. But there was treasure too. Gold wedges. Anchors rusting and lost. Heaps of pearls. And jewels scattered in the depths. Some of them were in skulls."

"A morbid picture to be sure," the jailor said. "I'm surprised you had the leisure to see the Deep Fathoms so."

"If that was the Deep Fathoms, I tremble to go there," Dunsdworth said worriedly. "I don't want to sleep again. Where is that maid with my dinner? I'm hungry."

"She'll be here anon."

Ankarette waited a few moments and then knocked on the door.

"That must be her," said the jailer. The door opened, revealing an ordinary soldier. He had no Espion ring. "What's your name, lass? Are you the new girl?"

"My name is Krysia," she answered simply.

"You'll wait while he eats so that you might clean? I need some time away from him," he added in an undertone.

"That is my instruction," Ankarette said.

The jailer nodded and then looked at the tray. "Looks like a pleasant enough meal. Better than the food the fish from your dreams were eating, eh? I'll be back in a little while."

"Bring me some more wine, if you would," Dunsdworth said. "I don't want to even dream tonight."

"Two bottles, then," said the jailer with a smirk. He looked at Ankarette, rolled his eyes, and held the door as she entered. She walked over to the little table near the bed. The room was unkempt, like his chamber in the Arbon. The door thumped shut.

"Bring the food over—" He stopped, sucking in his breath. He'd recognized her. She'd wanted him to.

"You're...you're alive," he said, eyes widening with fear. "Eredur said you'd died. I was condemned for murder because I'd killed you!"

"The Fountain-blessed are not easy to kill," Ankarette said.

He backed away. He was desperate to get away from her. She saw the panic quivering in his cheeks. The dread. He was trying to flee from death.

But there was nowhere to run. No way to escape her

justice. A poisoned needle injected by her ring finger stopped him instantly as he raced toward the door, making him collapse to the floor like a marionette.

Ankarette made him drink the mandrake. She watched him swallow it. Dosed with the poison from the needle, he'd been helpless to prevent it. His eyes were wide and feverish. All he could do was blink nervously as the poison worked through his system. The blinking slowed and then he fell asleep. His breathing slackened. Once he was totally unconscious, she dragged him to his bed and left his body there.

She waited the half hour before he stopped breathing.

Ankarette met the jailer coming up the steps as she went down.

"He wasn't too much trouble for you lass, was he?" the jailor asked, lifting the bottles of wine in his hands. "I appreciate you giving me a break from this awful duty."

"No trouble. He fell asleep." She shrugged with unconcern.

"Fancy that," the jailer said. "He'd just told me how scared of his dreams he'd been. I'm surprised."

Ankarette moved past him on the stairwell and continued down.

It wasn't a surprise at all. The dose makes the poison.

EPILOGUE

SHX

L ord Senetra Hux felt the rush of magic from the Tay al-Ard. He was used to the sensation of falling now, but it was always an unsettling experience to be standing on solid ground one moment and then, like hurtling through a trapdoor on a gibbet, to feel oneself plunging. He arrived deep in the Brythonican woods, at a place whose location was protected by the rulers and forbidden to all outsiders. The dense pack of trees blotted out the sun, creating shadows that concealed the carpet of rotting leaves. A large mound of boulders were clumped together, and before them stood a horizontal stone slab with a bowl chained to it.

This was a place brimming with Fountain magic. A trickle of water came from the boulders and a solitary oak, from which he quickly averted his gaze. A magical creature inhabited that tree, one that could steal memories and all sense of self. That was the warning he'd been given by the Wizr with the dark book. The trickle of water, the damp smells, made him uneasy. He looked around the grove cautiously, keeping his gaze from wandering back to the oak tree with clumps of mistletoe clinging to the branches.

He gazed at the design on the ancient bowl. The Gradalis. It was a piece of awful magic, one that could open a gateway between worlds. That was his very purpose, though. He had a special poison in his pouch, one that had been carefully acquired. A poison that would render an immortal being mortal.

Hux was going to travel to another world to kill the Wizr Myrddin. The prophecy of the Dreadful Deadman's return would be thwarted.

He'd trained for this. He had studied the lore. This was no easy challenge, but he had the skills. He had the courage. The boulders blocked the way, but his magic could shatter them.

Hux carefully approached the plinth of stone and bent to examine the bowl. It was a simple ceremony. The runes carved along its edges depicted a scene long lost to the chasm of time. The magical energy pumping through this place fascinated him. The chain and spike kept it bound to the Brythonican grove. But he had the ring now. The ring that would protect him from the damage he was about to unleash.

Years before, he'd entertained hopes of bringing Ankarette to this place, to teach her these secrets few mortals knew. Of Wizrs. Of swords found in wells. Of a dead king yet to be reborn. Of a plant that could cure almost any ailment. Its addictive properties were unfortunate, but it would forestall her death against the ravages of the poison.

His enthusiasm to share these things with her was dashed when she was under the influence of nightshade. He learned the truth about her feelings, her loathing of him and his methods, her fierce loyalty and trust in the Argentine rulers, and her unwillingness to ask him for help. That resoluteness had persuaded him to allow her to go over the falls. To learn from her own pain and suffering what rejecting him meant.

His keen senses alerted him to the fact that he wasn't alone. He sensed the apparition from the oak tree. The urge to look at it was powerful, but he steeled his mind, refusing to be distracted. Then he heard the crunch of a boot in the thickest part of the trees. Not from the oak but farther away.

A knight emerged from the trees, sword unsheathed. His armor had an ancient cast to it. It lacked the frills and designs of modern armory. Hux felt a jolt of fear upon seeing him, as this wasn't part of his plan.

"You are trespassing," the knight said, a little growl in his voice.

Hux straightened, wondering if he should draw a dagger first or the Tay al-Ard. When he had come to this place before, he hadn't stayed long. No defenders had come forward.

"Whom do you serve?" Hux asked. The man's accent was from Ceredigion. He was not Brythonican, nor was he armored as a knight of Ploemeur.

"I've served many Argentine kings," the knight said. "Long ago. You are trespassing."

Hux felt Fountain magic awaken in the knight. Magic that was strong. This knight was Fountain-blessed. His magic was the most powerful Hux had ever felt.

Hux frowned. "Who are you?"

"My name you need not know. Nor will you remember it after this. I am a guardian of the grove. And I was sent here to stop you."

"Sent by whom?" Hux demanded.

Then he felt the presence of another Fountain-blessed. He turned and saw a little girl with golden hair standing by the boulder. Where had she come from? If it were possible, the magic she was wielding was even stronger than the knight's.

They had been waiting for him. Somehow, they'd known of his intent, even though he'd shared it with no one.

He reached for the Tay al-Ard, pulled it from his belt, but it was yanked out of his hand. It flew to the girl's outstretched one.

"You have magic that does not belong to you," the girl said simply. "You are a bad man."

Hux felt a spasm of fear. Without the Tay al-Ard, he could not vanish from the scene. He had brought himself into terrible danger and now had no way to escape.

"Who are you?" he demanded of the girl.

"I am a water sprite. We have come from the Deep Fathoms to stop you. You meddle in things you do not understand. You are a servant of the Hidden Vulgate."

He did not understand what that meant. The knight was advancing on him, a grim look on his brow.

"If you are a water sprite, then you probably think you're immortal," Hux said. "But I can kill you still."

The knight charged. Hux drew a dagger and sent it flying at the warrior, who dodged it with shocking ease. Hux summoned his power to avert blows. The knight's blade would not pierce his skin. He would be immovable, like one of the boulders.

Still, doubt prickled in his brain. He'd fought knights before. Knew their skills, their temperaments. But this was no ordinary knight.

His sword was longer that most knights', a bastard sword of Occitanian make. One that was swung with two hands. Hux twisted around and evaded the first swing and then tried to kick out the man's knee but found an elbow coming into his face instead. Only the quickest of reflexes prevented a broken nose. Hux tried a grappling technique, but the man was made of iron and didn't budge. The fight raged between them, the knight forcing him to retreat beyond the bounds of the boulders and the oak tree. Hux flung another dagger at him, but the second one was deflected by the sword and ended up embedding into the bark of a tree.

Relentless. The knight was relentless! Hux decided to flee on foot, to get away from the guardian he'd unwittingly released.

As he turned, he found the young girl blocking his path. She said a word that he didn't understand, and a wall of invisible energy blocked his way forward. Turning back, he saw the knight swinging the sword down against him and felt it shear through the magic inside him, running him through.

Hux gaped in surprise, staring at the hilt of the bastard sword that had cut through him. His legs turned from stone to jelly. The knight gripped him by the front of his shirt and pushed the blade deeper before the poisoner slumped to the forest floor, blood oozing from the wound. Nausea swept through him.

"He must not die, Sir Ransom," the girl said. "He has another part to play in this. Carry him back to the Dryad tree."

The knight grunted, sheathed the sword in a shoulder scabbard, and then hoisted Hux off his feet as if he weighed no more than a sack of grain. He marched back to the grove with the bowl and the boulders before dropping the poisoner on his back on the stone plinth. Hux gasped in shock and pain, his body bent double as his inner organs twitched and spasmed with agony.

"I don't like poisoners," the knight said brusquely.

"I know," the little girl replied. "But he still serves a purpose. He will forget this place. He will forget what he was sent here to do."

Hux thought about the plant in the damp pouch attached to his belt. The root could heal his injury, but it could not bring back his memories. He tried to grab it, but the knight seized his wrist and held it away.

"We will leave him for his king to deal with," the girl said. "Bound to a tree. Powerless."

Hux began to shiver in pain and dread. Not Lewis. Not after all of his betrayals. He bared his teeth at the little girl, who had powers beyond his own.

"I will make you—"

"Be silent," the girl said, and his voice vanished in his throat. The power of the Fountain had overruled his ability to speak.

And then a beautiful woman stepped up beside the little girl. Her beauty made Hux's heart ache with reverence. Her eyes were the most startling shade of green. They drew him in. Bewitched him. He gaped in dismay. This was another spirit creature. This was—

She blinked, and he remembered nothing.

HUX AWOKE, tied to a tree at the edge of a forest. His arms were secured behind his back, and a rope was stretched around the trunk and over his chest. Delirious with confusion, he gazed around and heard the noise of horses. Mounted sentries wearing the raven badge approached him.

Raven—Brythonica.

Why was he in Brythonica? He couldn't remember what had brought him there or who had tied him to a tree. Looking at his shirt, he saw a piece of moldy bread sticking there. No daggers. His belt was gone. Blood stained his tunic. He'd been injured. Why didn't he feel any pain?

He squirmed against his bonds as the mounted soldiers approached. His head ached as he tried to remember how he'd ended up in such a predicament. Where was the...the...what? Had he taken a blow to the head? There was something that was supposed to help him escape, but he couldn't remember it.

"Just as the duke said," one of the knights muttered darkly.

"He's Occitanian. You can tell by his tunic," said another with a scowl.

"I was waylaid by bandits," Hux said, trying to calm his voice. "They took everything."

"You're a liar," said the first knight after dismounting. "I've orders to take you to the border of Occitania. There's talk that you're a wanted man by King Lewis himself."

Hux flinched at hearing the words. So many times he'd threatened Lewis. Used his influence and fear of poisoning to keep the Occitanian king in line. This...this was impossible. How had he, the most powerful poisoner in all Pisan, been reduced to such a reversal of fortune?

"I will pay you," Hux said boldly. "Release me and you'll be rewarded." Loyalty and trust. There it was again.

"Your promises are smoke," said the knight. "I obey my master's orders. Get him on the spare horse. If you try anything foolish, you'll suffer for it."

Hux helplessly waited as one of the knights drew a dagger and sawed through the ropes across his chest. He felt no pain, despite the bloody tunic. Something had healed him. But what? He couldn't remember anything. Where he had been. What he'd been doing. He'd been struck so hard that his memories had all emptied out. Why was he in Brythonica at all?

As the knights manhandled him over to the spare horse,

they removed the wrist bonds and then secured his wrists to the saddle horn.

A blue butterfly fluttered past him, its wings like sapphire. A feeling of dread seeped into his bones. Morvared wouldn't be able to protect him this time.

Lewis would get his revenge at last.

AUTHOR'S NOTE

Let me tell you the story of how this book came to be. When I began partnering with Tanya Anne Crosby at Oliver Heber Books, I did some research to find a plot for *The Widow's Fate*. You already know that Ankarette's story was inspired by my deep interest in the War of the Roses. I went back to some of the historical books on my bookshelf to reread some of the events. Then I took another look at the story of Ankarette Twynyho, whom my poisoner is named after. Lo and behold! I found a reference I had never seen before all these years later. A record that when she was arrested by the Duke of Clarence (the horrible Dunsdworth) she was judged, found guilty, and executed along with a man who had been captured with her. A man named John Thursby.

Thus the character of the night watchman was born in my mind, a love interest for Ankarette that I'd introduce in *The Widow's Fate*. Because I'd written *The Maid's War* first, I obviously hadn't considered him back then, but that story didn't require him. The period I researched for this included the story of Devereaux taking a castle (John de Vere, Earl of Oxford), which led to a siege and his eventual capture and imprisonment in Calais. I thought it would be interesting if John Thursby had been one of his soldiers. That would allow me to bring our favorite watchman into both books. Since the events in this novel were described briefly by Ankarette to Owen and Evie in *The Queen's Poisoner*, I reread that section to make sure things would remain consistent. And lo and behold again. These lines of dialogue jumped off the page for me: *Only one in a hundred can survive such a plunge. It was not the Fountain's will for me to die. It broke my neck and much of my body, but I survived. My fate was kept a secret. The queen cared for me herself and helped me to heal—not just my body but my heart as well.*

But my heart as well.

I confess when I originally wrote that line, I was thinking about Isybelle and Ankarette's grief over having accidentally killed her friend. But I now saw that it could also mean that Ankarette had lost someone she loved in that encounter with the waterfall as well. The image on the cover of this book, for me, was John Thursby's boat going over the falls first.

I also wasn't intending to do an epilogue chapter, but the idea of Lord Hux getting defeated by Ransom came to me, along with Ankarette meeting Sinia, and I thought it just worked so well. After besting Ankarette so many times, I felt he needed a comeuppance, one that would start his career decline and lead to the events in *The Poisoner's Revenge*.

For those who think one of Dunsdworth's men killed Davern—he did not. Lord Bletchley wielded the knife in that instance. I could not reveal it in the story because there was no one present to witness it. Astute readers will remember that Bletchley was the head of the Espion when Severn came to rule and that he was responsible for doing away with Eredur's nephews and blaming Severn for it. I looked forward to introducing him in this book. But Davern's demise was a steep price to pay for it.

For the historical curious, Devereaux will escape his confinement at Callait (he jumps into the moat and swims away, which is where I got the idea of how John Thursby escaped Averanche). He joins the insurrection against Severn Argentine and was there at the Battle of Ambion Hill. Where he dies before the events of *The Queen's Poisoner*.

I don't have any more plans to write another Ankarette novel, so the Poisoner of Kingfountain series has reached an end. However, during a recent trip to Europe with my wife celebrating our thirtieth wedding anniversary, I was inspired to write a new fantasy series, which Oliver Heber Books will start publishing in the summer of 2025. Stay tuned for more!

SPECIAL BONUS: THE POISONER'S REVENGE

The POISONER'S REVENGE

THE POISONER OF KINGFOUNTAIN

JEFF WHEELER

WALL STREET JOURNAL BESTSELLING AUTHOR

THE
POISONER'S
REVENGE

THE POISONER OF KINGFOUNTAIN

JEFF WHEELER

OLIVERHEBERBOOKS

ONE

A KINGFOUNTAIN TALE

A nkarette's wrists were bound, as were her legs, and a little splash of water came over the edge of the canoe as it hurtled along the river. She heard the roar of the falls coming as she gritted her teeth and fought against her bonds. The ropes on her wrists were beginning to give, loosening under the strain and pressure of her movements. She'd been trained at the poisoner school to escape bonds. But never had she needed to do so against the urgent rush of dwindling time. The canoe was heading toward the falls. The king's brother wanted her dead and had arranged a midnight arrest, a false trial, and now had taken on the role of executioner himself as well. The image of his face leering at her helplessness was scalded into her mind.

"My wife is dead because of you," he'd rasped with vengeance in his voice. *"You failed, Ankarette. Now embrace my revenge."* She could still remember the sour smell of wine on his breath. It had made her want to vomit.

Jerking hard one last time, she freed her wrists and quickly unraveled the ropes. The confinement of the canoe hedged her in, but she managed to sit up, just enough to see the stunning sanctuary of Our Lady, its tall spires lit by torches in the night. It sat on an island in the midst of a churning river, at the head of the falls. The palace was on her left—dark, foreboding. The king was visiting the fortress of Dundrennan in the North. He was days away, too far away to learn about her plight. Too far to save her.

The river was ink black, the sky devoid of moon but straddled with stars. There were no cheering crowds lining the bridge, watching in macabre fascination as another victim of justice was thrown into the waters, a life paid in tribute to the Fountain.

She started working on her legs, realizing the futility of escaping. She had a minute left, at the most. Even if she had oars and paddles, it would be an impossible labor to steer toward the sanctuary in time. Her heart was pounding in her chest with the dread anticipation of coming death. The plunge was just beyond the sound of the roar.

Still she fought to untie her legs. The need to survive, at any cost, drove her. Soon the bonds were loose. But it was too late. The boat began to shake as the violent surge of waters nearly upended her. A childhood memory of jumping off a massive boulder into a river came spurting into her mind. And then the void opened up before her, the waves acting as a catapult as they shoved the canoe into open air.

Falling, falling, falling.

SHE AWOKE WITH A GASP, as she always did at that part of the dream. It was too terrible even for sleep. The room was predominantly dark, save for the fat stub of a candle she'd left burning on the table. The curtains on the bed blocked most of the light, and she sat up, damp with sweat, her heart still pounding at the memory. She'd dreamed it a dozen times since it had happened. And yet, each time, she felt the terror anew.

The night King Eredur's brother had tried to murder her.

Then she heard the footsteps marching up the stairs to the tower where her room lay. The person made no attempt to hide the sound of their approach. The poisoner's tower in the palace of Kingfountain was her private lair, her peaceful domain. There were no servants who came to light the brazier for warmth or to clean her linens. All the ways leading up to it had been secured long ago, and only the Espion tunnels led there now.

The person approaching was making noise deliberately. They were probably afraid she might kill them.

Ankarette parted the curtain and slid her legs off the bed. Her stomach cramped painfully, and it took a moment for it to subside. At the top of the bedstead were some small shelves that held some of her little treasures of memory. From one she removed a vial with a screwed-on cap and quickly twisted it. She took a little swallow of the ichor, cringing at its awful flavor before it slithered down her throat. It would ease the pain in her stomach. She rested a moment, clutching the bottle to her middle, and then put the cap back on and returned it to its place.

The newcomer arrived at the door. She saw the light from his lantern at the base and saw the marks of shadow. There was a hesitation. She rose, fetching the dagger she kept near her pillow, and waited.

A timid knock sounded.

Ankarette rose from the bed and came forward, her bare feet silent on the rug. She waited to respond, drawing closer.

Another knock sounded.

Ankarette reached it, watching the handle to see if it would move. It didn't.

"Yes?" she asked, whispering just loud enough to be heard.

"The . . . uh . . . the king," said the muffled voice. "Wishes to see you."

Eredur never summoned her during the night. Not anymore. The news must be dire. She shifted her grip on the dagger. "Very well," she answered. She said no more. Whoever the messenger was, probably some Espion lackey, he waited a moment longer and then started back down the tower steps. She rested her forehead on the door, feeling the grain of wood against her brow. A knot of dread entered her heart.

Who would the king want her to kill next?

COMING down from the tower was an agony. Ankarette's insides were still ravaged by the poison she'd been given years before by the Occitanian poisoner, Lord Hux. He'd also provided the vial, and several others, with her name engraved in beautiful letters, containing not the antidote, but a serum that would forestall its effects. She'd spent years trying to unmask a cure and had failed. Whatever plant his poison came from remained a secret to the best apothecaries in Ceredigion, Brugia, and even, on her secret trips, in Occitania. But she had a suspicion that the poison came from farther afield. The East Kingdoms, perhaps? After so many journeys, Eredur had finally forbidden her to leave court in search of the cure. Perhaps her absence was just what Lord Hux wanted before he struck at Eredur. The treaty between Ceredigion and Occitania that had been signed years before was still in force, but Ankarette felt the Occitanian king was only biding his time, waiting for Eredur's power to wane.

She reached the royal bedchamber through the Espion tunnels and opened the secret latch to the room. There was plenty of light beyond, and she found the king standing before the remains of the nightly fire. He wore his breeches and a comfortable robe, which was open, revealing his massive chest and unwanted girth. He was no longer the soldier of his youth, the young man who had fought in brutal wars to become the wearer of the hollow crown. He did not look ready for war.

Queen Elyse sat at the edge of the bed, also wearing a night robe. Her flaxen hair had some silver in it now, but she was a stately woman, and her eyes were full of concern as she stared at her husband. She was the first to notice Ankarette's arrival.

"She's here," Elyse said and rose from the bed to come and embrace her. The two were friends, having shared many adventures as well as many tragedies together. Ankarette's nickname among the Espion was the Queen's Poisoner. The two embraced, and Elyse pressed a kiss to Ankarette's cheek. "You look pained."

Ankarette smiled sadly. "It will pass soon."

The king turned away from the hearth and faced her, his eyes containing the secret. Some of his chest hairs were silver now. He looked weary, weighed down, depressed.

"You summoned me?" Ankarette asked, tilting her head. After the king's brother Dunsdworth had sent her over the falls, her survival had been a closely guarded secret. She did not walk the corridors of the palace now, keeping to the shadows where she could advise the king and queen in secret. Sometimes her recommendation went counter to the king's privy council. And more often than not, he heeded her advice over theirs.

"A messenger from the North just arrived," Eredur said. "From Tom." Ankarette's eyes narrowed. Even after so many years, hearing his name made her flinch inside, made the ache flare anew. They had loved one another. But that had ended when he'd married Duke Horwath's daughter. They had a little girl, Ankarette knew. Lord Thomas Mortimer believed Ankarette was dead, that she'd been killed at the falls in an act of treason by Dunsdworth. She wanted to keep it that way. His marriage had not been an overtly happy one. But there was no doubt he doted on his daughter.

"What did it say?" Ankarette asked. She gave an air of unconcern, which she knew didn't deceive Elyse. Their hearts were knit too close for such deceptions.

It was Elyse who answered the question. "Morvared is dead."

Ankarette turned, gazing sharply at the queen. That was unexpected news. "When did this happen?"

"King Lewis has kept it a secret for the most part," Eredur said, his look turning darker. "The Espion didn't know. But Tom has friends in many distant ports. Someone who thought he would want to know that Morvared hated him as well. He sent me word right away."

"Ankarette," Elyse said warily, shaking her head. "We don't know for certain if it is true. The old queen's health may have been failing. Or perhaps she was . . . poisoned."

A feeling of dizziness had come over Ankarette. She felt like she needed to sit down. Lord Hux had told her that as long as Eredur spared Queen Morvared's life, that Ankarette's own would be spared. He had provided, in ways mysterious, replenishment vials to replace hers. Ankarette had used them sparingly, trying to keep extra in reserve. At least twice a year the replacement would arrive. She had an entire vial that had not been opened yet.

Eredur folded his arms. "Why the Occitanian king has kept it secret, I don't know. But I don't trust Lewis. He may have replaced Hux as his herald, but I don't believe he means to keep the terms of the treaty. We've been collecting the tributes he's paid. But I knew they might come to an end eventually. He wants his daughter to marry our eldest son. To keep the peace between our realms. To unite Occitania and Ceredigion once again. Or is that a pretext as well? They're both children."

Elyse nodded in agreement. "Has he been intending to call it off all along? We don't know. But Morvared's death comes at a suspicious time. And we couldn't help but remember the warning Lord Hux gave you, in particular, Ankarette."

She mastered her feelings and gripped the queen's hand in return. "You didn't summon me in the dead of night simply to share the news with me. You want me to go to Occitania and find out if she's truly dead."

Eredur smirked and let out a low chuckle. "Yes, that was our exact intent, Ankarette. Tom's message said she died at the castle in Dompier."

Ankarette nodded. "Then that is where I will go. Do you know where Lord Hux is? Has there been any word from him?"

Eredur shook his head. "Unfortunately no. Lewis chose a new herald years ago, and so Hux's movements are a mystery. He's probably still at Shynom." The king looked at her pointedly. "Are you going to seek him out, Ankarette?"

The queen also looked at her worriedly.

Ankarette and Hux's rivalry had lasted for years. He was the master poisoner. The most powerful one serving any kingdom. Yes, she'd managed to outsmart him on occasion. But it seemed like conflict between them was inevitable now. It was impossible to guess his actions or his reasons.

"It may be best if I did," Ankarette said. "If I could get him to breathe a little nightshade, I could force him to tell me the secret of the cure."

The king's lips were pressed together worriedly, and he stepped forward. "I can't afford to lose you, Ankarette Tryne-owy. Not when my children are so young. I'm feeling my age more every day. In ten years, my sons will be ready to rule in my stead, and I can relinquish more power to them. For now, I have to rely on my brother, Severn."

The queen's look darkened at that statement. Yes, there was bad blood between the Duke of Glosstyr and the queen. Severn was Eredur's right hand, the leader of his armies and keeper of peace of the realm. Eredur relied on him, but Severn's biting sarcasm and inability to forgive had earned him many enemies, including members of Elyse's family. It was strange, but Eredur and Elyse's oldest child, the queen's namesake, had a great fondness for her uncle. The boys, on the other hand, preferred their mother's family.

"You don't think I should seek out Lord Hux, then," Ankarette said.

"I won't forbid you to," he replied. "I trust you too much. I know you won't act out of spite or without reason. Go where the trail leads you. If it leads you to Hux . . ." He paused, shrugging. Then his eyes turned deadly earnest. "Then ensure he cannot interfere in our realm any more than he already has in the past."

"I will," Ankarette said, nodding. "I will take a ship at first light. Dompier is west of Averanche in the heart of Occitania."

"If you need anything, send word to Duke Kiskaddon in Tatton Hall," Eredur said. "I have Bennett stationed there. He'll help you if you need it."

Ankarette tilted her head and thought a moment. Bennett was a solid Espion and had been her friend many years. But she trusted her own instincts best and her Fountain magic.

Going alone would be easier. "Does the duke know I'm still alive?" She had fond feelings for the duke and his family. She'd helped their youngest son at his birth. It was the first and only time she'd used her Fountain magic to bring a stillborn back to life. As a young woman, she'd been trained as a midwife. That was how she saw herself—a bringer of life, not of death.

Eredur shook his head. "None of them know, Ankarette. That is how you wanted it."

She wondered how the duke's little boy was doing. But saw no reason to break free of her self-imposed concealment. She especially didn't trust the king's other brother not to attempt to continue what Dunsdworth had begun. Killing Dunsdworth still caused her pain. But Eredur had ordered it. She hoped he would never order her to kill his other brother too.

She was about to leave when the door handle turned and the door to the hall opened. All three turned, trying to see who was entering their room in the middle of the night without knocking. Ankarette had reached for her dagger, but it turned out to be their eldest daughter, named after her mother. Another child Ankarette had helped save during childbirth.

"What is it darling?" the queen asked, coming to meet her.

"I heard voices . . . one I didn't know," said the young woman who was sixteen and looked so much like her mother. "Who is she?"

"I will tell you later, Daughter. Go back to bed," Elyse said to the girl, who eyed Ankarette with interest and curiosity.

THE FORTRESS of Averanche was illuminated by torchlight as the ship approached from the north with the tide. The ramparts were set in rows of jagged teeth, and it was clear there were sentries patrolling them by the glow of the flames that moved along the upper walls. Ankarette had purchased passage on a Genevese trading ship with a cargo of green olives and mackerels. The pain in her stomach had subsided with the dose she'd taken the day before. She stared at the walls of the fortress, which was built on a cliff above the harbor. This fortress was part of the Occitanian lands, and she knew that once she stepped foot on the docks, she was in enemy territory. No doubt King Lewis had spies in all the major port cities. Her cloak concealed much of her features, but she would take no chances. She'd prepared the implements of her trade—poisoned rings, daggers, hairpins, along with small cylinders containing other devices that would disable or kill. Occitania was the land of Lord Hux, her nemesis, who could smile with charm while stabbing someone in the back. It had been years since they'd faced each other. Years since he'd defeated her and forced her to drink the poison that was slowly killing her.

She had trained more rigorously since then. She was older, more experienced. He'd be approaching fifty now, so she had some natural advantages this time. When she next brought out her dagger against him, she did not expect to lose.

Within the hour, the ship had reached the docks, and the captain began shouting orders to prepare the vessel to be inspected. He gave her a curt nod as the gangway was lowered, and she swiftly descended and entered the town. She was fluent in Occitanian and knew how to disguise her voice to change her age just by the inflection she used.

The first thing she did was determine if she was being followed. She went to a nearby tavern, which was loud and rowdy, and ducked inside. Immediately she went to the kitchen, walked past a bewildered cook, and then exited out the back. In the shadows of the alley, she made her way past a chicken coop, through a short gate with squeaky hinges, and then walked a little distance to the next street and turned the corner. There, she waited, listening, opening the hood of her cloak to hear better.

After several minutes, where all she heard was the scrape of leaves being dragged by the breeze and the nearby bluster of the tavern, she heard the squeak of the gate. She carefully looked around the corner, spying two men. They looked confused, unsure of which way she had gone. They obviously decided to split up, because one went the other way while one came in her direction. She twisted her poisoner's ring, exposing the needle. Divide your opponents' forces. Remove the lesser pieces one by one. Just like the game Wizr.

Ankarette pressed her back against the wall, listening for the sound of advancing footsteps. The man was being especially careful, but she did make out the subtle scuffing sounds that increased in volume as he approached the corner. He was walking quickly, which meant he was trying to catch up, believing her to be much farther ahead than she was.

His shadow suddenly appeared around the corner. He had a knife in his hand, the blade pointed forward.

He saw her.

Too late.

Ankarette gripped his wrist to control the dagger and jabbed her hand against the side of his neck, where the needle pricked his skin and caused a little rivulet of blood when he jerked in surprise. Suddenly his elbow jutted at her face, but she dodged it, keeping his wrist gripped firmly. He grunted at the pain and tried to call out in warning. She twisted and covered his mouth with her hand, the ring slashing part of his lip in the process. He was strong, vigorous, and terrified, which added to his strength. He tried to twist the dagger around to stab her in the stomach, and it took all her effort to keep the blade pointed away.

Then the poison finally worked, and he slumped in a heap on the cobblestones, but she still held his wrist and neck and gently laid him down. Although her heart was racing at the sudden violence, she listened keenly for the sound of his partner pursuing her. Nothing.

She quickly disarmed him, taking his weapons for herself, as well as his pouch of coins. Then touching his throat, she ensured he was still living. The poison would last for hours, and he'd have no knowledge of where she'd gone. She dragged his body deeper into the shadows to make it more difficult to find in the dark. They might not discover him until morning, by which time she'd be well away. Twisting her ring again, she concealed the tip. Then she left the alley.

Each kingdom had a network of courier horses. Messages were dispatched and returned at all hours of the day and night, depending on the severity. The king had his own royal couriers to use, but messengers could be dispatched for the right amount of coin. She had no intention of waiting until day to buy a horse, which would be conspicuous. Her goal was to steal a horse and ride to Dompier directly, in the disguise of a courier. She had perused the Espion maps of Averanche in the Star Chamber of the palace before leaving and knew where the porter doors were. These doors were locked during the night, but guards were stationed there in case riders appeared. A watchword was required to gain access.

'When she reached the porter door, she saw two men sitting on chairs and dicing, chuckling at one another in the cool evening. They shared a wineskin between them, no doubt adding to the humor

Waiting in the shadows, she watched the two dice and steal each other's coins. Patience was one of her specialties.

She watched them, listening to their banter, studying the wineskin they continued to pass to each other. It was still full, which meant they intended it to last through the night. Soon enough, one of them rose from his chair and went to relieve himself in the garderobe inside the small gatehouse. There was a brazier by the chairs to keep them both warm, and the other rose and stood over it, rubbing his hands above the coals. Ankarette approached from behind swiftly. The light of the fire kept her shadow behind her. She took the flagon dangling from the back of the chair and then pulled the chair back slightly. Twisting open the cap, she dumped a small packet of powder into the wineskin. The man sniffed, rubbing his hands continually over the brazier, unaware that she was standing just behind him. She set down the leather bladder and stepped back into the shadows again. The man came back to sit down, but the chair had been moved, so he fell on his rump and let out a bark of confusion and pain. She pressed her back to the wall, her dark cloak absorbing light. The other fellow returned, tying up his pants, and started to laugh at his friend who was still sitting confused on the ground.

They shared more wine. Within the hour, both men were sound asleep, one of them snoring obnoxiously loud.

Ankarette borrowed the key from one of their belts and unlocked the porter door. She returned the key to his belt and went out into the darkness, shutting the heavy door behind her. She'd left no trace of leaving Averanche. It would take days before news of her arrival reached King Lewis or Lord Hux.

That was all the time she needed.

THE COURIER THUNDERED down the road well past midnight, and she heard him coming from a distance. She'd chosen the spot of ambush along the road from Averanche to Pree, choosing a small area with dry scrub and some thick yew trees. It was a great place to conceal herself, and the yew had provided branches and leaves to help in her plot. She'd broken off several large branches and dragged them into the middle of the road, making it seem like they'd fallen naturally. A horse would sense the obstruction and halt. That would give her time to subdue the rider.

The sound of the galloping hooves grew louder, and she waited behind the trunk of the largest yew where she could watch the approach and attack from behind the rider. Although she was weary, she kept her senses alert and focused. It was just a single rider, a courier. She didn't know if it was a royal one or not but would find out soon enough.

The pounding hooves came up the road swiftly, and she waited, eyeing the road until she saw the smudge of black silhouetted in the moonlight. The rider reached the road in front of her hiding place, and the horse suddenly snorted and banked in.

"What is this?" growled the rider, trying to see in the darkness. The branches and leaves appeared a much more formidable barrier than they really were. Ankarette slipped out from behind the yew and stabbed a needle into the rider's leg with a quick-acting paralytic. He would remain conscious, but wouldn't be able to move his body.

"Ouch!" he gasped, turning in shock at the source of the pain. He tottered off the saddle, and she caught him, grunting herself at his weight. The horse became even more agitated, but she knew how to handle animals and had grown up riding with the Duke of Warrewik's daughter. She tethered the reins to one of the branches of the yew she'd hidden behind, and then dragged the man to the scrub. He was blinking rapidly, his face worried. He wore the uniform of King Lewis and the royal badge of the fleur-de-lis.

Even better.

"Who are you?" he said, his voice quavering. His whole body trembled under the effects of the poison.

Ankarette withdrew a small packet of nightshade and judged his weight by having dragged him over. She dumped a dose into her gloved palm and then approached him.

"Who are you!" he said, panicking.

She didn't answer and blew the dust into his face. Almost immediately, his body relaxed as the toxin took effect. Too much would have killed him. The right amount made a victim particularly pliable to answering questions.

"What is the watchword for the gates?" she asked him, leaning closer. She touched his throat and felt his heartbeat racing.

"Alys. The king's mistress," he said in a slightly giddy voice.

"What does she look like? Is she pretty?"

"I don't know," he babbled. "I've never seen her. The king has seen no one in weeks."

Ankarette knitted her brow. "Is the king at the palace in Pree?"

"No, he's hidden himself at his estate in Plessis."

"What do you mean?" Ankarette pressed. "Hidden himself?"

"He's made a prison for himself. No one can see him. He's fearful."

"What is he afraid of?" Ankarette asked, growing even more concerned.

"He's afraid of being poisoned," said the man, laughing. "There is a fence around the chateau. An iron fence. Four hundred archers patrol it. And sixty crossbowmen. No one comes in unless summoned. Or they are killed."

Ankarette blinked in surprise. The Espion had not been told of this. Then again, it was difficult keeping able people in Lewis's court. This was troubling news. Why was Lewis so afraid? Or had he had a falling out with Lord Hux? Was he afraid for his life from his one-time poisoner?

"Where is Lord Hux?" she asked.

"Who?"

"Lord Hux."

"I don't know that name. Lord Hux? I don't know Lord Hux."

She jostled him to keep him coherent. "Where is the king?"

"I told you that," he said. "He's at his chateau in Plessis."

"Where is Plessis? What city is it near?"

"It is by Vierzon. But you cannot go there. If you are not invited, the archers will slay you."

She did know the name of that city. It was deep in Occitania, far from the machinations of the court of Pree. What was going on? Had Lord Hux turned renegade against his master? Had another king managed to win Lord Hux's loyalty?

The man started to snore.

"Wake up," Ankarette said, jostling him again.

"Wha—what?" he groaned.

"Queen Morvared. Where is she?"

"The Queen of Ceredigion . . . is dead," the man said, mumbling.

A spasm of dread went through Ankarette's heart. Yes, Morvared had once been the Queen of Ceredigion. She probably considered herself the queen still, even though she'd lost the crown years before. Thanks to Ankarette's help, Eredur's queen wore the crown. But the thought of something happening to Elyse made Ankarette dread the words.

"What is your name?" she asked him.

"Marion, but they call me La Fleche. I ride like an arrow."
He sniffed, and Ankarette could sense the change in his voice,
the sound of someone rousing from the thrall of nightshade. It
was like someone realizing they were talking in their sleep.
Another dose, so soon, would kill him. There was much she
still wanted to know. But she'd learned much so far.

King Lewis was afraid. Morvared was indeed dead.

But could Ankarette be sure? Could she trust the report of a
courier?

No. She needed to know for herself. Because if Morvared
was dead, it meant Lord Hux would stop providing the cure.

And then Ankarette would die.

THE TOWN of Dompier was on the Orle River, which had acted
as a natural moat against the invading armies of prior decades.
The castle was on a hillside above the town, behind a vast
fortified wall interspersed with small guard towers. The
fortress itself was beautiful, constructed in the Occitanian style
that was different from the palaces of Ceredigion. Dompier
was a square chateau with four large towers at each corner
with tall angled roofs made of adjoining panels that rose to a
central peak. The shingles were made of dark slate, all uniform
in color, while the blanched gray walls were a similar, lighter
patina. The towers weren't rounded but hard edged. At the top
of each tower was a spike of bronze. The front façade, which
faced Ankarette from across the river, had a beautifully
constructed gatehouse behind massive stone walls. It was the
kind of castle that could withstand a siege for years. While the

townsfolk below might be compromised, the keep itself was highly defensible.

It was late afternoon by the time Ankarette had arrived. She wore the uniform she'd stolen off La Fleche and had practiced all day speaking in his tone of voice and accent. She'd bound up her hair in twisting braids and concealed it against the broad hat he'd been wearing. No one had bothered her along the journey, nor asked where she was going.

She rested on the horse, gazing up at the fortress, wondering whether she should keep her disguise or trade it for another. Yet, it was probably the best way to enter the castle without being questioned. No one knew she was coming. Messengers were not always the best informed of people either, although they relished gossip. She hoped to confirm the rider's news, but she'd need to be careful. The castle looked truly formidable. There was no ivy growing on its walls, no trees to use to climb to one of the upper windows. Even the chimneys, which the structure abounded in, seemed too narrow to squeeze through. She continued to study it, watching it for signs of activity. It was quiet and still. No bustling servants. What was happening on the inside, it was impossible to know.

Darkness was a friend, so she waited until near sunset to approach the river. A ferryman was loitering below, and when he saw her approach and noticed the badge, he directed her to bring the horse on the ferry, where she dismounted.

"Good news, sir?" the ferryman asked her inquisitively.

She frowned at him and turned away, adopting a haughty pose.

The man, chagrined, continued about his work, and soon they were launched in the river. There was a guide rope that helped the barge against the current, and in a half hour they'd crossed and darkness had settled over the town. It was smaller than Averanche, and she bought some food from the sole street vendor before riding up the slope to the walls.

The outer gate didn't even ask for a watchword. They just let her in, and she wondered at the lax standards in the realm. Though it was not a time of war. Or was trouble on the horizon?

She'd already read the courier's message, which he'd been taking to Averanche. It was orders to the mayor to prepare for an inspection of the city defenses by one of the dukes. She'd then forged another document, using the same handwriting style, requesting in similar language an inspection of the fortress of Dompier, and she'd pried loose the seal and reaffixed it to her note. She rode with the bearing of a man, giving the illusion that she was La Fleche. The real man she'd tied up and left back in the yew trees. She'd chosen not to gag him so that he could, eventually, be discovered and freed. But he'd not remember her or know where she was going. By the time Lord Hux discovered she'd been in Occitania, she'd be back at the palace of Kingfountain.

The horse's hooves clopped up the ramp heading to the fortress. The torches were not lit yet, and the walls looked like bleached bones in the sunset. Looking back, she saw the glimmer of the waters of the Orle River. She was tempted to use her Fountain magic to discern danger, but if she did and Lord Hux was there, he would know it—just as she could sense his power when he used it.

As she neared the doors, they opened, and two guards came out holding pikes.

"Welcome to Dompier," one of them said. "We didn't know you were coming."

"You weren't supposed to know," Ankarette replied, making her voice more husky. She handed the message to the guard. "But it will be clear soon enough."

The guard looked at the seal and then up at her. "What's the watchword?"

"Alys," she answered, sounding bored.

The other guard nodded, and the first handed the note back to her. "Bring your horse inside the courtyard. The castellan is eating dinner. We'll take you straightaway."

Ankarette nodded and urged the horse forward. Once inside, they shut the doors as she dismounted. There were two other guards inside. Four total watching the front doors. Hardly a strong defense. She imagined the entire castle had fifty men assigned to it. Formidable—but not impossible. Not that she'd try to fight them all at once, but she felt confident she could escape if she needed to.

After they took her horse, she was brought into the castle of Dompier. The inner corridors were lit by burning torches. Tapestries with colorful Occitanian fashions adorned the walls. The interior had been decorated with the subtle touches of a woman's hand. It was not a military garrison. No, it was more like a castle had been transformed into a manor house fit for a queen.

What if Morvared was still alive? Would she recognize Ankarette after all these years? The last time they'd met, Ankarette had thrown a dagger and impaled the old queen's wrist. But people saw what they expected to see. A rider, a courier. Someone of no importance. If Morvared were dead, Ankarette would inspect the corpse for the scar. That would be the evidence she'd trust. And why she had needed to come quickly before more decay happened.

But Ankarette did not suspect the old queen was alive. The news would not have traveled so quickly to Eredur otherwise. No, this was just a confirmation.

The castellan did not have a family or even a wife. He was a thickset man with wavy hair combed forward in the Occitanian style. His doublet was fine, his fingers greasy from the dinner, and he chewed rapidly before mopping his lips with the napkin. He glanced at Ankarette and then held out his hand for the note.

She delivered it and stood back again, hands clasped behind her back, studying the chamber, looking for the various doors.

He broke the seal and quickly scanned the note.

"An inspection? What for?" he said, sounding angered. "This makes no sense."

Ankarette shrugged mildly, continuing to gaze around the chamber.

"Why would Duke Brabant be coming again so soon after the funeral? The king isn't coming here. He's not going anywhere."

Ankarette sniffed. "I don't know, my lord."

"Of course you don't know. You don't know anything." He threw down the message. "Go to the servants' quarters and get a meal. The duke is paranoid, that's all."

Ankarette bowed and then slipped out. She was led to the kitchen where the cook pulled together some food for her and where she quickly learned that a funeral for Queen Morvared had been held recently. Not many dignitaries had attended, but the Duke of Brabant was one of them, and so it did seem odd that he'd be coming again so soon. Ankarette listened and applied some subtle questioning to learn that the queen had been interred in the crypt below the castle. A stone sarcophagus had been carved for her, depicting the queen in tranquil repose. Some visitors had already come to pay respects to it, some leaving flowers for the dead queen that needed to be cleaned up later.

That was all she needed to know.

Ankarette found out how to get to the crypt to pay her

respects, and since the castle was so quiet and the guards had already eaten, she was able to visit it alone without anyone accompanying her.

The crypt was at the bottom of some stairs, and torches had been set in wall sconces to illuminate the way. The steps were made of stone, and it would be easy to hear if anyone followed her. Still, she waited after going down, listening for the sound of pursuers. No one bothered with her.

So Ankarette followed the pathway, past stone columns into a vault-like room. The ceiling was low, but not enough to make her duck. The sarcophagus was plain to see, set in the middle of the room. There was a stone lip around it, with kneeling cushions for those wanting to come pay their respects. Ankarette saw some dried flowers as well and a small stone decorative fountain, which had two dozen coins shimmering in the bottom of it. The final respect paid to the dead.

Yes, all appeared to confirm the news that Sir Thomas bore. Everything, except seeing the corpse for herself. Ankarette could not turn back now, not after coming this far. She felt a sense of dread staring at the carving of the queen. It resembled the woman, and the visage brought back memories from Shynom palace and a command pavilion that she'd sooner forget. Memories of a voice that sounded almost childlike but was full of vengeance and pride. The woman had lost her only son in that final battle against Eredur. And Ankarette had helped in that defeat.

She stood for several moments, trying to quell the memories of the past that haunted her. Sir Thomas, she'd thought, had declared himself to her . . . only to forsake her for Duke Horwath's daughter. Pain clenched in her heart.

Now was not the time to be maudlin. She cocked her head, listening again for the sound of anyone coming. The little decorative fountain was still, causing no interference in her ability to hear. If she tried dragging the stone lid away, it would make a sound. She bit her lip.

She had to do this. She had to know for certain.

If Morvared were laid out in the same manner as her effigy, then the wounded wrist would be on one side. Ankarette let out her breath and then pressed her hands against the stone. It should be able to slide off. If it was set in, then she'd have to lift it up. Ankarette tried pushing against it. It didn't budge.

Why would it be easy?

She sighed and then stood at the head of the lid, bending her knees, and then hefted against it. She felt it giving, scraping softly stone to stone. She held her breath, prepared for the odor of decay. Surely they'd have embalmed her. But no one relished the smell of death.

Ankarette's muscles strained, but the lid moved up. There was a torch nearby, offering light on the shadowed crevice. Higher it went, higher. Then she saw the bleached face of the dead woman, the sunken cheeks, the grayish skin. The dark cushion of hair. It was horrible and mesmerizing to look at.

Then she heard the sound of a strand breaking.

And an iron gate crashed down against the stone at the bottom of the stairs. There were locking noises, the click and snap of machinery. The torches wavered as the realization struck her in the pit of her stomach.

She was trapped in the crypt with a corpse.

THE SOUND of boots came down the steps hours later. The castellan carried a lantern in his hand and approached the bars warily. Ankarette had realized the trap had been set, and she was caught in it. Gears had locked the gate from above, and she'd tried everything she knew in order to budge the iron bars, but they were immovable.

The castellan approached and looked at her suspiciously, then shook his head. "I'll admit, you surprised me," he said, cocking his head. "I really thought you were a royal courier and that your message was real. Thankfully, Lord Hux isn't such a fool." He shone the light on her face, but she didn't flinch from it.

The gnawing feeling of desperation wriggled inside her. She had to escape. She had to find a way out.

"If you release me, you will be a very wealthy man," Ankarette said. "The King of Ceredigion—"

He laughed at her face. "Now you're mocking my intelligence. Hux designed this trap himself, and only he has the key. Even if I wanted to help you—and I don't—I couldn't. Besides, your king will not be king for much longer." His eyes flashed malevolently, his tone revealing the depth of his hatred. "The queen gets her revenge on you at last. She's been here for years, Poisoner. Plotting it. Planning it. Waiting for your guard to go down to strike. I'll say no more, my dear. You can remove your disguise whenever you wish. I'll have a chamber pot and food brought to you. Hux said he'd come for you himself. Eventually."

Her feelings roiled with intensity. She had to get free! She stared at the castellan, wanting to hurl a poisoned dagger into his belly. But what good would that do? One man with a crossbow could end her life just as easily. Maybe death would be preferred.

Ankarette came to the bars, clenching them with her hands. The castellan flinched and backed away. He might be angry, but he was still afraid.

"You could batter down these bars," she said. "If you

wanted to. But I swear to you, if you do not release me, you will suffer. I won't kill you, sir. I'll make you wish you were dead. You have no idea what I'm capable of."

He smirked, staying well out of reach. "Oh, I think I do. I've a friend named Vauclair who was tricked by you years ago, when you were a young thing." He gave her a nasty smile. "I know who you are. You're good at betraying your friends as well as your enemies. I have one more thing to tell you. A message from Lord Hux. 'Threat. And mate.'"

THE ONLY TIME Ankarette had been imprisoned was when Lord Dunsdworth had arrested her and then sentenced her to death for the murder of his wife. She'd hated the helpless feeling then, but this was much worse. There was no sun to reveal the passage of time. New torches were brought daily, along with a meager set of rations, brought twice a day. They'd gone through the saddle bag from the courier's horse and brought her gown down to her, which she'd changed into. But her poisoner bag, which she always kept at hand, held nothing that would solve her problem in time.

And time was something she had now in abundance. Time to pace. Time to think. She wished she had her needles and thread, and although she'd ask for a set, she'd been denied. She'd used her Fountain magic to try to find a way to escape. But she may as well have been buried with the corpse of Queen Morvared. She'd examined the remains and found the tell-tale scar on her wrist. At least Morvared had escaped her exile at last. There was no way out of the confinement for Ankarette, however. She'd also examined the gears and locking mechanism. The keyhole was on the other side of the bars, higher than she could reach. Her cage had been designed by someone who knew the poisoner's arts.

Days passed. Each one making her agony grow. After a week, the effects of the vial she'd drunk before leaving King-fountain began to ebb, and the pain started again. It was an acute form of torture, trapping her in her agony, with no way to find relief. After the second week, her frantic feelings had grown worse. Eredur knew where she was. Had he sent Espion to try to find her? Surely King Lewis and Lord Hux were expecting it. And by doing so, her king had deprived himself of those who could best protect him.

There was no doubt in Ankarette's mind that Lord Hux was going to try to kill Eredur. He would have to get past the Espion, of course. But without Ankarette there to warn him, he would be vulnerable. She ate her rations, feeling the oppression of her confinement.

After a month, while her insides chafed with pain, the temperature began to cool. Winter was coming soon. Guards brought two braziers to the bottom of the steps, leaving her some degree of warmth. And then another month passed. She took small sips from her near-empty vial, to prolong her life. She'd bent her hairpin into a needle and had used the courier's uniform as her canvas. Sewing had been her passion, a skill she'd adopted from her mother. Needlework strengthened her Fountain magic, gave her insights. She came to realize how trapped she truly was. But the worst part was the torture of suspense. Not knowing what was happening in Ceredigion. Being helpless.

The Espion tried to rescue her on midwinter's eve. She only knew it was that day because one of her jailors had mentioned it.

She heard the noises of alarm coming from the castle

above. There were shouts, even the clash of arms. She was so sick and weak, but still she rose and went to the bars, listening to the sounds, trying to understand what was happening. Her mind quickened with hope. She'd been a prisoner for several months, her vial almost empty of the syrupy ichor that sustained her life. Hux hadn't provided anything new.

There was a crashing noise above, which startled her. The noises of conflict made her pulse race. Eredur had sent people to rescue her. She was certain of it. A battering ram would open the gate. Even metal would give to the use of force.

The door at the top of the steps opened, and a figure came rushing down. He was bleeding from a wound on his scalp, but she recognized his face. Bennet—one of the Espion who was her friend.

"Ankarette!" he said, seeing her at the bars.

Her heart swelled with gratitude. "Bennet," she said, reaching for him through the bars.

He was smiling, overjoyed to see her. "We found you at last. The king ordered this rescue a month ago, but it's taken time to slip into the country unawares."

"Bennet," Ankarette said, shaking her head. "The king lives?"

"Yes," he said, nodding vigorously. "We need to get you out of there."

"Lord Hux has the key," Ankarette said. "But the bars can be broken with enough strength."

"You look so weak," Bennet said. "Here . . . the king said to give you—"

The twang of a crossbow sounded, and the bolt struck Bennet in the back. Pain contorted his face, and he slumped against the bars. He gasped, trying to breathe. His legs crumpled as his broken spine lost its ability to support him. She cried out in anguish, trying to clutch him through the bars. He had something in his hand, something he was about to give her.

Another vial of the serum. The one she'd kept in reserve at the palace in her tower.

"Ankarette," Bennet wheezed, then his eyes rolled back in his head.

Two guards, each holding a crossbow, came down the steps. She managed to slip the vial into her pocket, but the tears she shed were very real.

Within the hour, the noises had faded. The castellan came down, mopping the sweat from his brow. "Well, my dear," he said grimly. "Your king fancies you for certain. I lost twelve men tonight. But we killed them all, I think. Some fled into the snow. They'll be easy to hunt. I've sent the dogs to go after them. One by one, they'll be slain. Like this one." He nudged Bennet's body with the toe of his boot. Then he spat on him.

Ankarette lunged against the bars, trying to grab the castellan. But he'd wisely stayed out of her reach.

"Still some fire left in you," he said with a smile. "Good. Hux said you had spirit. And he wanted to see it crushed."

ALTHOUGH SHE COULD NOT SEE the sun, she kept track of days by carving into the stone sarcophagus. Meals were brought twice a day, so she had a way to measure it. By her estimation, she had been confined for four more months since the attempted break-out.

There was no way to escape the prison. She'd examined it from every angle. She'd used her magic on it again and again, then replenished her stores by stitching with the courier's uniform. She'd worked over the cloak, the tunic, using threads from other parts to stitch with. In the cell, she'd even made friends with a little gray spider who spun a web in the corner to catch moths that were attracted to the lights. Ankarette liked watching the spider at work, and studied its elegant legs as it spun and wove its silk-threaded net.

The day Eredur died, she felt it. A ripple within her Fountain magic announced it to her. Maybe it was his ghost whispering to her before departing to the Deep Fathoms. She had the nightmare about the falls again that night. The speeding canoe as it rushed to the edge of the waters. Only, she didn't awaken on the fall. The canoe smashed on the churning water. Ankarette had survived the attempt to kill her, but it had broken her body. It had taken months to heal, and the injuries added pain to her life daily.

The death of her king was a new pain. It was a deep sadness that evoked her darkest thoughts, one that drained her spirit. The king's brother, Severn, would be chosen as the protector of the realm. And while she did not like the duke, she knew he was loyal to his brother. Queen Elyse didn't like him either, nor did she trust him as much as Eredur did. Ankarette wished she was back at the palace to advise the queen. But it wasn't possible. Morvared would have her revenge from beyond the Deep Fathoms. To make Ankarette suffer in confinement.

The castellan brought the news the next day, a smug look on his face. But she'd already known.

"King Eredur has died," he said. His smile broadened. "I received the message from Lord Hux just now. He's enjoying his stay in your city. It's a beautiful spring day. He may return soon. Or he may not. He wanted you to know."

Ankarette gave him a listless look and then turned away.

She'd known it would happen eventually. There was nothing she could have done to prevent it.

"I'm having a lamprey pie for supper," said the castellan. "I'll have one made for you. I think that was the dish, if I'm not mistaken, which killed your king. We can both celebrate . . . in our own way. No Eredur . . . no threat of war."

Ankarette sighed. "You don't know the king's brother like I do," she said.

The castellan snorted. "Oh, I'm convinced Lord Hux has plans for him as well."

That night, or what she thought was night, Ankarette poured her ration of water into the small dry fountain at the head of the sepulcher. And she tossed a coin into the waters, listening to the sound of it splash. And then she wept.

In ALL, she had six months in which to plan her revenge. She knew Lord Hux would come to gloat when his mischief was over. Would he try to woo her into his service? She doubted that. There could be no trust between them after this. He would know without doubt that she would get revenge on his king. Which was why, she had come to realize, King Lewis was hiding at his estate in Plessis. He'd hidden there to prevent being abducted by the Espion. Or killed, in case Ankarette escaped. Yes, Hux had thought of everything. Including how he would face her at the end. Was this his final act as poisoner before he retired? His grand drama? She imagined so. He would protect his king's interests and provide years of security for himself by causing instability—and probably civil war—within Ceredigion.

So Ankarette had made her plan, woven together night after night, day after day, in the solemn drudgery of her prison. Little snips of hair. Food rations withheld and preserved. Same with her water rations. She was biding her time. Preparing for the confrontation she knew was coming. Hux didn't want to fight her. He wanted to prove he didn't need to.

Ankarette was determined that it wouldn't happen on his terms. She would make him come to Dompier the only way she knew how.

By making him think *she* was dead.

She set her trap with care. Refusing to eat the food brought to her. Sitting listless and sullen, wrapped in her cloak. Moaning when the servants came with her meals. Then she lay still, exposed to the light of the torches, letting her shoulders rise and fall slowly. Her actions unsettled the guards. The castellan came to speak to her, asking if she needed anything, and she refused to respond to him, only moaning.

Then, on the third day of not eating or drinking, she set the trap.

She knew the castellan was in communication with Lord Hux. Her strange behavior would be reported. And he would respond.

When he arrived at Dompier, she sensed his Fountain magic as just a faint ripple. He had no reason to disguise it. She waited patiently, like the little gray spider that spun its web in the corner. Sounds came, the door opened, and Hux and the castellan came down the steps. She felt his magic probing, reaching, trying to find her. She'd used up her reserves already, giving herself nothing left for him to find.

"How long has she been dead?" Lord Hux asked. She recognized his voice. She'd heard it many times. He didn't sound confident now. He sounded worried. From her concealment, she saw his face. His goatee, which was new, was well streaked with gray.

"Four days, Lord Hux," said the castellan. "She stopped eating and drinking. Look, she's not even moving. Not breathing."

"I can see that," Hux said. He sounded disappointed. He hadn't gotten the full dose of revenge he'd wanted. Or that Morvared had wanted.

"She's not moved in days. She was moaning in pain. And the smell. She *smells* like she's dead."

"She had more serum," Hux said with suspicion. "One of the Espion smuggled it to her. It can't be gone yet."

"What if she drank it all at once?" the castellan said. "I think she killed herself in despair. That's blood on the floor."

"There is only one way to find out," Hux answered. "Fetch a guard with a crossbow. I want to make *sure* she's dead."

"At once, my lord," said the castellan.

Ankarette watched Lord Hux's face. He was gazing intently at the floor, not at her. He could see the blond hair coming out of her cloak.

Soon a guard appeared, holding a dreaded crossbow.

"Aim at the corpse's back," said Hux dispassionately. "Even if she's feigning death, she couldn't help but flinch in pain." He changed his voice. "If this is a trick, my dear, you'd best reveal yourself now. I have no hesitation killing you."

Ankarette smiled and waited.

The guard hefted the crossbow and brought the front to the bars. He wouldn't miss, not at that range. The crossbow twanged, and the bolt went true. The sickening crunch of bone sounded. The corpse was rigid.

She waited, breathing slowly.

"She's dead," Hux said, frowning. "I thought she would

have lasted longer. Years even. But when hope is stolen away . . . it breaks the spirit."

"What do we do, my lord?" the castellan asked.

"Throw the body in the moat. She can feed the trout. I'm going back to Kingfountain."

"Very well. Where's the key? You have it?"

Hux produced it from his belt and handed it over. Then he departed up the stairs.

The castellan ordered the man to fetch a ladder, which he did, but it took a quarter hour for him to return, and then the castellan, grumbling in impatience, climbed up to the keyhole that was well beyond Ankarette's reach. He inserted the key, and the locking mechanism clicked once, then twice. On the third time, the castellan climbed back down.

"Grab the bars. It will take two of us to lift it," he said to the guard.

The two men grunted and heaved at the bars, and the gate lifted up. It was heavy for two men, but they were strong enough now that the locking mechanism had been disabled. When it reached the height, another clicking noise sounded, fixing the gate to where it had been concealed before.

"There," the castellan said, rubbing his hands together. "Now, you grab her legs, and I'll grab her arms."

The two men started toward the body.

And that was when Ankarette sprung her trap.

From her concealment inside the sarcophagus, which she'd wedged open just enough to see out of, she shoved the lid up. The trigger inside had already been reset, and the gate came slamming down on both men, pinning them to the floor. As she had known, they were both larger than her, providing enough room to wriggle out.

Ankarette shoved the lid off completely, letting it crash to the floor, and then vaulted out of the tomb. The corpse on the floor, which had been facing her all the time, showed Morvared's grinning skull, the head cushioned by Ankarette's own hair.

The castellan was groaning, blood streaming from a gash in his head. The gate had landed on him first. The other guard, in a panic, was squirming to get free of the bars. He was a smaller man and desperate to get away, and he was one of the ones who had frequently tormented her. Ankarette struck him in the neck hard enough to break it. He went rigid and then still.

The castellan, blood streaming into his head, looked up and saw her looming over him, wearing the dead queen's gown. By the expression of fear on his face, he knew he was a dead man.

She didn't disappoint him.

THE VILLAGE of Aynan in Occitania was a humble one, but it had a comfortable inn called the Speery, and it was there that Lord Hux had chosen to spend the night after leaving Dompier. Ankarette hadn't followed his horse. No, that would have revealed her. But after poisoning one of the guards, she'd learned what Hux's stallion looked like and had asked those she'd passed on the way about it until arriving at Aynan.

The Speery had a warm fire and many guests. Lord Hux was clearly well known throughout the realm, and she saw the delight in the faces of the patrons as he regaled them with stories of Ceredigion. She'd joined the crowd, concealing herself, and listened to him speak.

"How King Eredur died, I'll never know," Hux said disingenuously. "He was rather fat at the end. Apoplexy, I should think."

"You knew the king, though," said the innkeeper. "You were once the herald, Lord Hux!"

"Yes, I knew him," Hux said. "A handsome man. A valiant warrior, to be sure. But too greedy, as all those from Ceredigion are. And foolish to sign that peace treaty. But he's gone to the Deep Fathoms now. And the kingdom is roiling because of it. They will not seek to fight us again. Not for many, many years."

"Not while the boar rules Ceredigion!" someone said with a sneer.

"Indeed not," said Hux slyly. "He murdered his own nephews to seize the throne. I'm shocked, truly. Eredur trusted him so much."

Ankarette listened in silence as the patrons laughed. There was a stab of pain in her heart. A small ember still lived on apparently. Now it was truly dead. Eredur and Elyse's sons were murdered as well. She regretted that she hadn't been there to stop it. Grief wrenched at her heart. Poor Elyse. Poor devastated Elyse.

"Here's another round to peace with our enemies!" said the innkeeper. A cheer went up among the group. Ankarette had already noticed which young woman had been serving Lord Hux. She'd followed the girl with her eyes as she went to go get another bottle of wine.

Ankarette rose from the table and crossed over behind the girl, brushing against her, and dropped a coin on the floor by her foot. The girl, hearing the sound, bent down and retrieved this.

"Is this yours, madame?" the girl asked, seeing Ankarette.

"Yes, I dropped it," she replied. "Thank you. But you keep it. I needed to pay for my meal anyway. You can save the rest for your honesty."

"Why thank you, madame!" The girl pocketed it with a smile, and then carried the wine bottle and the goblet over to the table.

Ankarette chose another table, one closer to Lord Hux, who was busying himself with the wine cork and popped the lid off. Of course he'd open the bottle himself. He still couldn't trust people. Nor should he.

"Let us have another drink, then!" said Lord Hux. "To the future king of Ceredigion!"

"And who is that?" chuckled the innkeeper. "You don't think the boar will live long, Lord Hux? Are you a Wizr to make such a prediction?"

"I am not a Wizr," said Lord Hux. "I'm just a retired herald who will live the remainder of his days in peace and solitude." He poured himself some wine and took a sip and smiled broadly. "Excellent! No, I think the boar will not rule long. A rival has been seeking an army from His Majesty, King Lewis. A rival who will invade Ceredigion and claim the throne himself. Then, my friends, we shall all live in peace. Let's drink to it!"

"To peace!" everyone shouted, raising their cups.

Lord Hux drank his down and leaned back in his chair, a wistful look on his face. He rubbed his mouth thoughtfully, watching the patrons. He had such a kindly face, an agreeable air. It was what made him so deadly, Ankarette realized.

She watched and waited, arms folded, studying him.

He smelled something off. His nostrils flared. His eyes darted around the room. Then he pulled his hand away from his face. His brow wrinkled in concern. Holding his fingertips near his nose, he smelled them.

The serving girl was walking toward the kitchen, clutching her stomach. She disappeared behind the doors. The coin dusted in poison was doing its work.

Hux's brow began to dot with sweat. Ankarette kept

watching his face, realizing the symptoms he was now feeling had alerted him to the poison running through his system. Poison that hadn't been in the drink. Poison he'd touched on the goblet.

"Are you well, Lord Hux?" asked the innkeeper. His smile was fading, becoming worried.

Tremors began to seize Lord Hux's muscles. He tried to reach for something across the table, but he couldn't coordinate himself, and his arm jostled the plate and overturned the wine goblet, spilling the red liquid on the table. It looked like blood.

Ankarette had just a little Fountain magic now. It was seeping into her pores now that she was free. Just a hint of it. She'd need to find some needlework to recuperate the rest. But she invoked it, letting the power exude from her.

Lord Hux turned his head in astonishment, seeing her at a nearby table. Ankarette inclined her head to him, as if asking a silent question. *What's wrong, Lord Hux? Do you not feel well?*

The tremors began to convulse through him. It was a powerful dose. Enough to kill him. More than enough.

"Someone fetch the apothecary!" the innkeeper shouted in concern. "He's sick!"

Ankarette rose from the table and approached. "I'm a midwife," she told him.

"Help him! Help him!" the innkeeper said, looking relieved.

"Carry him to a room," Ankarette said.

While Hux trembled and shook, several of the men lifted him and carried him to one of the nearby rooms in the inn. They laid him on the bed.

"I need a basin of water. Go!" she told the innkeeper, and he hurriedly left.

Hux was choking. He stared at her in terror, especially after they were alone. She removed the packet of nightshade and poured plenty into her palm. She blew the powder into his face, and he was unable to stop her. She waited until his tremors began to subside. A dizzy look came into his eyes. It was a powerful dose.

A fatal dose.

"What is the cure for the poison you gave me?" she asked him in a whisper, bending near his ear. "Do you have it with you?"

He blinked several times, his body relaxing despite the poison raging inside his body. "There is none," he said. "Only the serum to halt its progress. But not forever. Even it lessens with time. Surely you've felt it. You were always going to die."

His answer didn't surprise her. He'd controlled her life for years, ruining any chance of having children, having a life outside her deadly trade.

"I thought that might be the case," she answered. "I did look hard for one."

"Are you killing me, Ankarette Tryneowy?" he asked her calmly. His face had become pale. The poison worked quickly.

"Yes, dear Lord Hux," she answered. "And then I will kill your king. We both lose this game. I will leave a note with your body. To warn him I'm coming."

COMING BACK to the city of Kingfountain felt like a dream—or more appropriately, a nightmare. Ankarette had purchased fare on an Atabyrion trading vessel, which delivered her to Kingfountain just after noon at high tide at the end of summer. It was less than a year since she'd left, but felt more like a lifetime. She had been to the city so many times, but it felt otherworldly to her now. The roaring of the falls gave her a premonition of dread, but what was even worse was not seeing Eredur's banner anywhere. It had been replaced with the black banner of the White Boar, the standard of King Severn Argentine. She'd loved to embroider things with Eredur's banner, the Sun and Rose. She didn't have a fancy for dark thread, though.

She walked the streets of Kingfountain, picking up clues of the events she'd missed out on during her imprisonment. News used to invigorate her, stimulate her mind, even replenish her Fountain magic. But she was a woman with a death sentence, one that had been secured by Lord Hux years before. There was no cure for the poison he'd given her. Only a delay. She'd come to terms with her possible death years ago. She would never become an old woman. Instead, she would stay alive until the last sips of the vial were gone. She'd last another year perhaps, if she used it sparingly. Not enough time. But then, life was full of vagaries anyway.

It did not take long to reach the bridge that straddled the river over the falls and connected to the island of the sanctuary of Our Lady. All the reports suggested that Queen Elyse had sought sanctuary there—one last time. Memories from the past flittered through her mind. The Duke of Warrewik. Eredur, when he was younger. Sir Thomas arresting her from the inn across the street. A sad smile came to her. She'd lived an interesting life, even if it would be short.

She watched the gates of the sanctuary, observing the sanctuary men—the rogues of the city—going in and out, passing news and stolen goods amongst themselves. Although she wanted to see Elyse again, she dreaded the interview. But, not one to flinch from duty, Ankarette rose after finishing her meal and raised her hood, crossing the road and entering the sanctuary grounds.

There were many families there, people coming to toss in

coins. There was no shortage of prayers to the Fountain these days. Ankarette stopped at one of the pools, pausing to gaze up at the monumental structure. Her faith in the Fountain felt diminished. She'd been shattered by her experiences. For so much of her life, she'd had success. Until now. She'd fallen for Hux's trap and been unable to prevent her king's demise. Failure was a bitter thing. No one enjoyed its flavor.

There was a man sitting against the rail of the fountain, a very fat man whom she noticed because he stomped and frightened away the pigeons. Then he chuckled and started sending out crumbs again to lure them back. He had a foreign look to him—Genevese perhaps. Something about him felt off, and so she reached out with her Fountain magic, trying to discern something about him. He didn't turn his head at her intrusion of magic. But it was revealed to her that he was part of the Espion, trying to infiltrate the sanctuary men.

Knowing this, she remained out of his view and approached the sanctuary steps and mounted them. When she reached the doors, she was about to lower her hood, but she felt a premonition not to. Walking inside, she felt the solemnity of the place. The windows in the upper walls let in the streaming sun, but it still was darker than the courtyard outside, and it took time for eyes to adjust.

She was about to lower her cowl again, to show respect for the Fountain and those assembled to honor it, when she saw a little girl, probably six years old, with a braid in her dark hair, gripping her father's hand. The little girl talked in a gush.

"But why can't we take the coins from the fountain, Papa? It's not like anyone *uses* them. Don't they just get rusty?"

The man who held the little girl's hand was Sir Thomas, and it made Ankarette stop dead in her tracks. They were heading right for her. She turned, ducking around a nearby column, her heart panging in alarm of being recognized.

Sir Thomas's voice was full of humor. It made her ache to hear it again. "What? You don't think the coins disappear in answer to the prayers?"

"Don't be ridiculous, Papa," the little girl said. "That doesn't happen."

From her secret vantage point, she watched the two of them banter as they left the sanctuary. Sir Thomas had some gray in his hair, but not much. He was still hale, strong, a warrior born for the saddle and the battlefield. Ankarette brought news of the pretender's intention of invading Ceredigion. A challenger to Severn's newly won throne. Sir Thomas would be called on again for his experience and loyalty to the Argentines. She watched him and his daughter descend the steps, hand in hand. She remembered the little girl's name suddenly. Elizabeth *Victoria* Mortimer. She smiled at them in secret, then continued deeper into the sanctuary.

When she reached the deconeus's chamber, she didn't pause to knock. After twisting the door handle, she cracked it open and found an aging man sitting there, alone, reading from a book. She pushed the door open and then shut it.

When he looked up, he stiffened. "Who are you? Why are you here?"

"Where is John Tunmore?" Ankarette asked in surprise.

The man snorted. "The Deconeus of *Ely*? He's in Brakenbury Dungeon in Westmarch. Who are you? Why are you here?"

"I'm a servant of Queen Elyse," Ankarette said. "I have news she must hear. Can you bring me to her? I need to see her alone."

He gazed at her, his expression dumbfounded. He leaned back in his chair, looking perturbed. "She doesn't get many visitors these days. But you knew my predecessor?"

"I did. The queen knows me. She will vouch for me."

The man sniffed. "She's with her daughter right now. I'll ask the princess to come and see me. I have another letter for her anyway, which arrived this morning. The queen has some visitors, on occasion. Well, those that do come want her daughter's hand. The sanctuary has been busy of late."

"Thank you, Deconeus."

Elyse's private chamber in the sanctuary paled in comparison to her regal apartments at the palace of Kingfountain. The official queen of Ceredigion was Severn's wife, Nanette. But in Ankarette's eyes, it would always be her friend, her confidante.

"Blessed be the Fountain, you're alive!" Elyse said in wonder, rising from her writing table and hurrying across the room.

The two women embraced, the tears flowing freely. Their friendship had been born of years, had survived childbirth and wars, and now even death.

"You cut your hair," the queen finally said after wiping her nose and lowering Ankarette's cowl.

"I didn't want to, but it was necessary," Ankarette said, smiling. "I am glad to see you again. But my heart aches that I was not here to stop Eredur's death."

The queen sighed, nodding firmly. "You were imprisoned," she said. "I think my husband would have invaded Occitania to rescue you. If it weren't for the winter storms, he might have."

"That was part of Lord Hux's plan," Ankarette said. "There is much we must speak of."

"Come, sit with me," the queen said, bringing her over to a humble couch.

Ankarette did, and they held each other's hands. "News should be arriving soon. I wanted you to be the first to hear it. King Lewis is dead."

Elyse's eyes widened. "That *is* news. I've heard he's spent much of the last year hidden at his estate in Plessis under heavy guard. He wouldn't see our heralds, refused to outright. He wouldn't even see most of his own nobles. Some feared he died during the winter, but he would summon some of them, randomly, and disinherit them. Just to prove that he was alive ... and still the king."

Ankarette nodded. "He died in Plessis."

The queen couldn't help but smile. "How did you . . . how did you do it?"

Ankarette stroked the queen's hand. "I'll share this one secret with you, but I ask you to keep it to yourself. Some secrets should remain so. One thing I learned in Pisan is the power of believing. If someone believes they are sick, they can become sick. When I finally broke free of my prison, after hearing about the death of your husband . . . your *sons*"— Ankarette's throat caught, but she persisted—"I wanted to be sure that our enemies who planned this were brought to justice. After I killed Lord Hux, I put a message on his body, one that I knew would be found and brought to Lewis. It was a warning that I was coming for him."

Elyse nodded eagerly. "I'm sure he was racked with worry, then."

Ankarette smiled. "I never tried to break in to his manor. Instead, I broke in to his mind. I made him worry that every meal might be his last. I injured his guards. I made him doubt everyone he trusted. He was already agitated enough, with enemies to spare, that he quickly went mad. The last message I sent him was that he'd already been poisoned. He died yesterday morning after being awake all night jumping at shadows. I watched from outside the bars. The prince came to take his body back to Pree for internment. He wasn't killed by poison. He only *believed* he'd been."

Elyse stared at her somberly. "And Morvared is truly dead as well?"

Ankarette nodded and then quickly told her about her imprisonment and how she'd finally escaped. She also told her the news she'd learned from Lord Hux, that there wasn't a cure. There had never been one. Once her vial was empty, Ankarette would die.

The queen embraced her, and the two friends held one another, mourning for the losses they'd endured.

"But you are not dead yet," Elyse said, sniffling. "There is one more thing you can do for me."

"I cannot bring your sons back," Ankarette said, grieving.

"No, you cannot. Severn has asked to see me, here in the sanctuary. He even sent his young son to try to convince me. The poor dear is so upset that his cousins . . . are not here. Not that Severn would trust the truth to his child. It pains me so much. The anguish of losing a child. I wouldn't wish that on anyone. Not even Severn. So I have continually refused. He says he wishes to tell me what he knows of my sons' deaths. But I . . . I just cannot bring myself . . . to *trust* myself to believe him. My mother's heart *wants* to believe he didn't murder my sons. But I feel too vulnerable to deceit. He has a way when speaking," she said, shaking her head. "He's powerful. And persuasive. If I see him, I would like you to be there, in secret, of course. That way, I may know whether he speaks the truth or not. I don't believe you, with your Fountain magic, would be deceived."

"I can do that," Ankarette agreed. "Have the deconeus invite him to the sanctuary."

"I will," Elyse said, squeezing her hands firmly. "I want you to stay with me . . . here at the sanctuary. Let us spend your time together. I will take care of you."

Ankarette shook her head. "I can't," she said, staring at the walls, at the prison they were. "I couldn't bear to live here, listening to the roar of the falls day and night." She pursed her lips. "I think it would drive me mad."

"Where will you go? I need you *near* me, Ankarette."

"I will always be near you," she said. "I was going to return to my tower. Who is running the Espion now? Whom did Severn choose?"

Elyse frowned. "Dickon Ratcliffe. Utterly ambitious. Utterly incompetent. But not like Bletchley. That man . . . he was a knave. Eredur never trusted him. But Severn did. To his downfall."

"Bletchley was in league with Lord Hux, I think," Ankarette said, nodding. "It wouldn't surprise me. But he's dead now, isn't he?"

Elyse nodded. "Be careful, Ankarette. Severn knows about you. Not your name. Many times I heard him plead with Eredur to reveal your identity to him. He doesn't know all that you've done for us. He would try to kill you. He's . . . changed so much since Eredur died."

"We all have," Ankarette said.

It was the same nightmare again. Ankarette thrashed against her bonds, trying to escape the canoe as it hurtled toward the falls. She felt the rushing river beneath her, the splashes of water that kicked up over the rim of the boat. Could smell the river. The power of it, churning, carrying her relentlessly toward death.

But this time, she awoke before plummeting over the edge. The feeling of the river had roused her. The tingling of power, the ripple of magic coursing through her. Ankarette sat up in bed, looking at the stubby candle that was still halfway down, the flame strong and bright. She was in her room again, at the poisoner's tower. The smells of dried herbs were familiar, friendly. She saw her works, the needlecraft she'd done since returning to the palace.

The magic was racing inside her, filling her with alarm. She blinked, summoning the power that was already there. People were coming up the tower steps to do her harm. Ratcliffe's men. Liona, the cook, had warned her the day before that the Espion had discovered Ankarette's presence in the palace. And the king had ordered them to hunt her down.

Ankarette rose from the bed, grabbing the knife under her pillow. The men on the stairs didn't make any noise. But she knew they were coming all the same. The magic of the Fountain had warned her.

Why?

She didn't understand, but she accepted its help. They would try to murder her as she slept. Perhaps she'd need to start sleeping during the day instead.

Three men.

Ratcliffe had no idea what he was up against. She'd defeated an entire garrison at Dompier.

Ankarette leaned over and blew out the candle.

AUTHOR'S NOTE

I've said many times that the events of the Kingfountain series were inspired by real circumstances during the War of the Roses. This story was no exception. Queen Margaret of Anjou, wife of the mad king, died unexpectedly on August 25, 1482. The cause of her death was unknown. Edward IV, king of England, died a few months later in the spring of 1483. Some historians believe he was poisoned. His premature death triggered the power grab and conflict between his brother Richard and the queen's family. In June, Richard declared his brother's children illegitimate due to a prior marriage and assumed the throne as Richard III. The sons were later put to death, although there are claims one of the brothers survived and was hidden in another country. Edward's and Richard's enemy, King Louis XI of France, died on August 30, 1483, hiding in his estate, surrounded by archers and crossbowmen as if he feared for his life. Some say he died of a hemorrhagic stroke. Some believe he was poisoned.

I'll leave that to your imagination.

ABOUT THE AUTHOR

Jeff Wheeler is the *Wall Street Journal* bestselling author of over thirty epic fantasy novels, including his bestselling and beloved Kingfountain novels and the first book in his newest series, *The Invisible College.* Jeff lives in the Rocky Mountains and is a husband, father of five, and devout member of his church. Learn about Jeff's publishing journey in *Your First Million Words*, visit his many worlds at www.jeff-wheeler.com, or participate in one of his online writing classes through Writer's Block (www.writersblock.biz).

Printed in the USA
CPSIA information can be obtained
at www.ICGtesting.com
LVHW091531290724
786793LV00009B/97

9 781648 396601